from

with love

3:13 AM

by Catherine G. Lurid

Prologue

"So it does exist after all!"

"What?"

"Life after death."

"Of course it exists." He lowered his head back onto the plush armrest. "Have any of you ever seen a crab shed its shell?" No one answered, but Rapshmir didn't wait. "Death is an important necessity when it comes to things with varying expiration dates. That's why the death of the physical body should be perceived as no more terrifying than a seasonal molt."

"Louis"—Marian drained her glass as if it held courage instead of champagne—"there are rumors that the Masons are patronized by the very ..."

"The Devil?" Rapshmir was surprised.

"There are rumors." Marian nodded slowly.

"I implore you, if we were required to worship anyone, we would have chosen someone less controversial," Rapshmir assured her. "We worship ourselves, Marian. We are our own judges, gods, and even devils. Contrary to numerous legends, we have fairly simple principles and not-so-strict rules. As you can see, we admit people of color to the order. Moreover, our lodges are scattered all over the globe. Initially the order was formed as a small circle of people focused on studying the universe. Our prerogative is not faith; the strength of Masonry lies in knowledge."

"Terrible deeds are attributed to you," Raymond mused.

"Our most terrible deed over the centuries has remained unchanged—at the outset we slipped from the Church's control, and now we've escaped the grip of the authorities."

Suddenly El grimaced, clutching his chest, and asked Marian for water.

"It was a great pleasure to meet you, El Roberts." Rapshmir moved to the edge of his bed and extended his palm. El didn't say anything, but he shook Louis's hand.

"I think we all need to rest." The yacht owner bowed gallantly and left the room.

He walked down the corridor to his cabin and knocked. His bodyguard opened the door, leaving him alone. Low clouds shrouded the sky, and soon the window was streaked with slanted rain. The yacht rocked more as the storm intensified, lulling Louis. The last thing he remembered was the crystal chandelier swaying on his cabin ceiling. For the fifteenth time, he fell asleep.

"Louis," someone whispered softly into his ear, rousing him from slumber.

Louis Rapshmir had a penchant for games. He glanced at the clock, which read 9:39 p.m., smiled, and rose from the bed. The storm had passed, and the yacht was cruising smoothly at a moderate speed.

"Marian?" Louis surveyed the dark room.

A shadow glided by the panoramic window—someone persistently beckoning Rapshmir to leave his warm bed. He slipped his feet into his moccasins, draped a blood-red velvet robe adorned with the family crest around his shoulders, and stepped onto the deck.

An eerie mist spread across the black ocean—these waters were forever shrouded in fog, with or without Raymond. Rapshmir walked along a narrow balcony and reached the blue pool. A transparent black blouse had been left on one of the loungers, and a slender silhouette flickered, leading down the staircase.

"Dr. Flay, if I'm not mistaken." Louis tied his robe and had just sneaked down to the lower deck when every light on the massive yacht was suddenly extinguished.

Rapshmir jerked nervously—his sinful thoughts instantly gave way to anxiety. He couldn't tolerate such antics even from the living, let alone the dead. He turned and headed swiftly for the captain's bridge.

"Louis ..." Marian said sensually over his shoulder. Drops of cold sweat formed on his forehead.

3:13 AM

Ever since that very night when he was not yet fifteen, he had despised that bone-chilling fear. For the remaining years he had preferred not to acknowledge it, and now something had lured him out onto the deck after sunset and turned off all the lights. It seemed that she had not only managed to cut the power to the illuminations but had also lulled the entire crew.

Rapshmir was breathing heavily, trying not to turn around, when he felt ghastly touches under his robe. Cold, moist hands wound around his torso, aiming to descend into his silken pajamas. He froze.

"You must set me free," a tender voice whispered in his ear. "And you will know pleasures you never knew before ..."

Rapshmir mustered all his strength, but even that was insufficient to utter the word "no!" In that moment, he was only able to think about refusal.

The Gorgon breathed icy, noxious air onto the back of his neck, dragging his helpless body towards the edge of the deck.

The words "You're already dead" resounded in his ears, and he felt the sensation of hundreds of thin serpents enveloping him, tickling repulsively and invading his ear canals. They crawled into his nose and throat, writhing there in living tangles. They filled his sinuses and coiled around his eye sockets, tormenting him incessantly with an endless itch beneath his trembling eyelids.

Medusa had ensnared him in her chilly embrace. He swayed weakly and leaned over the low railing. Now, instead of her voice, he heard the rapid propellers of a powerful engine. They were just an instant away from engulfing him, ready to chop his flesh to pieces.

"Louis!"

Rapshmir snapped awake, finding Raymond's frightened face before him. He lowered his gaze—Raymond was holding onto his robe, attempting to pull him away from the edge. He grabbed his savior and took a step forward. He gazed at the churning waters—another second and they would've consumed him.

"What was that?" His stare darted around the deck. "Why did the lights go out? Did you turn them off?" He glared fiercely at Raymond.

"Hey, boss, if I wanted to kill you, I wouldn't bother saving you, would I?" Raymond raised his hands as if surrendering to an enemy. "And the lights didn't go out. I've been chilling out here for about two hours."

3:13 AM

Chapter 1

El ushered Marian Flay to the window. She smiled warmly and began to examine the giant wings of the airplane.

"Is everything all right out there?" El couldn't help but ask.

"Yes, yes." Tension appeared on her face.

"Marian?" She turned around, trying to listen to every word of her superior. "You're not afraid of flying, are you?"

"Me? No, why?" She smiled only with her lips.

***

When El was choosing a new partner, he was given a whole stack of personal files. Each file had a long number instead of a name, and under the number was the standard small print: *Counter-Terrorism Department*. First of all, El divided the agents by gender. He found women more efficient, more methodical, and, most importantly, he knew they were harder to seduce. Thailand was a beautiful country, El thought, but devious, and he would have to fly there often. Besides, female agents always smelled good, ate less, were less likely to be addicted to alcohol, and took up less space.

After quickly scanning the photos of young men, El began to focus on the "agents in skirts." Skirts have long disappeared from the uniforms of special agents, but the sticky nickname remains. Thirteen folders on the right and only three on the left. Carol—hair dark as night, smooth black skin—looked at El from the first folder. Her serious, focused gaze spoke of perfectionism and a tendency towards aggression. Carol would only be efficient until El started working outside the regulations. At the first opportunity—and there would be plenty of those—Carol's settings would immediately falter, and she would resort to hidden, and then possibly quite unhidden, sabotage.

The photo from the second folder stared back with calm gray eyes. Slightly hooded lids and near-perfect facial symmetry spoke of a remarkable inner balance. El loved balance. He loved minimal makeup, unremarkable features, typical height, typical weight. Agents like her were hard to describe verbally and therefore hard to make a composite sketch of. An Asian wouldn't be able to recognize this woman among a selection of similar faces; they would easily mistake the secret agent for one of the numerous tourists from England, Australia, and the USA.

Marian Flay, El read under the photo. *Thirty-two years old, legal education, impeccable service* ... He flipped the page.

Among her special skills were sprinting and swimming. Marian wasn't afraid of fire, water, or heights. She was a good shot, had awards in kung fu, and knew chemistry and poisons. According to the next two paragraphs, the fair-skinned blonde with a moderate scattering of freckles not only had a whole set of particular abilities but also a squeaky-clean reputation.

3:13 AM

Just what I need, concluded El and didn't bother opening the third folder.

***

The flight attendant politely asked the passengers to fasten their seat belts and to make sure the folding trays were in an upright position. The airplane was taking off. The heavy Boeing with 360 passenger seats started to move, and Marian flinched visibly.

"Do you have problems with flying in general or just takeoffs and landings?" asked El.

"The last ... two," Marian replied through gritted teeth.

"Do you know why we're flying to Thailand?"

"No. I only know what I was told by you."

"Our destination is Bangkok. We'll stay there for the night and take a flight to Phuket the next day."

"Why wait overnight? Why not head straight to Phuket?"

"You've never flown to the other side of the planet, have you?" El squinted. Marian pressed her lips together and shook her head. "Even in business class, twelve hours of flight will take its toll, believe me. Especially since we're not just flying on a huge airplane. It's also a time machine, by the way."

"How so?" Marian frowned.

"It's currently 7:45 p.m. in London on a rare Sunday evening without rain, right?" El looked at his expensive watch.

"Yes," confirmed Marian.

"We'll arrive in Bangkok at lunchtime on Monday, which is eighteen hours later, if the numbers are to be believed. But when we fly back, we'll save time thanks to the rotation of the Earth."

Marian finally looked out the window. The plane had reached a sufficient altitude for her to relax and enjoy the flight as much as she could. She closed the window shade and breathed a sigh of relief, leaving her seat belt fastened.

"So why we are going to Thailand?" she remembered to ask.

"Let's prepare for the flight, get comfortable, order a glass of champagne ..." Marian gave El a worried look. "Just for a better sleep. Sometimes there's turbulence over the Himalayas, and I don't want you to have a panic attack." El shrugged.

"No, no, I handle it well," Marian protested.

"Don't even object. One glass of light sparkling wine won't hurt you," he insisted.

"Honeymoon?" asked the flight attendant, Penchan, in a simpering tone.

Of course, no one could have guessed that El and Marian were secret agents. The long flight had forced them to dress in comfortable sportswear and sneakers. They wore no badges, and instead of classic black briefcases, they carried two backpacks. Their clothing was in suitcases, the necessary equipment would be provided upon arrival, and the top-secret documents were stored in the most secure place—El's mind.

El grinned but preferred not to answer. Penchan politely handed them embroidered satin pouches containing various flight necessities. El let Marian go ahead, and she disappeared into the restroom.

"This ordinary soap smells like a whole spa in London," she said upon her return.

El noticed that she really did smell very nice. "You ain't seen nothing yet." He smirked. "The smells of Thailand will stay with you for the rest of your life."

Marian narrowed her eyes, sensing the irony in El's words. Within moments the flight attendant appeared again with a selection of foil-covered trays and champagne. "I don't ..." Marian began, only to falter when El accepted two full glasses.

The beef steak, vegetables in spicy sauce, and shrimp salad were just as delicious as the food in a good restaurant. The sauce proved too hot for Marian, and she quickly reached for the cold drink.

"I suggest you start getting used to spicy food. Besides, not all restaurants in Thailand serve chilled champagne."

Marian laughed. El glanced at her sideways—he enjoyed her laughter as much as he was enjoying their dinner.

“So why are we flying to Thailand?” Marian asked, once again bringing up business.

“There’s a man there named Raymond Lee.”

“An Asian?” Alcohol had loosened Marian up—now she was trying not only to listen attentively to her boss but also to engage in lively conversation.

“An American.“

“Sounds like a Chinese surname.”

“Presumably some great-grandfather.” El shrugged nonchalantly.

Despite the fact that Lee was the most common Chinese surname, nobody would have thought that Raymond had even a drop of Asian blood. Except maybe for his almond-shaped eyes or his dark hair—darker than the usual North American brunet.

“So, what’s our assignment regarding Mr. Lee?” wondered Marian.

“B1,” El said succinctly.

“Personal conversation? That’s it?” Marian choked on her drink. “Twelve hours of flying just to talk to someone?”

3:13 AM

"Fourteen hours of flying, two hours in a Thai taxi, and forty minutes on a motorboat in the Indian Ocean," replied El, taking a sip of champagne and staring at the tiny bubbles clinging to the thin glass.

"Raymond Lee lives without internet or mobile connection?" whispered Marian.

"Why not? Mr. Lee has access to all the luxuries of the modern world. Only for a short time each day—just a couple of hours—but it seems to suit everyone involved."

"So why can't we contact him over the internet? It's just a B1. It doesn't even need a lie detector."

"This man predicts the future." El paused. "And quite often we communicate with him through satellite connection, no worries ... but sometimes he makes predictions", El paused again, leaving Marian breathless, "that we'd rather hear with our own ears."

Marian opened her mouth to ask something but suddenly fell silent. Fueng, Penchan's friend, collected the trays and refilled El's champagne. Marian declined politely, twirling the glass in her pale fingers.

The orange lighting in the cabin changed to a subdued purple. Soon, Penchan appeared with the bedding sets, including a soft blanket and a flimsy pillow. The business-class seats allowed the agents to recline almost completely for sleep, which could not be said for the cramped economy seats.

El couldn't sleep. Marian lay down and turned away from him towards the window, but he knew she wasn't one of those who fell asleep quickly. Especially now, after hearing all that.

***

The first time El met Raymond Lee was on the steps of a typical apartment building located to the north of Greenwich Village in Chelsea. This neighborhood covers a large area to the west of Sixth Avenue between 14th and 34th Streets and is considered one of the most attractive places in New York. The area, almost entirely devoted to residential property, combines various architectural styles, from elegant nineteenth-century townhouses to modern industrial lofts. Narrow rows of three-story apartments with external fire escapes fit snugly into the autumn landscape of one of the picturesque streets of the city. Here, one could easily run into a famous TV presenter rushing to their Porsche or an up-and-coming pop star running errands. Beside them lived the unknown Raymond Lee.

The bright brickwork of one of the apartment buildings seemed to reflect the fiery foliage of the abundant maple trees. The black railings of the high entrance were covered with a thin layer of road dust—the person who lived here seldom left the house.

El unbuttoned his austere black coat and reached for the doorbell. The carved door opened before he could touch it. On the threshold stood a dark-haired man with pale skin and expressive blue eyes. Both froze for a moment, then Mr. Lee slammed the door shut and locked it right in front of El's face.

The agent leaned his ear against it. Mr. Lee's heavy footsteps indicated he was running. *You can only run that fast if you're running downstairs*, El guessed.

He flew up the steps and, after a few yards, leaned against the door of the neighboring apartment. Pressing the doorbell, he pulled his ID from his pocket and, ready to introduce himself on the spot, opened it up. A frightened woman cowered by the open door as El rushed inside. All the flats had the same layout; in these multi-level narrow apartments, it's practically impossible to change anything. In the hallway, the staircase led up, with the basement door underneath. El pulled the handle and ran into the darkness. A tiny ray of light pierced the heavy curtains.

French window, El calculated, and the next moment, he appeared in the inner courtyard. He jumped onto a rickety table, pulled himself up by some metal bars, and, jumping over the low fence, stepped into the road.

"Stop—don't move!" He cocked his gun.

The fugitive stopped dead in his tracks in the alley and raised his hands. El approached him and said, hardly out of breath, "I'll put away my gun, you'll put down your hands, and we'll return to your home for a normal conversation."

***

"What department are you from?" Raymond washed his hands thoroughly with soap and dried them with a disposable towel.

"International Counter-Terrorism Department." El pulled out his identification again, meanwhile inspecting the spacious living room.

The huge cement wall was whimsically decorated with a strange portrait in a grotesque frame. Tall windows without curtains allowed in plenty of daylight, which was reflected by the massive low-hanging crystal chandelier. Between the warm brown leather sofas was a glass coffee table. Everything looked clean. Too clean—not a speck of dust, not a coffee cup ring, perhaps not a single fingerprint.

"What brings you here?" Raymond Lee sat down in an armchair and leaned back.

"Shall we calm down, Raymond? Our conversation might take longer than we anticipate," replied El.

"Have I broken any laws or been seen with terrorists?" Raymond looked to be in his thirties, with well-manicured hands that had never seen hard work. He could have worked in IT. However, there were no computers around—not even a television or a phone.

To live these days without gadgets? There must be some clues. El looked around again.

3:13 AM

Instead of a ceiling, there were wooden beams above. Up there was an open space, and if one moved into the kitchen area, one could see a huge bed. So much air and light—such a stark contrast to El's London apartment, where every inch counted as useful living space.

"How do you support yourself?" El knew the answer but couldn't help asking.

"I got lucky."

"How lucky?"

"A horse I bet on won a couple of races. And there's the Mega Millions," Raymond replied modestly. "Everything is documented, my taxes are paid, the amounts in my account match those with the IRS. I don't sponsor anyone, and no one sponsors me. The counter-terrorism department can sleep peacefully."

"Then why run away?"

"I thought you were a burglar."

"Is there anything worth stealing here?"

Raymond put his hands in his jeans pockets, looked down, and smiled. "Steal me, not something from here."

After just two races at the Pegasus World Cup, the embodiment of American extravagance, Raymond had made eighteen million dollars. Amazingly, after such luck, he had stopped betting on the races and switched to the national lottery. Three winning tickets had added another ten million to his savings. But when he returned to the races, the organizers immediately contacted the intelligence services.

After numerous checks, Raymond turned out to be completely clean. He had lived with his mother in New Jersey, graduated from high school, and got a job as a janitor in the psychiatric hospital where his mother had been sent by a medical council decision. After her death, he had disappeared for a while, but within a year he had sold his apartment in New Jersey and moved to New York.

His life in the big city seemed typical—he lived on the outskirts, searched for a job, and went to interviews. And El would have never learned about Raymond if it weren't for one terrifying scene captured by one of the street cameras that are everywhere in New York City.

"I want to show you a video." El pulled a Sony Vaio P from his spacious coat pocket—a full-fledged laptop almost half the size of a netbook.

"Not bad. Your company is well equipped."

"The department is well funded." El flipped through the files, opened the black-and-white video, and handed the latest gadget of 2010 to Raymond.

It was a recording from the CCTV outside the subway on Greenwich Street. On the left side of the screen was the date, 9/11/01, and on the right, the time was frozen at 8:40 a.m. Raymond tapped a button and the recording began to play. He didn't need to watch it; he remembered that New York morning vividly.

Raymond emerged from the subway and stopped at the gray barricade. He tried to take a step onto the street, but for some reason he couldn't. A young woman stopped beside him, arguing with someone on the phone and clutching her right arm. Raymond glanced at her and tried again to step past the barricade. His foot hovered above the asphalt and then returned to its place. Suddenly he looked up at the sky. The recording cut off at 8:42 and resumed with a close-up of his face. His nostrils flared as if he was inhaling an unknown scent. He closed his eyes, taking deep breaths, then suddenly he flinched as if he had heard a sharp, frightening sound. He looked around in fear and grabbed the chatty woman by the shoulder. He said something quickly. She cursed him and pushed him away. Raymond released her and ran back underground in an unusual hurry. Three minutes and forty seconds later, the first explosion shook the North Tower of the World Trade Center, also known as the Twin Towers. A terrorist-controlled plane had crashed into it.

Chapter 2

Raymond's eyes fluttered open, greeted by the lavender light seeping through the verdant jungle thicket and onto the gossamer mosquito netting above his bed. The roosters crowed incessantly, their clucks and caws echoing around the bungalow like a chorus of chaos. Raymond rolled over and buried his head in the pillow, attempting to drown out the pre-dawn activity that he had never quite grown accustomed to during his three-year stay on Koh An.

It was no secret that Mr. Lee had a fondness for his island, but there were moments when he yearned for the bustling metropolis of New York City, particularly during Christmas time.

Today it was the relentless rain that roused Raymond from his slumber. Glancing at the clock, he saw that it was nearly nine in the morning. He sat up in bed and rubbed the sleep from his eyes. The damp air carried with it the piquant aroma of patchouli, permeating the bungalow with its spicy scent. Raymond clicked on the coffee machine and made his way to the shower, relishing the feel of the lukewarm water cascading down his body. It wasn't long before he spotted a speckled lizard frozen on the ceiling. There were countless such creatures on the island, and they had become Raymond's closest companions, voraciously devouring the insects that plagued the equatorial region. The standard practice in these parts was to leave gaps between the walls and the ceiling to promote ventilation and drying. But in a climate where the humidity reached one hundred percent, mold was an ever-present threat—one that only the natural drafts could mitigate. As a result, crawling, flying, and scurrying beasts could easily find their way into Raymond's bungalow were it not for the ever-hungry lizards that patrolled the premises.

Sometimes he found frogs in his clothes, but only during the rainy season. Furthermore, the wide bed, a sacred place of rest, was meticulously covered by a canopy during the day and night. After checking his slippers for signs of life, Raymond slipped his feet in and picked up a cup of coffee. He walked out onto the veranda, inhaling the smell of rain, and settled into a wicker chair. One night he had left his sneakers right there, and in the morning, someone had placed small yellow eggs in them, thoughtfully covered with slime. Since then, no matter where he left his shoes, he always checked for repulsive contents before putting them on.

"Mr. Lee!" A burly Thai man with an umbrella ran up to the bungalow. "Khidaw?"

"Yes, thank you," Raymond replied. He knew that "khidaw" meant "fried egg" in Thai, but that was about all he understood in the local language.

The jungle was shrouded in a translucent haze. It began beyond Raymond's garden, where the workers had built a high fence. On such a small island, there were no monkeys—the fact had pleased Raymond considerably when he had bought the land—but an incalculable number of snakes lived there.

Obviously, the fence only protected against the snakes that swarmed the land at every moment, and no one was surprised by their tracks in the sand, left from night parties, as if hundreds of cyclists had taken a ride at dawn. No one poisoned their burrows or touched the serpents—the Thais knew how to live in a prudent neighborhood, and Raymond learned from their example. Only occasionally the snake-catching service came to clean up the inhabited part of the island, taking the most hectic ones back into the jungle.

In front of the house, parasitizing on the trees, purple orchids bloomed, sapodilla filled with juice, and plumeria shed its flowers into the shallow pool.

The downpour beat mercilessly against the palm leaves and the sprawling reed roof of the cozy villa, occasionally pouring down in heavy streams. In the distance, thunder rumbled.

"It will end soon." Kiet placed the tray on the veranda table and leaned out from under the roof.

"Forget it—we're not in a rush," said Raymond.

Kiet laughed. "After lunch, they'll bring the groceries." He bowed politely and, opening his umbrella, ran off again.

The aroma of breakfast permeated Raymond's nostrils like a narcotic potion. He looked at the tray—amidst the cucumbers, crispy bacon, and homemade potato chips, a khidaw dish was beautifully presented.

3:13 AM

Raymond loved the morning. He loved the rain. He loved Koh An.

The tropical downpours always ended as abruptly as they had begun, as if someone had opened the faucet and closed it half an hour later. Raymond changed his white shorts for swimming trunks and descended from the high veranda. The best houses were the ones on stilts. Floods couldn't reach them, and it was harder for any wildlife to get to the living space, although as it turned out, for these creatures, nothing was impossible.

The wet paths had taken on a deep gray color, and thin streams of rainwater still dripped from the enormous leaves. Along the beach, the crowns of tall coconut palms were swaying in the wind. Some of them had bent heavily over time, deciding to rest on the white sand.

Raymond had not yet seen the ocean, but he had already heard it. The first half of the day it was always calm, the tide usually coming in. It was pleasant to swim at this time, because by noon the ebb began and the ocean receded hundreds of yards, exposing the sand and sharp corals. By evening the ocean returned, but the timing of these fluctuations constantly changed. At the end of the beach, along the rocky cliff, the depth was greater, making the ebb less noticeable. There lived the varans, and neither Raymond nor Kiet wanted to disturb them.

Raymond walked to the sand, removed his sandals and white shirt, and hung his towel on a bent palm tree. The temperature of the Indian Ocean, which spread out like a turquoise strip at his feet, was always the same 80 degrees Fahrenheit, both in winter and in summer. He waded in waist deep and looked around. The water was crystal clear: Small shoals of tiny transparent fish flickered past, and spiral-shaped shells with thin legs ran along the bottom and buried themselves in a rush.

Raymond lay on the water's surface; the ocean perfectly held his relaxed body. His ear canals filled with water; now he could only hear the sound of the sea and his own breathing. He looked at the rocky cliff and dense jungles covered by low mist. There were cumulus clouds on the horizon, fishermen's boats, and the silhouettes of rounded rocks hovering over the ocean—the constant evaporation turned this world from real to ghostly.

Raymond closed his eyes. His body almost merged with the ocean, became a part of it, swaying in its leisurely rhythm.

***

He was lying in a bathtub in a New York rental apartment. After working as a waiter in a busy restaurant, his legs were so sore that the hot bath was the only place where he could recover before the next day.

Suddenly his hands went numb. His body slowly slid down and disappeared under the water. The dim light of a bare bulb penetrated the strangely greenish water. At that moment, Raymond was thrown forward with force and hit something as hard as concrete. He was no longer in his cramped bathtub;

his paralyzed body was being thrown back and forth by a powerful mass of water. Sharp glass shards, heavy logs, and dead people crashed into him at tremendous speed.

Raymond didn't feel any pain. Pain is just a signal from the brain that something is wrong with the body. But when you're almost dead, those signals don't make any sense, and the brain simply stops sending them. He had bumped into some metal structure, and something slippery underneath had pushed his torso up to the surface. Now he could see the destroyed buildings of an Asian coastal city. Dirty water had flooded the shore up to the tops of the tall palm trees, sweeping house roofs and broken boats deep into the jungle. Everywhere there was only mud, pain, and death.

Someone grabbed Raymond's leg with a dead grip and dragged him back under the water. He thrashed in convulsions with his last bit of strength and resurfaced in his own bathtub. Everything was just the same except for the screams and inconsolable crying that still echoed in his ears. He knew ... knew for sure that very soon, something terrible was going to happen somewhere on Earth.

Since early morning, New York had been covered with thin snow. The country was getting ready for Christmas, and the restaurant schedule was packed. Raymond left his apartment earlier than usual and got to work only slightly late.

He put on his uniform and entered the kitchen. It was unusually empty for the beginning of the workday. Somewhere at the end of the huge space, people huddled around a small television screen—a terrible tragedy had occurred on the other side of the planet. A nine-point earthquake in the Indian Ocean had caused a deadly tsunami that had hit the shores of Indonesia, Sri Lanka, southern India, and Thailand. The waves were over fifteen meters high, and the ocean had advanced hundreds of miles into the jungle. It had happened at 7:58 a.m. Thai time and 7:58 p.m. New York time—just when Raymond was taking his bath.

The tragedy claimed over 200,000 human lives and became one of the most destructive in modern history. When Raymond bought the island, the coastal service required him to install an evacuation route indicator in case of a tsunami. Such indicators can work in coastal cities, where it becomes entirely unclear where to run if water is literally everywhere, but not on Koh An. If a tsunami ever came there, no one would have a chance of survival.

***

As Raymond opened his eyes, he surveyed the rare low clouds and shifted his gaze to the rocky cliff. There stood a man, and Raymond saw him. Not with his eyes, but he knew for certain there was a man up there. He knew what he was wearing, where he was looking, and what position he was standing in. When he had purchased the uninhabited island, he had sincerely hoped that there were no people and therefore no ghosts. But as it turned out later, one eerily lucky tourist had crashed onto the rocks after a failed jump from a height.

3:13 AM

Just one, but always ruining the view, thought Raymond, closing his eyes again.

When he finally decided to stand, the water only came up to his knees—the ocean was retreating. Athit, Kiet's wife, was cooking delicious beef with wood mushrooms in a spicy kiwi sauce, and the aroma of the exotic dish spread all over the beach.

Raymond uncorked a bottle of cold Riesling, grabbed a glass from the kitchen, and walked out onto the wooden veranda that extended onto the sandy shore. Several woven chairs were arranged there for guests, along with a couple of tables.

He wasn't expecting anyone today except for the guy on the motorboat who delivered groceries to the island each week. He filled the polished glass and sipped the wine. The sun warmed his shoulders, and he looked straight out at the ocean. It turned crimson.

Raymond lowered his gaze. His heartbeat quickened. He took a deep breath, drank some more wine, and raised his head. Mangled corpses floated on the brown foamy waves. Not one, not two. They were everywhere—as far as the eye could see.

Athit, wearing Vietnamese flip-flops, approached carrying a tray with a plate full of food.

"Not now." Raymond struggled to swallow his saliva. His neck tensed, his stomach felt unpleasantly tight, and heartburn crept up his throat.

The elderly woman immediately turned around and marched back to the kitchen.

Raymond no longer dared to look at the eerie ocean. He picked up the bottle from the table and walked to his bungalow. He took out his mobile phone from the cabinet, turned it on, and sent a single message to the only number he had saved.

Something terrible is coming. Massive. I've never seen anything like it.

He left his phone on the bed and stepped out of the room. He settled back into the wicker chair on the sprawling veranda and took two large gulps of wine, inhaling the stale midday air. These spontaneous, chillingly realistic visions had plagued him for seven years, ever since he had met El Roberts.

***

"You have to learn how to predict this stuff ahead of time so we have hours, days, months, and years to prevent it, you understand?" El's stern face loomed over him. His sharp, straight nose, strong chin, and intense brown eyes made it seem impossible to resist him.

"But I can't. I don't know how to control it!" Raymond blurted out.

"Correct me if I wrong, but you can somehow predict the lottery and horse racing results ..."

3:13 AM

"A lottery in a day, horse racing in just a few hours. I don't understand how I can help you by reporting on a tragedy just one hour in advance. And how can I know if it's one hour or one minute, one day or one year?"

"You must come up with something. Develop some sort of system, train your abilities ..."

"Easy for you to say." Raymond stroked his hair. "What if I can't?"

"Then we'll have to add a couple of new clues to the case," answered El calmly.

The tension made Raymond's temples ache. "No, you can't pin Christine's death on me. You know I didn't kill her!" he shouted.

"Think, Raymond. What's more important: your life, Christine's life, or the lives of three thousand people? People who died. People whose death you predicted. And that's just what you got caught on. How many more deaths have you foreseen in your life? How many times have you known in advance and stayed silent?"

"This isn't my choice!" He swallowed.

"True. But for some reason, God or the Devil—I don't know who's in charge up there—gave you this ability." El glanced at him fiercely.

A faint line of sweat broke out along the edge of El's graying hair. It wasn't easy to have this conversation. Threatening the poor kid with prison ... he was demanding the impossible. However, it was only impossible at that very moment.

"And how much time do I have?" asked Raymond, calming down.

"Three months," El squeezed out.

"You have no idea how hard this is! Just throw me in jail right now. Why drag it out for three long months?" Raymond exploded.

"Six months." El softened slightly.

"And if I succeed?"

"You'll be able to participate in any horse race, make any bet. If you want, you can even buy yourself an island and move there. No one will stand in your way."

***

The phone beeped quietly on the bed. Raymond didn't budge. White plumeria flowers circled lazily on the surface of the shady pool. They hypnotically attracted his gaze, and soon he didn't have the strength to tear himself away from their unhurried movement. Four digits were spinning in his head, and he waited patiently for them to arrange themselves in the right order. Another message came through—Raymond didn't even flinch. He took another sip of wine and finally saw the number. It appeared as dark blue veins at the bottom of his pool.

3:13 AM

Kiet materialized around the corner in a flurry. "Mr. Lee, your lunch is ready!" The butler lifted a copper tray with a domed lid.

"Bring it over—let's eat." Raymond waved his hand.

"You're thinking too much again," Kiet remarked. "Mr. El might be coming soon?"

"I think he will ..." Under the lid was an appetizing dish adorned with miniature corn cobs. "You don't like him, do you?"

Kiet pretended he didn't understand the question. "If you go for a swim, I'll clean the pool, sir." He bowed obligingly.

Raymond nodded. He poured more wine, but it no longer made him drunk. On the contrary, the drink sobered him, relaxed his brain, which had been inflamed with strange visions, allowed him to step back from direct participant to indifferent observer.

In the six months that El had given him, Raymond had visited almost every casino in the country. He tried to guess as far in advance as he could, and gradually he began to succeed. First came a strange vision, then he deciphered it, and then he searched for the date.

Once he had been sitting in a Las Vegas hotel trying to see the numbers of the roulette. Suddenly the building shook. He grabbed his passport and money and rushed out onto the street. He ran through the crowded hall, not understanding why no one else seemed to feel the vibrations. When he was outside, there was another explosion in the southern wing of the tower, leveling the rest of the hotel to the ground.

"There's a bomb! Oh God! There's a bomb somewhere!" he shouted.

Raymond was taken to the police station. It was the shortest detention in Las Vegas—ten minutes later, he was released. Soon El contacted him, and Raymond passed on all the information he had about his terrifying vision. From that day on, the hotel was put under surveillance. For eleven long months, there were no signs of terrorist attacks, explosions, or even ordinary shootouts. But exactly one year later, when El's superiors were getting tired of waiting for a miracle, information was received that an explosive device had been found in the southern wing of the hotel. A window washer working at height had eight kilograms of dynamite on him.

Since then, Raymond had known how the exact date was shown. He tuned this channel like the antenna of a radio receiver and now he also had the channel guide. He often withdrew into himself for whole days, looking for signs everywhere. They added up to digits, which in turn added up to a terrible number—and then he could say precisely how much time the department had left.

3:13 AM

Chapter 3

El glanced at the sleeping Marian. He didn't need a partner. He had flown to Asia alone many times before. He was never bored, he didn't suffer from bouts of loneliness, nor did he have a strong need for social interaction. So why had he meticulously chosen her; why did he bring her along? Now he would have to explain to her things that were sometimes inexplicable, convince her that it was all true, and look into eyes full of confusion. Why? Most likely because he wanted an objective witness by his side—someone who would acknowledge that he was not crazy. After all, after years of working with Mr. Lee, El had truly started to doubt his own sanity.

The agent turned over onto his other side, fluffed his pillow, and closed his eyes.

But as his consciousness began to drift into the realm of Morpheus, the plane suddenly plummeted into free fall. Five seconds felt like an eternity. After a warning signal resounded throughout the cabin, the clicking of seat belts added a further layer of anxiety, and the Boeing plunged into an air pocket, lifting El's body from his seat. Marian screamed and clutched the armrest with her right hand and El's forearm with her left. He just smiled. "Don't worry, we won't crash," he said calmly.

"How do you know?" Marian was losing her composure.

The plane once again gained altitude but soon desperately lost it. A wave of screams swept through the cabin.

“If this plane was destined to crash, Raymond would have said so.”

“What if he decided to get rid of you?” Marian pressed herself into her seat. “Would he have told you?”

And if Raymond had decided to get rid of him, El was taking Marian with him—the woman who, despite all her strengths, was damn similar to Christine. He had seen that unfortunate woman in the morgue in photos when he was studying the life of the boy in New Jersey. The young Christine, torn apart by a psychopath, no longer felt any pain. She had suffered through her own hell, but horror was forever frozen on her marble face with its black, ugly bruises. Unlike Raymond, El never confused the living with the dead. But now, in the dim light of the emergency lamps, Marian’s face shone with a deathly pallor. Red capillaries spread across the whites of her tired eyes, which were instantly filled with the same fear of death as Christine’s.

***

“You promised me!” Raymond yelled. He was beside himself with anger.

“I’ve kept all the promises I made to you, Raymond.” For the first time, El’s voice filled with concern.

3:13 AM

"In Las Vegas I only asked for one thing—for Clifford to stay in jail till the end of his shameful existence. For Christine and my poor mother!"

Raymond paced back and forth in the bungalow's living room. No one had told him that Clifford, the rapist and murderer, had died in the mountain Alcatraz, the strictest prison in the United States. When the agency had received the news of his death, the death certificate was immediately classified. Not a single word about the strange incident in the prison bathroom, not a single mention of Florence or Colorado in any media outlet. How had Raymond found out? As always! El had never even dreamed that it would remain a secret for long. He was just biding his time.

"He's dead. I have no control over people's lives," El protested, outraged. "You should be happy." The agent reached for the coffee machine, noticing his hand was shaking. "You should be happy," he repeated, stuck in the stuffy air that filled the room. "Now that sadist is burning in hell."

The coffee machine sputtered and splashed hot water on El.

"What do you know about hell?" Raymond thundered.

"I'll stop by in a couple of days," El replied without turning around. "Maybe then you'll stop confusing a secret agent with Charon."

He left the bungalow, descended the stairs, crossed the tropical garden, and was on the beach in a minute. He had no intention of leaving the island so soon. As usual, he dined with Raymond under the stars until the night tide. The Thai man who piloted the motorboat slept in a hammock near the palm leaf canopy, unaware that the tenant was about to leave.

"I need to go back to Patong," El shouted, catching up with him.

The man jumped up and ran after him. Two hundred yards of wet sand tested El's patience—the driver had left the engine far from the shore, taking into account the low tide. They had just jumped into the boat when El's neck was pierced by a sharp pain. He lowered his head and massaged his neck, feeling his muscles like stone under his fingers. A second later, something made him turn around. Raymond was standing on the white sand, drowning in the mist of the jungle island. "Damn it," El muttered.

Soon, Koh An turned into a lonely hovering cloud over the water, and El noticeably calmed down. It was forty minutes to Patong from there, but it was dusk already. The fiery water swallowed the sun, forgetting to release the moon into the darkening sky. El strained, trying to see something, but blackness covered everything like a thick curtain. The Thai man turned on a dim flashlight that seemed to only blind the eyes and attract mosquitoes. They raced towards Patong's invisible shores without maps or navigation, relying solely on the sailor's memory and skill.

Suddenly the engine sparked and, with a loud bang, started smoking. The smell of kerosene mixed with fumes, and the deafening roar subsided. The boat drifted a few yards on inertia and stopped.

Damn it! cursed El. *Damn you, Raymond. Did you really set up a meeting with Clifford for me?*

The Thai turned on his flashlight and leaned over the engine, his shadowy figure merging with it, swearing loudly in his own language when the motor suddenly jolted.

"Damn it!" El cautiously looked into the water, standing in the middle of the boat and trying to hold on to the framework of the awnings.

The water below was black. It splashed and crashed against the sides, boiling and foaming. El strained his eyes.

"Holy mother!" The next moment, he fell to the floor.

"Mister, what's going on?" the Thai asked, climbing carefully around to him.

El breathed heavily, struggling with a horrifying vision. He stood up again, hunching over, and looked over the starboard side. Hundreds of dead gray hands reached out for the boat, vying to rock it. The nights here were hot all year round, but hallucinations like this sent chills down El's spine. He pressed the emergency signal button of the GPS on his watch, still not believing his eyes. The vessel was hit again on the right side, followed by a strange groan. The sailor fell off the board he was sitting on and crouched in the stern. Cold sweat dripped down El's forehead when he realized that he wasn't hallucinating.

"Phu tay thi mi chiwit," the Thai whispered uncontrollably.

"Who is that?" El tried to compose himself and wiped the sweat off his face.

"The living dead ..."

"Well, yes ... how did I not figure it out?" El muttered under his breath.

Both fell silent. Someone was quietly scratching the bottom of the boat. In the darkness, El felt as though the dead were already there, that they had broken through the bottom and would sink this damn vessel any minute and then start to tear their flesh to pieces. A bright spotlight appeared from behind one of the dark islands scattered along the Andaman coast. The sound of the boat grew louder, drowning out the eerie scraping beneath them.

The Thai jumped to his feet and started screaming—of course, he didn't know that someone was after them.

***

El took a long shower and collapsed onto the bed. *What was that?* he thought.

He couldn't believe that Raymond Lee was able to do something like this—such an act of blatant wickedness. And if he was, El simply wasn't prepared for this.

3:13 AM

***

"It's now 11:15 p.m., and Raymond Lee's interrogation is beginning." The recording given to El for review of the case in New Jersey began to play.

He listened to it four times and then fast-forwarded to the end for the fifth time.

"How did you find out about Christine?"

"She came to me," Raymond replied in a young, subdued voice.

"She came to you ... and you killed her?"

"She came to me hours after she was dead." The boy took a hard breath, clearly answering not for the first time.

"I haven't heard anything about the walking dead in my area, but lately there have been too many cases of one fucking rapist and psychopath," the investigator pressed Raymond.

"I see ghosts. They come to me." Raymond's voice was weak, devoid of any persuasiveness. "Christine came so clearly that I thought she was still alive. I wanted to help her sit down and then call the hospital, but when I got closer, she vanished into the doorway. An extremely pale and disfigured face appeared again, but this time behind the mesh screen of the front door."

"And at that moment, you remembered how you killed her?" The investigator slammed his fist on the table, making Raymond's voice tremble.

"I didn't kill her! I just followed her!"

"You followed her when she was alive?"

"I followed her spirit," cried Raymond, completely broken.

With such a testimony, there was no escape from prison. The boy had found Christine's body in the woods while it was still warm. There wasn't even a tiny chance of denying his involvement, and his mother took the blame for him. A childhood friend of hers, a psychiatrist who had always harbored feelings for her, managed to have her declared insane and spared her from the penitentiary. He also arranged for Raymond to work as a orderly at his clinic and allowed young men to spend the occasional night with his mother. Just as Raymond turned nineteen, Alicia was diagnosed with tuberculosis and passed away suddenly within the clinic's walls, as if she had been holding on until her beloved son matured and was able to live without her.

***

"If he saw dead people in the nineties, he could have easily learned to interact with them or even control them by now," thought El, splashing cold water on his face.

That night he couldn't sleep at all. He couldn't even stay in the stuffy room any longer—the incident at sea had stunned him, possibly even broken him in some way. He stepped out onto the balcony. There was a wicker lounge chair and a low marble table. He ordered coffee and, for the first time in ten years, opened a pack of American Spirit. Only a couple of yards separated his bare feet from the gurgling pool—the balconies on the first floor opened straight onto the water, allowing for round-the-clock swimming. The blue lighting beautifully shaded the tropical mini jungles. Planted in thick clusters, they served as a hedge for adjacent balconies, providing minimal but appreciated privacy. A delicate avocado scent wafted from the massage salon, while the bar, designed to resemble an island in the middle of the blue ocean, gave off a sharp bourbon aroma. El took a sip of coffee and lit his cigarette. The quality tobacco, skillfully blended with fragrances, calmed his brain like a professional psychologist.

Could it have been a hallucination? But what about the guy who ran the boat? Nothing matched, and after his second half-smoked cigarette, El decided to swim. The water now filled him with dread, but he couldn't go on like this. He needed to confront his phobias here and now, returning himself to his former idyllic, fearless state once and for all.

He descended the chrome staircase into the warm, transparent water. A plumeria flower brushed against his back as it floated by, and El jumped in fright—he was still far from an idyllic state.

He swam over to the bar and ordered a cold whiskey. It was that sleepless night when he decided to find a partner—someone whose purpose would be not to protect him from an unexpected supernatural attack but to at least be a witness of it.

***

The plane jolted again, and oxygen masks rained down from the ceiling. For a moment El was ready to believe that Raymond, despite everything, had decided to kill him and Marian, but their flight stabilized.

“The plane hit a zone of turbulence. We’re through the rough patch,” announced the pilot with a slight east Asian accent. “We’re gaining altitude again.”

Marian stared at the floor, slowly coming to her senses. “Don’t worry, we’ll definitely make it now,” said El, patting her shoulder. He reclined his seat and fluffed up the small pillow once again.

The scent of coffee woke him. The cabin lighting changed to orange, and people in economy class started bustling around. He stretched his back. Marian jumped up as if on command and soon disappeared into the restroom. El could have slept a little longer, but it seemed like pre-landing anxiety had taken hold of all the passengers at once.

He reclined his seat, handed the blanket to Penchan, and received a cup of filter coffee from Fueng.

“Coffee for your wife?” came the unexpected question.

3:13 AM

"You better ask her," El replied coldly, suddenly realizing that except for her special skills, he knew nothing about this woman.

"I'll have coffee, thank you."

Marian appeared out of nowhere and took her cup. Once again the scent of spring flowers, patchouli, and orange emanated from her, and El involuntarily turned his head to inhale more of this magical morning blend.

"You seemed much more confident ordering champagne for me than coffee." Marian gave a rather charming smile, but El caught a shade of sarcasm in her tone.

After breakfast, Marian asked for another cup of coffee and decided to open the window shade. Below them the ocean stretched out, an endless blue canvas. Rare clouds hung above it, casting sharp navy shadows. Some of them could easily have been mistaken for the rolling islands scattered along the coast of Phuket.

Marian stood in awe. "How beautiful!" she exclaimed. "It's so different from the Atlantic."

El knew that Marian had only flown across the ocean from London to America and from America to London—once to Canada and once from Philadelphia to Lisbon. And she was absolutely right. Everything was different in the Atlantic: the colors, the horizon, the coastal curves, and the air. Even when a huge iceberg appeared on the almost black water, the view from above did not stir the imagination with the same force as an island overgrown with misty jungles in the middle of crystal-clear turquoise.

The plane flew past the winding white line of the beach and soared over land.

“In forty minutes, Bangkok,” whispered El. “A massive city.”

Marian turned around and met his eyes unexpectedly close to hers. She blushed and hugged her coffee mug more tightly.

“When I first came here, it was night. Bangkok started shining with lights long before we landed. It seemed to me then like a gigantic living organism. Bangkok breathed, thought, lived, and the plane, like an annoying fly, circled above, trying to find a place to land. This city has lungs that it breathes with, it has a heart that beats. But God forbid you end up in his cloaca, Marian. Heaven forbid!”

She gave him an aghast gaze and set aside her unfinished coffee.

The plane circled the city and began to descend. This time Marian looked calmer and much more relaxed. She didn’t grip the seat and didn’t grab El’s arm, which disappointed her companion slightly.

The plane landed smoothly and, after taxiing for another ten minutes, came to a stop. The agents left the aircraft and walked through the bright corridors of the airport. Stretching their muscles, they waited in a long line at passport control and, after all checks, finally arrived at the giant hall where their identical black suitcases were spinning alone on the conveyor belt.

They crossed the registration hall of Suvarnabhumi Airport, where Marian was fascinated by the twelve-meter demon statues. Under ornate and gilded costumes, creatures with lavender, turquoise, red, and blue skin peered out. Their wild gazes, half revealed by sunken eye sockets, were complemented by fangs and frightening grimaces. Domed hats towered over their elvish ears; they brandished an array of enormous weapons in their hands.

“Perhaps more than anything else, Thais believe in spirits, especially the restless ones.” El stopped and lifted an indifferent glance to one of the demons, seeing Marian’s interest. “There used to be a cemetery here, right under us, and these guardians were installed to calm the souls of the dead. According to legend, they must not let the spirits from the world of the dead get into the world of the living in case they create another mass grave here.”

“Isn’t there enough space in Bangkok? Why destroy the cemetery?” protested Marian.

“Come and see for yourself.” El smirked and strode towards the exit.

Thailand’s air greeted them with nearly a hundred percent humidity and 86-degree heat. Marian took a breath and grabbed on to El. Her lungs hadn’t expected this, and she suffered from oxygen deficiency, swiftly causing severe dizziness.

“Are you okay?” El supported her.

“I can’t breathe here,” she replied weakly. “It’s like a real steam room. I’m not even kidding.”

“You’ll get used to it.” El took Marian’s bags. “And you’ll even come to love this air. You’ll see!”

3:13 AM

Chapter 4

Raymond looked at his phone. He finally glanced at the messages. All of them were from El.

I found a new agent to work with you, El had written.

She's an excellent specialist. Young and trained. I'm sure it will be much easier and more pleasant for you to work with Marian than with me. If you have any questions, don't hesitate to ask.

You can find the agent's dossier in your email. Take care.

"Don't tell me you're scared, El!" Raymond grinned.

He didn't bother to open his laptop and look at Marian Flay's dossier. He knew for sure that El would soon enter this room again, but not alone this time.

***

"The pool is ready, Mr. Lee." Kiet bowed and placed the long scoop net on the stakes near the bungalow. Raymond nodded and sat back in his chair. He finished his late lunch to the strange cries of tropical birds and, grabbing the remains of his wine, headed to the shady pool. Sitting on the edge, he dipped his feet into the clear blue basin. The water didn't cool him down; it just washed away the drops of sweat that inevitably covered his body in the equatorial climate. He took a sip from the bottle of wine and, without taking off his clothes, plunged into the pool. Like the plumeria flowers, Raymond spread his arms and lay on the water. He looked up at the sky but saw the cabin of the plane that would take off from London at 7:45 p.m. in a week and a half. A couple of agents would be sitting in business class sipping champagne—El Roberts, who had become a pain in the ass, and young Marian Flay, who looked a bit like Christine. In his vision, Raymond approached the woman's chair and leaned in.

"Maybe in profile view, but not from the front ... not from the front ... You wasted your time, El," remarked Raymond.

He paused for a moment, staring at El as if deciding his fate. But was he really deciding? Probably not. Although those who are tightly intertwined—intertwined so undeniably and constantly—could possibly shape each other's destiny, even if they don't always realize it.

Raymond exited the plane at an altitude of six miles above the earth and hung in free fall, contemplating the slightly curved horizon. The snowy peaks of the mountains gave way to the ocean, its blue waters framed by islands and coastal shoals. From this height, the dense forest of the jungle appeared like a downy duvet, perfect for a soft landing.

Raymond had left his body on Koh An, meaning he was now headed for the tiny dot in the middle of the vast ocean. After flying over large cities and small settlements, he glided towards the winding coastline. Here, the sky had turned a deep shade of purple-red, casting the same hue over the water. The waves were awash with burgundy, and corpses stood in them, reaching all the way to the skyline and staring at each other's backs. Their clothing, soaked in blood, revealed fatal wounds, and their faces were impossible to identify by age or gender. They were all the same, and they were all dead.

Raymond wobbled gracelessly. His usual indifference was replaced by alarm, grounding him to the Earth. He was losing altitude when suddenly the corpses raised their heads to the sky and he realized that all of them had finally seen him. Fear robbed him of his wings. When he fell into the ocean, he found himself in blood instead of water. Through the ruby liquid filled with black, slimy clots, hundreds of lifeless blue hands pursued him. Blue fingers scratched his body, tore his clothes, and drowned him. He struggled to find the bottom and pushed himself up in a panic, emerging from the pool.

His body was gently enveloped by transparent water. Somewhere in the jungle, the birds still screamed. And down here, plumeria flowers swirled smoothly around his shaking hands.

He caught his breath and approached the bottle of wine. Alcohol helped again, instantly relieving the severe pain in his temples. He hadn't had visions like this in a long time. How long? Actually, he had never experienced anything like this before.

He climbed out of the pool. He didn't feel like swimming today or for the next few days. He took off his wet clothes and walked naked to the banana grove, where a chrome shower stand sparkled among the trees.

Raymond changed into a clean shirt and shorts, grabbed the keys to his yacht, and headed to the beach.

"Mr. Lee, are you leaving?" Kiet flew up to him immediately.

"I'm sailing to Koh Phi Phi," he replied shortly.

"Not waiting for dinner?"

"No."

Kiet stayed behind, and Raymond walked alone to the rocky cape. The narrow path led him back to the water, where a mini Riva was hidden between two smooth stones at a short pier with a wooden awning. Taking just two steps along the pier, he jumped onto the white deck of the yacht. Finished with polished wood, the Riva looked fancy with a milk-colored leather salon. Raymond started the engine and carefully maneuvered his vessel between the rocks out into the open water.

If you're going to describe an equatorial sunset, you cannot do it without shades of purple. All of its hues captivate, transporting Europeans and North Americans to another universe. And no matter how long someone from New Jersey may live here, the raspberry-red sky with its intensely plum cumulus clouds will never cease to amaze them.

3:13 AM

Raymond breathed in the scent of the ocean and surveyed the picturesque giants of the Andaman Sea islands. An incredible place. If you're looking for paradise, it's there.

Raymond slowed down and entered the azure waters of Ton Sai harbor. The long pier was covered in colorful motorboats, and he eventually parked his yacht near a similar white one. The watchman courteously took the rope and tied it to the mooring. Raymond hopped off the pier and, after handing a few notes to the Thai man, walked towards the center of the island, where the music never stopped and the revelry only subsided for a few hours in the morning. He walked along the bazaar to the restaurant overlooking the lagoon. True to his habit, he ordered white wine with the fish.

As he took his first sip of Australian Nepenthe, the dusk warmly embraced him. The wine's bouquet was dominated by passionfruit with a hint of blackcurrant, and the aftertaste, with notes of green apple and freshly mown grass, stretched out the drinking time. The taste was rich but elegant and the color almost transparent—just the way he liked it.

The fish with lemongrass exceeded Raymond's expectations, not to offend Athit—Kiet's wife cooked wonderfully.

Darkness fell. A singer as black as the night took to the low stage. Raymond turned towards her and was absorbing the velvety nuances of her skin when he caught the predatory glances of the local women sipping cocktails at the bar. When he had moved to live on the islands, the local nightlife had taught him the bitter truth—the most beautiful, long-legged, and well-mannered Thai women are not really women. Well, they are in all senses except the anatomical. Since then, Raymond had gifted them with sweet smiles but only flirted with European and Australian ladies. The tall, well-built, and highly attractive American had plenty of choice, and on top of that, none of the lovely ladies even guessed his millions.

Raymond settled the bill and left the restaurant. He walked through the stinky streets of the center, teeming with bars, cheap hostels, and perpetually drunk tourists. His destination was on the other side of the island, where the picturesque bay hid the Slinky Bar—a place that Raymond had once fallen in love with. This time the spacious sandy beach of the club was strewn with flowers. Half-naked girls jumped around in circles to monotonous music. Raymond approached the bar, admiring the young bodies reddened by heat, noon sun, and drugs.

Raymond leaned over to the bartender. "Manhattan."

"In honor of the festival of the god of ultramarine"—the bartender grinned and nodded towards the beach—"we only have cold beer in the bar."

Raymond had already learned the local rules and knew perfectly well that MDMA and ecstasy suppress the body's ability to thermoregulate. Very often, their use in hot countries leads to overheating and heatstroke. In a hellish combination with strong alcohol, it can cause hyperthermia of up to 104 degrees. And since there are no hospitals on the islands or medical help close to civilization, those who mix

3:13 AM

MDMA with vodka are much closer to the grave than to euphoria.

He cast a farewell glance at the naked revelers and disappeared from the beach into the hubbub of street bars. From each bar blared Thai versions of James Blunt and Adele, and after some searching, Raymond found a deserted corner and sat down, ordering another Manhattan. Beautiful songs succeeded each other, and after his second cocktail, he even started to hum along. Blocking out the musicians, a wobbly blond girl in a bright and impressively short sundress appeared before him.

"Hey!" She grinned.

"Hey," Raymond replied curtly.

"You're American?"

"Yeah."

"I'm from Dublin."

"Beautiful city."

"Have you been there?"

"Never been."

The girl beamed and lowered herself onto a barstool next to Raymond. "Mireille." The rosy-cheeked blonde extended her hand.

"Raymond."

"Where are you staying? I haven't seen you here before."

"I rented a bungalow on the other side of Koh Phi Phi."

"In one of those expensive hotels?" Mireille's thin eyebrows shot up towards her sun-bleached hair. "So we'll go to your place tonight?"

"I'm afraid, Mireille"—Raymond paused—"we'll barely be able to make it to your place."

The girl traced her finger along the curved neckline of her dress and, with her half-closed eyes fixed on Raymond, called out to the bartender, "Rum and Coke, with lots of ice."

They left the bar at half-past two in the morning, huddling in the shadows as they made their way to a cheap guesthouse. A bright streetlamp shone into the narrow room, illuminating two beds. And in its light, Mireille appeared completely naked within moments. She took charge of everything and then repeated the act. The third time, Raymond politely declined and went into the bathroom.

He turned on the light and stared at a massive black cockroach the size of a matchbox. The insect seemed to stare back at him. Raymond was afraid to slap such a behemoth; doing so would be like committing a full-blown murder. He didn't want to disturb the creature, so he turned off the light and closed the door to the bathroom tightly.

3:13 AM

Mireille was already asleep. Raymond covered her with a sheet and searched for his clothes on the floor. His wristwatch showed 3:00 a.m.

A repulsive voice came from an armchair in the darkest corner. "How sweeeet!"

Raymond shuddered. He knew that voice and that disgusting way of drawing out words. He straightened up and stared into the darkness. "Who's there?"

"As I leeeearnt from them." The sound came again.

Now Raymond remembered. The voice belonged to the cleaner at his school—Christine's rapist and killer.

"Devil!" He clenched his temples with his palms.

"You've almost guessed it," the ghost hissed like a snake.

Raymond turned sharply and headed decisively towards the exit.

"How sweeeet," came from behind him. "Can I kill her? But not right away ..."

"Damn you, El," Raymond grumbled, motionless on the threshold. "Couldn't you have kept him alive?"

"She'll be fine with me. She won't even know it's me. She'll think it's you ... using her again like a whore."

"Damn!" Raymond leaned over the doorknob as Mireille moaned softly behind him.

“Ah, ah, ah, Raymond ... Raymond ...” The completely drunk sleepy girl was clearly feeling everything the insane Clifford was doing to her. “Oh God, how good,” she moaned. “Take me, Raymond ... take ...”

Blood pounded in Raymond’s temples. He rushed into the bathroom, jumped over the sleeping cockroach, and filled a bucket with cold water. When he thought he had enough, he grabbed it and ran to the bed. He hesitated as he watched the wildly aroused Mireille writhing on the crumpled sheets.

If Raymond hadn’t known Clifford, he would have left. Who knows how many freshly deceased perverts prey on drunk women for sex? It’s common for their spirits to weaken over time and become powerless. But Clifford wasn’t just a sex addict when he was alive—he was a true maniac.

Mireille rubbed her ample breasts, vibrating her hips as if someone was entering her body every few seconds. Raymond let out a deep sigh and poured the bucket of ice-cold water onto the woman’s pelvis. She screamed, jumped up, and pressed herself against the wall. “You’re insane!” she yelled.

Raymond didn’t bother explaining himself. “Try not to get drunk for the rest of the vacation,” he grumbled, then simply walked out of the room, listening to Mireille’s angry insults behind him.

He was sober again. Visiting spirits always sobered him up instantly, no matter how much he had drunk. Especially if the apparition was the ghost of someone who had killed the people he cared about most in his life.

3:13 AM

It was around four in the morning. The streets were noticeably empty, but they were never deserted in the center of Koh Phi Phi. Rage overwhelmed Raymond. He had known that the degenerate Clifford would come to him after death, and he had done just that. It's good when the body is burned—everything except the soul is burned. It's bad when it's mummified—all energetic shells continue to live for a long time. Clifford had clearly been buried, otherwise he wouldn't have been able to make Mireille feel all of that.

How about calling and asking them to burn the maniac? Who would take care of that? Agent Roberts always found it easier to lie than to do what Raymond asked. And before Clifford's soul was left without astral and mental bodies, before it went to the Hell of his insane desires, he would be happy to fuck the entire island. And that would be the most positive scenario. The main thing was that he didn't start choking girls in a fit of ecstasy, which Raymond did not rule out.

Raymond relieved himself off the pier, untied the mooring line, and jumped onto his yacht. He started the motor and raced across the black waters of the night ocean, eager to reach home as soon as possible. Today he had felt dirty—even more so after indulging in the pleasures of the Thai guesthouse. But now the dirt seemed to stick to him in a peculiar way. It had almost seeped through his skin, filling his lungs with a pungent mix of alcohol, mold, and animal sex.

Through the veil of the night, the pale face of Christine suddenly appeared before his eyes. Her dirty body lay in the moss under a fallen tree. Her eyes were open, reflecting the light of a flash like glass. Her lips were bitten and bleeding, and the bruised imprints of the maniac's hands were forever etched on her neck.

Raymond hastily stopped his yacht—he had to lean overboard. He caught his breath, took a gulp of water from a plastic bottle, and lay down on the white deck. The stars were shining. He knew and foresaw so much, but still he had no idea if there was someone, an all-seeing being, up in the sky—the one he prayed to, relied on, and wanted to believe in with his whole heart.

At dawn, he reached home. He took a longer-than-usual shower and called El.

"You have to exhume Clifford's body and burn it!"

He began without greeting, taking his usual place on the veranda with a cup of coffee.

"What's on the other side of the scale?" El sighed.

"Maybe a couple of bodies on Koh Phi Phi." Raymond blew on his coffee.

"Maybe sounds uncertain."

"Maybe ..."

"I'll report this possibility to the higher-ups," El interrupted. The wording meant only one thing—he wouldn't be handling this. He had more important matters to attend to.

"El"—Raymond tensed—"we can save them."

3:13 AM

"Both of them?" El clarified coldly.

"I don't know how many. The more energy the poltergeist spends, the weaker it becomes. I don't think this psychopath has enough for more than two, but who knows?"

"The agency doesn't deal with individual cases. But I'll think about your request."

***

A few days later, Raymond learned that two Americans had fallen asleep and never woken up on Koh Phi Phi.

Gillian Gris and Molly Carlo were found dead in their room at the Dawn Guesthouse. Gillian's heart stopped beating around two in the morning, while Molly's stopped around three. The girls were found naked with no visible signs of injury on their bodies, and the door to their room was locked from the inside, English news from Thailand reported.

"Damn, El!" exclaimed Raymond, dialing the agent's number again.

"When did this happen?" El asked dryly.

"Last night."

"I burned Clifford yesterday morning, as soon as I could reach Florence from London." El suddenly spoke up. "With my own hands."

"What?" Raymond was taken aback.

"You're surprised? I thought the all-knowing Raymond was already aware."

"No ... I ..." Raymond didn't know what to say. "But what about those two?"

"I don't know. It's a fresh case. But I can call the Phuket police. Although if it's not Clifford, those poor girls were probably killed by drugs, heat, and alcohol."

Raymond fell silent.

"Did you really burn him?" he asked again, bewildered.

"Raymond, you're a wealthy man. Order an exhumation and you'll get your answer."

El hung up. Raymond breathed a sigh of relief. He chuckled, looked at the rainy jungle, and took a sip of his fragrant coffee.

3:13 AM

Chapter 5

In the taxi Marian finally took a breath. “Are there air conditioners everywhere here?” she asked with a hint of anxiety.

“I haven’t really noticed.” El looked at Marian sternly, as asthma hadn’t been mentioned in her file. “But most likely yes.”

It had happened a long time ago, in her childhood. But at six years old, it had all gone away as if the illness had never existed. One day Mrs. Flay took the blond girl to a strange old house.

“Come in!” a hoarse voice shouted, and Marian’s mother opened the door, letting her daughter pass.

The dark corridor was heavy with smoke, and the little girl started to cough immediately. But her mother stubbornly pulled her by the hand into one of the rooms, where a plump woman sat on the couch.

“What do we have here?” The host, an imposing black woman, leaned towards Marian. “Asthma?”

“That’s right, Madame ...”

“Abangu.”

“Madame Abangu, Marian has had asthma since birth,” Mrs. Flay explained.

"Why wait until she was six to come to me?" Madame Abangu grumbled angrily.

"We had no idea that the illness could be cured by coming here." Marian's mother tried her best to stay calm.

"I'm a sangoma, and I can do a lot of things." Madame Abangu slowly reached for another cigarette. It seemed like the room disappeared in the cloud of smoke; she lit up again, and Marian began to lose consciousness.

"Perhaps we should step outside for some fresh air? My daughter will stop coughing, and we can come back again." Marian's mother spoke apologetically, supporting the girl, who had collapsed to her knees from the severe attack.

"It's not the air that's the issue." The sangoma leaned over the child and looked into her eyes. "It's the power within your daughter that her body cannot handle. A strong spirit destroys a fragile body. Air has nothing to do with it."

Madame Abangu placed an open palm on Marian's chest and yelled something with an inexplicable fury. She shouted something incomprehensible, her voice echoing through the room. Within minutes, the girl took a deep breath of the smoke-filled air. She fell into her mother's arms and whispered with bluish lips, "Mom, I can breathe!"

Large maternal tears fell onto her mother's pale cheeks. After that day, Marian never struggled to breathe again. She achieved firsts in sprints and long-distance races, dived with spectacular breath-holding abilities, joined every sports team, and hardly ever tired.

Outside the window of the fuchsia-colored taxi darting through the bustling city, skyscrapers, rundown buildings, and bazaars were strung along the elevated metro tracks. An endless haze hung over everything, turning the city into a phantom apparition. The taxi wheeled off the main road and headed into the heart of the city's prestigious neighborhoods down a broad boulevard lined with tall, slender palm trees. They crossed a bridge over the dirty Chao Phraya River, whose banks were lined with longboats and fishing homes on stilts. On the other side, towering golden domes rose above the buildings and parks. Piercing the low sky with its sharp peaks, the temples contrasted so sharply with the city's style that for a moment Marian wondered if she was hallucinating. But no, those colossal structures were more than real.

"Can we ..." Marian hesitated before asking, "Can we go there?"

El glanced at his partner from the front seat. Not finding a reciprocal look, he inadvertently stared longer than he should. Her adamantine eyes shone with a lively excitement—a true rarity in the ever-tired London.

"Maybe." He turned away, observing, as the taxi crossed the bridge, dozens of colorful motorboat roofs beneath.

The car rushed past street vendors and souvenir shops, clusters of rectangular residential buildings adorned with lush greenery, and gleaming mirrored skyscrapers.

The driver parked his taxi near a black high-rise hotel, which was embellished with genuine tropical gardens on its ledges. El paid the fare and helped the bellman with the luggage. Marian slipped out of the taxi and made her way to the lobby as fast as she possibly could. El gave her a dissatisfied glance but didn't dwell on the incident. They checked in at the reception and headed to the glass elevator.

"So high!" Marian couldn't help but remark, gazing at the rapidly receding ground beneath her feet.

During the past day, El had developed the feeling that absolutely anyone off the street could become an agent and that what was written in the files of young agents was only half true. Marian was definitely afraid of flying, suffered from acrophobia, and had had asthma, which she had conveniently left out when she had signed up for the job. Agent Flay was far from perfect, but she brought some movement into the stagnant waters of Agent Roberts' many years of service.

"I'll be waiting for you in the lobby at eight-thirty," El said and went into the neighboring room.

Marian went inside and took off her sneakers. She removed her socks and walked barefoot on the soft carpet. Approaching the panoramic window, she looked out at the strange landscape of the unfamiliar city. Roofs, roofs, and among them, piercing the clouds, skyscrapers shrouded in a thin mist. Even from a relatively modest height, post-lunch Bangkok looked like a flying island. After gazing for a while, she soon realized that although the capital was mesmerizing, it was definitely conducive to sleep.

The hotel showers were polished and almost sterile, but they lacked soul. Marian, however, didn't suffer from a lack of soul in the bathroom's interior. She suddenly recoiled from the door as she undressed. On the inside hung a wooden mask of one of the many Buddhist guardian demons. Its bright green skin was adorned with a scaly pattern, and a blue tongue twisted between its sharp fangs as it stared at Marian with bulging, insane eyes, making her freeze with fear. She didn't dare remove the totem from the door, but she had no intention of taking a shower under the strict supervision of the sea devil. Throwing a towel over the mask, Marian turned on the water and hurriedly stepped into the shower stall. The water relaxed her muscles, and the fragrant shampoo transported her from the anonymous hotel room to the heart of the jungle during a summer rain. The small room filled with white steam, the scent of coconut, and the freshness of bamboo. Overwhelmed with pleasure, Marian closed her eyes, inhaling this unknown world. Mysterious aromas intertwined with an ancient belief, giving rise to an irresistible desire to explore this enigmatic land.

The only thing a man fears—the thing he cannot explain ... In Marian's mind echoed the words spoken by someone, somewhere, at some time.

She wiped the water off her face and looked at the door. The white towel lay on the floor, and through the steamed-up glass, a crazed demon stared back at her. Strangely, he no longer frightened her. She wrapped herself in a plush robe, wiped the idol dry, and left the bathroom. Soon she sank into the soft bed and closed her heavy eyelids, a burning sensation lingering underneath. She turned to look at the white mist in which the endless Bangkok disappeared and fell asleep once again.

A knock on the door jolted Marian awake—the room was dark. Through the vast panoramic window, the metropolis glimmered with a million lights.

"Wait a minute!" she shouted, trying to figure out where she could turn on some lights.

Soon the room was delicately illuminated around the edges of the bed, and then a tall floor lamp in the corner smoothly flickered to life. For a moment Marian thought someone was sitting in the plush armchair—a dark silhouette was imprinted under the lamp. She froze, staring at the empty corner, but the insistent knocking interrupted her thoughts and instantly sent her to the door.

"It's 8:45." El was standing in front of her. "And you're not ready yet." He was dressed rather unusually for an agent—light jeans and a casual black shirt.

"I'm sorry. I didn't think it would be so hard to wake up."

"I forgive you the first time. Let's chalk it up to the time difference. I'll be waiting for you in the lobby in five minutes." El looked at his watch. "If you want, I can order you a strong coffee."

3:13 AM

"No, no, I think I've slept enough. But I'm afraid five minutes won't be long enough to get ready." Marian adjusted her hair, hinting to El about the necessity of at least minimal styling.

"Agent Flay, it won't be five minutes before your skin starts to glisten with sweat. Even after sunset, there's no relief from the heat. We're at the equator, Marian. You better get used to it," said El, heading towards the elevator.

"But five minutes ..." she pleaded.

"Don't worry. Even in that robe, you'll be the most beautiful woman out there," he replied without turning around.

"Where?" she asked, flustered by the unexpected compliment.

"On the streets of Bangkok," came his response from the elevator.

Marian rummaged through her suitcase and found a pair of comfortable jeans and a loose gray T-shirt. She tied her blond hair in a tight knot and slipped her feet into soft ballet flats. She stepped out the door, but before reaching the elevator, she returned. She switched her forbidden gadgets for a wristwatch and added a few drops of fragrance to her neck before leaving the room again.

El stood up silently when he saw his partner. They walked out onto the street, and the hotel's air conditioning was replaced by humid heat.

“Let’s take a walk to the restaurant.” El gestured gallantly to the left.

After about ten minutes of leisurely walking, Marian got used to the lack of fresh air and air in general. They crossed a narrow street and, at El’s command, turned between tall buildings. There, right in the center of the city, an evening bazaar unfolded.

“Do you need anything from Gucci?” El smiled.

Marian silently surveyed the piles of knock-off goods for any taste and of any brand. As they walked past, someone from the upper floors poured water onto the tarpaulin canopies, which emitted an exceptional stench.

“Oh my God, what’s that smell?” Marian covered her nose.

“Probably waste,” El replied. “Thai cuisine is not always refined. Even the middle classes eat meat and fish that have gone bad due to the hot weather. When combined with fragrant spices, such dishes are normal for Thailand. Not to mention delicacies like insects and snakes that are part of the local diet.”

They passed a place where a local vendor was relieving himself against the wall and suddenly emerged onto a well-kept street. Here, low, intricately trimmed trees twisted in a pink glow, polished paving stones sparkled, and the aroma of freshly cut garden flowers mingled with that of a gilded, carved house. The expansive roof, in the finest Asian architectural tradition, was adorned with an array of miniature temple offerings. There was everything here, from candle lanterns to fans to fragrant incense. Among the household items, thoughtful Thais had left fruit, cookies, and a bowl of milk.

"And what's this?"

"A spirit house," replied El shortly, as if London streets were just littered with such things. Marian became embarrassed and fell silent, gazing at the towering skyscrapers ahead that gleamed in the distance.

"Welcome to san phra phum." Suddenly lowering his tone, El began to speak. "These are not to be confused with ancestral homes or shrines for the gods Brahma and Ganesha. Here in this land, believing in spirits is not considered unusual or strange. On the contrary, beings from the other world are taken seriously. From the poorest of the poor to the successful businessmen on Forbes' list, all social classes honor the spirits and carefully tend to their abodes. The tradition of placing spirit houses and their design is comparable in Thailand only to the industrial feng shui in Singapore. The proper location of these incorporeal beings' homes determines the prosperity and health of the house's inhabitants, or even, as in this case, the entire street."

They turned into a narrow alleyway once again and emerged before a breathtaking structure. Woven from tropical plants combined with glass and illuminated by delicate fixtures stood a popular Indonesian restaurant.

"I think you're going to love it here." El smiled with his eyes.

The dimensions of the interior were stunning. Giant crystal chandeliers hung from the 65-feet-high ceiling. This fusion of high tech, bohemian, and jungle transported visitors to another planet. Marian's heart beat faster. She froze, dissolved in the beauty of this unique space, and then quickly followed El.

The dishes had a delicate flavor with no spicy seasoning.

"This is a Balinese recipe." El sipped his cold wine. "The only set of exquisite dishes without any chilli sauce. Enjoy! In Patong and on the islands, even if you beg the waiter not to use any red pepper, the food will still be too spicy."

"This is an amazing place," Marian exclaimed, "and it's not just because of this exquisite carp." She held the crystal glass delicately in her fingers and raised her eyes to the ceiling. "For so long during all my years of service ... I just want time to stop right now."

El squinted and gazed at Marian's ecstatic face for much longer than allowed by regulations.

"I told you you'd love Thailand," he said finally, and Marian smiled broadly.

It was eleven o'clock when the agents found themselves on the city streets again—poor and rich, exquisite and dirty, all mixed up amidst slums, gilded temples like diamonds lost in the rubble. Someone had drunk the milk and eaten all the cookies at the house of spirits; the bazaar was closed. Instead of tables, semi-naked Thai girls stood in the light of lanterns hung under the same tarpaulin canopies.

“Sir, come with us.” They came alive. “We’ll serve the madam too. Don’t pass us by.”

The doors swung wide open where just a few hours before, the street vendor had been squatting to relieve himself. Club music blared from the stuffy room and the spotlights glittered. Naked women were dancing on tables overflowing with liquor. Marian found herself gawking until El took her hand cautiously and led her away.

“It’s like Heaven and Hell, only side by side,” Marian observed.

“Exactly.” El smiled. “Unfortunately—or fortunately—the concepts of Heaven and Hell are not absolute. What seems like Hell to one person could be someone else’s idea of Heaven.”

They arrived at the hotel and stepped into the fresh, fragrant lobby. “There’s a bar on the top floor. Would you like to join me?” El asked politely.

“No thanks. Bangkok is dizzying enough without wine. Have a good evening.” Marian bade him farewell and got out of the elevator on her floor.

She entered the room, walked up to the panoramic window sparkling with billions of lights, and rested her slightly sweaty forehead against the cool glass. The temperature change made her temples throb. She took off her jeans and sank into the soft sheets. Her eyes closed and through the haze of sleep, she saw a man sitting in a chair. She snapped her head up and stared into the corner. Of course there was no one there, but Marian felt like there was.

Like an insistent thought or a speck in her eye, this place troubled her and deprived her of sleep.

Damn! Marian sat up in bed and clasped her head in her hands. *What's wrong with me? There's no one there! Can't you hear me? Just sleep! There's no one there!*

Suddenly she felt better. Somehow, using one of the main senses a human has, she realized that she was alone in the room. She looked at the chair—it was empty in every possible and impossible sense of the word.

She glanced at the clock—it showed 11:11 p.m. In some unique way, Marian had been catching duplicate numbers on any electronic clock too often since childhood. She drank some water, closed her eyes, and fell asleep calmly this time.

3:13 AM

Chapter 6

Sunsets. They distinguished these horizons from the others. It was the sunsets that filled Raymond's anxious mind with tranquility, and the cold wine sealed that state until morning.

Raymond wasn't afraid of the night. Perhaps in the past he might have been, when it was difficult to differentiate a coat rack in the hallway from a silent stranger. And only when the coat rack advanced toward him from the darkness would he realize that it was neither of the two. He would quickly retreat from the apparition. Sometimes someone stood by his bed all night, and, groping for his sleeping lover, he would realize that it wasn't her at all. In those semi-conscious moments, Raymond found solace in the thought that the girl wasn't a psychopath. However, that joyous thought didn't save him from the cold sweat that covered his back.

He could easily have lost his mind, like many other hypersensitive people. But he didn't. Despite everything he saw, felt, and shared his living space with, Raymond didn't contemplate suicide, nor did he think about the end. He knew for sure that physical death didn't make things any easier, unfortunately.

***

"Live, do you hear me?" Skinny fingers tightened around Raymond's hand, and strong nails dug into his young flesh. "I'll watch over you from above. I'll see everything from up there—who would know better than you?"

The young man nodded and wiped away all the coming tears. Alicia was worried about leaving her son alone in this cruel world, but most importantly, alone with himself.

For an entire year he still smelt her scent in the house. In the mornings he heard the sizzle of eggs coming from the empty kitchen. In the evenings, when he turned on the television, he saw her favorite channel playing—a channel he himself never watched. She didn't frighten him, never entered his room. She simply lived with him for the year granted to her by the rules of the afterlife. And then, on the anniversary of her death, she quietly disappeared. She left without a fuss. She kissed her sleeping son on the cheek, lightly tapped the mosquito net, and flew away with the cry of migrating birds.

The cluttered rooms suddenly became empty. Unbearably empty. And Raymond put the house up for sale.

***

"Kiet, I feel like having a steak tonight," Raymond declared as he entered the kitchen.

Kiet nodded and relayed his request to his wife. Athit retrieved a tightly packaged piece of red meat from the refrigerator and slapped it onto the table. Raymond found the scene amusing, and with a smile, he walked out onto the open veranda adorned with woven chairs.

3:13 AM

Suddenly a brilliant white yacht appeared from around the cape.

"Oh no, not her!" Raymond closed his eyes, hoping it was just his imagination. But the yacht not only didn't disappear, it approached the shore.

"Kiet!" Raymond shouted towards the kitchen. When the Thai man came into view, he added, "Two well-cooked steaks and chilled champagne. She only drinks champagne ..."

Kiet glanced at the immense vessel, quite out of place in their modest harbor.

A dinghy was lowered onto the water and a slender figure descended into it, dressed in something just as white as her yacht. A servant ferried the woman ashore and returned to the mini ocean liner. Standing on the wet sand was the long-legged Ann Jay. Korean or Japanese, and with obvious European ancestry, she looked stunning. Her sun-bleached, straight-as-rain hair fell over a loosely fitted men's shirt, revealing hints of pajama shorts underneath. In one hand Ann Jay held flip-flops and in the other, a dew-covered bottle of Piper-Heidsieck.

"Kiet, no need for champagne." Raymond reclined in his chair, his gaze fixed on his guest. "She can keep it to herself."

"Last week you were on Koh Phi Phi." Ann Jay stepped onto the wooden platform, slipped on her flip-flops, and moved closer to Raymond's chair. "And I thought you missed the embrace of a woman!"

“The embrace of a woman is significantly different from a spider’s grip, Ann Jay.”

She smiled and placed the weighty bottle on the table. “One day you’ll realize that we were made for each other.” She rested her sharp elbows on the table, her hands supporting her delicate face with its cherry-red lips.

Raymond had first seen her at a renowned restaurant in Phuket. Her outrageously expensive one-shoulder dress and luxurious hair had distracted him from his dinner. She had walked by, leaving a trail of intoxicating fragrance and a dozen questions.

While buying the island, Raymond had been obliged to attend lunches with the wealthiest Asian families, who always tried to set him up with someone. But during these encounters, Raymond had never encountered such elegance and beauty among their daughters.

Ann Jay skillfully set her traps—after all, she had gone to that restaurant for Raymond.

Did he have an affair with her? Yes, he did. Did he love her? No. Not because Ann Jay was a dominant, spoiled socialite. Raymond didn’t fall in love with her because he couldn’t. One morning he got out of bed, looked at her flawless body, luxuriant hair, and succulent lips, and realized he no longer desired them. It happens when one overindulges in oysters or expensive liquor. If someone truly loves oysters, they will return to them again and again. But if they simply wanted to try the delicacy, once they're satisfied, they'll forget about the dish.

But with Raymond it was even more than that. When he grew tired of Ann Jay, she continued to feed him with herself, and he became sickened. Now, whenever he saw the pristine white yacht entering Koh An harbor, he felt nauseous.

Kiet brought champagne glasses and popped the tight cork. The bottle exhaled and a faint wisp of smoke escaped, resembling a genie. The guest took a sip of the sparkling drink and looked at Raymond with a melancholy gaze.

"I miss you so much." She poured out her soul.

But those words didn't make it any easier for either Ann Jay or Raymond. He tried not to look at her, and only when she was admiring the island would he admire her. He wasn't missing her; he was simply astonished by her natural perfection once again. Suddenly, elongated hieroglyphs flashed on her hand through her unbuttoned cuff.

"Did you get a tattoo?" Raymond raised his expressive eyebrows high.

Ann Jay frowned. "No"—she emptied her glass—"but if it helps bring you back, I'll get one."

Raymond tensed. He stood frozen on the ocean, contemplating the strange vision.

Once he had witnessed something similar in a prestigious clinic in Bangkok. An old man in a wheelchair had been covered from head to toe with such tattoos.

Death marks? An unsettling thought passed through his mind. *Fine for an old man, but Ann Jay!*

He glanced briefly at the woman, who, not receiving any chivalry from Raymond, refilled her glass once again. A bronzed hand with a gold bracelet brushed back her hair, revealing a delicate neck. Underneath her hair, black, slightly faded hieroglyphs became visible.

Raymond closed his eyes and massaged the corners. He didn't want to see all of this. He didn't want to think about Ann Jay, but her impending death overwhelmed him.

"Are you in good health?" he asked inappropriately.

Anger immediately flashed across her beautiful face. "I'm throwing my heart at your feet," she erupted, abruptly standing up from the table, "and you shamelessly trample on it!"

"No, that's not it ..."

It was too late to justify himself, and Raymond caught Ann Jay's hand. She flinched and lowered her almond-shaped eyes to Raymond's.

"I didn't mean to offend you. Please sit down."

3:13 AM

A symbol consisting of two hieroglyphs appeared on her smooth forehead.

Quite complex characters, but if I sketch them right away… Raymond thought and bent to the sand. With a stick, he traced a schematic resemblance of a Chinese house, a cross with a slanted wall, and triple roofs.

"What does this mean?"

Ann Jay circled the hieroglyph. "It's 'kūki' in Japanese, meaning 'air.'"

"Are you flying somewhere?" Raymond sat back down. Ann Jay pondered the symbol before taking her previous seat again.

"I'm flying to Vietnam the day after tomorrow."

"Don't fly," Raymond said curtly.

"Why all these games? Do you want me to stay here? With you?" Ann Jay pleaded, ignoring Kiet with his steaks.

"No!" Raymond moistened his dry throat with champagne. "I just don't want you to fly to Vietnam."

Ann Jay covered her face with her hands and let out a heavy sigh. "How am I supposed to understand you, Raymond? How? Is there anyone on this earth who can truly understand you?" Raymond wanted to joke about a whole counter-terrorism department, but he restrained himself.

They had dinner and strolled along the twilight shore. The sky filled with blue, the misty jungles with green, and the horizon sparkled like a Christmas tree with the lights of the anchored yachts.

The evening ocean dizzied them much more than the alcohol, and soon Ann Jay took Raymond's hand. She pressed herself against him with her whole body. "I'll stay with you tonight." She leaned towards his lips.

"You can't stay," he replied quietly.

"Then kiss me. I don't want to fall asleep tonight without your kiss."

Raymond kissed her. One kiss was not enough for Ann Jay. Her lips truly resembled cherries—delicious, but impossible to eat too many of.

She didn't say goodbye. She simply turned and walked towards the yacht, which had floated ashore. Raymond watched her until she reached it—perhaps today he was seeing Ann Jay for the last time. Death marks don't simply disappear. If she refused the dangerous flight, the air hieroglyph would vanish, but it would be replaced by a hieroglyph of water, earth, fire, or who knew what else. Death holds tightly to those she has marked. Raymond had not the slightest clue why she did this or, better to say, for whom. He knew so much yet nothing at the same time. It was always the same: One newfound answer raised dozens of other questions.

3:13 AM

***

The image of old Frank froze in the air. The cramped room filled with the scream of a nurse—*he's wet the bed again*. The old man plopped himself down on the meshed mattress, waiting for a clean one, and the door of the ward closed with a bang.

"Don't be angry with her." Raymond placed the tray of lunch on the narrow table.

"She doesn't have much time left anyway. There's no point in getting offended over such sins," Frank replied indifferently, peering curiously at his plate.

"What are you talking about?" A rather young Raymond, working part-time at the psychiatric clinic, often engaged in conversations with the patients.

"She has the marks of death." Frank wiped his fork with the only napkin and started on the pasta with chicken sauce.

"Where, exactly? I didn't notice ..."

"Everywhere." The old man continued eating heartily. "They appear here and there."

"And what do they look like?" Raymond persisted.

"Sometimes like words, sometimes like symbols."

"And who puts them there?" Raymond narrowed his eyes.

"Death puts them there."

"Why?"

"So as not to get confused." Frank looked up at him with clear eyes.

Four days later, the rude and condescending nurse was hit by a bus. The doctors couldn't save her.

"Frank, did you hear? She died!"

"Ah, I warned you," the old man said with frustration.

"You warned me?" Raymond frowned.

"For the first time, I saw black fire on her body. It seemed to cover her entire hands and part of her face. *Georgina!* No, not quite." The old man paused. "'Georgia,'" I said, "'you're engulfed in fire! Check the gas in the kitchen, or better yet, don't cook anything until the weekend.' I don't know if she believed me, but on her shift on Saturday, her hands were as clean as a baby's. Well, not even a week passed and the signs appeared again ..."

"And what did you see this time?" Raymond choked out.

"I saw road markings, tire tracks, and a sign."

"A sign?"

"Yeah, 'New Jersey—Baltimore.'"

***

3:13 AM

Raymond filled his lungs with the cool night air, gazed at the starry face of the late evening, and walked towards the wooden porch. “Kiet? Has the champagne chilled enough?”

“Yes, sir—as cold as the night in London.” The Thai man tried to make a joke.

“Bring it here.” Raymond smiled. “Kiet?” Kiet froze with the sweaty bottle in his hand. “Where do Thai people go after death?”

“It depends on whether they served good or evil.” He shrugged.

Raymond frowned as if he had bitten into a lemon. “And what if they’ve served none of it?”

“I’m afraid I don’t understand,” Kiet stammered, pulling out the tight cork and releasing another pop of vapor.

That evening Raymond drank, futilely trying to push thoughts of Ann Jay away. She had everything, and that *everything* couldn’t make her happy. But it was capable of making her dead.

“What’s wrong with this world?” Raymond clasped his head in his hands and stared at the floor. A plump black snake slithered between his feet. Perhaps if a mark of death were to appear on his body today, it would take the form of a snake and three bottles of alcohol.

The creeping creature brushed against Raymond’s leg with its forked tongue, paused in contemplation, and slithered away.

He fetched a glass of water from the kitchen and stumbled back to his bungalow. He sat on the veranda, and when the Milky Way sliced across the sky from east to west, he entered the house. He took a cool shower, washing away his heavy thoughts, and stepped with wet feet onto a thin towel. His body stiffened from the cold—a coldness unimaginable for the equator.

Raymond donned his robe and glanced at the air conditioner casing—the blinds were shut. He nervously spun in place, expecting anything but this. Someone was lying on the bed.

The gauzy canopy was stained with crimson blood, attracting a swarm of black flies. A quiet moan revealed that the midnight visitor was more alive than dead. Raymond quietly approached the dresser, finding the clock there by touch.

3:14 a.m. They come after three. Raymond grew wary. *And who is it this time?*

He approached the bed, barely making a sound. The stench of decaying human flesh hit his nostrils. Through the dirty bandages he could discern deep, oozing ulcers. The guest's clothing was soaked in slime in some places and firmly stuck to the wounds in others. The face was unrecognizable—emaciated and worn, resembling that of a mummy. The dying figure turned and lunged forward, spraying Raymond with a cocktail of blood and pus.

He flinched, stumbled backward, slipped on his own wet tracks, and collapsed onto the floor.

3:13 AM

***

Through the reed blinds, the rosy haze of early morning seeped in. Chickens cackled beneath the house, and roosters crowed in the garden. Raymond raised his head. The bed was empty, clean, and neatly made. He leaned on the dresser and checked his body for any clinging insects. Finding no parasites, he crawled on his knees to the bed and slipped under the covers.

Chapter 7

Marian opened her eyes. The alarm clock emitted short beeps, urging her to wake up. White light seeped into the gap between the curtains; she could hear through the thick glass the distant beeping of cars trapped in a traffic jam.

Marian emerged from the bed, took a shower, and tied her hair into a tight knot. She slipped into a loose-fitting shirt and wide-leg trousers, laced up her sneakers, and stepped out of the door. Silently, she walked across the soft carpet of the long corridor, heading straight for the elevator. Just a few seconds later the adjacent door opened and El appeared in the hallway. He approached her room, paused, and listened, causing Marian's mind to fill with questions.

The elevator arrived, a short ding sounded, and El immediately turned around. They locked eyes—a startled El and a bewildered Marian.

"I thought you were still asleep as usual." El approached the frozen Marian and pointed to the elevator, its doors sliding open. She snapped out of her reverie, lowered her gaze, and stepped into the little compartment.

"And do you often eavesdrop by the door?" Marian managed to conceal her smile, speaking with difficulty.

3:13 AM

"Only when I don't have the equipment for proper surveillance." Marian barely held back a laugh. "You have a great style. I like it," added El unexpectedly.

She was flattered by his attention. Moreover, she enjoyed being in the company of a real secret agent, even though she had never actually worked for the counter-terrorism department. She didn't practice kung fu and had only fired real combat weapons a couple of times in her life. Undoubtedly, Marian Flay worked for the government and, in a sense, for the security service, but she certainly wasn't a secret agent like El.

***

"I got scared, you know?" El took a sip of his beer from the slender, long-necked bottle.

"Well, well, well, El, what are you going to do about all of this?" Aldridge asked, pausing for a moment before posing the question.

El scanned the miniature bowls spinning on the conveyor belt of the Japanese restaurant. He picked up a marinated squid with capers and armed himself with chopsticks.

"I'm thinking of quitting working with Raymond." El glanced sideways at the forensic investigator, his best friend by association.

"El"—Aldridge furrowed his brow—"I don't think Raymond wants you dead. In my opinion, that's the last thing he wants for you. But making some adjustments to your work is definitely worth considering." The balding man cast a glance at the pink tails sticking out of the green broth.

They ordered another bottle of beer, and Aldridge pulled his phone from his pocket. "Hold on a minute. Louise is nagging me not to get drunk. "

"Can you even get drunk on this?" El raised the miniature bottle of unfiltered beer.

He wants to sever ties with Raymond, typed Aldridge quickly and sent it to the only number in his phone that wasn't named.

Three minutes later, his phone vibrated.

Plant the idea of a young agent as his partner!

"Is she angry?" El pierced Aldridge with his gaze.

"You know my Louise." The man shrugged. "She's always ready to find fault by the second cup of morning coffee. So, you say Raymond completely lost his mind on his island?"

"You know, he's actually not a bad guy ... I mean, not the completely off-the-rails guy he appears to be." El smirked.

At that very moment, Aldridge realized that Agent Roberts would continue flying to Bangkok until the last day of his retirement.

"Sometimes I feel sorry for him. Just imagine how a young, handsome, and far from stupid person must feel, choosing a life on a deserted island instead of bustling cities, friends, and society."

"Oh, come on! This guy has set himself up pretty well."

"No matter what, a person needs another person."

"So your Raymond doesn't have anyone at all?"

"A sad story. His girlfriend died at the hands of a maniac, and a few years later his mother—his only relative—passed away in a psychiatric clinic. I don't know if Christine was his first love, but she was definitely a close one. As far as I know, he's never had a true friend since then."

"El!" Aldridge snatched two bowls of white crab meat and wood mushrooms from the passing table. "And what if I find you a partner?" he proposed, his voice filled with intrigue.

"To be honest, I thought about it that night when I left the island."

"I can say more: What if we find a charming agent from New Jersey? Would he drown a fellow native?"

"Raymond? No, he's not bloodthirsty. Just impulsive."

It seemed that El had already given up on the idea of a partner when Aldridge raised his beer bottle in the air and proposed a toast instead. "I'll prepare the files of the most talented young agents. Do it just once—not for Raymond's sake but for yourself, El. You deserve good company."

"Well, if the company is really good."

They clinked their bottles together. "I promise by the end of the workday tomorrow, there won't be a single slacker in the stack of folders on your desk."

Aldridge didn't disappoint. By the end of the workday, there was a stack of folders on El's desk filled with the personal files of young agents. The thought of a partner faded away immediately. Thailand was too tempting for men—two bachelors couldn't walk a few blocks in the evening without stumbling upon adventures that would put their badges to the test. If they were to fly, it had to be with a female agent, but Aldridge had only brought three folders belonging to women.

***

She doesn't look like Christine. Aldridge leaned over the morgue photos. *Maybe a bit in profile, but not face-on.*

"He won't see her until the airport," came the emotionless voice from the receiver. "And let the makeup artists work their magic before the photoshoot. The only thing required of El Roberts is to choose Marian Flay himself. So do your best!"

And Aldridge did his best. From the photo attached to Marian's personal file, a grown-up Christine stared at El. Her hair, nose, and neck had been blurred by a few pixels, inexorably forcing the viewer's brain to concentrate on clearer details—her expressive gray eyes and sensual lips. In addition, the computer had mirrored her face for complete symmetry. Such a technique could put a person into a trance-like state—surprisingly, our gray matter simply revels in all things symmetrical. Makeup artists, graphic designers, and Marian herself, who had never been a plain Jane, provided El's neurons with true aesthetic pleasure, and Agent Roberts made the right decision.

***

They stepped out of the elevator onto the rooftop of the building. A magnificent view unfolded before them.

"Almost among the clouds," Marian whispered softly.

Beneath the glass canopies a blue pool murmured, while comfortable wicker chairs glistened. The two agents occupied one of the tables, and a waiter promptly approached with a silver thermos in the shape of a teapot.

"Coffee?"

Marian nodded eagerly and took the hot beverage. Soon its aroma mingled with the smell of scrambled eggs, sizzling bacon, cucumber, and freshly baked bread. After breakfast they headed to the airport, and at around half-past eleven they checked in for their flight to Phuket.

The smaller Boeing didn't intimidate Marian. Instead, after takeoff, the turquoise ocean and the cluster of blue islands dispelled her fears altogether.

"You know, Marian, our plan was to get settled in the Patong hotel and then go to the pier. From there, I usually rent a boat to reach Raymond's island. But we won't sail there today."

“Why?” Marian turned her attention away from the mesmerizing view and looked at El. “Isn’t Mr. Lee expecting us today?”

“On the contrary.” El glanced out of the window, intruding on Marian’s personal space. “I think he’s expecting us precisely today.”

Marian sank back into her seat, watching El, and tactfully said, “If Raymond never makes mistakes, I’m sure he learned about the date of our visit long before us.”

El smiled discreetly. He liked the way her mind worked. He liked her style, her gaze, and he really liked her scent. He had brought her along with the intention of connecting her to Raymond, but he himself had somehow become connected. This had happened too quickly for El and completely unexpectedly.

The plane touched down. Retrieving their luggage and bypassing persistent taxi drivers, the agents stepped onto a reed-covered street where a parked white minivan awaited them. Behind the wheel sat a Thai man.

“Good day, Mr. El!” The driver grinned, revealing a row of yellow teeth. “Welcome to Thailand, madam.”

Their route took them past roadside thickets that closely resembled real jungles, adorned with green-molded houses, treacherous cliffs, and steep hills. Within thirty minutes the view of a sprinkle of islands appeared from one of them, the azure ocean glistening. Marian leaned against the window, admiring the picturesque view.

"Are we sailing there?" She gracefully pointed at the islands through the tinted glass.

As they approached Raymond's dwelling place, El became less inclined to take Marian to Koh An. "We'll see. Perhaps Raymond is in Patong and we won't have to wander around the ocean in a motorboat."

Marian's face tensed. She squinted at the horizon, realizing that the plan could abruptly change, but she immediately resumed her role and innocently asked, "What's that over there?"

"That's Patong beach, the largest one. But it usually gets stormy after lunch."

The white minivan descended the hill, paused at two intersections, and pulled up at tall ornate gates. Through the gilded multi-armed goddesses, a tropical garden, a massive turquoise pool, and a semicircular six-story hotel could be seen. Soon, a slender Swiss bellboy in a red velvet suit with golden trim appeared on the arched bridge. Everything in this place exuded oriental sophistication, scented with patchouli and jasmine, blooming and leaning toward the azure water. Abundant with fruits and refreshing drinks, the lobby resembled a Buddhist temple, not without its statues of demons to ward off restless souls. The agents' rooms were located on the ground floor, side by side once again.

"I'll talk to you about our plans later. In the meantime, relax," El briskly told Marian, and she disappeared into her room.

The luxurious decor held little interest for her now. She approached the immense window overlooking the pool and leaned against the glass. "Damn," she whispered. "Did you really change your mind about introducing us?"

All right, Marian, focus! If Roberts is heading to the island alone, for example, I can also sail to Lee's place alone, but I need to know the island's name. I can't contact headquarters ... Damn! Everyone was sure he was bringing me to meet Lee!

Marian darted from the window to the bed.

Fine—let's assume I follow Roberts and remember the name of the boat. Then I'll pay the guy double and he'll take me to Lee ... Marian ran her slender fingers through her light hair. *The important thing is that he takes me there. Well, and that he isn't one of Roberts' men. It'll be much easier if they meet somewhere here in Patong. In that case, surveillance will be significantly simplified.*

Marian understood perfectly—the situation had drastically changed, and now she would have to follow Agent Roberts' every step.

***

As soon as Marian had taken off her protective suit, a phone call came through on the office's landline. Removing her gloves as she went, she circled around the desk and grabbed the black, rectangular receiver.

"I'm listening."

"Dr. Flay?" The voice sounded painfully familiar.

"Good afternoon, sir—or is it evening already?" Marian glanced up at the darkening window.

"You're about to go on a trip."

"Alaska again?"

"No. This time to the islands in Thailand."

Marian pondered for a moment while the voice continued.

"You're required to hear the testimony of a certain Raymond Lee."

"Testimony?"

"Accounts of his visions and premonitions, just like the other two cases."

"Do his descriptions match? Are you expecting a similar description of the disease symptoms from this"—she paused, trying to remember the name—"Raymond?"

"I don't expect anything from him. And you shouldn't either. Your task is to familiarize yourself with his stories and draw parallels—if it is possible, of course—with the visions of the other two oracles."

"Understood. When do I fly?"

"You'll be flying with an agent—El Roberts. He'll contact you and arrange the assignment."

"Got it."

"And one more thing." The caller paused briefly. "You'll have to work undercover as a young security service agent. A copy of the fictional dossier will be in your mailbox at nine p.m. We decided not to change your name, but you'll need to study your new biography thoroughly."

"Why all the complexity?" Marian frowned.

"El knows nothing about the other oracles. He's always worked solely with Raymond, and I've decided to keep it that way."

"Hmm. So why does he need a partner?"

"It seems Raymond Lee has acquired telekinesis and frightened Roberts. He wants support to avoid such situations."

"I see. And this Raymond—does he know about the others? Or about me?"

"I can't say for certain. He's the most powerful of them all but also the most unstable. He only communicates with Roberts. We've sent our guys to him before, but the experience had unpleasant consequences for them. Since then, very few in the department are eager to work with him."

3:13 AM

"Very few?"

"Actually, no one ... Good evening, Dr. Flay."

"Good evening ..."

Marian hung up the phone and stared out of the window, where twilight had given way to darkness. Exactly at nine o'clock, as if from nowhere, a lavender folder appeared in her mailbox. Among the papers, underneath her new biography, lay a couple of photographs. The stern yet vibrant gaze of Agent Roberts and the cold, transparent blue eyes of Mr. Lee both looked at her from the surface of the lacquered desk. She brought her cup of hot tea from the kitchen, blew on it, and, forgetting to take a sip, put it down. The photo of Mr. Lee fully caught her attention.

His pale skin contrasted with his dark hair, which framed his high forehead in large carefree waves. Her inquisitive gaze skimmed over his straight nose, then shifted to his pronounced cheekbones and masculine chin and finally settled on his thin lips.

Her heavy head touched the velvet cushions. In her hands flashed the photo of Raymond.

***

The means of communication was left for El in the same spot—at the minivan's door. El took up his phone, checked his email, and had just sent a few short messages to headquarters when there was a knock on his door. Marian stood on the threshold, dressed in a black knit dress and sandals.

"I'm going to the ocean. Are you okay with that?" she asked.

"I wouldn't recommend it. There's a storm brewing," El said, noticing how well black suited Marian.

"Don't worry. As you learned from my dossier, I'm an excellent swimmer." Marian was determined, and although El wasn't thrilled by her initiative, he eventually meekly closed the door behind her.

He went to the spa, took a dip in the pool, and ordered coffee in his room. He felt the desire for cigarillos again, not out of shock but due to the memories—this balcony was where he had last smoked them.

The human brain is uniquely wired. If something contradicts its common sense, it simply moves it from the folder labeled "reality" to the folder labeled "illusion." El's brain lacked originality—it slowly but surely moved the lifeless hands rocking the boat to the "illusion" section.

Suddenly, under the pointed roof of the round bar, El spotted a familiar figure. No, this time it wasn't his imagination—Raymond Lee was sitting in this hotel, practically opposite his room. Raymond was leaning over the bar, sipping a foamy piña colada through a straw, and thanks to the fact that the hotel was populated by wealthy retirees, not a single night butterfly had settled around him yet. El stood up before he had even had the chance for a proper sit down and quickly left his room.

“What are you doing here?” El didn’t bother with greetings.

“Stop pretending to be surprised.” Raymond laughed suddenly. “You don’t have to be psychic to find you in Patong. You always come to the same hotel and get a room with a poolside view, and they are practically facing the bar ...”

“So you decided to surprise me?” El interrupted him abruptly.

“I wish I’d come here with the intention of surprising you.” Raymond took a sip of his cocktail. “I can’t sleep in my own house. They literally drove me out.”

“Who?” El frowned.

“The walking dead, El; the walking dead.” Raymond sighed as if he was talking about an invasion of ants or, worse, rats.

Chapter 8

On the nightstand, a glass of cold water and an aspirin came into focus.

"Damn ... Kiet! It feels like I'm this close to confessing my love to that guy," Raymond muttered, tearing open the wrapping of the tablet.

It fell into the water and started fizzing. Suddenly, amid the fizzing, Raymond distinctly heard a whisper. He jumped up and looked around—the canopy was bathed in warm afternoon light. Through it he could make out the wicker chest of drawers, a massive television, the built-in blinds on the wall cabinets, a comfortable armchair, and a small corner bar with glasses, strong liquor, and a coffee machine.

He froze, still listening to the silence. In the jungle wild birds were squawking, the pool was gurgling in the courtyard, and water was dripping in the shower, splashing heavily onto the gray tiles of the stone floor. Soon the aspirin tablet would dissolve completely, taking with it the secret of the strange whisper.

Raymond hated being frightened. The dead, essentially, shouldn't scare him. Especially for someone who had grown accustomed to their presence and learned to coexist with it. Leaving a message should suffice; after all, appearing in a dream would make him understand everything. But these dead ones followed their own scheme, and Raymond couldn't comprehend either them or their motives. They didn't speak to him, didn't ask for help—they seemed to have simply come across him once and surrounded him without any apparent purpose.

He took a refreshing sip of the medicine and, after lying in bed for another half an hour, finally got up. He brewed some coffee and hastily put on a shirt—clean, without the scent of Ann Jay or any trace of her lipstick. If only he could help her—the heavy thoughts tempted him to drink again. But Raymond, without any unnecessary drama, closed his eyes and breathed in the damp jungle air.

***

No one can help us but ourselves, said the man whom Raymond had once met in New York.

"Hey, kid," a strange old man had called out to him in the street, "aren't you afraid to lead them?"

"Who?" Raymond glanced behind him.

"The dead!" The homeless man gestured wildly toward Central Park West.

"There are no dead people here," Raymond replied calmly with absolutely certainty.

"They're there," the old man insisted. "And there are countless of them, Raymond, an entire ocean ..."

Raymond frowned—he had definitely not told the stranger his name. “Are you hungry?” He raised his eyebrows, trying to recognize in the old man someone familiar to him or his mother.

“Am I hungry?” the homeless man countered. “No, I am not hungry, Raymond. Don’t run away from them, do you hear? Don’t run. They are your destiny, your inevitability.”

Raymond, despite his respect for street prophets, did not like the vagabond’s words.

“Sir, I would like to help you, but alas, I don’t know how.” He decided to intelligently end the conversation.

“No one, do you hear, no one is capable of helping us except ourselves.” The vagabond waved his dirty hand at Raymond and pushed his trolley, apparently stolen from a grocery store.

“Who are you talking about now? People like you and me?” Raymond shouted in surprise.

“What’s the difference?” the old man grumbled. “You, me, all the living—everyone will be dead very soon.”

***

Chills ran down Raymond’s arms from the memories.

“How can one see so far into the future?” He squinted and took a sip of black coffee from a white cup.

The recent rain had just passed, and the shady garden was filled with bright colors. Thin streams of water still dripped from the giant palm leaves, the towering plumeria showered the pool surface like a white carpet, and purple orchids released fresh root tendrils. The scarlet heliconia collected rainwater in its pockets, while the giant strelitzia revealed long bright-blue pistils emerging from its yellow petals. On that rainy day, Raymond was absolutely certain—nothing could evict him from his heaven.

How wrong he was.

Raymond passed the mango trees, whose whimsical roots seemed eager to reach into his pool, and walked along a narrow path that led to the ocean in search of the azure water. He trudged across the wet sand, from which small seashells and coral branches emerged, exposed by the receding tide. He walked for over a hundred yards until the water finally reached his knees.

"I'll take a dip here," he decided and lay down in the transparent, warm water. Out of habit, he surveyed the billowing clouds that had brought rain and that were now drifting away from Koh An. His half-closed eyes wandered over the hills of green jungles until they settled on a rocky cliff. Usually a ghost stood there, but today there was no one in that spot.

Raymond lifted his head and stared intently at the shore. In that moment, he felt with his skin that someone was watching him from the depths of the dense jungle. Not one, not two people—there were watchers everywhere. A rissoid running across the seabed brushed against his back, startling him.

What's happening to me? I'm not easily frightened, he thought, hastily retreating to the dry sand.

Something stirred and darted among the trees off to the side—Raymond caught a glimpse of movement out of the corner of his eye. It was as if his deserted island had suddenly become inhabited, so vividly did he see it all.

Struggling to maintain his composure, Raymond reached the porch and collapsed into a chair.

"Mr. Lee? Wine?" Kiet hurriedly asked.

"No, no wine. Enough!" Raymond blurted. "Not far from losing my mind completely ..." he whispered to himself.

"Coffee?"

"Yes, please ... and water! Ice-cold water."

Kiet sprang into action as if Raymond was dying of thirst and very soon returned with a dew-covered pitcher, a glass, and a mug of frothy coffee.

The island's master reclined in the chair, his gaze lifting to the pristine beach where the tide had scattered dozens, perhaps hundreds, of intricate seashells. And there, at the edge of the jungle, he saw Ann Jay.

She watched him from a distance, refusing to come closer. Raymond could easily assume that she had left the yacht beyond the cape. He was even willing to believe that Ann Jay had climbed over the ridge of those sharp rocks to reach the beach. But the blood-soaked clothes, twisted limbs, and eyes lost in darkness vividly conveyed that Ann Jay's beautiful body was not there anymore.

Perhaps she had listened to Raymond's words, but in her own way. Instead of waiting until the day after tomorrow as planned, she had flown to Vietnam the very next morning, hastening her own demise. Raymond's hand trembled. He struggled to avoid spilling his coffee, placing the hot beverage carefully on the table and grabbing a pitcher of water. Without taking his eyes off Ann Jay's disfigured form, he filled a glass and poured icy water directly onto his crown.

His body twitched; his breath faltered. He let out a sigh of relief—the sandy shore was empty. Only a pair of monitor lizards basked on a dry tree nearby. They raised their heads and extended their black forked tongues as if sensing the restless spirit of Ann Jay. Raymond stood up, grabbed his mug from the table, and, trying to keep himself composed, strode along the narrow gray tiles amidst the tropical trees. Thoughts swarmed incessantly in his mind. Could he have saved her by keeping her on the island? By lying, as he had done countless times before, about missing her? Not missing her soul, to be honest, but her voluptuous body. Had Ann Jay's presence in this place altered the course of her destiny? Could he have forewarned her about her death by revealing everything he knew—about how differently he saw the world, how intricately he explored life in all its manifestations, and how acutely he sensed death? There were no answers to these questions.

He reached the bungalow and ascended to the veranda.

It was calm here. The pool murmured pleasantly, and the trees swayed with the sudden gusts of wind—a storm was brewing. Like a colossal unknown organism, it loomed from the direction of the open ocean. It didn't creep forward, trying to remain unnoticed. On the contrary, it surged with unprecedented force, engulfing everything in its path, striving to uproot things from the earth and devour them.

Large raindrops drummed on the palm leaves, and the azure pool became ruffled. Twilight joined the dark clouds, and soon Raymond's paradise garden sank into semi-darkness. The gusty wind transformed into an outright hurricane. As the palm groves bent, revealing the chrome shower stand, a black figure appeared before Raymond. The guest stood motionless, leaning his forehead against the mosaic tiles. His skin had darkened, his clothes were soaked in blood, and someone had haphazardly cut his hair. In the mango thickets among the upturned roots, another intruder stood frozen, while a third one watched Raymond through the reed sticks.

Raymond didn't want to succumb to panic and continued sitting in the chair. He drank cold water and convinced himself that there was nothing to fear until he glanced at the surface of the pool. There, floating in the thick blood, were corpses. The rain washed their bodies, and decaying wounds gaped through torn clothing.

Even after witnessing that, Raymond stubbornly remained seated, even as his heart raced and futilely attempted to burst out of his chest. He closed his eyes and counted to ten in a measured rhythm. He took a deep breath, inhaling the scent of rain, and opened his eyes again—only to find the pool empty. However, this time the corpses, every single one of them, stood in coagulated blood, fixing their murky gazes on him.

Raymond jumped out of the chair and rushed into the house. He locked the door—the same one that he had only closed during his first two nights there out of unfamiliarity and fear of snakes and monitor lizards. He surveyed the room, closed the shutters, and slumped into a chair near the window. He could no longer see the jungle, but he could hear the rain drumming on it and the massive wet leaves lashing against the walls of the bungalow.

Outside, night had completely fallen, and Raymond's dwelling was engulfed in gloom. He lit a torch and brewed a pot of fragrant tea. Only now, battling primal fear, did he unexpectedly note the downsides of being single.

What's the point in having company if I'm the only one seeing the dead? Raymond took a sip of the hot drink, closed his eyes, and sank into the soft pillows. Suddenly, amidst the sound of rain, a familiar eerie whisper reached his ears.

"What do you want?" Raymond shouted. "I don't understand your whispering! Speak normally or go away."

The whisper ceased as abruptly as it had begun. Raymond listened intently, took a gulp of tea, and reclined in the chair.

"That's better."

After finishing his drink, he changed into comfortable pajamas and settled into bed. He decided to take a sleeping pill. Since a whole tablet would make him groggy until the following evening, he only took half of the long pill. The medication was more soothing than the rain—Raymond's eyelids grew heavy, and his consciousness plunged into oblivion.

He opened his eyes expecting the morning, but it was still night. His head felt as if it were filled with lead, and no matter how hard he tried to focus his gaze, the picture blurred. The wind howled outside. The sound unsettled him because it was closer than usual. Something was banging in the distance, preventing peaceful sleep. Raymond pried open his extremely heavy eyelids and eventually discovered the source of the noise—the front door, which he had locked that evening, was swinging open. The canopy, stained with crimson marks, fluttered in the wind. In front of his bed stood people. Dark silhouettes of the dead surrounded Raymond, fixing their lifeless eyes on him.

"What do you want?" he whimpered, attempting to sit up.

Amidst the roar of the wind and the relentless pounding of the door, Raymond discerned a monotonous murmur. The corpses whispered once more, depriving him of his sanity. He grabbed a pillow and covered his head with it. After a moment, cold hands touched him beneath the blanket—he instinctively curled up, hugging his legs to his chest, his entire body trembling. His body had transformed into a bundle of fear.

3:13 AM

Somewhere beneath the house a rooster let out a frantic cry, and Raymond jolted on the bed. Daylight seeped through the shutters. The room was empty, and the door was closed.

Raymond pressed his palms against his face and exhaled with relief into his trembling fingers. Dead ... They had never touched him. They appeared, frightened him, watched him indifferently, replayed the moment of their death, but the ghosts never ... never touched him. Oh no, these deceased were not mere visitors. They required something greater than a mortal writhing in fear. Moreover, when Raymond demanded answers from the spirits, they always spoke. But these ones showed no inclination for heartfelt conversation. Beyond everything else, Raymond was concerned with one solitary question: What were their intentions? What reaction did they expect from him? What were they pursuing? They had made no attempt to warn him of anything or divulge any information. It seemed that he had simply been careless, disturbing them by delving into places too dangerous to explore.

He got out of bed, brewed coffee, and approached the door. His tired gaze landed on the lock, hanging by just one screw—the rest lay at his feet in a halo of small wood shavings.

Raymond furrowed his brow. *The dead must have gone mad ...* He disdainfully flicked the white screw with his slipper and nudged the warped door with two fingers.

That morning he lingered on the veranda, refusing food. Closer to noon, he packed a small sports bag and headed to the beach.

"Kiet!" he called, examining the corals brought in by the ocean and embedded in the planks of the wooden platform.

"Yes, sir?" The Thai man emerged from under the shelter.

"I'm leaving for Patong for a few days. Can you fix my door? By the way, you and your wife can visit your daughter and your grandchildren if you like—I won't be here."

"Understood, sir. When do you plan to return?"

"Perhaps after the weekend."

The Thai man nodded and bowed politely.

Raymond made his way along the wet sand towards the yacht hidden beyond the cape. The storm during the night, the water sweeping over the palm trees, had evicted the slumbering reef-dwelling inhabitants from their underwater realm. Raymond came to a halt. He bent down and pulled an open oyster shell from the sand. In the pale yellow layers of the mollusc's flesh shimmered a large droplet-shaped pearl.

Rare! With a hint of pink. Raymond admired it, and after detaching the precious find from the slimy tissues, he tossed the oyster back into the ocean.

He rounded the bald rocks and reached the wooden pier. The large waves didn't reach this place—they crashed against the reefs surrounding the tall cape. Raymond started the engine, guided the mini yacht along a winding path free of underwater rocks, and sped towards the shores of Patong.

An hour later the azure bay appeared, framed by a white strip of sand and a coastal town immersed in the jungle.

Raymond approached one of the docks in the harbor and moored the yacht. He paid the attendant, hoisted his travel bag onto his shoulder, and set off towards the town. Before long he hailed a rickshaw that took him to a hotel with exotic carved gates. It was not far from where he had once met El, where Agent Roberts had imprudently praised the decor and comfort of the rooms that led directly to the pool.

A bellhop rushed to the gates. "Welcome, sir!"

The inner courtyard truly resembled Eden, and Raymond noted that the agent had excellent taste and perhaps even a budding affinity for luxury. Stepping across the humpbacked bridge that stretched over the sprawling pool, he cast his eyes upon the cozy balconies with their woven sofas. Banana palm and reed thickets separated each of the rooms, each of which had its own individual descent into the water. His gaze froze on three rooms to his right and one on the other side of the simulated island, which served as a breakfast spot and a bar at the same time. In some inexplicable way, Raymond could sense the presence of El Roberts. He had stayed there before, so he would stay there again this time.

"Good day, Mr. ...?" A round-faced Thai woman in close proximity greeted him.

"Lee. Raymond Lee."

"Did you make a reservation, Mr. Lee?"

"No," Raymond declared firmly.

"I'm very sorry." The receptionist smiled apologetically, folding her hands as if preparing to pray. Raymond sighed and pulled an unremarkable yet highly prestigious piece of plastic from his pocket—a Centurion MasterCard. Not only did its owner have to spend no less than a quarter of a million dollars per year, but there was also a charge of three thousand greenbacks just for its maintenance.

"What type of room are you interested in?" The Thai woman leaned in towards the screen. "We have a VIP suite with a private rooftop pool or a duplex with a six-person jacuzzi."

"A room for six people?" Raymond frowned.

"A jacuzzi for six people, Mr. Lee. And if you need people—"

"I understood, thank you!" he hurriedly interrupted. "I need a ground floor room with direct access to the pool."

"Yes, we have one available—an end unit, the most spacious." She clicked the mouse twice.

Raymond closed his eyes for a few seconds. Before him appeared El's broad back—he was walking along the red carpet of a corridor adorned with intricate demon statues and huge vases filled with tropical plants. Raymond saw in El's hand a hotel card when the agent stopped at a carved door.

3:13 AM

The number 1313 manifested itself. In Raymond's vision, El turned to see Marian with her light hair tied tightly at the nape of her neck. She entered room 1312.

"I need 1311." The millionaire declared his desire with precision, sliding his Centurion card across the marble countertop.

"But it ..."

"No? Well, I'll have to search for another hotel, then ..."

The senior manager, who had rushed to the reception desk as soon as he had spotted one of the most prestigious bank cards in the world, nudged the receptionist aside. "Of course it's yours, Mr. Lee!"

"By any chance, have there been any deaths here?" Raymond calmly inquired.

The manager stared at Raymond in astonishment but a moment later apologized and shook his head.

"And there isn't an ancient cemetery beneath the hotel?"

"No, sir," the manager said fearfully.

"Then why did you place guardian demons in the corridors?"

"For decoration, Mr. Lee." The manager slid the golden-framed guest welcome message towards Raymond.

He signed it without providing any further personal information, without filling out forms or showing his passport.

Within three minutes he had checked into the room he had chosen, and within another five minutes—at precisely 1:13 p.m. local time—an exquisite lunch and a bottle of chilled champagne were brought to him. Raymond immediately exchanged it for Australian white wine and remained quite satisfied.

“If only they could banish the ghosts, I may live here,” he pondered, opening the balcony door and stepping out to the gurgling pool.

3:13 AM

Chapter 9

In his dream Raymond stepped through the door and froze in the narrow hallway. The sound of running water echoed from the bathroom. He turned and had just taken a step towards the source of the noise when an ugly demon face emerged from the doorway. Surrounded by a green haze, it bared its fanged teeth and hissed like a serpent, its long tongue nearly brushing against Raymond.

"Goddamn it, those guardians!" Raymond exclaimed, recoiling.

He walked over to the panoramic window and gazed out at the mist-covered Bangkok. Soon Marian entered the room, wrapped in a robe.

"You have quite a modest budget," Raymond remarked, but Marian didn't hear the guest, nor did she see him. She collapsed onto the soft bed and closed her reddened eyes, deep in thought.

Raymond sank into a chair and focused his gaze on the agent. He didn't have to watch for long before he was able to enter her recent memories. A white veil of clouds obscured his view.

***

"We're flying over the mountains, Dr. Flay, so there might be some turbulence," warned the pilot of the small six-seater plane.

The screen of her phone displayed 2:45 p.m., and Marian shifted her gaze to the oval window. Below them lay the deep green mountain peaks, covered in a thick carpet of massive evergreen forest. The surroundings felt so soft and cozy that it deceptively gave the impression that nothing bad could happen, even if one of the planes were to lose attitude and fall.

The plane shook, and the woods instantly lost their enchanting allure. Marian pressed herself into the seat, inhaling and exhaling deeply through slightly parted lips.

“How much longer until Juneau?” she asked.

“Twenty minutes, ma’am, no more,” replied the pilot, and he was right.

Before twenty precious minutes had passed, the mighty pass curved towards the green expanse of the bay. Here, on both shores of the breathtaking strait, lay the capital of Alaska. Cities like Nome, Juneau, and a few others could only be reached by plane—there were simply no highways leading there. But even this place was not her destination.

The landing was smooth, but once the flight was over, Marian was glad to be behind the wheel of a ground vehicle. “Do you have something smaller than this?” she inquired, surveying the old pickup truck.

“Believe me, for the roads you’ll be driving on, this is the most suitable vehicle.” A burly rental worker examined her from head to toe. "Even though it's spring now, there's still plenty of snow outside the city."

He tucked his chubby hands into the pockets of his work overalls and pulled out the keys. Marian reached out for them as the guy playfully clenched the jingling keychain in his fist, disgustingly smacking his lips on a chewed matchstick.

"Will you leave a phone number? Just in case." He chuckled. "Otherwise, wherever you go, you might easily end up on a list."

"What list?" Marian sneered contemptuously.

"Missing persons."

Leaving the city, Marian drove thirty-seven miles along a picturesque forest road. Occasionally, wooden mansions with boats parked for the winter could be seen nearby. In the entire duration of the drive, only six cars passed in the opposite direction.

The social distance is impressive—six miles per person! Marian noted.

After two hours of driving on the winding yet monotonous road, oncoming traffic disappeared altogether. Tall pines gave way to rows of similar pines, with the distant northern sun flickering between them. Marian felt drowsiness creeping over her—her eyelids grew heavy, and it seemed like all thoughts vanished from her mind. On the left, a mesmerizing strip of lake emerged. Marian hit the brakes and pulled over on the shoulder. Out of habit, she crossed the empty road and made her way over the steep pebbles to the water's edge. The lake, saturated with emerald-green hues, proved to be astonishingly pure and cold. Marian washed her face and, with a keen eye, observed her surroundings.

According to the map, the road circumvented the gleaming mountain and disappeared into the wilderness. Somewhere out there an old man lived—in a place that no one had given a name. In Alaska there are numerous solitary houses identified by the road they are near. And that's the best-case scenario. In the worst, the road is marked only by a weather-worn number.

The velvety firs soothed her weary city eyes, and the smooth surface of the water carried her thoughts away from the hustle and worldly troubles. Suddenly a figure appeared on the opposite shore. Whether a hunter or a fisherman, he stood frozen, studying Marian as if she was a rare creature. She immediately jumped to her feet and hurried towards the car. For the next couple of hours, sleep was far from her mind—she didn't even consider stopping or dozing off, locking herself inside the vehicle.

As the numbers she'd been searching for came into view at the roadside, darkness engulfed the place. Only the last remnants of sun-kissed snow illuminated the narrow forest road, and through the black branches, a warm glow of electric light flickered.

3:13 AM

Marian parked the car on a cleared patch of the yard and ascended the creaky wooden staircase. The front door opened right away, revealing a bearded, slender man. Ethan Parker had looked much older in the photo, and Agent Turner had referred to him as an old man multiple times during their conversation.

"Good evening, Dr. Flay!" Parker opened the wooden door wide, spreading his arms warmly. "Tired, are you? There's hardly anywhere for a helicopter to land here. Just forests all around," he mumbled apologetically, not allowing Marian to get a word in edgeways.

Marian took off her jacket and boots, receiving soft rabbit fur slippers from Parker in return. "The floor is cold," he explained. "Are you hungry?"

"Yes, thank you," she replied curtly, hesitantly standing on the threshold of the spacious room.

It had everything one needed for life in the forest, including a shotgun hanging above the fireplace. Soft armchairs and a table stood near two large windows. Opposite the fireplace was a couch on carved wooden legs. And against the stone wall, a round table and four homemade chairs were arranged.

Marian's gaze was drawn to the roast potatoes with pheasant.

"Please, please. You must be hungry, of course!" Parker continued bustling. "For breakfast, I managed to get duck eggs. There won't be any bacon—I get my meat from birds and fish."

"Don't worry." Marian waved her hands. "I appreciate any treats and I'm grateful for such hospitality."

Parker beamed and slowly sat down on a stool. "And I also have teas! A large collection of herbal teas! Doctor, do you like tea?"

By that time Marian's mouth was full of food, and she could only nod. But it was enough for Parker to keep talking, and talk he did without pause.

"Alaska is an amazing place. I used to live in Denver and had no idea how incredible it is to reside outside the city and away from people. I used to anxiously wait for spring every year, like a fool, going to work, worrying about neighbors. I would be late for the bus, upset if I got my feet wet. Denver has so much rain, you can't even imagine. Much more than in London—you flew here from there, didn't you?"

"Not a direct flight, of course." Marian wiped her mouth with a napkin and took a sip of water.

Ethan Parker sounded like someone not entirely sane. *Either he's spent too much time alone in the woods or that's the price of having superpowers*, she thought.

"No, no, don't say that! I didn't spend too much time alone in the woods. And it's hard to call it loneliness," Parker declared as if Marian had spoken her thoughts aloud.

But Marian knew for certain that she hadn't uttered a word. She froze with a fork in her hand, staring at the mind reader.

3:13 AM

What ... what the Devil?

"The Devil has nothing to do with it," Parker added, looking embarrassed.

"But how ...?" Marian mumbled, deciding that it would be mentally healthier for her to communicate with Parker using her vocal cords.

"What?" Parker exclaimed in surprise.

"How can you read my thoughts?"

"And you haven't spoken to me, have you?" Parker genuinely seemed baffled.

He got up from the table and started to fill the kettle with water. The stream trickled weakly and Marian noticed his trembling hands. Finally she saw to what extent Parker was afraid—he was afraid of himself.

"I was talking to myself, but it seems there's no secrets from you." She tried to ease the situation, knowing who she was heading towards and why. "Tell me, Ethan, how do you do it? Do my thoughts ... hmm ... they sound in your head? Or do you simply know what I'm thinking as if you just thought of it yourself?"

"I don't know," came the rather unexpected response. "I can't say if your voice sounded as a sound in my ears or as a thought in my head. I simply ... I simply receive information from you."

“You receive information?”

“Do you think the forest is silent? And all these animals? They all speak, each carrying its own information.” Parker crossed the room and approached the window.

“And you hear them?” Marian narrowed her eyes in disbelief.

“Yes, I hear them. I hear the forest scream in pain when it’s being chopped down. I hear the deer express gratitude for a handful of hay during the harsh winter. I hear the fatally wounded hare begging for an end to its suffering.”

“But how do you hunt, then?”

“I don’t hunt. Fishermen and hunters come to me—I help them, they help me.”

“I understand how they help you, but how do you help them?” Marian pressed for an answer.

“I tell them where the fish will feed, when and where the pheasants will fly. Sometimes I have to share the whereabouts of deer or bears. But I never disclose the locations of mothers with their young, never!” Parker raised his voice.

“Yes, I understand.” Marian set aside the pheasant leg, her hunger suddenly dulled. “So, what have you seen that you must tell me?”

“I didn’t see anything.” Parker shrugged. “Unfortunately or fortunately, I don’t see things, but I hear them.”

3:13 AM

"Speak to me." Marian bustled about, retrieving a recording device from her belongings.

"Whispers."

"Whose whispers?" She pressed the button.

"At first I thought it was the trees whispering." Parker's speech was interrupted by the whistle of the boiling kettle.

He poured hot water into a teapot in which aromatic dried herbs and berries lay. He placed two clay mugs on the table and, shuffling his feet, filled them with a greenish tea.

"Let's go to the veranda. I'll tell you—it all happened right there."

Carrying the mugs, Parker went out onto the wide veranda that surrounded the entire house. Marian followed him closely, her footsteps echoing softly on the wooden planks. The cold air rushed into her lungs. Taking a deep breath, she could even distinguish the rich scent of pine resin and the familiar smell of snow. Oh yes, snow has a smell! In reality, the melting snow carried the familiar scent of rain. Marian knew it well, having grown up in Canada, where winters were filled with snowy landscapes and the promise of spring showers. The fragrance of damp earth mingling with the cool freshness of the air brought back memories of childhood and the anticipation of new beginnings.

***

The scent, combined with the surrounding forest, unfailingly transported her back to one spring. That very day when she had first laid eyes on a mangled corpse. The man lay motionless at the bottom of a ravine. Thin streams of melting snow trickled down to his feet. It was springtime, but not the fragrant and sunny kind; it was gloomy, rainy, and slushy.

"Hey, mister!" Marian shouted, having sneaked out of her house for a secret rendezvous with her high school buddy Willie. "Hey, can you hear me?"

The man didn't budge. As the girl walked along the edge of the cliff, trying to catch a glimpse of the stranger from a different angle, her feet slipped. Mud separated from the bank, dragging Marian downward. In a panic, she clutched the loose soil with her fingers, but it did little to impede her rapid descent. With great speed, her boots collided with rocks. Her body spun around, jerked up, and plummeted to the ravine floor. Her head spun, her hands had scraped against the rocks, and her clothes were soaked in places.

Marian lifted herself up and her gaze fell upon the lifeless body.

Maybe he fell just like I did but hit a rock and lost consciousness, she speculated.

"Hey, mister," she touched the man's shoulder.

It was wet, cold, and far too rigid. As if it wasn't a person but a dummy. Marian stood up and circled the discovery. She felt foolish: She had gotten dirty, soaked, and bruised descending to assist a lifeless piece of plastic. But when her eyes beheld the face of the find, she lost her balance and fell to the ground. It was human. Well, it used to be. Before her lay a corpse, its facial skin, unlike its rock-solid back, sagging and splitting. The nose seemed transparent, revealing its large triangular cartilage through the wounds. Insects had settled in one eye, making themselves a temporary dwelling. The other eye, clouded and covered in a murky film, stared at Marian. She would have thought the unfortunate had caused his own demise if not for the rectangular piece of silver tape securely covering his mouth.

After minutes of sheer horror, a sense of curiosity awakened within Marian. She often found herself mentally returning to that face. Death now held a peculiar fascination for her. This had seemed abnormal until she had pursued a career in medicine.

***

Parker placed his mug on the table and moved his chair to the right of the door.

“I was sitting right here, in this spot, when I heard a faint whisper. I didn’t like it. No, not at all! It made my hands tremble, just like they are now.” He brought the mug to his lips and Marian noticed the tremor in his hands. “I listened carefully and heard my name: ‘Ethan, Ethan,’ they whispered, ‘come to us, Ethan!’ I said I wouldn’t go.” He shook his head convulsively.

Marian felt uneasy. It wasn't about the strange whisper; she wasn't afraid of it. It was Ethan Parker that truly frightened her.

Turner, this guy is not himself... She lifted her gaze to the sky, mentally sending a message to her boss. Naturally Turner couldn't receive her message, but Parker could.

"Yeah, I'm out of my mind," he repeated.

"Damn," Marian whispered.

"Yet your department keeps sending their agents to me. So is the madman not as crazy as he seems?"

Marian struggled to swallow. "Did they whisper anything else? Maybe they mentioned under what circumstances they'd died?"

"The dead?" Parker clarified, and Marian gave him an anxious look. "The dead said they're more alive than all of us. 'Compared to us, Ethan, you're dead. You're dead and we're alive!' That's what they said. And then, as proof, they snapped branches in the woods and scratched my house. They scratched everything down there!"

"Did you see the scratches?" Marian began to rise and approach the balcony railings to look down, but she stopped herself.

"No. They'll only appear in nine years."

3:13 AM

Marian took a sip of the herbal tea, which tasted surprisingly decent, and rested her head against the wall.

"I know, Ethan Parker, we live in different worlds. And ... I apologize for that."

Parker took a big gulp as well and exhaled with relief, his breath forming white vapor in the cold evening air.

"The authorities in the center listened to your and another oracle's stories. They believe that a terrible disease is approaching the world. That's why they've sent a doctor to you. I need to know the symptoms of this sickness, you understand. But the fact that these people are dead and whispering is not a symptom. I need to know what they died of and how. Do you understand?"

"Yes, I understand," Parker responded, albeit not immediately. "The next morning I asked the forest if it had seen my nocturnal guests. Because, as I've mentioned, I only hear things, I don't see them."

"You said." Marian nodded.

"The forest replied that there was no place to go at night—the dead were everywhere. Bald walking corpses, rotten to the core, they surrounded my house. Their eyes were clouded white like dead fish. And their bodies were covered in fatal wounds ... so severe that the snow turned red."

“So that’s what the forest said?” Marian squinted, noting how poetically the forest could speak. Parker lowered his gaze and nodded.

“Well ... Did the forest mention where they came from?”

“From the water, from the future. In nine years, the glacier upstream will melt. If I survive, my house will stand on the shores of a magnificent lake.”

“You know so much, yet you don’t know if you’ll survive.” Marian frowned.

“Death, it’s only here.” Parker touched his almost-gray hair. “If your mind is dead, your body won’t live.”

Marian fell silent and imagined a corpse that fit the description.

If there are many people, it means it’s viral or infectious. It spreads quickly. The body resembles someone affected by plague or leprosy. Could it be a mutation of the plague bacterium? A unique form of leprosy caused by leprosy bacteria with predominant skin lesions? In the final stage there is severe damage to the front chamber of the eye and the upper respiratory tract—they could very well produce whisper-like sounds. Leprosy has been officially classified as a neglected disease by the World Health Organization, but that doesn’t mean nothing is capable of resurrecting its new, or perhaps even old, form. The source of infection could be water, perhaps from the melting glacier. Only God knows what has been frozen in there for millions of years.

3:13 AM

"Can't argue with that." Parker instantly responded to her thoughts. "But there's one other point."

"What is it?" Marian asked, not surprised anymore by his ability to read her mind.

"Their bodies were dead, but what was here"—Parker tapped his finger against his head again—"what was here was alive, Dr. Flay."

"How is that possible? Bacteria that kill the body but leave the brain untouched?"

"I don't know, Doctor. That's where you come in! This guy with freckles and a poetic last name comes to visit me." Parker paused.

"Lenny Levitan?"

"That's the one! He's a meteorologist, isn't he?"

"Geophysicist, as far as I know."

"We have many conversations when he visits."

"I have no doubt," Marian said with a sigh, recalling how talkative Lenny could be.

"We talk about nature, the weather, ecology. I had nothing to do with the dead before. I had no dealings with you before. And in Denver, do you know, Marian, where I worked before, the wind told me about the deadly hurricane Katrina back in 2005? Before, they didn't believe me when I tried to warn the rescue services of Louisiana and Massachusetts for a week. Who was I before all this?"

"I don't know."

"I was the right-hand man of George Brown himself, the founder of the most prestigious funeral bureau in Colorado. I worked there for fifteen years, Dr. Flay. Fifteen wonderful years in excellent company. And never, hear me, never did a single dead person speak to me in all those years."

"What am I supposed to think based on your statement?" Marian asked, her mind racing to grasp the implications of Parker's words.

He gestured defiantly into the void, emphasizing his point. "These corpses, though they may appear lifeless, are actually alive."

Leprosy … It's a rather peculiar disease. Marian's thoughts slipped out.

"How peculiar is it?" Parker couldn't hide his curiosity.

"Leprosy … It's a rather peculiar disease," Marian pondered aloud in an attempt not to lose her mind all in one evening. "It involves the peripheral nervous system. And imagine if the infection were to produce an additional irritating effect on the nerve endings as well as the spinal and cranial nerves. Then a nearly dead or even fully dead person could exhibit some movement and even produce sounds."

3:13 AM

"Is such a thing possible?" Parker's eyes widened as he gazed into the dark woods, contemplating the unimaginable.

"It's been four hundred years that doctors have been studying the human body, both externally and internally, yet no one truly knows what this body is capable of."

The veranda fell into silence. Somewhere in the distance an owl screeched, and Marian spoke again.

"Ethan?"

"Mm?"

"I know that in the early days of Lenny's work in Alaska, he brought a lie detector to you."

"Yes. It's in the attic."

"Would you mind telling me the same things tomorrow but with the equipment connected to you?"

"You won't believe it, but I'm actually looking forward to the interrogation procedure," Parker suddenly confessed.

"Why?" Marian was genuinely surprised.

"It's a marvelous opportunity to find out if I've completely lost my mind," he remarked with a hint of humor.

Marian burst into ringing laughter, a laughter unusual for her reserved demeanor.

***

The persistent knock transported Raymond from the cold of night in Alaska back to his hotel room in Bangkok. From the darkness someone shouted "Wait a minute!" and soon the room was bathed in soft electric light. Marian was staring at him intently from her bed.

"What is it, Doctor? Can you see me?" He leaned forward.

The knock echoed again, and Marian, leaping out of bed, rushed to the door.

"It's eight forty-five." El's voice resounded. "And you're still not ready!"

Raymond approached the door as well. Of course, at that moment, no one could see or hear him.

Where did you dress up like that, El? Raymond smirked, surveying Agent Roberts from head to toe.

3:13 AM

Chapter 10

Raymond enjoyed a delicious dinner, went for a massage, and returned to his room. He put on his swimming trunks and stepped out onto the balcony.

“What a beautiful night.” He breathed in the scent of blooming patchouli bushes and descended the chrome ladder into the illuminated pool. Soft melodies wafted from the bar’s rooftop, accompanied by the clinking of bottles behind the counter.

Raymond swam towards the bar island, where a waiter promptly approached him.

“Care for something to drink, sir?” He bowed.

“Some chilled white wine,” Raymond replied.

“Riesling?”

“Chenin blanc.”

“Very well, sir.”

“Mmm, excellent wine, superb hotel! And you don’t have to be a millionaire,” Raymond mused, leaning on the pool’s edge and observing the whimsical design of decorative jungle foliage beneath the water.

He fended off a couple of young ladies who had been discreetly sent to him by resourceful lobby staff, and after grabbing a bottle of the favored Chenin from the bar, he returned to his balcony.

Raymond shrugged off his robe and took a sip of wine. The pool's blue hue blurred, and the playful laughter of millionaire hunters gradually faded. He was once again in Marian's room.

Marian was trying to sleep but couldn't. She tossed and turned, closing her pale eyelids and then opening them again. She anxiously watched the very chair where Raymond Lee had comfortably settled.

"Damn it!" She suddenly sat up on the bed, dramatically clasping her head in her hands. "What's wrong with me? There's no one there! Can't you hear? Just go to sleep already! There's no one there!"

"Hmm, I'll come back later." Raymond stood up from the chair and moved from the dark corner of the Bangkok city hotel to the balcony in Patong.

"She can sense me." Raymond smiled at the swimmers and took another sip of the chilled wine. "Dr. Flay can sense me! The Department of Counter-Terrorism becomes less mundane ..."

He swam a bit more, drank a little more, and thought of Marian. He didn't want to frighten her. He had gone through similar fears himself—a most unpleasant experience, especially when you know so little and can do even less.

3:13 AM

He entered his cool air-conditioned room, slipped under the covers, and decided to pay a visit to El this time.

The agent sat on the bed, scrolling through his emails on the screen of a small gadget. Raymond settled into an identical chair in an identical position to Dr. Flay's room. He focused on El's stern countenance and whispered softly, "Come on, Agent Roberts, care to share your secrets?"

Not a muscle twitched on El's serious face.

***

At the very next moment Raymond found himself in a dark oak-furnished office. It was filled with books, a massive desk, and a comfortable brown armchair. A strong, dark-skinned woman in a black judge's robe entered the room. El followed proudly behind her.

"Mr. Roberts." She spoke assertively, taking her place behind the desk. "I wasn't born yesterday."

"I can see that," El replied, attempting to lighten the serious conversation with humor, but to no avail.

Judge Lawrence looked at the agent with a reproachful gaze. "When the cases of inmates awaiting amnesty for good behavior landed on my desk, your department called me immediately. Immediately! Not even five damn minutes had passed!"

"Thank you. We work quickly," El replied with a satisfied smile on his face.

"At the same moment I realized that something was fishy with this guy's case—Clifford's case. You don't know how to play it clean, do you?"

El remained silent.

"I called my assistant"—the judge pointed her red-manicured finger at the black telephone—"and he brought his file into my office. And you know what I found there?"

"I'm eager to find out." A three-meter wave washed the satisfied smirk off El's face, replacing it with unpleasant apprehension.

"There was planted evidence! I know how your boys operate—it's their clumsy handwriting."

"I don't quite understand, Judge Lawrence, which evidence you're referring to. The evidence was found during the investigation of Christine Moore's murder. Nothing more, nothing less."

"Of course!" She burst into fake laughter. "El Roberts, how do you sleep at night, sentencing an innocent man to life imprisonment?"

"Clifford is guilty. That's why he's in prison. And that's why I sleep perfectly well every night."

Judge Lawrence narrowed her authoritative eyes and shook her head, contorting her plump lips into a peculiar shape. "Did you ever hear anything about amnesty, Agent Roberts?" Her voice was eerily calm.

3:13 AM

El left her office and immediately contacted the warden of the Alcatraz east wing.

"Yes, Agent Roberts?"

"Martinez, Clifford Anderson will soon be released under Colorado state amnesty."

"Yes, Agent Roberts."

"He must not be released."

A suffocating silence hung on the line.

"Are you sure he's guilty?" Martinez asked a single question.

El stared intently at the glass surface of the huge window. It seemed like he didn't blink at all.

"I'm sure," he said finally. His thin lips remained slightly parted, as if he wanted to say something more but was unable to.

Their conversation was over. The very next day El learned that Clifford had met an untimely demise due to a bathroom accident. He had slipped on the tiles, fallen, and hit his head on the tile. The injury had proven fatal. Moreover, by the time he was discovered, he had lost a significant amount of blood, lying there under the hot shower. They couldn't save him. They tried their best, but it was all in God's hands.

"Roberts! I will get you!" an enraged Lawrence screamed into the receiver.

El was certain that someday someone would eventually get him, but in his opinion, luckily or unluckily, it wouldn't be Judge Lawrence.

***

Raymond rose from his chair and approached the agent. The latter had fallen asleep, leaning against the headboard—an aging, solitary servant of the law.

"El ..." Raymond sat at his feet. "Damn you, El. Damn you!"

If Raymond could have had his body with him, he would have squeezed a tear from it.

"You killed him! Killed him for me ..."

Raymond opened his eyes. He was lying on a massive bed, gazing at a ceiling adorned with golden ornamentation. A bitter residue of past mistrust gnawed at him—mistrust that El didn't deserve.

He turned towards the window. The balcony door was slightly ajar. White translucent curtains swayed in the gentle breeze. Someone was swimming in the pool.

Raymond glanced at his phone screen. It seemed like he had just fallen asleep, but the green digits ominously displayed 3:03 a.m. He struggled to lift himself from the overly soft mattress and listened intently.

Through the floor-to-ceiling window he could see the swimmer cross the pool, propel themselves off the wall, and splash into the water once again. The sound of splashing approached, growing quieter until it ceased right in front of the balcony.

"Raymond ..." A soft whisper echoed, sending chills down his spine.

He stood up and slowly approached the balcony door. The elongated whisper repeated, "Raymond, come to me ..."

The psychic knew all too well that one should never heed a haunting call. A polite summons, with respect for the living, almost always sounded different. But this strange voice captivated him. It held an indescribably repulsive yet pathologically alluring quality. Such a cocktail of emotions stirred his curiosity. If it hadn't been for the horror of the night before, Raymond would have, by God, stepped onto the balcony and peered around the corner. But this time he simply closed the door and drew the heavy curtains.

He heard the sound of a wet body climbing onto the tiles. Raymond took a step back in a horror as a tap came on the glass.

"Magnificent Mr. Lee," the ghost whispered.

The only person in the whole wide world who called him that was Ann Jay.

Raymond didn't want to see her. Guilt or longing, or perhaps both, tore his soul apart. But not being able to see her was unbearable as well.

He cautiously pulled back the velvet curtain—the balcony was empty. However, the wet mark of her hand remained on the glass, and a glistening puddle of water adorned the small blue tiles. Raymond slowly opened the door.

"Let's go for a swim, Mr. Lee." Laughter emerged from the darkness of the decorative jungle. Within a moment, she sprang into the water from somewhere and swam away once more.

"I've had enough of swimming, Ann Jay." Raymond grabbed a bottle of wine from the bedside table and stepped onto the balcony. He settled into a wicker chair and poured himself a fragile glass. "Would you like some wine?" he inquired politely.

"I want to, but I can't." A pale face appeared at the edge of the pool.

She clung to the chrome railing with slender fingers adorned with black nails, her anger-filled slanted eyes fixed on Raymond. In the blue light from the pool, her deathly pale skin appeared bluish to him. Once magnificent, her body was now covered in black Japanese characters, and her plump lips, instead of a vibrant cherry hue, were the color of ink.

Raymond let out a heavy sigh and, never taking his sad gaze off Ann Jay, took a sip of wine.

"You knew. You saw them ..." The girl extended her delicate hands, displaying the marks.

3:13 AM

Raymond struggled to force the wine down his petrified throat. "I warned you not to go to Vietnam."

"You could have saved me, but you didn't," Ann Jay hissed.

Suddenly Raymond remembered Ethan Parker. "You know, Ann Jay, I've been contemplating for so long why we can't escape death. Who marks us for it and why?"

A lump that had been sitting in his chest unexpectedly turned into tears. They welled up and filled his clear blue eyes. Through the watery haze, his vision became worse, but without the lump, it was considerably easier to breathe.

"And who is it?" Ann Jay whispered.

Incredible—even the dead know shit!

"It's ourselves, Ann Jay!" Raymond leaned fearlessly towards the pool. "When something dies here"—he tapped his temple with his finger, just like Parker had—"that's when the body meets its end. You understand? We lose the fire of life, faith, or whatever else in our minds ... We deprive ourselves of it and switch ourselves off. We sign our own death warrant by keeping somewhere deep inside us one single thought—unwillingness to live. All this gets started because of some minor upset that goes deep down and causes disappointment in life. That's the whole problem."

"I didn't want to live without you, Raymond ..."

"Yes, Ann Jay. In some remarkable way, you managed to stuff that thought into your enchanting head. You had everything, but you needed me. You needed me to the point of death! You know, Ann Jay, the more spoiled a person is by their whims, the greater the risk that one day they'll condemn themselves to death."

"You could have saved me, Raymond."

"No, Ann Jay. No one can save us except ourselves. That's how the world works, darling. Those are its rules. Love life and you live. Don't love it and you die."

"But—"

"No buts!" Raymond stumbled over his words, interrupting a ghost for the first time in his life. "Death doesn't know words like 'but,' 'if,' or 'maybe.' It doesn't understand thoughts like 'I'll live only if ...' For death, either you want to live or you don't."

"Stay with me ..." Ann Jay began to emerge slowly from the pool.

She no longer heard Raymond, nor did she understand his words. It was just the same as in life. "One last time, my love, be with me ..."

Raymond jumped up from his chair in fear and retreated towards the balcony door. He wouldn't have agreed to sleep even with a living Ann Jay, let alone a dead one.

He grabbed the bottle from the wicker table, hurried back into his room, and locked the balcony door. This time Ann Jay didn't knock. She slowly but surely turned the metal lock.

3:13 AM

Raymond rushed out into the corridor and called for the managers on duty in the lobby. Then he selected the two most fearsome demon guards, who, with a snap of his fingers, instantly teleported into his room. The bewildered staff couldn't understand where to move the statues. After a sweaty twenty-minute struggle with the wooden sculptures, the ominous blue demon took its place by the balcony door while the fiery red one stood guard at the entrance.

"Much better," Raymond assessed, closing the door behind the confused and deathly tired staff.

"Better for you to go into the light, Ann Jay!" he shouted from behind the demon nearest the balcony. He drank a glass of cold wine to help him sleep and wrapped himself in a soft blanket.

The night passed peacefully. Raymond stretched out in bed, realizing that he had finally gotten some rest, and ordered coffee over the phone. The waiter who entered the room bumped into the demon statue and recoiled, almost spilling everything he was carefully carrying. Raymond smiled and handed the young man a good tip, including compensation for emotional damage. "And also please inform me when my neighbors move in," he added.

The young man nodded and rushed out of the room as if scalded. Raymond sipped his coffee, contemplating where the third oracle might reside, but he couldn't find the answer within his own mind. Only Marian knew the answer. Well, he would have to figure it out the very next day.

***

Raymond had breakfast and headed towards the ocean. Here at Patong beach there was always a sea of people. The stretch of sand next to the azure harbor was never empty—throughout the year, at any time of day, there would inevitably be a plump Thai man lying there fully dressed, a couple of teenagers launching something into the sky, three or four Japanese women in hats and all-white attire diligently working on their selfies, a pair of muscular Europeans in tight swimming trunks strolling from one cape to another. In addition to all these characters, as soon as you stepped onto the white sand, you were bound to encounter hundreds of passers-by, onlookers, swimmers, runners, lovers, families, but above all, sex workers. They worked on Bangla Road at night and hunted for customers on the beach during the day.

Raymond struggled to break free from the crowd, took a swim until low tide, which was at noon, and returned to the hotel. After a relaxing massage and meditation in the smoke-filled, fragrant room, he settled down at an open-air restaurant near the bar. He savored some spicy beef with a tropical salad and ordered a revitalizing coffee—the aromatherapy oils had made him drowsy.

Soon a couple of agents appeared on the inner courtyard road. It's worth noting that they looked good together. Even the thirteen-year age difference didn't spoil the aesthetics at all. Both were dressed in sharp, well-pressed minimalist attire, with neat hairstyles and identical black suitcases. Expensive watches adorned their left wrists, as their right hands were usually occupied either with a gun or with reports to be typed. Their focused gazes seemed to constantly supply their brains with information, which could very well be classified. In that case, they needed to rush to their rooms and report to headquarters as quickly as possible, followed by the procedure. Classifying tons of information ...

Raymond almost couldn't help but laugh, nearly giving away his presence. He glanced at the graying head of El till he disappeared through the lobby doors, the at-least-ten-years-younger blond lady following him. Raymond missed Roberts indeed. He was genuinely glad to see him.

Before Raymond could finish his coffee, Marian appeared on the road. Clad in a black knitted dress and carrying a cloth bag over her shoulder, she marched towards the gate and left the hotel.

Raymond moved to the bar counter and ordered dessert. From there he could see El heading to the spa salon, taking a swim in the pool, and returning to his room. It's amazing how, if a person is confident that no one is watching them, they will never notice surveillance, even if the observer is right under their nose.

On his second cocktail, Raymond caught a glimpse, out of the corner of his eye, of El stepping onto the balcony, freezing for a moment, and then darting back into the room.

Well, finally! He sighed with relief.

***

“What are you doing here?” El forgot to greet him, but Raymond was happy to see him even without the formalities.

“Stop pretending to be surprised.” Raymond chuckled. “You don’t have to be psychic to find you in Patong. You always come to the same hotel, get a room with a poolside view, and they are practically facing the bar ...”

El smiled subtly and sat down next to him. “So you decided to surprise me?”

“I wish I’d come here with the intention of surprising you.”

El frowned and ordered a cup of coffee from the bartender.

“I can’t sleep in my own house. They literally drove me out,” Raymond confessed.

“Who?”

“The walking dead, El, the walking dead.”

“Is it that bad?” El brought the miniature cup of hot espresso closer.

3:13 AM

Chapter 11

Dusk was setting in. They stepped out of the hotel and walked along the streets, tinted crimson by the setting sun. As they reached the busiest and at the same time most debaucherous street on the entire coast, they noticed a two-story restaurant on the crowded Bangla Road. Half-dressed courtesans of indeterminate gender grudgingly made way as El and Raymond entered the dimly lit ground floor. It was here that the seductive music played loudly, while the second floor offered more light and tranquility. At that time of day, few visitors to Bangla Road would have thought of having dinner there, and as the sun finally disappeared into the depths of the jungle, they were left alone on the spacious balcony.

El pushed aside a low glass filled with ice. By the end of their conversation the whiskey bottle was empty, and Raymond asked for a couple of cold beers.

"Nine years, huh? And what is it—an epidemic, an eco-catastrophe, a war?" It seemed that in the span of three hours, El had aged another year.

"I don't know. But if it was an illness, they would have sent a doctor instead of you. Wouldn't they?" Raymond glanced at the agent.

"I'll write a report, request them to send one. But right now, you yourself aren't sure if it's an illness. Perhaps there's another reason for this mass death?"

"They don't behave like the dead, El. And they don't say anything. That's the whole problem."

"Maybe they'll say more." El scratched his temple.

"The main thing is that it isn't too late ..."

"Nine years is a considerable time."

"Considerable." Raymond took a sip of his beer. "But any impending event should be viewed not from the perspective of a specific time frame, but perhaps based on the concept of the point of no return."

"You mean the time when we can no longer change anything?"

"Exactly, Agent Roberts. When no one can change anything anymore."

El raised the narrow neck to his lips. "Hasn't the point of no return arrived yet?" he asked before taking a sip.

"No."

They spent another twenty minutes in silence, finishing their beer.

"Back to the hotel?" El slammed the empty bottle onto the table.

"Perhaps ..."

"I'm even scared to go down to the first floor." El lazily got up.

3:13 AM

“Scared? You?” Raymond smiled with his eyes.

“You know, I used to fear nothing. But that was before you, Raymond, before you ...” El patted Raymond on the shoulder.

“I’ll take that as a compliment.”

They laughed, supporting each other. Drunk, lonely, sharing horrifying secrets—the kind that only a scant handful of people in the world have an inkling of.

El and Raymond descended the stairs, although it would be more fitting to say they rolled down. A great cover band, by Thai standards, was performing on the low stage. The two men walked past, swaying slightly, not intending to dance, but the atmosphere caught their rhythm. The crowd swarmed around the millionaire with his own island in a perpetually crumpled shirt and the well-groomed but heavily intoxicated federal agent. The entire bar was dancing. And they were dancing pretty well, by the way. It was hard not to notice the tall, well-built foreigners amidst the short Thais and sunburnt tourists. But they didn’t hide either.

Raymond started clapping his hands above his head to the beloved beat, right wrist adorned with a Rolex. The guitarist began a solo. And now the whole bar was clapping along. It became truly lively, and the bassist only added to it. The drums came in for support, and an English-speaking choir came to the aid of the singer. Even those who didn’t understand the words tried their best to sing along.

Someone requested an encore and slipped ten bucks to the singer. The band played it again, and so did the bar, led by El and Raymond. They couldn't get enough on the third round, but they left amidst enthusiastic whistles and never-ending applause.

As they stepped outside, they immediately bumped into Marian.

"Looks like you're on tour," she joked, forgetting to laugh for some reason.

Raymond and El tried to stand still and not stagger, but they weren't doing a good job.

"Raymond Lee." El introduced his touring partner. "Marian Flay, my colleague," he whispered to Raymond. "But how did you find us?"

"In Patong, there's nowhere else to look. If you didn't call a taxi from the hotel, then you headed on foot straight to Bangla Road. And here"—she pointed at the still-whistling crowd—"I could find you just by following the whistles."

They managed to make it back to the hotel and dispersed to their respective rooms. Marian paused in the corridor, casting at them a judgmental glance. El flawlessly passed through the doorway but soon stumbled over something and collapsed. Raymond, upon entering his own room, was startled by the presence of the three-meter-tall statues and recoiled against the wall. After a moment he remembered why they had been brought in, muttered an indistinct curse, and closed the door behind him.

Marian was indignant. El and Raymond had talked without her, and everything had happened without her involvement. She had no information to offer, and she wouldn't have any if they intended to drink themselves into oblivion every day.

***

Raymond opened his eyes. The pool outside appeared a deep blue, with the sun not yet risen. He reached for his phone but dropped it on the floor. After taking a shower, he wrapped himself in a clean robe, picked up the phone, and glanced at the screen.

4:10 a.m. I missed the ghost party, and Marian must still be asleep ... It would be nice, Dr. Flay, if you were the one getting drunk instead of me and freeing your mind. But it seems we have no choice! he thought, glancing at the demons. He dragged a chair to the wall, sat down in it, and closed his eyes.

***

A pleasant warm breeze blew in her face. Marian stood facing the ocean. Judging by the pristine white sand, she was on the Pacific coast. The low mansions to her right, with impeccably clean windows, reflected the bloody sunset of Los Angeles.

Her mobile phone rang in the pocket of her denim jacket.

"Flay, are you there?"

"Yes, Frank."

"And how do you like it?"

"It's a fancy place. Just missing the sound of a saxophone."

The coordinator chuckled discreetly. "All right, send me your location."

Marian moved the phone away from her ear and sent her location.

"You're on the right track. Walk down this street. The third mansion with a black façade—that's the one. Call at exactly 6:06 p.m. Not a minute earlier or later. You have twenty-four minutes for everything. By 6:30, you must leave that house."

"Why such precision? I hope you didn't plant a bomb there!"

The coordinator chuckled again. "Rapshmir has a client at seven."

"I see ..."

"Signing off, Doctor. Good luck!"

"Thank you, Frank."

Marian had to leave her rented car at the gas station—the only place she could legally leave a car. According to the satellites, the rest of the coastline, which was more than six miles away, was completely empty and lifeless. Any car parked near the mansions in this wasteland would disappear within minutes, as if it were a mirage in the Sahara. Then it would be a search-and-find game in the parking lots for abandoned cars.

She stopped in front of a round courtyard paved with black cobblestones. The low, sprawling mansion made of glass and marble resembled a memorial. Only the tall vines of ivy and wild grapes gently softened its sharpness.

Marian glanced at her watch. She had a minute to spare and made a leisurely approach to the tall arched door. At exactly 6:06 p.m. she reached for the bell, but the door opened by itself. A dark-skinned man in expensive glasses and a cashmere sweater the color of wet sand stood in front of her.

"Dr. Flay?"

"Louis Rapshmir?"

She knew what he looked like; there was no time to act out surprise.

"Pleasure to meet you indeed, Doctor!" Louis's gaze slid over the guest, taking in every detail from head to toe. "I'm delighted to have such an attractive guest. Please, come!"

The mansion owner walked through the marble hall towards the leather sofas, and Marian followed him.

"Would you like a soft drink?" Rapshmir intertwined his slender fingers, studying his guest.

"I have twenty-four minutes, Mr. Rapshmir. Well, now twenty-three." Marian briefly glanced at her watch.

"Actually, we have the whole evening at our disposal. The strict twenty-four minutes are reserved for agents who don't please me. But you please me, Dr. Flay." Louis trailed a languid gaze over her, taking in her figure-hugging midi-dress and lingering on her slender ankles. Marian swallowed and straightened up, attempting to maintain a professional demeanor.

Rapshmir revealed his unnaturally white teeth and thoughtfully touched his lower lip. The moment when the meeting ceased to be purely business arrived too quickly.

"Ines, bring the champagne," Luis called out towards the end of the hall, where a maid appeared and promptly disappeared.

"Shall we begin, Mr. Rapshmir? I will listen attentively to you and make notes, if you don't mind." Marian opened a small suede bag with a long strap, revealing a notebook and pen.

"Where would you like me to start?" Louis settled comfortably on white leather, crossed his legs in their tailored, slim trousers, and resumed studying the already-flustered guest.

"You may start wherever you deem necessary, but personally I would be interested to know how you foresee the upcoming events."

"From my dreams." Rapshmir shrugged as if it was extremely obvious.

"And that's all?"

"That's all."

3:13 AM

"You don't see spirits, hear voices? You simply have prophetic dreams?"

"Exactly! Of course, if my clients need to communicate with deceased relatives or departed geniuses, I summon their souls for a conversation. But they come to me in dreams as well."

"That's intriguing."

"It's safe. I've established a relationship with the spirit world in a way that doesn't interfere with my life. I've seen those prophets who end up spending their days in straitjackets—such people simply can't handle their affairs."

Ines brought a pair of tall glasses and Rapshmir fell momentarily silent, inviting Marian to partake in the sparkling beverage. She took a glass from the tray and Louis reached out towards her.

"Cheers! To our acquaintance!" Rapshmir took a sip of champagne, never averting his lustful gaze from Marian.

Marian took a sip as well, hoping to relax even just a little.

"So you saw the forthcoming event in a dream?" She was trying—completely in vain—to divert Louis from his lascivious thoughts.

"Right! That night I had an appointment with the spirit of a grieving widow's late husband. He was supposed to reveal the hiding place of the family diamonds. He simply didn't have the chance to do it in his lifetime," Louis explained. "But the spirit never came. I was waiting for him in my dream, standing by the window at night, when suddenly there was a strange movement in the ocean. At first it looked like a huge wave, but then I realized that what was approaching was people ..."

Rapshmir sighed deeply, processing his own words. The room fell into a momentary silence, filled only by the crackling of the bio fireplace.

"You know, Marian, it was terrifying. They were marching towards my house under the light of the full moon ... an army of the dead! Emaciated, battered, hairless, with clouded eyes. I couldn't bear to watch. I drew the curtains. I paced around the room, looked at my sleeping body until I heard their whispers: *Louis, come to us ... Louis, you're already dead ... no need to pretend ...*"

Lost in his thoughts, he took a sip of champagne and pursed his lips, mentally returning to his horrifying dream.

"I was damn scared at that moment. My alarm clock is set to exactly four in the morning, and it's supposed to wake me up. I wanted to wake up from the dream, which meant I had to go back into my body. I tried to return, but nothing worked. And then this utterly devastating thought came to me: *What if I've really died?*"

Marian listened intently, completely forgetting about her notes.

"And so"—Louis sighed again—"I was tossing and turning, trying everything to get back from that nightmare, when the window suddenly flew open. You know, during my out-of-body experiences I have full control over the space around me. In my dreams, doors and windows can't just open on their own. I either open them myself or they're opened by the souls of the people I invite. But that time, when I turned around, the window was torn out of its frame. The whispers were calling me; they literally demanded that I look at them. Well, stepping over the broken glass, I finally looked. The entire beach and the entire ocean to the horizon were littered with the dead. Suddenly, all of them, as one, raised their hazy eyes towards me. They ... they ... Marian, they were dead, but at the same time, they were alive. Dead individually but alive as one large organism. Do you understand?" Rapshmir squeezed his eyes shut.

"So someone was commanding them?" Marian asked cautiously.

"Commanding?" Louis paused. "Perhaps, but I wouldn't dare to say that with certainty."

"Did you notice any specific damage to the skin—anything other than their clouded eyes?"

"Hmm, I'm not sure. I'm not a doctor." Louis shrugged.

"Try to imagine for a moment."

Marian caught his intense gaze on her fingers, in which she twirled a ballpoint pen.

"What was wrong with those dead folks?" Louis closed his eyes for a moment. "Nothing else, just they were dead!" He saw them again in his head.

"Well, maybe there was something else. Just try to imagine and mentally compare the images you've got. Every detail is important in symptomatology," Marian pushed.

"There were no children among them."

"Excuse me?"

"I couldn't determine their ages or genders, but all these people were adults."

"That's more interesting." Marian blinked rapidly and quickly wrote something in her notebook.

"Besides their sunken eyes, by the way, they weren't blind—they could still see with those eyes. So, apart from the strange look, lack of hair, and numerous wounds, I don't remember anything else. And their voices sounded more like a hoarse whisper than a human voice. But that happens with the deceased. I often hear whispers instead of their previous voices from my visitors. They say that the voice is the first thing the soul forgets." Rapshmir picked up a glass from a low table and stood up. He walked around the hall, glancing at Marian from a distance. "Don't stay silent, Doctor!" he exclaimed, pulling her away from her notes. "Tell me your thoughts. What does your charming bright mind think?"

3:13 AM

Marian scanned the sofas with her eyes, trying not to turn towards the homeowner.

"I think that with severe eye damage, people cannot see well, especially at night. But with impaired vision, hearing often becomes sharper. They might have heard you and raised their heads in response to the sound. At that moment, it might have seemed like they were looking at you."

"Very good, Marian."

The millionaire—or rather billionaire—Rapshmir walked past Marian, pulling out the wooden hairpin that held her hair up. Her white-blond locks cascaded over her shoulders and onto the back of the leather sofa. Marian froze, while Louis, unfazed, continued walking calmly. She finished her champagne, keeping the glass in her hand for self-defense.

"Skin damage," she continued, "can be explained by the influence of bacteria or microbes. But the absence of hair is also a distinctive feature that unites all these people. However, there are three possible explanations for it."

"What explanations?" Louis settled himself brazenly on the arm of the sofa.

"Either in the early stages of a disease, the hair is cut for some reason, or it falls out due to the illness itself, or it falls out as a result of treatment, such as the medication used in chemotherapy."

"How interesting." Rapshmir leaned closer to Marian and started twirling a strand of her blond hair around his finger.

Marian was taken aback. "I've gained a lot of useful information from you, Mr. Rapshmir," she exclaimed, getting up. "Thank you for your cooperation. Your help is invaluable."

"Two nights ago the ghost I was expecting finally came to me. And besides the jewels, I asked him about the dead," remarked Louis casually.

Marian turned around, casting a startled glance at him.

"One more glass and I'll tell you about it." He shamelessly examined her again. She sat down, soon receiving another glass of sparkling beverage.

"What did your ghost say, Mr. Rapshmir?" She sipped the drink.

"He said that in nine years, Phorcys will release his monstrous daughters, and they will destroy the world."

"What?" Marian frowned.

"In life, this esteemed man, whose name I cannot disclose, was passionate about history. As far as I know, he dedicated ten years of his life to excavations. So it's not surprising to encounter such interpretations."

Louis leaned closer to Marian's neck and inhaled her powdery scent. Her consciousness seemed to vanish into the history of the ancient world, where she futilely tried to remember

Phorcys and his daughters. She snapped out of it when she felt Louis's full lips touch her neck.

"Mr. Rapshmir!" she whispered. Her voice was husky, her eyes widened, and her hands almost automatically packed the notebook and pen back into the suede bag on the thin strap.

"Louis," Rapshmir corrected her.

"Louis, I have to go."

"Promise me we'll meet again." He squeezed her hand, awaiting her response.

"I promise." Marian decided to tell a lie, but as it turned out later, it wasn't a lie after all.

Chapter 12

Marian had breakfast in the restaurant in proud solitude, glancing occasionally at El's and Raymond's balconies. She went to the beach, sipped a cup of coffee, and at precisely 1:30 p.m. she descended to the pool. She had just managed to swim to the edge when the balcony door of Room 1311 opened. Disheveled, Raymond wrapped himself in a robe and stepped out, armed with a mug of coffee.

"Good morning!" Marian smiled, attempting to be friendlier than on the previous night.

"Morning," Raymond mumbled.

Marian swam closer, hoping to seize the chance to arrange a private meeting with the psychic. "Do you come here often?" she asked.

"Quite often."

"And what about Roberts?"

"I don't gossip about friends behind their backs, Dr. Flay, same as you, isn't that right? Conveniently, all of them knew nothing about each other ..." Raymond stared casually at the restaurant visitors as Marian froze. *Did he say that accidentally? Or does he know something? What if he knows and so does El? Or maybe El has found out everything already.* Unpleasant shivers ran down her spine.

3:13 AM

“Why do you think El hired you?” Raymond spoke again, not bothering to shift his sleepy eyes towards Marian.

“Even in our department, experienced individuals sometimes need assistance. Maybe not of a physical or intellectual nature, but as a fresh perspective from an outsider,” Marian responded confidently.

“And what do you see from your fresh perspective? With your clear eyes?” Raymond finally looked at her, and his piercing gaze made Marian feel a sudden heat.

He could conquer any heart, even now, in that ridiculous robe, with tousled hair. With that cold look, observing the bustle of life without much interest. A man who knew so much, who saw right through all of them. A demigod to some, the Devil to others ...

From the adjacent hotel room, they heard a splash, and soon afterward, El emerged near Marian.

“Good afternoon! What are you guys talking about?” he asked.

“About you!” Marian replied candidly.

“About me?” El looked surprised. “I’m flattered.”

“I suggest taking a dip in the ocean,” said Raymond.

“I already swum before low tide while you were still sleeping,” Marian retorted somewhat reproachfully.

"I don't mean the beach." Raymond took a sip of his coffee. "I mean the open ocean."

Marian and El exchanged glances. "Is it safe?" El asked.

"It's a completely different experience," responded Raymond rather vaguely.

"How different?" Marian frowned, realizing that El was already halfway to embarking on another adventurous idea of Raymond's.

"A sense of complete freedom."

Everyone fell silent. Even Marian couldn't find anything to say this time.

***

The taxi driver dropped the travelers off at the pier. El helped Marian step onto the gleaming floor of the snow-white Riva. Raymond started the engine. The yacht roared to life and, following every turn of the steering wheel, swiftly moved away from the shore. As they departed from the semicircular harbor, Marian was stunned by the views around her. Now she didn't regret for a single minute agreeing to this ocean excursion. Besides, leaving those two alone together was no longer in her plans.

"El, take the helm!" Raymond shouted.

El walked over to the miniature wheel and took the captain's seat with caution. "Just keep it steady?" he asked.

3:13 AM

“If there are any boats or ships in our way, you can make a turn.”

El smiled discreetly. Raymond took a chilled bottle of wine and glasses from his bag. Marian grew wary. Raymond noticed her unease but didn’t show the slightest concern. Calmly he uncorked the bottle, poured a glass, and approached Marian closely.

“Here in Thailand, even on the open ocean, it’s very difficult to be completely alone.” He handed her the dewy glass and added, “It’s not Alaska, Doc!”

Marian’s face contorted as if a ghost had appeared in front of her instead of Raymond.

“Have you been to Koh Panyee?” Raymond kept talking nonchalantly, keeping an inquisitive gaze fixed on Marian while sipping his wine.

She merely shook her head weakly, still contemplating the remarkable coincidences in Raymond’s speech earlier.

“How about you, El? Have you been there?” Raymond handed him a glass and returned to the helm.

“No, I haven’t. By the way, this is excellent wine.”

“Thank you.” Raymond nodded gratefully. “They also call one rock there James Bond Island. So, El, it’s almost destiny for you to visit there.”

“Hah.” El felt a bit flustered.

"Once, this island bore the typical Thai name Tapu and didn't enjoy much popularity even among the locals. But in 1974 the situation changed drastically: A film crew arrived on the island to shoot a new movie about the legendary spy. After the release of *The Man with the Golden Gun*, Tapu suddenly gained immense popularity and became known to the people in honor of the fearless agent 007. About ten years after the filming, it became part of the Phang Nga Bay Marine National Park. And today, James Bond Island is one of the most photographed spots in all of Thailand. It's almost like West Cliff Drive in California."

Marian felt a chilling wave wash over her for the third time that day. *He knows everything, damn him!*

She refused to look at the almighty Raymond and instead stared at the azure ocean, dotted with yachts, speedboats, and the green hills of the islands.

They rounded the picturesque cape of Phuket and entered the waters of the Andaman Sea. Marian stood up and looked around. It felt like she had stepped into one of those magical souvenirs they still sell in bookstores today. When she was just a little girl, she couldn't let go of a glass half sphere that revealed a blue ocean with whimsical islands underneath. White sand surrounded intricate slopes, and above the tallest mountain in the center of the exhibit, an airy cloud hung in the sky. Marian turned the toy upside down and gazed into the sphere once more. Now the entire space of that fairytale place was filled with a fine golden rain. Back then, at the age of ten, she would have given anything to shrink to the size of a mosquito and fly to one of those islands. To lie there on the soft sand and gaze at the blue sky while the warm ocean waves tickled her feet.

Well, twenty years later those dreams had come true. Now she was here, in the middle of a glass sphere in an utterly unreal world.

The yacht glided past a fantastic coastline where cozy hotels, quiet docks, and pristine white beaches basked under tall palm trees. After half an hour of leisurely cruising, the Riva entered the waters of the national park. Here, on the turquoise smoothness, spread green giants of mountainous islands. These jungle titans seemed even taller in the company of the low-hanging clouds. Any moment now, one of them would graze the quirky rock and suspend itself on the very peak.

"We're on another planet," Marian whispered.

The Riva slowed down.

"What shall we call it?" Raymond asked with an air of Amerigo Vespucci.

"Call what?" El inquired, and Marian threw yet another anxious look at Raymond.

"Another planet." Raymond scanned Marian, clearly testing her endurance.

The yacht drifted until a peculiar rock appeared near the islands. It seemed suspended, barely touching the water's surface. Raymond selected the best vantage point, anchored the Riva, stripped down, and jumped overboard. El followed suit. Only Marian couldn't tear herself away from these unique views she seemed to have dreamed of her entire life.

They returned at sunset, tired from the heat of the day, and as darkness fell, they were glad to gather at the bar under the rising moon. This time Marian stayed in the water while El and Raymond resumed their drinking spree. Over and over again she swam closer, eavesdropping on fragmented conversations. Time passed, and the bar emptied as guests retired to their rooms or strolled to Bangla Road.

One more swim to the mural and I'm done for today, Marian thought, pushing herself away from the pool's edge.

Casting an inquisitive look at the bar, she stopped swimming and stood up. Raymond pointed to one of the balconies not far from her. Marian swam closer to the bar and climbed out.

"El, he's been standing there for quite a while," Raymond explained and called out to the man he saw. "Hey, buddy, turn around! I'm talking to you! El"—he turned back to Roberts—"should we aim a gun at him or something? Make him turn or scram."

"Raymond, there's nobody there," El said softly, covering his eyes with his hand.

"Damn, they found me." Raymond jumped up from the table and headed to his room. Marian, glancing apprehensively at the empty balcony, descended into the water, crossed the pool, and went to her room as well. She swiftly wrapped herself in a robe and dashed into the corridor. Approaching the door of the adjacent hotel room, she listened carefully, then gave a knock.

3:13 AM

“Raymond, please let me in! We need to talk.” Marian knocked in vain at Room 1311, wrapped in her robe. “I saw it.” Her voice trembled with deceit. “Raymond, I saw it too!”

The door opened. The psychic’s face wrinkled as if he had just swallowed a lemon. “Who did you see?”

Marian rushed into Raymond’s room and quietly closed the door behind her. “There was a man standing there, bald, with horrible sores and dull eyes. More like a dead man than a living one. Isn’t that right?”

Raymond burst into laughter. “So you think I yelled at El to shoot a dead man?”

Marian frowned in confusion.

“Or do you really believe I’m as crazy as Ethan Parker? Or perhaps as obsessed as Louis Rapshmir? I could fly off the handle and spill all the things I told El yesterday, right? Or I might end up revealing even more than I did to him.”

She couldn’t utter a single word, just stood there, immobilized.

“So El is in the loop? Did the Center spill about the oracles?”

“The Center?” Raymond’s eyebrows shot up toward his hairline. “I have my own center, far less fallible.” He tapped his temples with his fingers.

Raymond took a sip of wine and came closer to Marian. He cradled her head between his palms and leaned in so close that their lips almost touched. She froze, speechless, motionless.

"As soon as you fall asleep, Dr. Flay, I can easily step into your mind. I'll open the door, dust off the desk, brew strong coffee, and approach your shelves. I will find plenty of books there, suited to even the most discerning taste, from erotica to dark secrets, Doc. I usually pick a book based on my mood, settle into a chair, and read all night long. And when you wake up the next morning, I'll know everything about you. And not just about you. Everything that's here"—Raymond squeezed his palms tighter—"is in my power. All these trips, people, every word, every glance—I know it all!"

"Only about me?" Marian managed to force the words out of her constricted throat.

"About everyone. I know everything about everyone! For me, there are no doors, no secrets, Doc. I can repeat any word spoken by you or the oracles, in Alaska or sunny California. Everything said by that enigmatic Turner or your playful coordinator Frank. How many glasses of champagne Ines brought, how many times Rapshmir mentally undressed you, and how many times you stared at my photo, still tucked away in the secret pocket of your bag. One can only wonder why you lingered over it so long before sleeping in that cramped hotel room in Bangkok."

Marian managed to stay on her feet, trying not to collapse from shock. When Raymond finally released her, she staggered backward, fumbled for the doorknob, and quickly rushed out into the hallway.

She burst into her room and, for some reason, locked the door behind her. She was trembling—shaking violently with an unceasing shiver. She grabbed her clothes from the chair, intending to remove her robe, but froze, staring at the wall. The very wall that separated her from Raymond Lee. Marian retreated into the bathroom, but even there, she felt uneasy. Paranoid, she changed her clothes, hiding from imaginary observers.

One phone number remained etched in her mind—just one, but its importance grew by the minute. She couldn't call it whenever she pleased. It was reserved for moments of life or death—or when confronted with something extraordinary, inexplicable, and as frightening as Raymond Lee's newfound abilities.

Marian sprang into action and rushed to the phone. She dialed the country code and, trembling, entered the coveted number. Three rings later, she hung up. Not because she had changed her mind, but because it was the code.

She couldn't sit, lie down, or do anything else. She paced around the room, while Raymond Lee's words kept repeating in her mind like an endless melody. His icy gaze froze before her eyes, penetrating her to the bone with Arctic coldness on a hot evening near the equator.

How could she ever think that someone other than God Himself could monitor her every step, thought, action, body—her entire life? Damn it, her whole life! The problem was, Raymond was nothing like God. Or if he was, she wasn't ready to accept it, but who could blame her?

About thirty minutes later, the phone in her room rang. Marian leaped up and hurried to the nightstand.

"Dr. Flay?" A voice devoid of emotion answered.

"Sir, it's an emergency." Marian spoke breathlessly.

"I'm listening."

"The oracle, he ... he knows everything."

"Please clarify the information."

"He possesses incredible abilities."

"What kind of abilities?"

"I don't know how he does it, but—" Marian suddenly fell silent.

"But?"

"He can extract any information from anyone's mind. In just a couple of nights, he took out my meetings with other oracles. Everything, from words to glances. He knows places, names," Marian babbled. "He knows things that only I or only you know. It's impossible to guess. He truly reads people like books, sir."

"Only those nearby?"

"I think it's possible from any distance. Because ..." Marian stumbled again.

"Because?"

"While I was sleeping in Bangkok, he ... he came to me when he was on his island in the Andaman Sea."

"Confirm the information." The voice on the phone remained steady. "The oracle can remotely access any events from anyone's mind while they sleep. Is that correct?"

3:13 AM

"I think so ..."

"Yes or no, Doctor?"

"Yes, sir."

Silence hung in the air.

"Dr. Flay, where is Raymond Lee at this moment?"

"What? Where is he?" Marian was even more flustered than before. "I suppose he's here, in the hotel. In the room next to mine."

"Thank you for contacting me. We strongly advise you to take a walk on the beach within the next hour."

"Why?" she blurted out, but no one heard her.

Marian placed the receiver back, replaying the conversation in her mind. What had she, Dr. Marian Flay, just done? Had she killed Raymond Lee? The thought sent a shiver down her spine. She stood up, but her legs wouldn't cooperate. Clinging to furniture and stumbling, she made her way down the corridor and knocked on the neighboring door. Raymond didn't answer. Her heart began pounding in her chest, and she rushed to El's room. The agent didn't open it immediately, but eventually he did.

"El! Where's Raymond?"

"My God, what's wrong with you?"

"Where is he? El, where is he?"

"He sailed to his island. Why?"

“When?”

It was a rhetorical question; she knew perfectly well when he had sailed away.

“About thirty minutes ago when he came to say goodbye. I suggested he take a stroll, but he said he’d already called a taxi.”

“El!” Marian burst into his room and closed the door behind her. “I killed him! I killed him, do you understand?”

“What? Hold on.” El shook his head. “Let’s sit down, and you explain everything to me.”

“No! We don’t have time! They’ll be here within an hour!”

“Who will be here, Marian?”

“From the Center ... Oh my God, what have I done?”

“Don’t worry. If they’re coming for someone, they’ll definitely inform me.” El hurried to pour his partner a glass of cold water.

“No, no, no! El, I don’t report to you. I never did. I’m directly connected to the Center. And besides, I’m not an agent. I’m a doctor.” Marian sat on the bed and clasped her head in her hands, while El stood frozen with an empty glass. “I thought I was doing the right thing, but I made a big mistake tonight. I killed him ... Oh God ...”

“So, what did you do exactly, Doctor?” His voice was filled with skepticism.

“I told them everything ...”

3:13 AM

"Yes. What did you tell them?" El wondered patiently.

"He can penetrate any mind, El. He can extract any information from our memory. From any distance, from anyone's head! Do you understand?"

The agent went rigid in his tracks and, it seemed, didn't blink for several seconds. Then he sprang into action, took an empty suitcase from the closet and turned it over. He pulled a black pistol from a plastic cover hidden inside and quickly put it all in a small backpack along with his wallet and a black zip-up hoodie. Without saying a word, he stepped decisively out of the room.

Chapter 13

"El, wait! I'm coming with you!" Marian rushed out into the corridor.

"No," he snapped harshly.

Marian dashed into her room, grabbed a black backpack from the wardrobe, and snatched her purse from the chair. She caught up with El outside.

"Marian, I can't take you with me. You stay here," muttered El, noticing her beside him.

"Please. It's my fault, and I want to help!"

"Listen." He swiftly turned around and grabbed her shoulders. "If you're following me, there's no turning back now. And if you truly believe that I'll psychoanalyze you, absolving you of guilt, you're sorely mistaken, Mari. I'm leaving, and you're staying here. In this place! That's an order."

"El!" Marian ran after him once more.

He stopped and closed his eyes, cursing under his breath. "I need a taxi!" He spoke in an urgent tone to the receptionist.

"One of the cars is waiting at the gate, sir. Where will you be heading?"

3:13 AM

There was no answer. El headed to the road, opened the door of a pink sedan, and sat in the front seat. He heard someone slide into the back.

"I don't have time, Marian. But if you want to stay on the dock, it's your choice."

"El, please forgive me. I thought ..."

"You thought?" El exploded. "Did you really think the Center would let a person who knows everything live? Is that what you truly thought? Or maybe you thought they'd throw a party in the department over it?" He turned to Marian, scorching her with his gaze. "Oh God," he added and turned back to the scared taxi driver and the winding road bathed in the soft light of the streetlights.

Marian sniffled, and El realized she was crying. "Knock it off." He frowned. "I don't need any hysterics right now."

"I was scared!" she yelled. "I was scared to death! What should I have done?"

"What should you have done?" El smirked, piercing Marian with a heavy gaze in the rear-view mirror. "Come to me and tell me everything! Instead of calling the Center. Then we'd all be safe right now. And we'd figure out together what to report to the higher-ups and what not to."

"I'm sorry," Marian sobbed from the back seat.

When the pier came into view, El took out his phone from the backpack and dialed Raymond's number. There was no answer. He quickly typed a message and hit the Send button. He waited for confirmation that the text had successfully reached the recipient before getting out of the car. He walked along the wooden pier, hearing Marian's steps behind him. Passing the boats, El "accidentally" dropped his phone into the water, and his wristwatch followed the same way.

"Do you have any electronics on you?" He turned to Marian at last. She shook her head, wiping away tears. "A phone?"

"No."

"A watch?"

"A watch?" She looked at El with reddened eyes.

"Yes, a watch!"

The watch, forever frozen at 10:10 p.m., was lost on the same pier, and they soon rented a boat to Koh An for a decent sum.

"I hope it won't stall," grumbled El as he settled down under the colorful canopy.

"Yes, mister!" The Thai man bowed happily. El shot him a scorching look, but the sailor nonchalantly switched on the flashlight, started the engine, and steered away from the dock without any rush.

"He knows where to go?" Marian asked as the shoreline turned into a faint string of lights.

"He knows," El replied confidently.

3:13 AM

Soon darkness enveloped them, and the moon migrated to another part of the sky, faintly illuminating the ocean and the darkened silhouettes of the islands. Marian was starting to feel a little calmer, and the wind dutifully dried her tears.

"Are you okay?" El softened his tone.

His words brought Marian an unprecedented sense of relief. She grabbed his strong shoulder and leaned against him, caught in a surge of emotions.

"Thank you," she whispered helplessly.

"So, a doctor, huh?" El turned his face towards her, and the unspoken word "charm" raced through his mind. "Well, spill it." He sighed heavily.

"There are three oracles—at least, I know of three. One lives in Alaska, another in California, and the third one is here in Thailand. I visited the first two, collected their testimonies. Both were visited by the dead. According to their accounts, the dead behaved strangely, as if their minds were still alive. Ethan Parker spoke of nine years before it happened, and he said that water was to blame for everything. Both psychics provided some details about the appearance of the infected. And Louis Rapshmir, as a medium, managed to convey a message from one of the spirits about an upcoming event. He was a historian ..."

"Rapshmir?" El interrupted.

"No, the spirit that came to him."

"Ahh."

"So, this person whose spirit came to Rapshmir was a historian in his lifetime and conveyed this phrase: 'In nine years, Phorcys will release his monstrous daughters, and they will destroy the entire world,'" Marian explained.

"Phorcys? Who's that?" El furrowed his brow, delving into his memories.

"According to Greek mythology, he's a chthonic sea deity or the god of the raging sea. He commands all sea storms and terrorizes sailors, giving birth to sea monsters from the depths of the ocean. His daughters, the Gorgons, are also considered, according to ancient myths, true monsters."

"The Gorgons? Including Medusa?" El interjected.

"Exactly! This seems to confirm the role of water as the source of the disease."

"So this is a disease?"

"Yes. It strongly resembles the plague, but it's even more like leprosy. In short, it looks like an extensive bacterial infection that affects the central nervous system and possibly even the brain."

El should have hated the deceiver, or at least become disillusioned with her. Despite these feelings, he inevitably felt deep sympathy with Marian as she revealed the truth, acting differently and shedding her mask, standing on equal footing with him.

3:13 AM

The darkness covered them, for without it, he would never have dared. El leaned in towards Marian and touched her tender lips with his own.

To say that Marian didn't expect it would be an understatement. But with the twists of fate, this day had already filled her veins with adrenaline. Perhaps fueled by epinephrine, she was even somewhat pleased with this initiative from Agent Roberts. A kiss somewhere in the middle of the night ocean with a secret agent who had a gun in his backpack stirred her imagination and pushed thoughts of their actions aside. Absorbed in each other, they wouldn't have stopped any time soon, but the Thai man, noticing the peculiar activity in his boat, impudently announced, "In twenty minutes we'll arrive at Koh An, a private island."

Not surprisingly, the sailor had spilled the beans when they were almost there; it would have cost romantics several times more to get from there to another destination.

"We know," El said, tearing himself away from Marian with an effort.

The boat entered the bay of Koh An and came to a stop in the shallow water. The agents jumped ashore and made their way through the darkness. The motorboat sailed away, leaving the island engulfed in darkness.

"It's so dark here." Marian clung to El's hand once again.

"Normally the beach is lit up all night because of the snakes," El whispered, causing Marian to almost jump onto his back.

"Snakes?" she gasped and froze, hesitant to take another step.

"Of course. After sunset the beach is crawling with them." He didn't intend to comfort Marian. "We need to walk carefully once our eyes adjust."

And as their eyes gradually adjusted, Marian could make out hundreds, maybe even thousands, of black, wriggling bodies on the contrasting sand. She felt sick, as if a snake had coiled around her shoulders and was squeezing her throat. Her forehead was covered in tiny beads of sweat, and her legs resisted moving forward. Suddenly a thin beam of light from a pocket flashlight pierced the night.

"El, watch your step," Raymond warned. From the darkness, a familiar hand with a Rolex on its wrist appeared, handing El another pocket flashlight.

"Where's Kiet?" El asked immediately.

"He's in the village with his grandchildren."

"That's good."

After that, maneuvering through the writhing snakes became much easier. Some of the reptiles reacted to the light with dangerous jerks, brushing their slippery tails against the shoes and even the bare ankles of the late-night visitors. Marian did her best to hold herself together, but after another fairly loud scream, she clamped her hand over her mouth.

They passed through the chirping and rustling tropical garden, where every second something would slip off a branch, jump from leaf to leaf, and screech loudly at the moon. Upon entering the house, Raymond turned on a dim light and opened one of the cabinets. He spun the lock of the safe and, looking at El through the half-open door, said slyly, "Take my travel bag and put the bottles from the bar inside."

It seemed that even this guy might get bored of hiding from death without a couple of drinks. "They'll make a noise," Raymond continued. "Wrap each one in a towel." El promptly got to work.

Raymond filled the black sports bag with money, and when the stacks of bills ran out, a shiny Colt gleamed in his hand.

"A gun?" El was surprised.

"I'm alone on this island." Raymond spread his arms.

"Raymond." Marian used the pause. "I didn't think you—"

"Would get scared just like you?" he interrupted her.

Marian fell silent. Clearly this wasn't the right time for explanations. In any case, she was glad that El had found Raymond before the assassins.

"Let's go," El commanded, and Raymond hoisted the bag onto his shoulder.

They left the bungalow, descended from the veranda, and passed the pool, heading into the heart of the banana palm forest. Soon the ground gave way to sand—a sure sign that the beach was close. In the distance they heard the sound of an engine, and all three understood that their guests had already arrived. The thin beams of their flashlights went out, and without a word, they silently continued their journey. The trail led through a densely overgrown jungle cape and descended into a secluded cove hidden from curious eyes. Between two sloping rocks, nestled against the wooden pier, stood the Riva.

Behind them, a bright flashlight flickered through the black foliage. El and Marian quickly boarded the yacht. Raymond untied the mooring rope and jumped onto the white deck too. He started the engine and was guiding his vessel between the rocks when the first shot rang out from the jungle. All three dropped to the floor. The agents took cover under the table, and Raymond crouched at the helm.

"Faster!" El shouted.

"I can't go any faster; there's a coral reef behind us!" Raymond calmly steered the Riva through the winding path to the open ocean before finally turning the fast boat and rushing into the darkness of the Andaman Sea. He knew those waters like the back of his hand—perhaps even better. But after flying at full speed for a few minutes, he suddenly called out and slowed down.

"El, take over! I think I've been hit."

El and Marian rushed to the helm. Raymond was standing in a puddle of his own blood.

"Oh God!" Marian exclaimed, raising her hands.

3:13 AM

El took the helm, and the doctor helped Raymond to the sofa. "There's an island nearby; we can anchor there," he suggested.

"This island?" El asked, nodding at the navigation display.

"Yes, this one." Raymond groaned. "Sail towards it. Reduce the speed in half an hour. Go carefully near the sharp cape and then just turn the key. The engine will shut itself off. Then press the button to the left of the wheel—we'll drift until we reach the shallow waters, and then drop the anchor."

Marian clung to Raymond, inspecting his blood-soaked shirt. "Here, I found it on your forearm. The bullet … the bullet grazed your shoulder," she muttered nervously. "Where's your drink? Where are the towels?"

El nudged the travel bag toward Marian. She found a bottle of whiskey wrapped in clean towels. She treated the wound and tied the terry cloth fabric tightly as a tourniquet.

"What about anesthesia, Doctor?" Raymond groaned and immediately received the same bottle that had been used as antiseptic just a minute before.

The agents exchanged glances, the yacht flying through the pitch-black ocean like a fly trapped in a sea of tar.

Soon the shooting ceased. El guided the yacht into a miniature harbor, turned off the engine, and dropped the anchor. When the Riva came to a stop, he approached Raymond and sat down next to him.

"How do you feel?"

"I'll live ... Right, Dr. Flay?"

Marian cast a guilty look at El. He took the bottle from Raymond's hands and, taking a sip, passed the whisky to Marian. She took a sip as well, coughed, and glanced at the blood-soaked floor of the Riva. After a generous dose of bourbon, Raymond managed to change his blood-stained shirt for one of El's black hoodies he found in the backpack. He dozed off on the couch while Marian and El wiped the sticky blood from the deck. After a few minutes, he began shaking feverishly. Marian rushed to find blankets and, discovering a couple in the storage compartment, carefully covered him.

When they had finished cleaning up, they saw the owner of the yacht lying on the soft seat in a deep slumber. The two agents settled down on the floor. Bright stars lit up the sky, and the ocean murmured beneath them.

"What'll happen now?" Marian whispered, snuggling against El's chest.

He hugged her, breathing in the scent of her disheveled hair. "I don't know, Mari."

"Do you think there's a place on this planet where we could hide from them?"

"I don't think so. I'm certain such a place doesn't exist."

Marian grew somber and pressed closer to El.

3:13 AM

Suddenly something hit the stern, and the yacht shook. A chill ran down El's spine.

"What is it? What's out there?" Marian asked.

El couldn't voice his suspicion, but when the jolt was repeated, he flinched as if hundreds of lifeless bodies had once again extended their blue-tinged hands over the side of the boat. He left Marian and crept to the edge of the Riva, where the moon's silver light revealed a sharp fin.

"Just sharks."

"Just sharks?" Marian exclaimed.

"They were attracted by the blood. That's not surprising," said El, trying to erase the horror from his face and returning to Marian. "Let's lie him on the floor. God forbid he falls overboard and all our efforts go to waste."

Marian let out a restrained chuckle. El was clearly trying to lighten the mood.

The sharks circled the boat and then swam away. El and Marian calmed down and lay back on the checkered blanket. They couldn't sleep. They looked at the sky, listened to the ocean, and kissed each other, fully aware that it might be their last night alive.

Soon Marian changed Raymond's bandage, noting that his hand was no longer bleeding. His brief nap, more like a trance, had miraculously seemed to heal his wound.

"How I crave coffee," he moaned sleepily. "I'd sell my soul to the devil for just one cup."

"Haven't you already?" El grinned.

"No. As you can see, I'm constantly negotiating the price."

"Where to next? I hope we're not settling on this island." El looked up at the jungle-covered rolling rock ten times smaller than Koh An.

"No. I've had enough of islands," grumbled Raymond. "We'll cross the Andaman Sea and head to Krabi port. There we'll take a taxi to the airport. We'd better be on the plane before sunrise."

"Raymond, I hate to break it to you, but we won't get through passport control."

"I have my own plane."

"Your own plane ..." El repeated thoughtfully.

"It's mine, but due to significant tax differences, it's registered in the name of a local wealthy man. Such planes rarely face scrutiny, especially in Thailand and especially for a stack of cash." Raymond winked.

"All right, even if we manage to board the plane without any checks, where will we fly to?" El frowned. "Wander around developing countries until we run out of money?"

"We can seek protection from Canada," Marian interjected.

3:13 AM

"Citizens of Britain and the United States?" El looked mournfully at Marian.

"I'm a Canadian, El, and my father is a diplomat."

El looked anxiously at his companion, trying to fathom just how many more secrets her charming head held.

"Well, it seems like we've charted our course," Raymond said, lowering his head back onto the blanket and groaning theatrically. "What other surprises do you have for us, Dr. Flay?"

El looked at her with eyes full of tenderness and fear at the same time. She remained silent, apparently keeping plenty of secrets. Raymond, ignoring their conversation, stood up and started the motor. He steered the yacht out of its hiding spot and the navigator set the course for Krabi port. With all the lights turned off, he skillfully maneuvered the Riva through the maze of Andaman Sea islands.

Chapter 14

Somewhere in the distance, the black skies parted, and a bright beam of light pierced the agitated sea.

"They switched to the helicopter," El stated, and Marian felt an unnatural chill in the otherwise sweltering night.

"Are we going at full speed?" she asked Raymond.

"At full speed."

"Maybe we should find someplace to hide? There are more islands in this sea than water."

"I think that's exactly what they're counting on." El glanced nervously at the sky.

The bright beam of light seemed to draw nearer and then recede, making Marian's heart pound in her chest.

"El, take over. Marian, have a look at my hand," Raymond said, relinquishing control to El and turning his attention to the doctor. She reached over, lifted his sleeve, and peered under the bandage.

"Give me more whiskey, Doc." Raymond kept his eyes fixed on the beam, not even noticing the disapproval that crept onto Marian's face.

"Maybe that's enough," she retorted.

"What's enough?" The clairvoyant gave her a cold look.

3:13 AM

"Getting drunk ..."

"Doc, give me this damn bourbon if you want to stay alive." Even in the darkness, his eyes sparkled with fury. There was a threatening undertone in his voice.

Marian wasn't afraid—what else could she fear anymore? She was furious. While El had bravely saved Raymond's life, it seemed that the guy didn't care at all. She stood up, struggling, pulled out a faceted bottle from her bag, and handed it to Raymond.

She headed towards the helm, hearing the bottle open behind her. Just a minute later, a thunderclap roared somewhere near the shores of Phuket. Marian turned sharply. Raymond was still sitting on the checkered blanket, gazing upward, where the first sinuous lines of lightning soon appeared. Suddenly the whole sky over the Andaman Sea became obscured by low storm clouds, and the first large raindrop fell directly onto Marian's forehead.

El turned around—the helicopter's beam disappeared hopelessly in the thickness of the newly formed mist. Raymond nonchalantly pulled a black hood over his head, grinned smugly, took a sip of bourbon, and closed his eyes. When raindrops splashed on his pale face, he laughed. His laughter echoed with a powerful rumble and drowned in the stormy ocean.

"El ..." Marian shuddered, unable to tear her gaze away from Raymond. "Is he doing this right now?"

"I don't know, Mari ... I don't know ..."

"Look, he's summoning a storm! Look at him," she demanded.

The situation grew more mysterious and unsettling by the moment. Marian couldn't help but watch in both awe and trepidation as Raymond's enigmatic behavior seemed to intertwine with the rising tempest.

"If he's the one doing this, we're in good company." El grinned, but Marian had little room for amusement.

"In that case I suppose he could handle it without us." She still regarded Raymond with suspicion.

"A person needs another person, Mari. Perhaps each of us is capable of much more when we're not alone."

Marian softened suddenly, perhaps due to the rain, as she blinked several times. And who knows, maybe it was only the motion of the sea that drew her closer to El.

After three hours of wandering the night ocean, the shores of Krabi appeared on the navigator screen, marked with winding rivers. At 4:14 a.m. local time, the Riva rounded the gigantic finger-like rock and entered the waters of the bay. The mouth of the Chao Fah River was faintly lit, and the long Klong Jilad pier could be seen.

El slowed down and maneuvered the yacht towards the high pier. There was no one around. He took a gun out of his backpack, slung his bags around himself, and silently climbed the narrow stone steps. Marian and Raymond followed him.

3:13 AM

The long jetty was dimly lit by round hanging lanterns. From the giant bushes near the water, someone chirped loudly.

“It looks clear,” whispered El as he straightened up. The recent rain had stirred up swarms of small, pesky insects. They buzzed around, finding their way into their noses, eyes, and damp necks with every step.

Leaving the port building, which resembled a hangar, the fugitives made their way up the street. Beneath a banana palm, they spotted a lone taxi with a Thai driver sleeping peacefully in the front seat.

El tapped on the roof and the driver jolted awake, casting a frightened glance at them. He half leaned out of the window and mumbled something in the local dialect.

“Khun wang him?” Raymond grumbled.

“Chi-chi!” The driver nodded, starting the engine.

El reached for the door handle, but Marian stopped him. “I’ll sit next to the driver! If there’s a pursuit, you can take me hostage,” she said, her voice dripping with deceit.

El frowned but agreed. The car started and drove them away from the ocean, heading towards Krabi International Airport.

Raymond was leaving behind the Andaman Sea and his beloved Riva. He gazed wistfully at the misty jungles and the dark tangles of the whimsical philodendron, which, as was customary, adorned the local roads with its luxurious foliage. He already missed everything he had soaked into his thin skin over the past five years. He longed for the purple sunsets, the lavender dawns, the might of the azure ocean, the ghostly jungles, and Athit's incredible culinary skills. He so often woke at dawn to the clucking of hens, the crowing of roosters, and the bustling of restless Kiet. And just as often, he cursed them all. Too often to be nostalgic now, but that's just how people are. How much he would give to return to the past!

If only he could turn back time. To that luxurious restaurant where he would never respond to Ann Jay's alluring glances. To that distant time when he still knew how to keep his secrets and, with some effort, could distinguish the living from the dead.

The car drove through the city streets and turned onto the highway, and the driver picked up speed. Nobody understood where the police car came from, closing in on them from behind. Flashing all its lights and blaring its siren, it rapidly chased the taxi on the empty road.

Marian's heart pounded furiously. Her ears were clogged with excitement, and the bourbon, drunk who knew how many hours ago, rose into her throat.

El quietly drew his gun from the holster at his waist and took a deep breath, poised to shoot back at their pursuers. Raymond leaned over the bag and felt for the Colt inside; any second now, he would have to take the driver hostage.

The wailing of the siren grew louder, and the tension inside the cabin escalated. It felt as though a single cry or sudden movement could force someone to pull the trigger. The police car pulled alongside, bathing the pale faces of the taxi passengers in red and blue lights, then raced past them.

3:13 AM

Raymond leaned back in the soft seat, closed his eyes, and chuckled softly. El holstered his pistol and let out a silent sigh of relief. Ten minutes later, they reached the airport checkpoint. Sleepy workers glanced at the taxi and retreated behind their small windows.

“Arrival or departure?” asked the driver, with a strong accent.

“VIP terminal,” commanded Raymond, and the Thai man immediately turned and maneuvered around a shabby one-story building.

He stopped before the security barrier, and a sturdy guard with a rifle approached the car. Someone among the three passengers swallowed audibly.

“Can I help you?”

“My plane is here at your airport. I would like to see it,” Raymond admitted, his voice calm and composed despite the tension in the air.

“One moment,” the guard replied and disappeared through a tinted glass door. Soon afterward, a strong and confident Thai woman emerged, holding a portable fingerprint scanner.

Marian’s heart raced with anticipation, unsure of the outcome. El glanced at Raymond, understanding the gravity of the situation. Airport security was conducting a thorough check, and the escapees couldn’t afford any mistakes.

Raymond leaned forward, extending his hand. Devoid of emotions, the woman expertly placed his fingers on the scanner and the device hummed to life. Seconds felt like hours as the results were processed. Everyone froze. Even the taxi driver seemed to hold his breath, anticipating airport security's decision.

Finally she nodded, apparently satisfied with the scan. "You're good to go, Mr. Sombun Na Taku."

This decision surprised everyone except Raymond. The Thai woman thanked him and disappeared again behind the black doors; the very next moment, the security gate opened. They disembarked near the glass gates, where a VIP zone employee rushed to meet them.

"Your luggage, Mr. Na Taku?" The well-built young man grinned effusively.

"I have none this time," Raymond replied.

"When are you planning to depart?"

"Right now."

"Do you need a pilot?"

"Yes, that would be helpful."

"Please, the shuttle will take you to the aircraft. Which city are you flying to?"

"We are flying to Canada."

The obliging Thai man paused, staring at Raymond with a bewildered look. "But usually before such a long journey we ask for a minimum of three days' notice!"

"My apologies, but it happened this way," Raymond stated matter-of-factly. "We are taking off now."

3:13 AM

"But Mr. Na Taku, with all due respect, please give us at least an hour! Besides scheduling your flight and bringing in an experienced pilot, our technicians need to check the aircraft and refuel it."

"Fine," Raymond grumbled reluctantly.

"Thank you," the Thai man said with a sigh of relief. "We will send provisions, champagne, and the passport control services for you and your guests."

No more words were spoken after that. All three got into the black van and soon found themselves facing the elegant Gulfstream jet.

"It's so beautiful," exclaimed Marian before stepping into this $65 million flying wonder.

The velour cabin, the color of creamy custard, was adorned with soft sofas and comfortable leather seats. There was a television, a video link to the pilot, retractable tables, and even a minibar.

"Home, sweet home!" Raymond exclaimed, flopping down on the sofa and sinking into its softness.

"Don't get too comfortable yet," chided El. "We still have an hour to wait, not to mention passport control. How for God's sake are we going to handle this?"

Raymond either didn't want to answer or didn't know how to respond. Everything that evening had happened spontaneously, and he didn't seem to be in a hurry to break the tradition.

Marian cautiously settled into a chair and stared out of the round window. "Raymond, dim the lights," she whispered, and he immediately obliged, using the internal control panel.

El leaned over and looked out of the window. A group of uniformed staff was walking towards the plane.

"The visa service and baggage inspection." Raymond reached for the illuminator, catching El's stern gaze. "Trust me. We're in Thailand! You can buy anyone here except CIA agents. But for some reason, I'm sure they're still looking for us somewhere among the islands of the Andaman Sea."

Even if the Riva didn't sail into open waters, even if it docked at the same pier where the fugitives had disembarked, someone would simply steal the well-maintained yacht with the ignition key left as a gift. The not-so-foolish local criminals, after seeing bullet holes, would realize that it was better to hide such a find from prying eyes. After patching up the expensive Riva and waiting a few months, they would sell it with fake documents in just a couple of days—and that would be the end of it.

Of course, it wouldn't work that way with the plane. The investigation of Raymond in Thailand would inevitably bring the Gulfstream to the surface. No matter how much money they paid for silence now, it would inevitably come out sooner or later. But most likely not until after their sixteen-hour flight.

Outside, there was a knock, and Raymond, grabbing several sizable stacks of cash from his bag, went to the fuselage door. He spoke only briefly, and within a couple of minutes the team of handlers had descended the stairs onto the deserted airfield.

3:13 AM

"That's it." Raymond reentered the cabin. "Mr. Na Taku has long planned a trip to Canada with his childhood friend Liman Hongsvan," he said, clasping his hands prayerfully and bowing to Marian. "And, of course, he didn't forget his old friend Virot Wongart." Raymond turned to El with a bow.

El glanced at Raymond's antics and resumed pacing up and down the cabin.

"Someone's running toward the plane," Marian suddenly whispered, keeping watch near the illuminator.

Raymond crossed the narrow cabin with calm steps and briefly glanced out of the round window. "It's the same guy." He headed to the door. "They probably told him we're giving out money here."

"Mr. Na Taku," the visitor panted, "do you need anything? A flight attendant?"

"No, no, thank you. Ms. Hongsvan will be delighted to serve her old friends and the pilot."

"Provisions for the entire journey will be brought any minute now. We remember your allergy to caviar!"

"I also have an allergy to chatterboxes, but they're not working today, are they?"

"You're in luck! Today, only the most reliable team is on duty. The pilot is already on his way to the airport, and within half an hour, you and your friends will be airborne."

There was a pause, during which Raymond undoubtedly rewarded the employee. And now the satisfied voice chirped with double the optimism, "If you need anything, just say the word! My team will do everything in our power."

"I was just wondering where we could find some cozy clothes. We got caught in the rain and got soaked."

The visitor briefly glanced at Raymond's shorts, stained with peculiar crimson streaks. "Yes, sir."

"And it would also be nice to get something for Canada. I've heard it's still cool there at the end of spring."

"Yes, sir. My brother-in-law has a store in the airport. He'll bring some clothes to Departures. What style do you and your friends prefer?"

"Sporty." Raymond peeked out from behind the polished wall and examined Marian from head to toe. "Yes, we love sporty!"

"Of course, sir."

"And here's something for your relative for the trouble."

"Thank you, Mr. Na Taku! Thank you!"

Technicians outside got to work inspecting and refueling the aircraft. The minutes until takeoff seemed to stretch into eternity.

"God, why is it taking so long?" El sighed, peering at the pre-dawn sky with an anxious gaze.

"We have too much adrenaline in us, that's why it feels like a long time," replied Marian calmly, softly massaging her temples.

3:13 AM

"What?" As if he hadn't heard, El turned away from the window and gave Marian a look that vividly conveyed his feelings about her.

"Raymond, have you ever heard of time distortion?" She paused her massage for a moment.

"Never heard of it." He shook his head, still lying on the sofa and admiring the cream-colored polished wooden ceiling.

"Time distortion is nothing more than a change in the perception of time. The phenomenon was recorded by the British Research Institute during experiments involving free-fall jumps. They equipped Chris—I think that was the subject's name—with a special watch. The device displayed numbers at such a speed that no one on the platform could call out the sequence on the dial. For everyone watching, there was just an infinite green flash. They raised Chris to a height of 160 feet and let him free fall. When they finally disconnected him from the bungee cords, he was able to accurately name a series of numbers he saw on the display during the fall."

"And how does that work from a medical standpoint?" El furrowed his brow.

"Chris was afraid of heights. The adrenaline in his bloodstream slowed down his perception of time. He saw things that no one else could. For Chris, time stretched during the fall, while for the doctors on the platform, it remained the same."

"That's interesting," Raymond commented, exploring the ceiling.

El remained silent. Marian's stories altered his perception of time. He stared at her, sensing that his life could stretch out under the influence of all the chemical elements that arose in his body next to her.

Footsteps sounded outside the aircraft. Someone ascended the metal steps of the boarding ramp at a leisurely pace. Raymond jumped up from the sofa and rushed to the door.

"Mr. Na Taku? I am your pilot, Niran Talang."

"Please. We have been waiting for you," Raymond said as the captain entered the narrow cabin.

"I'll check the instruments, and we'll be ready to take off in ten minutes."

"Thank you, Captain. I have a few personal requests, but we'll talk about them in the air."

"I was informed that you would be piloting, Mr. Na Taku."

"That's right, I am piloting. During takeoff, landing, and at your request—I'll be right there with you."

"I am most grateful." The elderly Thai man bowed, then proceeded to the cramped cockpit.

Provisions were brought to the aircraft, filling the tiny kitchen cabinets to the brim. The door of the Gulfstream finally closed, and the pilot started the engine. A pleasant excitement ran through Marian's body. They were flying—the fears and anxieties of the long night were over.

3:13 AM

She looked at the brightening horizon, where appeared a rosy halo of hope, when suddenly a black van emerged from behind the airport building. It raced towards the Gulfstream.

"Oh no ..." Marian whispered.

El and Raymond looked out of the window—the van was speeding as if possessed. Raymond stormed into the narrow aisle and froze in front of the cockpit door.

"Captain Talang"—he knocked—"can we take off now?"

"Please, come in. Another couple of minutes," the captain replied over the intercom, and with a decisive click, he unlocked the door.

"I'll join you in one second," Raymond replied and stretched out his hand towards El. El handed Raymond his silver Colt.

Raymond's hands trembled. He'd never thought he'd have to use this beautiful deadly thing.

El smiled. For so many years, he had been eaten away by the terrible thought: *What if Raymond Lee killed his childhood friend Christine? What if he's the real psychopath and murderer? What if—* Now El saw with his own eyes that Raymond Lee could be anything, but not a killer.

Chapter 15

"I can handle this on my own." El squeezed Raymond's shoulder. "Go to the cockpit and help the pilot take off. That's much more important right now."

"Wait! It's the guy with the bags," Marian whispered, peering out from behind the polished partition.

"With the bags?" El's face contorted with misunderstanding.

"Damn, it's the clothes!" Raymond exclaimed with relief. He handed the Colt back to El and gently pushed the agent out of the narrow aisle.

"Mr. Na Taku." The breathless visitor hurriedly handed the stuffed bags to Raymond.

"Thank you," he replied, quickly escorting the man away, hearing a rushed "Have a safe flight" as he left.

Raymond raised the boarding stairs and made his way to the cockpit. The dim lighting in the cabin faded even more, and the Gulfstream began to move.

"El, we're leaving! We're leaving!" Marian repeated endlessly.

El took a seat next to her and fastened his seatbelt. Hypnotized by the horizon, Marian gripped the armrests—she still couldn't believe they were going to escape.

3:13 AM

"What if they order the pilot to land during the flight?" she asked, keeping her eyes on the airfield.

"Where would he land, Mari? We'll be flying over the ocean."

The Gulfstream rolled onto the concrete runway, then sped off towards the brightening horizon. Gaining substantial speed, the aircraft lifted off the ground and soared into the sky. The engines roared as the jet tore through the humid equatorial air.

Marian and El remained silent, their gazes fixed on the unforgettable landscape of this peculiar land that had unexpectedly brought them together. At an altitude of over twenty thousands of feet the flight stabilized and the cabin brightened. Raymond emerged from the cockpit and disappeared among the food cabinets once more. A loud pop and the sound of fizz filled the air. He returned with a tray that he almost dropped due to his wound. Carefully, he brought out the champagne glasses one by one.

"Liman Hongsvan." Raymond bowed to Marian. "Mr. Wongart?" El chuckled and accepted a glass.

Everyone's mood was uplifted. It seemed like their problems had dissolved along with the outlines of the coast adorned with twinkling lights.

"Raymond, when did you realize that you could not only see the future but also control it?" Marian leaned forward. Her voice was tinged with wonder—she was incredibly curious about the incident with the rain over the Andaman Sea. El seemed interested too, but for some reason he had never felt compelled to interrogate Raymond about all his abilities.

"Once, I worked as a dishwasher in a New York restaurant," Raymond said, taking a sip of champagne and savoring a large shrimp. "I had nowhere to live, so I stayed overnight in the storage room, sleeping on the floor. I promised the manager that once my house in New Jersey sold, I would be able to rent a room nearby. He took pity on me and chose not to tell the owner of the establishment. In an effort to save money, the owner instructed the night security guard to turn off the heating every night, and he did just that. With the onset of winter, I started freezing on that thin mattress. At the time, I didn't even have enough money for a second mattress or a couple of extra blankets. One night, the low temperature hit hard—I woke up unable to feel my fingers. I warmed up with some tea and rubbed my limbs. I tried to enter the utility room to unscrew the valves and avoid freezing to death by morning, but the door was locked."

Raymond pulled the creaky blanket higher, as if the chilling memories from the past had visited him once more.

"Two months earlier," he continued, "in the middle of a work shift, I had gone into the boiler room and turned the valve that cooled down the radiators—it was an unusually hot day for November standards. So I knew what I was up against. That February night, I pressed against the door, closed my eyes, and imagined I was next to the boiler. In my mind, I reached out and turned that very valve that fed fuel into the boiler, which then heated the water pipes and activated the steam heating system. Fifteen minutes later, the room temperature became bearable for sleep. I kept doing this until spring arrived. In the morning, I would stop the boiler room work, and at night, I would release steam through the door again. When the weather warmed up, I finally rented a room, and a month later, I got promoted."

"Promoted? To what?" El choked on his champagne.

"To waiter," replied Raymond proudly, examining the bubbles in the expensive champagne that had cost no less than two hundred per bottle.

Marian remained silent, clutching the empty glass with delicate fingers, occasionally observing Raymond. It seemed she was getting to know a new Mr. Lee—the person who had never been so candid, so human, and so intriguing to her before.

"More champagne?" El reached for the bottle.

Marian flinched, pulling her gaze away with difficulty. "Um, yes, please," she stammered.

Raymond excused himself to use the restroom and took a detour to talk to the pilot. El had dozed off. Marian, on the contrary, was becoming more sober as she pondered, fixing her gaze on the darkness outside the window.

"I'll swap with the captain. You take care of him. Just don't pour any champagne in his mug," Raymond whispered, afraid of waking El.

"Of course!" Marian jumped up and hurried to the provisions compartment. Raymond entered the code, and the door to the pilot's cabin slid open.

"Captain Talang, I'll relieve you." Raymond's voice rang out.

Marian seated the captain in a leather chair, set up a table, and brought him a reheated dinner. "Tea or coffee?" she asked.

"Coffee, please." Niran nodded.

Marian prepared the invigorating drink for him and hesitantly made her way to the pilot's cabin. "How do I talk to him?" she whispered to Niran, peering out from behind the polished partition.

"Just press that button there." The pilot pointed.

"Raymond?"

"I'm listening, Doc."

"Can I come in?"

"Hm, not a problem." Raymond chuckled and opened the door.

Marian entered the incredibly cramped space. Decorated in the same way, the cabin was bright and cozy. On the left, in the senior pilot's seat, sat Raymond, looking relaxed.

"You really know how to fly the plane? I'm impressed!"

"I do, Doc."

3:13 AM

“Sir, may I sit next to you?” Marian stretched herself taut like a string and placed the edge of her palm to her forehead, mimicking a salute. Raymond laughed and granted her request.

“In reality, technological progress has advanced to the point where planes can fly without pilots,” he confessed, waving his hand over a dozen sensors and buttons on the control panel. “To be honest, it’s all automated.”

“Really?”

“Absolutely! If an aircraft company wanted it, this bird could fly entirely on its own.”

“Then why don’t they fly that way?”

“People aren’t ready for it.”

“What do you mean?”

“Not ready psychologically. The truth is, today, no passenger would board a self-piloting piece of metal.”

“Hmmm, I understand. You’re a fascinating conversationalist, Raymond,” Marian said with a bashful smile.

“Oh no, Doc, not right now!”

“What?” Marian was bewildered.

“When I’m wounded and drunk, flying this damn plane.” Raymond turned away in frustration. “You’re back with your interrogations ...”

“No!” Marian lamented. “No, really, I didn’t even mean to.”

“Ms. Hongsvan, thanks for the coffee.” Captain Talang entered the cockpit.

Marian and Raymond fell silent. Marian cast a quick glance at Raymond, forced a strained smile, and left the cramped room; there wasn’t enough space for the three of them.

Nine hours remained before they would reach the shores of Canada when Raymond stepped out of the cockpit. Marian and El were sleeping peacefully on the unfolded sofa. The doctor had rested her head on the agent’s shoulder, and he had gently wrapped his arm around her waist.

For some reason Raymond hesitated, watching them for a moment before scolding himself, dimming the lights, and slipping under the soft blanket. He carefully adjusted his bandaged hand and closed his eyes.

The plane jolted. Raymond was certain he hadn’t fallen asleep yet, but the cabin clock told him an entire hour had passed. At 10:25 a.m., the Gulfstream entered a zone of turbulence. It rocked from side to side, and the cabin lights flickered unpleasantly.

Raymond propped himself up and peered through the window shade. A white fog assaulted his eyes—the plane had entered a cyclone over the Pacific Ocean. He reached for the phone receiver on the control panel and pressed the button to contact the pilot.

3:13 AM

"Hello?"

"Do you need a hand? We're getting tossed around pretty badly here."

"We'll be through it soon," Talang reassured him.

"Thank you, Captain."

Raymond rolled over and closed his eyes. Suddenly, strange sounds reached his ears. The psychic listened intently—someone was handling scissors near the cockpit.

He unfastened his seatbelt, stood up, and had just taken a few hesitant steps into the semi-darkness when the noise momentarily ceased. The Gulfstream jolted again, and Raymond just managed to grab a chair back. The door to the lavatory swung open abruptly, its light coming to life as an unseen presence resumed its work with the scissors.

The cold scrape of metal blades made Raymond break out in a cold sweat. Taking a few more steps, he rounded the polished partition and burst into the galley. The plane went into a brief free fall, and the lavatory door slammed shut with a loud noise.

Raymond gathered his composure, turned on the overhead light, and approached the door, pulling at the handle. The lavatory light automatically turned on, revealing that it was empty. Only some long strands of chestnut hair lay on the floor, cut by someone. As Raymond examined the strange find, the hair seemed to writhe like a million thin snakes, slowly slithering towards his bare feet.

“Mother of God!” he exclaimed, slamming the door in horror. For a moment he thought someone was standing behind him. He turned around; there was no one there. Raymond backed away into the narrow corridor and turned swiftly. He looked around in fear, but there was still no one behind him.

He caught his breath, switched on the additional light, and peered back into the cramped lavatory—there wasn’t a single hair on the white floor.

“What does it mean?” He leaned his forehead against the fragile door. “How exhausted I am ... Oh God, how tired I am of all this ... Captain, do you need company?” He pressed the button on the pilot’s door, hoping to distract himself from the gruesome visions.

“Rest, Mister; the plane is in capable hands,” came the reply.

“Wine ... my favorite wine was somewhere,” Raymond whispered, moving from the cockpit to the kitchen compartment. He procured a pale Australian, uncorked the bottle, and took it to bed. A few sips—just a habit, brought from the islands, it seemed. However, his brain remembered the familiar scent and taste and realized that its owner was unwell again. The puzzle of how that intricate mechanism worked was still a mystery, but after exactly four sips, Raymond fell asleep.

3:13 AM

He opened his eyes. A call from the pilot's console armrest beeped.

"Yes, Captain?"

"We're coming in for landing. In about forty minutes we'll be in British Columbia, heading for Prince Rupert Airport."

"Already? Well then, I'm preparing some coffee and heading your way."

"Very timely," Niran responded happily.

The invigorating aroma stirred Raymond's drowsy mind. Soon, through a thin veil of clouds, he beheld the winding pre-dawn coastline. The inky-black ocean washed around carved capes and elongated, flattened islands. Some mountain summits still held white snow patches, and impenetrable wild forests glowed mysteriously with turquoise hues. Air traffic control connected with the Gulfstream, authorizing their landing at this coastal airport in British Columbia.

Due to an extremely strong breeze, the plane had to make an extra loop, and, bypassing the steep mountains, they finally emerged over a rich blue bay dotted with white multi-story liners. The coastal city still basked in electric lights, inviting them warmly into its cozy harbors.

"Beautiful," Raymond murmured. "Have you flown to Canada before?"

The captain was focused on the instruments, giving only a faint nod in response.

They arrived on the same day, a full two hours ahead of their departure time. That's how it goes when you're flying strictly northeast at a speed of 500 miles per hour.

The plane was moving faster than scheduled, and the landing turned out to be rough. They slowed down and came to a stop almost at the far end of the airstrip. The landscape on the ground was barely any different from that at the airport they'd left. Instead of jungles, they were surrounded by forests, and the horizon was adorned with a pre-dawn glow—this time of year, the north experiences early sunrises.

"Feels like we never left," Raymond mumbled.

In the cramped cabin, a call signal chimed. Raymond lifted the receiver and hesitated for a moment. He gave the pilot a peculiar look, offered an apologetic smile, and exited the cockpit.

Marian paced the cabin, peering out of the window.

"Welcome to British Columbia!" Raymond exclaimed triumphantly. "Marian? Something wrong?"

"You've never flown to Canada, have you?" she said finally.

"What's the matter?" Raymond leaned toward the window.

"They tricked us! This isn't Canada ... It's Juneau, the capital of Alaska!"

"Damn it ..." Raymond clutched his temples.

3:13 AM

El leaned over his pistol, absentmindedly massaging his scalp. Marian, exhausted from pacing around, collapsed into a chair.

“Captain!” Raymond spun around and strode heavily toward the pilot’s cabin. He dialed the access code, which should have granted him entry, but it didn’t work—the pilot had locked himself in.

“Damn it!” Raymond pounded on the impenetrable door. “Captain, I order you to open up!” he shouted, pressing the intercom button.

“I apologize, Mr. Lee. I cannot open the door for you.”

“Then take off! Do you hear me? Take off!”

“I’m sorry, I truly am. You’re being sought by the CIA. I cannot go against the law.”

“Curse you!” Raymond struck the door with force and collapsed on the floor, curling up in pain.

“Raymond!” Marian rushed to him.

“Don’t come any closer!” he yelled, halting her midway.

“We have visitors.” El had spotted a convoy of black pickups through the window.

“Close all the windows, El,” Raymond requested, his tone much calmer now.

He sat on the floor, leaning against the door, and closed his eyes. After a few seconds, a mechanism on the other side of the door clicked open. Raymond could have stood and entered the code with his fingers, but he remained seated—the code above his head was entering itself.

Finally, he stood and pulled the handle. The door swung obediently open. He was met by a terrified Niran Talang.

"You'd better run to Mr. Roberts. I'm not in the mood," Raymond growled through gritted teeth.

Niran pressed himself against the wall, cautiously bypassed Raymond, and darted into the narrow corridor.

"Not so fast, Captain Tulag or whatever your name is," El greeted him.

Raymond, now at the controls, taxied a few more yards and sharply turned the airplane. In the distance he spotted a line of black service vehicles blocking the way. He grabbed a set of headphones and flipped the switch for communication with the airport.

"Private Flight 358 is taking off. Clear the runway," he stated calmly.

"Gulfstream G650 Flight 358, repeat it."

Raymond repeated the message.

"Hey, kid, shut off the engines. You've landed." A rough, raspy voice came through.

"I have three hostages on board. If you want to keep them alive, clear the runway." Raymond confidently guided the plane into position for takeoff. “If you don’t remove your pickups, I’ll start killing innocent people in a minute.”

He disconnected, slowing down before the line of black vehicles that blocked the path. Then he grabbed the headphones and shouted into the built-in microphone, “Captain Niran Talang, Agent El Roberts, and the charming Dr. Marian Flay will die one by one in a minute. And by the time you bring the gangway, I’ll drop their lifeless bodies down it.”

In Raymond’s head, blood pounded with a frenzied rhythm, and on the twenty-first beat, the pickups scattered. He steered the Gulfstream onto the runway, gaining speed as the pickups moved aside. He was picking up momentum when a desperate scream echoed from the cabin.

“There’s no fuel left! We can’t fly! We’re going to crash, do you hear me? We’re all going to die!”

El and Marian exchanged glances. The plane howled, shook, and, burning the remnants of its fuel, lifted off.

“El!” Raymond shouted, this time leaving the cockpit door wide open. Footsteps echoed behind him, and soon Agent Roberts appeared. “Have a seat,” Raymond invited him, nodding to the copilot’s chair.

“Where are we flying?” El asked on an exhale.

“We won’t make it to Canada without fuel, but we can land somewhere nearby.”

“Without working engines?” El questioned.

"Without working engines."

As the plane gained altitude, Marian burst into the cockpit, unable to stay put. "I took his phone and locked him in the restroom," she announced.

"Excellent, Doc!" replied Raymond. " Among the three of us, it's only you who have been to Juneau."

Marian subtly recoiled, and he continued, "Is there any abandoned military airstrip or cleared area for landing?"

"I ... I don't know." Marian hesitated. "I rented a car and drove northeast along the highway, following it without deviating ..."

"Northeast, then." Raymond checked the location. "Were there any stretches of road without trees?"

"Without trees in Alaska?" She sounded puzzled. "Wait—there was one stretch. Rocky shore on both sides of the road, and water beyond it."

"How many miles?"

"From here?"

"How many miles long is that stretch of road?"

"There were definitely about two miles ..."

"A stretch like that should be visible from the air," Raymond muttered, turning the plane northeast.

3:13 AM

Chapter 16

Soon the drone of the engines subsided, and even the unflappable El felt uneasy. The small disc of the sun had fully settled above the horizon, casting its rays through the trees, which were adorned with a ghostly mist.

Below, endless hills of coniferous forests stretched out. The winding road vanished and reappeared amidst the dark green expanse.

Finally, among the greenery, a river the color of teal gleamed, and Marian exclaimed, “Descend—we’re close!”

“Are you sure? Without engines, we won’t be able to take off again.”

Marian hesitated for a moment, studying the intricate shoreline, and spoke much more confidently. “I’m sure. It’s about half an hour’s drive from here.”

Raymond input the parameters and the machine, powered by emergency batteries, calculated the necessary landing angle. “Due to the wind, we’ll have to circle to descend as smoothly as possible.” He focused on the instruments.

Ahead, among the rocky shores, an open stretch of road emerged, and Raymond hastened to deploy the flaps. The aircraft responded instantly and was soon gliding at a low speed. Raymond turned the control wheel. The Gulfstream, like a massive bird spotting its prey, swooped down in a spiral.

Raymond sweated, alternately cursing and coaxing the jet into submission. Suddenly, above the mirror-like stillness of the stagnant water, he realized he was flying faster than intended. He reached for the controls and, with a trembling hand, adjusted the interceptors. The aircraft straightened out and balanced above the line of stone-gray asphalt. The yellow markings guided him, and seconds later, the wheels touched the ground.

The Gulfstream gave a slight jolt, but soon gravity prevailed, and the plane transitioned into full braking. It rolled almost to the next bend and came to a stop, one wing immersed in the outstretched firs.

Marian was the first to laugh. El and Raymond caught her joyful mood. She unfastened her seatbelt and, leaving the narrow steward's seat, rushed toward the pilot. Embracing Raymond around the neck, she closed her eyes and murmured, "We did it! You ... you did it!"

Raymond exhaled and unbuckled himself. His hands trembled and his legs were wobbly.

El patted his friend on the shoulder, stood up, and left the cabin. "Doc, we better hurry." Raymond gently withdrew from Marian's embrace and rose from his seat. She remained alone, breathing heavily.

Sliding the bags of money, alcohol, food, and spare clothes over their shoulders, Raymond and El opened the door and lowered the retractable stairs to the ground. Marian slid the latch, freeing Niran Talang. She donned El's backpack, cast a final glance at the jet's luxurious cabin, and descended the stairs, stepping once again onto the Alaskan land.

"Faster—into the woods!" El grabbed her as the sound of helicopters echoed behind them.

They ran, resisting the urge to look back. The coniferous forest sheltered them temporarily, but search teams would soon begin combing every mile within the Gulfstream's radius. Intelligence agencies would find Niran Talang, and he'd reveal that among the jet's passengers, the sole hostage was him—a hired pilot from a Thai airline company. From that moment on, the order "Shoot to kill" would be added to the pursuit.

El surged ahead thanks to his endurance and physical preparedness. He leaped over fallen trees, feverishly seeking temporary shelter for them all. In the distance the river gleamed, and El dashed towards the water. He descended onto the rocks and quickly surveyed the tall, water-eroded bank. Beneath looming roots lay a dark crevice that could easily accommodate three people.

"Over here!" He waved to the others.

Marian and Raymond descended onto the damp stones.

"Why hide? Wouldn't it be better to run?" Marian whispered, squeezed between El and Raymond in the narrow cave.

"They won't deploy more helicopters immediately," El explained. "For about an hour, the mercenaries will search from the air. Ground transportation needs time to reach here.

So after scouring this area, the choppers will move to another spot, and we'll continue along the river, hopping on wet stones to confuse the dogs."

"Dogs?" Raymond tensed.

"Puppies, if you prefer. Sweet little Shepherds, trained to go for the throat."

Marian swallowed. "And then? What's our plan?"

"We're heading to your Ethan."

She turned quickly to El, her gaze troubled, caught in his brown eyes that in turn traitorously lingered on her pale lips.

"But ... why?"

"To get acquainted!" He grinned, sweeping a sultry look over her dirt-smeared forehead and her hair, which was tightly knotted and filled with pine needles.

Above them, helicopter blades thrummed. Raymond pressed himself into the sandy ground, while Marian huddled against El. The searcher swept over the forest, emerging near the shore. Descending a few yards lower, it could easily have spotted them from an acute angle. But the towering firs obstructed the view, and after a spin over the water, the helicopter shot upward along the river. Somewhere in the distance another chopper's roar echoed, but the fugitives had no time to wait. They emerged from their cover and dashed along the stones by the riverbank.

3:13 AM

Sticking to the trail, they occasionally ventured into the forest, altering their route intermittently.

"I can't go on anymore. Let's take a short break," Marian pleaded.

"We can't, Mari," El interjected. "Every minute counts. If we keep up the same pace, we'll sleep in a comfy bed tonight."

"But why are we heading to Parker's?" she protested. "There are plenty of abandoned houses around."

"That's exactly where they'll be looking for us."

"And what about Parker? Do you think he's on our side? He's practically a CIA agent, just a little eccentric."

"He'll tell them where to find us," Raymond chimed in, catching his breath.

"That's what I've been telling El!" Marian exclaimed.

"He'll tell them where to find us while we're sitting in his home." Raymond wiped his brow, leaned his elbow on his knee, and fixed his translucent eyes on Marian. "Ethan Parker speaks to the woods and reports everything to the agency. We don't stand a chance in this forest if he's on their side."

Without a word Marian took a water bottle from her backpack, wet her throat, and resumed walking. El and Raymond exchanged glances and followed her.

At 1:33 p.m. they arrived at a wooden mansion. Several windows were ominously boarded up for the winter, and a fishing boat was chained to the entrance.

“It’s a couple of hours’ drive from here to Ethan’s,” Marian informed them. “If only we had a car ...”

“If we had a car, the helicopters would find us in less than ten minutes,” Raymond retorted.

Copter blades drummed over the spruces again.

“Damn,” Raymond muttered, his gaze anxiously fixed on the sky.

“Over here,” El rasped, pushing the nose of the boat aside.

Marian, lamenting about rats and spiders, crawled into the dark space under the stairs to the front door. Raymond followed El closely just as the air search circled above the house. Their hearts pounded in unison with apprehension and fear. El found Marian’s hand, while she found a hand with a Rolex. But Raymond didn’t respond to her touch, and as soon as the sounds over the roof subsided, he tactfully moved away from any unnecessary contact. Darkness always exposes as much as it conceals.

“Raymond?” She suddenly spoke up, and Raymond thought that even the sound of the helicopter was more pleasant to him than her inquiries.

“Hmm?”

3:13 AM

"Why don't you use your strength against them?"

"Do you want the helicopters to crash? The people in them didn't give orders to kill us."

"No, I don't want that," she mumbled.

"So can you do that too?" El said with unmistakable tension in his voice.

"No, I can't."

It looked like the tension had reached its limit. El snorted, restraining laughter. However, Raymond also clamped his mouth shut, avoiding letting out a laugh. Marian sighed in annoyance.

They emerged from their hiding place and sat on the ground, leaning against the house. One of the bags contained cold chicken schnitzels, salad, and bread. Raymond found the partially consumed bottle of Australian wine from the night before and took a sip before any food reached his stomach.

"You drink every day." Marian pierced him with a disapproving look.

"So what?"

"As a doctor, I don't recommend you do that." She greedily took a bite of a yellow schnitzel.

"If I listened to doctors, I'd be right where my mother ended up," he retorted.

"Where?" Marian softened her grip.

"In the loony bin."

In the distance, the faint echo of barking dogs reached them, and Marian immediately jumped to her feet.

"They're a long way away," El reassured her. "The canyon just has good acoustics, but we shouldn't hang around."

The fugitives descended to the river again, removed their shoes, and crossed it at the shallowest point. The water stung them with cold. They scrambled up the steep bank and continued running through the woods.

"We'll have to cross the river a couple more times to confuse the tracks," El said, and before nightfall, they would ford the fast-flowing water several more times.

The sun set, casting a chilly darkness over the land. With the arrival of night, their anxiety subsided, and all three fell silent. They were utterly exhausted, their strength drained to the core. As twilight shrouded the forest, their hopes of reaching Parker before nightfall seemed to grow more elusive, a fragile wisp in the fading light. Raymond, it seemed, had been completely drained of his vitality, stripped of the extraordinary abilities he had once possessed. The sounds of helicopters grew scarce, but this in no way indicated a halt in the search efforts. In the darkness of the northern woods, those equipped with night vision binoculars held a distinct advantage—a sort of superpower against the befuddled Raymond. The ache of his wound throbbed once more, as if his weakened mind could no longer uphold the vitality of his body.

"I hope we find Parker's house, otherwise we'll starve." Marian persisted with her pessimism.

Perhaps she was taking revenge on Raymond. Or perhaps it was her nature—a doctor who kept everyone under control, deep down hoping for the best but always prepared for the worst. El remained silent, not understanding what was happening between the two of them. Or rather, he didn't want to understand. For years the hardened El hadn't dreamt that anyone could touch his petrified heart. And when Marian did, he felt a sharp need just to be close to her. To look into her lovely face, protect her, and hope that one day she returns his feelings.

A bottle gleamed in Raymond's hand. Disappointed, Marian turned away.

"I had a vision, Doc." He suddenly spoke to her. "In the plane, while you were sleeping, I saw someone trimming their hair in the bathroom."

"Hair—hair again," Marian muttered almost inaudibly. "But why were they cutting it?"

"Maybe because those hairs were moving." Raymond took another sip of wine. "And behaving like little snakes."

"Gorgons ..." Marian stopped. "Medusa!"

Through the trees, a reddish glow of artificial light sparkled.

“Careful here—we might be walking into a trap.” El tried to ground their conversation in the reality beyond the myths of ancient Greece.

“Let’s take a seat.” Raymond set their bags down beneath a sprawling tree. “I’ll go scout ahead.”

“Are you out of your mind?” El protested. “I’ll go.”

“Sit, El, sit.” Raymond grinned. “I’ll sit too. My ever-present intellect will handle the reconnaissance.”

“They could be nematodes.” Marian continued to mutter, lost in her own thoughts, paying no heed to the unfolding events. “They might infiltrate hair follicles or even replace hair entirely.”

“Doc!” Raymond scolded her and closed his eyes.

He concentrated intently, yet nothing materialized. He shut his eyes tightly and clenched his teeth, only to be met with a searing pain that spread across his scalp, igniting a migraine. He relaxed, releasing a cloud of vapor into the air. As the night approached, the temperature dropped, yet the chill seemed oddly invigorating. Suddenly he found himself in front of the house. Not a soul was in sight. He could hear someone bustling around on the porch, finally settling themselves into a creaky chair. There was a short ring, and Ethan picked up the receiver.

“I’ll let you know. When? When the forest’s creatures settle down, their activity diminishing,” Ethan explained apologetically. "You're well aware, of course, that hunting season is now underway," he continued, his voice carrying the weight of knowledge. "I'll call you back soon. I'll call with an answer. Yes, yes, certainly with a definite answer."

"We need to hurry." Raymond snapped back to reality. "Parker is on the porch right now, prepared to converse with the forest and the woods, it appears—willing to betray us without hesitation."

El eyed the sturdy tree trunks skeptically, swung his bag over his shoulder, and sprinted toward the house.

"El, the gun." Raymond hurried after him. "I think we might have to threaten him."

"Got it." El armed himself with a Colt, gripping it tightly in his hands.

They made their way stealthily to the terrace. Raymond ascended the stairs quietly, then in seconds unlocked the door, which was secured from the inside.

Silently, El stepped into the house, gliding through the spacious living room toward the porch. Ethan was swaying gently in the rattan chair, eyes closed, attuned to the symphony of nature. The rocking ceased abruptly, and Ethan froze. Frowning, he muttered something disjointed and spun around, met first by the muzzle of a gun, then by the gaze of El.

"Easy," El hissed.

"Ethan!" Marian reached out, ignoring El.

The psychic sat up, searching for solace in her, hoping she could shield him from the madman. "They're looking for you! But why?" He leaned towards her like a vulnerable child seeking refuge, drawn to her presence with an instinctive need for comfort.

"Let's go inside, Ethan. I'll explain everything," she answered, lending her support as she helped him to his feet.

When he entered the room, his eyes darted to the couch, where Raymond lay sprawled.

"This?" He gestured.

"Yes, one of the three oracles," Marian clarified. "They're after us because of him." Raymond yawned theatrically.

"What has he done?" Ethan froze, torn between entering his own home and backing away from the unfolding scene.

"He amplified his abilities, and the agency decided to eliminate him." Marian gestured helplessly. "Anyone working for them could face the same fate. That's why we've come here—not only seeking refuge but also warning you of the potential danger."

Ethan retreated, found a seat by the fireplace, and sank into it slowly.

El picked up the black phone from the porch floor, closed the door, and drew the thick curtains. "How long does communication with these trees usually last?" He gestured to the window and holstered his gun.

"About twenty minutes on average. I tune in, ask a question, and wait for an answer."

"Well then"—El turned to the wall-mounted clock—"in ten minutes, you'll call them and inform them that we're heading southeast to the Canadian border."

"But what if they don't believe me? What if they come here?" Ethan's nerves were getting the better of him.

"You'll tell them you lied at gunpoint," Marian replied with calm assurance. Ethan nodded weakly.

"And no tricks," El added firmly.

"All right."

"We won't stay for long," Marian reassured him, taking a seat at his feet. "We genuinely have nowhere else to go."

He cast a fearful glance her way, sinking into the chair, blinking rapidly.

"We need to save Raymond's life. We're fighting for him just as fiercely as we would for you. Besides, he holds the key to the impending epidemic. Last night he had a vision that pieced together all the puzzle fragments."

"Is that so?" Ethan frowned, side-eyeing Raymond, who was now asleep on his couch.

"Yes. It all comes down to the hair. This contagion occurs through the follicles."

"So that's why they cut off the hair of the deceased?"

"I believe that's exactly why."

***

Raymond woke in the middle of the night. The living room was deserted, and the fireplace crackled softly with dying embers. Groaning, he shifted onto his other side and fluffed the decorative pillow beneath his head.

A faint creak came from the porch. Raymond sat up, spotting the hood and slender shoulders of Marion in her roomy black parka. Wrapped in a blanket, she rocked gently in the rattan chair.

Raymond lowered his head onto the pillow and closed his weary eyes. The chair creaked again.

"Damn it." He got up from the couch and approached the door.

A rust-colored moon had risen in the sky, casting an ethereal glow over the sharp peaks of the massive Alaskan national park. He opened the door and whispered softly, "Hey, Doc, you did a great job with Parker. No one could have done better. But could you please stop rocking the chair?"

Marian remained silent.

3:13 AM

“Enough already, Marian. It’s time to rest. El must be waiting. We all need a good night’s sleep. Who knows, we might be running again tomorrow.”

Marian continued her rhythmic swaying, not uttering a single word.

Raymond stepped onto the balcony and leaned against the railing. The night was clear and windless, hinting at the approaching summer, yet its coldness seeped into his bones. His gaze descended from the high veranda to the foot of the woods, where corpses stood beside black tree trunks, their gruesome, clouded eyes staring up.

“Do you see that?” He turned toward Marian.

Hideous ulcers marred her skin, thin lips slackening into a crimson jelly of congealed blood. A gray film obscured her eyes, and her nose twitched incessantly, invaded by meandering white worms.

“Raymond,” she whispered, rising from her chair.

He recoiled, nearly toppling from the veranda to the barren ground below. Regaining his balance through sheer determination, he rounded the corner of the house and knocked frantically on the glass.

“What’s happened?” A disheveled Marian opened the window.

“Living corpses out there.” Raymond wasted no time squeezing inside.

"Corpses? Where?" Marian leaned out onto the veranda, rubbing her bare shoulders. "Raymond, I've been wanting to ..."

Marian fell silent, realizing she was alone again already.

"Please don't run away from me." She followed Raymond into the living room.

Before he drew the curtains shut, Marian managed to catch a glimpse of the veranda, bathed in the glow of the blushing moon. One of the chairs was slightly askew, and Marian froze, fixating on it. She could have sworn someone had just vacated it.

"A corpse was sitting there?" She couldn't tear her gaze away from the large windows, feeling the cold shivering up and down her spine.

Raymond nodded.

"What did it look like?"

"He wasn't in the best shape." Raymond fetched a blanket from the fireplace and fluffed the firm pillow once more.

"Raymond"—Marian approached him closely—"can't you see how similar we are? I sense them too; I can ..."

She was reaching for his lips when his voice cut in, chillingly matter of fact: "You can what?" He scowled, his cheeks tensing—not the most inviting expression for a kiss.

3:13 AM

"I can understand you and share in everything you feel and see."

This prospect seemed marginally better than the company of corpses. Moreover, Raymond knew with certainty that Marian could hardly grasp half of what she was saying.

"Go to sleep, Doc."

"But why? Am I really that repulsive to you?"

"Listen, we all need some rest, and tomorrow we need to focus on the task at hand," Raymond implored. He pointed toward the veranda, speaking much more calmly now. "You were sitting there. And you were dead. Dead just like all of them."

Marian fell silent. She massaged her temples, turned away, and softly uttered as she left the room, "Well, not a bad way to end the evening."

"Doc?"

She stopped and glanced wearily at Raymond.

"What do you mean?"

"I mean that according to your predictions, I'll survive until the infection. I'll die in nine years, Raymond. No one's going to shoot me in this damn forest tomorrow."

Chapter 17

Raymond's drowsy eyes struggled open. Wooden railings adorned with birds surrounded the veranda, filling the air with bustling chirps.

He rose and silently opened the balcony door.

"Ethan, why do you need so many eggs? Don't you live on your own?" came a voice from the porch.

"Well, you see ... the previous ones were chicks," Ethan stammered.

"Oh yes, our compassionate one." The hunters chuckled. "And where are they?"

"Who?" Ethan panicked.

"The chicks."

"I took them to the woods."

Raymond smirked and headed to the kitchen. He filled the kettle with water and placed it on the electric stove. Seating himself on a wooden chair, he pulled the bag he had taken from Jet and discovered a package of Brazilian coffee and some packets of brown sugar.

"Good morning." Ethan circled Raymond, hugging a small box of loot.

3:13 AM

"If you keep talking to them like that, they might show up at our doorstep by evening," Raymond quipped.

"I'm not very good at lying," Ethan admitted.

"Me neither." Raymond sighed. "I guess it's our distinctive trait. You need to learn, Ethan. Survival in this world often demands a touch of falsehood."

Ethan arranged the food on the refrigerator shelves, seemingly lost in thought, though Raymond couldn't care less what he was pondering. Raymond didn't press for conversation. He poured boiling water over the aromatic granules, added a sugar packet, and inhaled the bittersweet aroma. As he awaited drinkable temperature, he removed his T-shirt and glanced at the bandages Marian had applied back on the plane.

Ethan turned towards the table and, catching sight of the gunshot wound, almost dropped the supplies.

"Watch the eggs! If we have to buy them from the hunters again today, we won't escape the attention of the CIA."

"They shot at you?" Ethan's hands trembled again.

"As you can see"—Raymond gestured—"they aimed at a different spot."

Ethan slowly lowered himself into a chair. "I knew, I knew ... There's no place for people like us in this world."

Raymond grimaced. "Just a question of time and evolution. Perhaps in a hundred years, everyone will be like us."

"What kind of world would that be?" Ethan gave him an inquisitive look.

"A world without secrets?" Raymond hesitated.

"Make me your drink; it smells too good."

Both fell silent, gazing at the birds on the balcony. Maybe because Ethan could read minds, or perhaps for some other reason, Raymond wasn't thinking about anything in particular. He was attuned to the forest's noise, absorbing the northern pine-scented air.

"Are you in pain? Why did you take off the bandage?" Marian broke the sweet silence.

"It's fine. Just let it breathe some fresh air," he replied, his eyes still fixed on the woods.

Ethan looked at Marian, then shifted his concerned gaze to Raymond and gave a subtle smile. He rose from the table and started preparing breakfast. Soon the sound of sizzling eggs filled the air.

El approached the veranda, stretched, and took a deep breath. "What are we going to do? Does anyone have an escape plan?" He turned. "Or any kind of plan if there's nowhere to run."

3:13 AM

"El, I need to inspect the glacier," Marian declared unexpectedly.

El furrowed his brows and peeked around the curtain at the deserted yard. "Inspect as in admire? Right?"

"I need samples," Marian confessed, tying her hair into a tight knot.

"Samples," El pondered. "You're not seriously think about chiseling ice that's destined to melt away in nine years with a pocket knife?"

"There are crevices in the glaciers. That's where you can retrieve them," Marian replied, dead set.

"And then what? Are we going to turn Ethan's house into a lab? Find an antidote here?"

"It's not poison, it's a bacteria or virus ..."

"Stop, stop, stop! Yesterday you were talking about some kind of nema ..."

"Nematodes!" Marian's eyes lit up. "There are about a million species of them on Earth, and a significant portion parasitize in the bodies of humans and animals. Their shape is thread-like, hence the unofficial name 'hairworms.' These worms can be up to half a meter long and only about two millimeters thick—although there is a species that reaches up to two meters in length. Nematodes are some of the most resilient organisms on the planet; they've been found in fossil form from the Eocene period, which was around fifty million years ago."

"What does that have to do with the virus?" El tried to grasp the thread of Marian's narrative.

"The virus could be present in ice and later in thawed water, but it needs a host. Nematodes, on the other hand, are carriers of Nipah virus, which means many others too. Nematodes also cultivate bacteria for food."

"Okay, but what's the connection between worms and bacteria? As far as I know from school, one doesn't come from the other. They're entirely different biological groups."

"Yes, but bacteria can alter the worms. There was an article recently in the journal *Since* about the symbiosis between deep-sea worms and methane bacteria. The bacteria essentially changed the entire feeding system of the worms, helping them break down methane to gain energy. And this is bacteria that we've already studied. What nematodes could teach bacteria that science doesn't have any idea about, God only knows ..."

"So, are you saying there are bacteria there?"

"I can't say for certain. It could also be a virus capable of altering the DNA of all living organisms. Less likely there are frozen eggs of an unknown species of nematodes, more aggressive and rapidly multiplying."

"Less likely?"

3:13 AM

"The more complex the organism, the harder it is for it to survive. Although with any of this wild combination, we can imagine a rough picture of how the first Gorgona Medusa could have emerged."

"Wait, wait." El shook his head. "People haven't been drinking water from lakes and rivers for a very long time. Before it reaches our homes, the water is purified."

"We still keep swimming in it, irrigate our fields and gardens, and believe me, that's enough. Nematode larvae are about one thirty-fourth of a millimeter long. They can live in salad leaves and get inside us that way."

"This sounds like some kind of science fiction movie," El said skeptically.

"Ah, believe me, when you look down a microscope, all science fiction suddenly turns into reality. In the equatorial belt's rivers, there are worm-like parasites that enter humans' skin and spread throughout the body via the bloodstream. In a favorable environment like the human body, parasites multiply rapidly, and when they run out of moisture or space, they push their bodies outward through the skin, but more often they take easier routes out, like the eyes. Believe me, it looks very gruesome. More horror than science fiction."

"But then why isn't that our scenario?" El paused.

"Because our nematodes have learned to attack the brain," Raymond exclaimed, "turning their victims into walking corpses."

“Learned from what? Bacteria and viruses?” El’s face twisted in confusion.

“Exactly.” Marian blazed like a matchstick.

“All right.” El sighed. “Let’s suppose these nematode eggs, cunning viruses, or smart bacteria will one day put a hefty full stop to human existence. But why retrieve them? Or did you suddenly decide to bring about doomsday?”

“El, they’re waiting for my answer.”

“Who?”

“You know who!”

“Turner?” Ethan ventured thoughtfully.

“Ethan!” The doctor shot down the mind reader.

“Turner himself.” El smirked, dramatically touching his tense forehead. “Who would have thought ...”

“If I have evidence, I can offer him something in return.”

“In return for what?”

“Your lives.”

“Our lives?” El protested.

“So you’re completely sure they won’t touch you?”

“I ...” Marian glanced briefly at Raymond. “It seems I’ll live till I get infected myself. You guys stay. I’ll go alone.”

3:13 AM

"Not happening." El turned to the window as if his gaze could lock the doors of the house.

Marian put on her shoes and headed out into the yard. "Mari!" El shouted, but she ignored him. "What's gotten into her?" El wondered.

"Doc!" Raymond called out.

Unexpectedly for everyone, Marian froze in the doorway.

"Dr. Flay, Agent Roberts and I wouldn't mind taking a walk on the local glaciers, but it might be better to scan the woods first." Without getting up from the couch, Raymond arched his back to see her gray eyes. He gestured for her to return to the living room. And when she did, he took a sip of strong coffee and closed his eyes.

His consciousness passed through the balcony door and stepped out onto the veranda. Raymond leaned over the railing and surveyed the porch. But that wasn't enough for him. He mentally stepped onto the wide planks, pushed off, and took flight. Beneath his feet, the sharp peaks of tall firs shifted—there wasn't a single human soul in the forest for miles. Raymond looked from a distance at the glacier, which resembled a massive white tongue streaked with blue vessel-like patterns. It slid into the green waters of the lake, reflected in meticulous detail on its surface. Raymond vaulted over the coniferous forest and soared above the road. Cars sped along the picturesque highway—the only ones for tens, maybe hundreds, of miles. Raymond touched down at Ethan's house. He carefully scanned the edge of the forest, the sweeping branches of the tall trees, and the cluttered yard. He listened—no human voices, no helicopters, only the blissfully sun-drunk chirping of birds.

"It's clear. We can go," Raymond pronounced a moment before he opened his eyes.

"Excellent." As if on cue, Marian stood up.

"Stop, stop, stop! Not so fast," El persisted.

"We'll take Ethan's pickup, and he'll be the one driving it."

"No way." Ethan hesitated. "I agreed to shelter you in the house, but not there." Waving his hand towards the window, he attempted to leave the room, but Marian stopped him.

"This is a good idea."

Ethan looked at her uneasily.

"As you can see, Ethan, we have lofty goals, and I assure you, they align with yours. It's not us in danger, it's the whole world!"

"Let's go while it's still clear!" El burst out, grabbing a kitchen knife.

They rushed into the yard and settled into the three rear seats. Ethan started the engine and pulled away. The glacier was five and a half miles from the house, and within twenty minutes, after leaving the road, the pickup came to a halt amidst dense thickets. After following a forest trail for about three hundred yards, the travelers emerged before the colossal white giant.

"Good Lord, it's enormous!" Marian whispered. "How do we get to it?"

The viewing platform offered a magnificent panorama but no chance of coming into direct contact with this natural monstrosity. If El had been holding a knife, he would've dropped it, realizing his helplessness before this force of nature. Ethan, however, was less astonished, having been here more than once.

"Why didn't you tell us at the house that it's impossible to reach?" El glared at Ethan. His hope for Ethan's grip on reality was steadily dwindling with each passing minute.

"Maybe by boat," Marian mused thoughtfully.

"And certainly not with a nail file," El grumbled.

"Damn, it looked smaller from up high," Raymond muttered, heading back towards the car.

"Where are you going?" Marian stopped him.

"To the cozy cabin of the pickup. If you want to contemplate the creation of the late glacial period, I have no objections."

Raymond paused, his almond-shaped eyes fixed on Marian. Soon he continued on his path, and from behind, Marian's voice sounded irritated.

"Perhaps you could help in some way?"

"You've mistaken me for Superman, Doc."

Marian glanced at Raymond, then switched her attention to Ethan. "Do you have a boat?"

"All right, that's enough." El sharply interrupted the questioning and left the observation spot.

"I know—they're there." Marian continued and climbed into the cab.

The men fell silent. None of them had the slightest desire to climb the mountains to reach the glacier. Risking their lives to rent a helicopter or stealing a boat left behind for the winter wasn't an option. They all understood that the task required not only the appropriate gear, technology, and equipment but also experience working on glaciers. Even Ethan, who had seemed somewhat persuadable, appeared to grasp this, but not Marian. She fanatically sought ways to dive under the ice and emerge seconds later with deadly weapons in hand. An approaching car appeared on the opposite lane.

"Car!" Ethan yelled, slowing down.

El and Raymond flung themselves to the floor of the pickup, pulling the bewildered Marian from her seat. She fell into El's strong arms, and Raymond grabbed her red bag by its thin strap, sending its contents scattering onto the worn carpet as it flipped over. Marian shot him a piercing glare, and as soon as the oncoming car had distanced itself sufficiently, she began to collect the scattered IDs, plastic, and business cards strewn across the floor. Raymond helped her retrieve a fallen lipstick from beneath the seat. El, in turn, was handing her a golden compact when his attention was drawn to a folded piece of paper.

Call these numbers in your most challenging situation, Marian. Sincerely yours, L. R., the message read, accompanied by the extravagant handwriting of the mysterious L. R. and an American phone number. El silently handed the note to Raymond.

"Doc? Who's L. R.?"

"What?" Marian closed her bag and turned to Raymond. He held the find in his hands, and Marian squinted with satisfied sincerity.

"What's this?" She persistently feigned ignorance of the note.

"You're going to tell us what this is! I'm willing to believe in an ordinary admirer, but this version will need to be double-checked."

"Yeah, Raymond, but I don't know any L. R. And how did it end up in my bag?" Marian spun the note in her hands. "L. ... Louis Rapshmir! It could only be him!"

El shot a brief glance at Raymond, who nodded. Neither of them held out any hope that Pandora would reveal the truth on the first try.

"What ..." Marian continued, lost in thought, "what if I call him?"

“Doesn’t he work for the counter-terrorism department?” El quashed all her hopes.

“He ...” She hesitated. “You know, it seems to me that Louis is so self-sufficient and fabulously rich that he could afford not to work for anyone. Collaborate? Perhaps. But working for someone? Louis Rapshmir would never do that.”

Raymond tightened his jaw and broke into a smile. This was her revenge for the previous night. A skillful, subtle, feminine revenge. It wouldn’t be fair to say that the doctor had hurt Raymond Lee. But sting? Oh, she stung!

“His mansion is invisible on satellite maps.” Marian continued her battle with toothpicks. “His phone can’t be tracked or tapped. On top of everything, he’s a gentleman. If he can’t help as promised, my call will remain a secret. Mr. Rapshmir is a man of his word and honor.”

“Impressive.” Raymond couldn’t hold back. “After all this, I’m almost ready to call him myself. But where from? I might not be particularly attentive by nature, but I didn’t notice a single phone booth near the glacier. And all of Ethan’s devices are certainly under surveillance.”

El remained silent, gazing at the endless expanse of the Tongass National Forest.

“We’ll drive further away from Ethan’s house and wait for a passing car. I’ll step onto the road and ask the driver for a phone to make an important call. I’ll only need a minute to ask Louis for help and tell him where to find us.”

3:13 AM

“You’re planning phone calls pretty quickly.” Raymond laughed.

She ignored him and turned to El. “What do you say?”

“What is there to say?” he answered quietly. “We have to try.”

“As you say, El Roberts, as you say.” Raymond looked through the window.

“Ethan, turn around!” Marian perked up.

They had traveled two miles when a dark blue van appeared on the road. Ethan pulled over, and Marian, clutching Louis Rapshmir’s phone number, scrambled out onto the road. Raymond embraced the headrest of his seat and leaned forward. El visibly stiffened and armed himself with a gun. Marian hurried over to the van and conversed briefly through the driver’s window. Soon a phone appeared in her hands.

“An old-fashioned keypad,” Raymond commented.

“Call it luck. Modern gadgets can be tracked with a snap of the fingers,” El muttered.

Marian spoke briefly, and by the end of the conversation, she was beaming with a captivating smile.

“He’ll come for us the day after tomorrow,” she announced proudly, getting back into the car. “At three-thirty p.m. on Lincoln Island. It only has one dock, where we’ll need to arrive.”

“Arrive!” El echoed her a moment later. “And even if we get there, where will he take us and on what?”

“Mr. Rapshmir will kindly come on his yacht—on which, by the way, he completed a round-the-world trip. He’ll take us to Port Hardy in British Columbia. That’s where we were headed originally, but due to fate’s will or someone else’s, we never made it.”

“This is getting a bit too much,” Raymond reproached her. “I didn’t ask you to call the agency and rat me out!”

“You scared me to death!” Marian flared up.

“How? How could I have scared you so much that you sentenced me to death?” Marian fell silent, but Raymond continued. “Indeed, Marian! Why bother unraveling your own fears? You could just make one call and silence all the witnesses. Why be honest with others? Why be honest with yourself? Isn’t it better to make just one person shut up? But shut up forever.”

In a matter of seconds, Raymond received a slap across the face.

“That’s enough!” El thundered.

Finally they found the courage to voice all that had been gnawing at them for so long. Marian hadn’t fully grasped the extent of the damage she had inflicted upon Raymond’s tranquil life, was unaware of just how long he had yearned for that existence. The weight of her guilt for what she had done now bore down on her shoulders with great force. Her attempts to draw closer to Raymond seemed utterly foolish now. She felt a terrible ache within, yearning above all else to turn back the hands of time. In fact, it seemed best never to have known Raymond Lee at all.

In somber silence, they reached Ethan's house. They dined on roast pheasant, exchanging routine phrases. Raymond lay on the same couch he had favored the previous day, sipping his bourbon. As Ethan bustled about the homestead, El and Marian struggled to piece together a viable plan to get to Lincoln Island.

The phone's trill echoed through the air. Ethan shook his head, refusing to answer the call.

"Pick up the receiver!" El hissed through gritted teeth.

"No, no ..." Ethan retreated into the corner of the kitchen.

"Please, Ethan!" Marian pleaded. Drawing closer, she pressed his weakened, trembling hands against her chest. "Please ..." Her eyes glistened with tears, shining not only in supplication for salvation. Somewhere deep within her soul, an ocean of entirely different emotions roiled, but somehow it seemed to work.

Ethan relented and picked up the receiver. "Hello?" he said, his tone cajoling. "I don't see them on land," he fibbed. "Look on the water ... near Juneau." He listened intently to some instructions. "I'll inquire with the woods when night falls," he vowed and bid a curt farewell. "I need some time alone," he confessed, and, with a step back from Marian, he hurried into his room.

"He's going to betray us! He'll betray all of us!" El fumed.

"We don't have a choice." Marian paced the room.

"I'll sleep in this room. There's no other phone in the house," Raymond interjected. "As long as I'm here, he won't be able to contact anyone."

Marian let out a heavy sigh, her gaze lingering on the bourbon bottle in Raymond's hands. Without a word she left the room.

"Thank you," El said and followed.

After a few sips, Raymond drifted into slumber. When he awoke, the room was bathed in the gentle glow of the fire. Outside, the darkness was falling rapidly, as if someone had turned off the already dim light. The first stars appeared—so bright without city lights and so clear without the humidity of the equator. The fire crackled, warming the night air and Raymond's lonely soul.

"Forgive me." A voice came from near the couch.

In response, Raymond handed Marian a bottle. She took a sip and tried to return the bourbon to its owner. "Keep it," he croaked. "I've had enough for today."

He fluffed his pillow and turned towards the wall. Marian pulled a blanket off the chair and went out onto the veranda. Raymond didn't sleep. He heard her crying but didn't go any closer. He heard El cross the living room and go out to his Marian. They sat there for a long time in the chairs, gazing at the magic of the northern night. El took the bottle from Marian, took a sip, and handed it back. Marian reached for the strong whiskey, but, leaving it on the floor, she replaced the alcohol with El's reassuring hand. They held onto each other like this until nearly midnight. His fingers brushed against her hair and traced the contours of her face, undoubtedly thanking the Almighty. Not for her—Marian had her fair share of faults. He was thankful for the feelings that the Almighty had bestowed upon him. Those feelings were so new and precious.

Chapter 18

Before dawn broke, El tossed a black bag of money onto the seat and started the engine of the old pickup truck. He surveyed the darkened windows of the house; no lights had come on, which meant he hadn't roused anyone.

He fired up the heater, shifted gears, turned the vehicle around, and pulled onto the highway. A thin mist draped the forest, crawling onto the road from the lowlands. It slunk beneath the wheels, almost pleading with him to stop. To turn back to Ethan's house, slip under the warmth of Marian's blanket, and forget about the journey down the road that led to Juneau.

But El couldn't recall a time in his life when he had turned back. It was a rarity. Only once had he stopped, breathing heavily and silently pleading for the stillness to be broken by Rachel's cry. If she had called out to him, he would have turned around without hesitation. But Rachel Roberts remained silent. She finished her cigarette, gave her ex-husband a lingering gaze, and slammed the door shut, locking it.

For nearly ten years she had waited by that door. Ten years of sleepless nights. If El wasn't on assignment, he vanished with friends from the department. If he traveled on business, he always went without her, rarely informing her of his return.

3:13 AM

Did he love Rachel? A foolish question; of course he did. He had fallen for her back in school, asked her to the prom, and proposed three years later. But El's fiery temperament, his intense gaze, and his passionate nature did Rachel Roberts no favors. Did he cheat on Rachel? An even more foolish question. El Roberts used to wring every drop from life. After each assignment, he would drink with friends at bars, where he was inevitably found by someone like Mireille, and with her, Agent Roberts would lose himself. As he told his casual lovers about the scars from bullets and the dangerous escapades he'd been on, he sought to prove to himself that risking his life was worthwhile. And Rachel? Rachel always found out first. Not from El, but from the EMTs at the ER.

One day Mrs. Roberts had had enough. She gathered El's things and placed them outside the door. When he returned from a three-week trip, he found suitcases covered in dust on the doorstep.

Thirty miles later, the sky above the forest began to lighten. El didn't feel drowsy, but out of habit, he craved a strong cup of coffee. Within an hour his journey would come to an end, and perhaps he would be offered a mug of the traditional morning beverage.

El knew where he was headed. While Marian had been examining the treetops and Raymond, the agent had been committing the signs and road numbers to memory. A broken signpost with the carved words "Ranger Station" was etched in his mind. Yes, national parks had ranger stations. Sometimes more than one, if the park spanned hundreds of miles. These daring souls ensured the preservation of flora and fauna and prevented forest fires. They monitored the hunting season, aided injured animals, and occasionally saved people's lives.

Spotting the familiar writings El skillfully veered onto a dirt road leading deeper into the woods. The pickup truck crossed a rickety bridge over a mountain river, climbed a steep switchback, and pulled up to a compound surrounded by an armored fence. As soon as he braked at the gates, a restless early rising dog bounded toward him.

Exiting the vehicle, El surveyed the yard. Various modes of transportation were parked not far from the wooden, single-story building, ranging from a caterpillar tractor and ATVs to a fire truck and a helicopter.

The door creaked open, revealing a drowsy young man on the threshold. He hastily threw on a puffy vest as he rushed to the gate. Spotting him, the dog wagged its tail with joy and eagerly nudged its owner.

"Baggy, enough already. Your breakfast isn't coming anytime soon ... Sir, how can I help you?" The young man shifted his focus to El.

"I need to reach the glacier. I'll compensate you well." El got straight to the point.

"Is someone stuck up there?" The ranger tensed.

3:13 AM

"No one's stuck, thank God. I need samples of the ice that'll melt in nine years," El declared nonchalantly.

"Um, sir"—the young man hesitated—"the thing is, for such an expedition, you need special permission."

"My permission is right here in this bag." El unzipped it and displayed stacks of banknotes secured with straps.

The ranger looked around, doubtful for a moment, then stepped decisively towards the gate. "Just ice samples? Nothing more?"

"Nothing more," El assured him.

El entered a spacious room with lockers, monitors, a large table, and a sofa. Opposite the latter stood a small television, and an improvised kitchen was tucked away in a corner.

"Andrew Farrell." The curly-haired, sturdy guy extended his hand, holding a pause that El filled with a fabricated name.

"James Brickley."

"Coffee?" Andrew offered.

El nodded eagerly and placed a deposit on the table. "Half now, the rest upon return."

Andrew's eyes lit up brighter than a Christmas tree. He grinned, shook his head, and couldn't resist a question.

"Mr. Brickley, it's your right not to answer, but I'm bursting with curiosity. What do you need this ice for? Seriously, this kind of money"—he flipped through a bundle of bills—"for a piece of ice! Isn't that odd?"

"I'm not at liberty to disclose someone else's secrets. But let's suppose that a wealthy individual wanted to astonish his guests and add ice to their whisky that's not just hundreds or thousands but millions of years old."

Andrew froze by the coffee machine. After a moment, he raised his eyebrows ironically and burst into laughter that filled the entire station.

"I'm sorry to part with your advance, James, but in Alaska, there's no ice older than a thousand years. Such ice only exists in Antarctica. And let me dash your wealthy man's hopes—a drilling rig would need twenty years to reach ice that's over a million years old. That sort of ice lies more than two miles deep, my friend."

"Well, if you won't tell my client about this"—El pulled an additional stack of money from his bag—"then there's no one else to tell. I don't particularly want to fly to Antarctica."

"I understand." Andrew nodded. "But why choose ice that will melt in nine years?" The young man finally handed El a cup of filtered coffee.

"My employer's daughter is a microbiologist." El took a sip of coffee, letting it seep in and spread through his body. "So she stopped me by the car and asked me to bring blue ice from Alaska's glaciers no older than that. She believes the ice at greater depths could contain harmful bacteria or even deadly viruses."

"Damn, sometimes I regret not finishing at the Oklahoma Meteorological University." Andrew chuckled. "You tell your story so intriguingly that I want to believe it all."

"I'm a bodyguard, Andrew. It doesn't matter how much drilling it takes to satisfy a client's whim. For me, what's crucial is that he doesn't keel over from his whisky. And, of course, that he doesn't become a carrier of some unknown disease."

With a firm grip, Andrew approached the lockers, retrieved a folded map, and spread it out. "Which glacier are you interested in, Mr. Barkley?"

"Brickley," El corrected him. He never forgot his fabricated names.

He leaned over the map and traced the route he had taken from Juneau. He mentally marked the approximate location of Ethan's house and pointed to the lake where, visible even on the map, a tongue-like white mass descended.

"Hmm, got it. It's quite close." Andrew took a sip of coffee, pursed his thin lips framed by light stubble, and continued. "So, listen, James ... in Alaska, there are over seventy glaciers. On average, about three hundred and thirty pounds of ice melt each year. This one loses about four and a half pounds a year. On top of that, this ice doesn't melt like an iceberg—this glacier has to reach the water to melt. So the ice that'll melt in nine years isn't deep. It's"—Andrew looked at the ceiling and silently moved his lips—"just a couple of yards from the edge. But it's melting at a constant rate. However, compared to last year, we've observed an almost twofold acceleration in this process. If it continues geometrically, then ..." He approached the computer and quickly typed something. "And if it continues geometrically," he repeated, "you'd need to take samples at a distance of five hundred yards. Five hundred and eleven, to be precise."

"Is that how much will melt in nine years?" El frowned.

"In the best-case scenario."

"And in the worst?"

"In the worst case, the entire glacier will melt. But five hundred and eleven yards is what we can predict with a high probability." The meteorologist spread his hands.

El suddenly understood that in this business, missing the mark could mean being off by a mile. But he had no choice.

"If you like, we can take samples from the crevasse. You'll get beautiful specimens with a bright blue hue. Your boss will be pleased." Andrew started putting the money in the cabinet. "If you're ready, we can head out. Excursions to the national park glaciers start at nine in the morning."

El nodded and emptied his cup in three large gulps.

"These are crampons." Andrew handed El a pair of spiked boots. "No daredevil sets foot on a glacier without them."

3:13 AM

El smiled, recalling Marian's unstoppable urge to walk on the ice in summer sneakers.

"Do you have a thermos?"

El shook his head.

"Okay, we'll get some containers from the base. They're professional—keep things cold well. After all, if the ice melts, the color won't return after refreezing."

"Really?" El genuinely marveled.

"Of course! Ice is blue because it's denser. There are simply no air bubbles in it. That's all." Andrew shrugged like a child.

Andrew leaned a pair of telescopic poles, an ice ax, and a drilling apparatus against the door. He gave his new acquaintance a thorough once-over and tossed him a rust-colored puffy vest just like the one he was wearing.

They stepped out into the courtyard, where the first light of dawn was beginning to break. Baggy started leaping around, wagging his tail.

"We'll be back to feed you. Go on, get some rest." Andrew spoke to the dog.

Their gear was arranged on the floor of the helicopter and within moments the aircraft was lifting the adventurers into the sky. They soared over the forest, crossed a gray ribbon of road, circled a couple of lush green hills, and glided toward the picturesque Berners Cove. The helicopter skimmed over the malachite waters and circled around a massive white tongue of ice that sloped down into the bay.

“I’ll touch down between those mountains,” Andrew shouted. “We’ll have to take a little walk.”

El had no objections.

Ethan’s house faded into the distance, and as the helicopter began its descent, the landscape was enveloped by the blue mountains. The valley was captivating in its grandeur, and the crispness of the morning air added a sharpness to the scene, as if a massive lens was bringing the distant peaks closer to the eye.

From there, a trail led down to a perfectly smooth circular ice basin—the starting point of a millennium-old glacier. Rippled ice, like frozen lava, emerged from the mouth of the basin and extended toward the mirror waters of the lake.

“How was it formed?” El suddenly asked, accepting the ice ax and telescopic poles from Andrew.

“About eight hundred years ago, a meteorite struck right here.” The young man leaped to the ground. “Down in that basin, the debris formed the lake. Then it froze, and that gave birth to the glacier. Over time, the ice carved through the bedrock, and this monster broke free of its crater.”

El glanced at the wind-etched ice, then at Andrew, and blurted out, “I need ice from that 800-year-old crater.”

Andrew froze for a moment.

3:13 AM

“You’re not after that crazy lord’s stuff, are you?”

“No.” El’s expression remained unflinching.

“Triple the fee and I won’t ask any more questions.” The enterprising Andrew squinted.

“Deal.”

“Even if we find a deep crevasse, drilling will eat up the whole day.”

Andrew packed a bunch of ropes with carabiners for vertical descents into his backpack, along with thermoses and dried rations. He handed El an ice pick and sealed the helicopter shut.

“Hey, Mitch!” Andrew had dialed his colleague’s number. “I’m on a private tour for the whole day. Cover for me and feed Baggy, all right?” Andrew listened to the groggy voice of Mitch. “Don’t worry, I’ll share.” He chuckled.

El heaved up part of the equipment and followed the agile Andrew. They descended a rocky slope into a depression and, swapping their sneakers for spiked boots, stepped onto the ice.

Walking was challenging. The inclined spikes sunk far deeper than El had expected, but the risk of slipping was practically eliminated.

Suddenly, just a step away from the agent, a massive crevice appeared.

"Damn, that was unexpected!" El gasped, retreating from the edge of the abyss.

"We're lucky it's spring." Andrew grinned slyly. "In winter these crevices, covered with a thick layer of snow, are the deadliest traps."

"I can imagine ... Are you going to go down here?"

"No. This one's too shallow." Andrew surveyed the glacier and took a sip of water. "To get to the former lake, we need something deeper."

"Deeper ..." El whispered and carefully circled the daunting chasm.

What if all this effort is in vain and there are no microorganisms at all? Have the prophets tangled themselves in their prophecies, and has Dr. Flay gotten lost in science fiction? El thought.

Well, at the very least, he understood everything that fell within the range of his understanding and was doing everything within his power. From the dark-blue mountain, a massive slab of snow detached and crashed into the lake. El halted—here, he felt different. Throughout his life, he had carried a proud sense of self-importance. Agent Roberts saved lives. This gave him an intoxicating feeling and justified the considerable resources invested in a single goal.

But here, surrounded by ancient ice, El felt like a mere speck. Under the intense gaze of these stone behemoths that had stood for millions of years before him and would endure just as long afterward, Agent Roberts unexpectedly grasped how insignificant his life was.

"Halt!" shouted Andrew and rushed over, grabbing El by the sleeve.

El gave the young man a stern look, but he only nodded toward the ground. One more step and the federal agent wouldn't have been able to count his bones—an icy abyss lay ahead.

"This one seems suitable," Andrew said, unfastening a mat made of a sleeping pad from his backpack. "Lie on your stomach, James. You'll lower the drill."

El lay down, but the action only intensified his fear. Even to a person far removed from glaciology, the glacier's cross-section was mesmerizing. A few yards ahead, a gray layer of ice was interrupted by a band of earth that spread out gracefully, as if sending its curved roots into the bright-blue depths. The deeper El looked, the more the saturated color darkened, transitioning into azure and soon a foreboding black.

"The bottom's invisible!" El exclaimed, astonished, as he looked at Andrew preparing to set off.

The young man merely smiled and drove several long spikes into the ice. He secured the rappel, tossed El a safety rope and a line for hauling loads, and then slowly descended into the crevice of the glacier. For a while, El could still make out his deliberate movements, but soon enough, the young man disappeared completely into the icy cavern. El cautiously crawled closer to the edge, peering into the black abyss; his reflection flickered in the ice, revealing a faint beam from Andrew's headlamp. El swallowed and withdrew to his previous spot. Barely twenty minutes later he heard the faint sound of drilling. It persisted for about an hour, and when the monotonous hum ceased, El figured that Andrew must have reached the desired layer, but when the young man resurfaced, lay down on a camping mat, and requested tea from a thermos, El learned that the drilling had only just begun. At lunchtime they snacked on trail crackers and emptied a second thermos.

By evening, El couldn't bear to lie still any longer and dozed off. Suddenly a piercing cry of "James!" rang in his ears. He jolted to his feet and scanned his surroundings. One of the ropes securing Andrew had loosened and was slithering like a serpent into the crevice. El grabbed it, planting his boots straight on the ice.

"Hold on!" the terrified young man cried from below. "Hold on to me!"

"I've got you!" El shouted back, feeling the weight of a couple of hundred pounds in his hands. "Damn!" he yelled, leaning back with all his might.

An unnatural heat welled up in his palms; he realized he had forgotten to wear protective gloves. Another minute passed, and his palms were damp, but the moisture wasn't sweat—it was blood. El didn't know how much longer he would have to hold on or how much more pain he would need to endure.

He got lucky. Andrew had only been ten yards from the surface when the anchor had given way. El heard the sound of a pickax entering the ice, and just a moment later Andrew's curly head appeared on the surface.

"Damn, James, I owe you ..." the young man groaned. "And what's this? Oh, for God's sake, where are your gloves? You've torn your hands to shreds!"

"It's nothing. I've been through worse," El confessed, breathing heavily.

Fourteen hours later, at precisely 8 p.m., El held in his hands the sample from the crater. Cylinders of perfectly blue ice fit into the thermally insulated containers. Exhausted, Andrew loaded both backpacks onto El and practically crawled off the glacier. He received the promised payment, which infused him with renewed energy, and started the helicopter's engine.

"I hope it was worth it," he muttered to El, offering him a first aid kit.

El nodded, hoping much more than Andrew.

***

"El!" Marian cried, descending the stairs.

"It's okay, I'm here." He embraced her gently.

"Where is she?"

"Who are you talking about?" El's face contorted in confusion.

"The ice! Medusa! You have it, don't you?"

"But how ...?"

"Raymond checked the area and found the pickup abandoned at the ranger station," Marian babbled. "And when it got dark, Ethan asked the trees, and they told him about a helicopter, a glacier, and how there was no one for hundreds of miles except one person driving a car and heading towards the house. His house!"

"I see ..." *Glad my wife never had a friend like that,* he thought.

When the doctor peered into the containers of ice, her eyes lit up with an odd gleam. "It's so blue!" She gazed at the transparent cylinders as though they were made of colored glass. "Where exactly did you get it?"

"From the depth of a ten-story house, Mari. I wasn't the one drilling, but I provided ample assistance." El raised his bandaged hands.

"Oh my goodness, but why so deep?" Marian started examining El's palms.

"A meteorite struck there, creating a lake. That's what gave rise to the glacier."

"So what's in there?" Raymond peered skeptically into the container. "Extraterrestrial organisms? Microscopic bastards from another galaxy, poised to teach Earth's nematodes the art of conquering the world?"

"I hope they're in there ..." El mumbled.

"Well, well." Raymond looked into the sports bag, which turned out to be nearly empty. "I assume the expedition was on my tab?"

"My father will reimburse you," Marian said hurriedly.

"Don't worry, Mari. If there's a national lottery in Canada, there won't be anything to reimburse," El assured her.

Chapter 19

"El, Doc, get up! We need to clear out of this house; they'll be here soon!"

El sat up, his eyes wild as he stared at Raymond. "Who's coming? What are you talking about?" he demanded.

"Come on, come on! Get up! You know who's ready to roll up on us in the dead of night." Raymond began suiting up in his second sweater.

"Are you sure?" El jumped to his feet and pulled on his pants.

"Positive!"

"Parker?"

"Parker!" Raymond shot a fleeting glance at the bewildered Marian and left the room.

"That crazy psycho." El slipped into his sweatshirt and dashed into the hallway. He wanted to barge into Ethan's room, but the door was locked.

"Ethan! I'm starting to regret not unscrewing your damn head on the very first day!" he shouted.

"Mr. Agent, no need to yell at me! Stay in the house—they'll take care of us," Ethan naively replied.

"Take care of us!" El snapped. "Why? Why did you betray us? We were leaving after lunch anyway!"

3:13 AM

"You don't understand what we're dealing with! She talked to me! I heard everything ... Not only her. Many of them. They wouldn't let me sleep. They talked to me all night ..."

"Psycho," El muttered and went back into the living room.

This time Marian stepped into the hallway. "Who talked to you, Ethan?" She squatted down, tying her shoelaces.

"The ones frozen in the ice. The ones waiting for their day to ..."

"To what, Ethan?" Marian pressed herself against the door.

"To take over the whole world ... They ordered me to kill all of you and release the ice into the lake. They demanded my allegiance, Marian! Please forgive me, but I called for help ... I'm just a human!"

Marian lowered her gaze. She, more than anyone else, understood the psychic. Once, out of fear, she had acted just like Ethan Parker.

"And they, Ethan ... who are they?"

The prophet remained silent.

"Were they bacteria, microbes, or viruses, Ethan?" The doctor pressed for more details.

"They were the gods themselves, Marian! They are gods!"

Dr. Flay slowly stepped away from the door.

"Mari, let's go!" El called from the stairs with strong anxiety in his voice.

"He's saying something ..."

"Mari, he's insane! Let's go! Every minute counts."

They left the house and got into the pickup truck. "We're taking Ethan's car?" Marian was puzzled.

"Yes!" El started the engine and pulled out of the yard.

They sped down the road, cutting through the darkness. Despite the coolness of the night, the pickup's cabin was filled with a stifling silence.

"And where are we going now?" Raymond asked after a while.

"To Juneau," El replied curtly.

"Then I guess we can catch some sleep ..." Raymond pulled out the remnants of the whisky from his bag and reclined in the back seat. "Better than sleeping at gunpoint," he added and took a sip.

"What are you talking about?" Marian exclaimed, her head snapping towards him.

"About how I was sleeping by the crackling fire when suddenly someone yelled 'Raymond!' in my head. And I woke up to find Parker in front of me, holding a shotgun."

Now even El glanced at Raymond in the rearview mirror.

3:13 AM

"I wasn't exactly in control at that moment ... but when the gun hit Parker's jaw, he dropped it and ran out of the room."

"Oh my God," Marian murmured.

Silence fell once again.

"We need to tell Rapshmir to turn back." El sighed. "It won't be good if he sails to Lincoln Island and instead of us, he's met by the CIA."

"Why turn back? He's almost there!" Marian protested.

"Mari, Parker has betrayed all of us. Including Rapshmir ..."

"El!" Marian seemed to jump in her seat. "He won't betray Rapshmir!"

"Why is that?" El frowned.

"Ethan Parker has a terrible memory for names. He can't remember what to call Lenny—Lenny Levitan, the guy who's been visiting him for nearly ten years! I guarantee it"—Marian pressed her open palms to her chest. "Under torture, he won't recall the name of Louis Rapshmir. We only said it twice."

"Hmm." El snorted skeptically. "If you're guaranteeing it, Dr. Flay, I'm willing to take the risk." He shot her a brief glance. "We'll reach Juneau, find a telephone, and arrange a meeting at a different location."

"If he can get a signal out in the ocean," Raymond couldn't resist adding.

"Ethan ... he said some strange things." Marian turned pensively towards the window.

"No doubt about that," El grumbled, not wanting to succumb to paranoia.

However, Marian continued: "He referred to those frozen in the ice as gods—"

"He probably overheard our conversation about Phorcys and his daughters," El cut in.

"He reads minds and only human ones," Marian countered. "What if all these gods actually existed at some point?"

"It's all imagination." El clicked his tongue in displeasure and rubbed his forehead.

"No, really, El! It's one thing to come up with a human with a horse's body, but just think of the imagination it takes to come up with a woman with snakes instead of hair!"

"Are you serious right now?"

"But why not? Come up with one right now. Create a monster for me—one that has never existed anywhere, at any time, in any of the known myths. It's an impossible task!"

"Marian, eight hundred years ago is no longer Ancient Greece ..."

"If it was brought by an asteroid, I assure you, there's more than just one or two of those rocks in space. And they only fall to Earth after getting knocked off course in some Saturnian belt, which acts like a giant vacuum cleaner, pulling in everything that enters our solar system."

"So now we're talking about a meteor shower with a two-thousand-year interval! Correct me if I'm missing something."

"Two thousand years to us is just a moment in space," Raymond interjected.

"Okay, but even if that's the case, how do you think these microbes survived on a hunk of rock? Sure, they might be frozen in space and radiation might not affect them, but a meteorite burns up in the atmosphere," countered El.

"Microbes and bacteria can survive in extremely harsh environments on Earth. In the solidified lava of underwater volcanoes, millions of bacteria were discovered. I'm talking now about tremendous depths and airless spaces. They can live without sunlight or resources. It's the most unique survival mechanism we have on Earth. They can adapt to radiation; some even feed on metals. No, scientists haven't yet been able to prove that microbes can arrive on meteorites. But they haven't been able to prove the opposite either."

El furrowed his brow even more, concentrating on the road. Searchlight beams appeared over the forest on one side.

"They're fast ... Raymond, open my backpack. There are night vision goggles in there." El reached out expectantly.

Raymond leaned over the bags and soon handed El a complicated-looking lensed device. "Where'd you get those?"

"Bought them at the ranger station." El put on the goggles, which looked more like binoculars, and turned off the headlights.

The helicopters circled behind them, scouring the road and forest paths. One of them was inevitably getting closer to the pickup, so El turned into the woods, speeding through the sprawling bushes. He killed the engine and removed his elaborate eyewear.

The beam slowly sliced through the dark ribbon of the road and headed toward the state capital. From the other side, a second searchlight flickered through the forest trails. Everyone hid. Even Raymond stopped sipping his bourbon and feigned death.

The helicopter came very close. Its light illuminated the trees just a couple of meters from the tangled branches of the shrubs. Someone up there seemed to sense them. But sensing is not seeing. Soon the bright beam moved away, allowing all three escapees to breathe again.

El waited for about ten minutes, and emerged from the cover. Raymond unscrewed the bottle cap again.

"Don't drink." El spoke up. "I might have to be replaced soon. My palms are bleeding."

Raymond didn't reply, but everyone in the cabin heard him screwing on the aluminum cap. A minute later Marian put on the night vision goggles and took the wheel. The road and the landscape were bathed in an eerie green glow. El checked his gun and moved to the back seat. Raymond squeezed in beside the doctor, piercing the darkness through the windshield.

“Raymond?” Marian suddenly whispered.

“Mmm?” he murmured lazily.

“Why did Ethan say that?”

“I don’t know why your Ethan is saying such strange things,” Raymond said curtly.

“But you feel something too, don’t you?”

“From this ice?”

“Yes, Raymond.” Marian chimed in immediately. “From this ice. What do you feel?”

Raymond leaned over to one of El’s backpacks and pulled out a container. The metallic cylinder reflected the lights on the dashboard, and Raymond, unable to focus, shut his eyes. He sat like that for nearly three minutes, hardly moving, and then placed the container back into the black backpack before staring into the darkness again.

“I don’t feel anything,” he said. “To me, it’s just ice. Cold, transparent ice.”

Marian frowned, and ahead, the bright beam of another helicopter emerged. She immediately veered into the forest, racing among the trees in search of underbrush.

“There, there!” Raymond shouted. “To the right!” Marian turned her head, spotting a thicket of mixed trees.

“How did you …?”

Raymond himself didn’t know how he had sensed the bushes in the darkness. Apparently every cell in his body was attuned to survival. The pickup nestled in its improvised shelter as the choppers relentlessly combed the road.

“They’re increasing,” El whispered. “Just another hundred miles and we’ll be in Juneau,” he said, cross-referencing the distance on the instruments.

“Still a long way.” Raymond sighed, seeing three beams instead of the usual two in the mirrors.

Now two helicopters combed the road, moving in opposite directions, while a third skimmed over the water.

“He talked about the island.” Marian’s voice trembled. “Ethan talked about our plan. If they decide to check all the yachts entering the Gulf of Alaska they’ll easily find Rapshmir. Oh God!” She covered her face with trembling hands. “It’s like we’ve been caught in a whirlpool that’s pulling us in. And other people too …”

Soon a sniffling indicated that Marian’s nerves weren’t holding up.

Raymond opened the pickup’s door and stepped out.

3:13 AM

"No, Raymond! Don't do this! Not even for all of us. Your life is a unique gift. A gift to all humanity."

"Calm down, Doc! I just want to take over the driving." Raymond circled the vehicle and opened the driver's door. Marian stepped down, avoiding looking into his eyes.

Raymond sat down, gripping the steering wheel and gazing at the sky. He leaned back in the seat, closed his eyes, and took a deep, labored breath. With each exhale, the gusts of wind, seemingly from nowhere, grew stronger, sweeping around the car. The treetops bent over. A stormy wind was approaching Tongass National Forest. The chopper blades rattled, resisting the gusts, and it veered towards the city.

Marian tensed, her muscles coiling like springs. A faint smile played on El's lips, his eyes glinting with hidden amusement. Meanwhile, Raymond remained utterly unperturbed. He put on the night vision device and started the engine.

The forest concealed the winding road, and only on open stretches did the old pickup sway from side to side, not allowing the driver to go straight. Marian calmed down. As it turned out, the foul weather scared her much less than the Feds did.

Soon she grew tired of fighting sleep and closed her eyes. Her head involuntarily leaned to the side, and Raymond was left alone.

The road seemed like a negative to him. Here, the gray tones gave way to a dull green, and the sky emitted an unnatural acidity. His eyes were rapidly becoming fatigued. He wanted to curse everything, throw the device out of the window, and switch on the familiar headlights.

Black trunks replaced each other, and Raymond nervously pressed the gas pedal. Suddenly a massive shadow emerged in front of the hood. Its eyes glowed and its mouth opened in a soundless scream. Raymond swerved onto the shoulder, jamming the brake pedal to the floor. The pickup creaked, spun around, and, rear wheels dangling, tumbled into a ditch. El and Raymond were pressed against the glass, and only the securely strapped Dr. Flay remained seated.

"El! The containers!" Marian exclaimed.

The agent leaned against the roof, tucked in his legs, and crouched amidst the shattered glass. "The containers are okay," he said. "What happened?"

"I don't know." Raymond groaned. "She jumped onto the road."

"She?" El clarified just in case.

"A woman," Raymond breathed.

"Well, yes," El mused. "Why didn't I think of that?"

"Juneau is seventy miles away." Raymond glanced at the instruments. Gas was running low, the oil sign was blinking, and the clock read 3:33 a.m. The psychic cursed and shut off the engine.

3:13 AM

El was the first to surface. He opened the front cabin door and pulled out Marian. She hopped to the ground and took the bags. Next in line was Raymond. As he stepped onto the ground, it became apparent that he had injured his shoulder on the shattered glass and scratched his face.

"Hold on, I'll help you." Marian hurried over. She disinfected the wounds with bourbon, and Raymond downed the rest.

"Now, let's head toward the water." El loaded himself up with the bags and headed into the forest.

"And then?"

"And then we'll pray someone's left a boat by the shore." El sighed wearily.

The impenetrable forest filled with the crunch of branches and heavy breaths.

"What did she look like?" Marian asked, catching up with Raymond.

"I don't know. It was just a moment." Raymond shrugged. "Burning eyes, disheveled hair, and a wide-open mouth, as if she was about to scream."

"It's a Gorgon," Marian whispered.

"And what's known about them?" A surprising question from Raymond.

"About who?" Marian perked up.

"Gorgons. What do the ancient myths say about them?"

"Um"—the doctor bit her lip—"according to my memory, Medusa was originally a human, which is why she's the only mortal among the monsters. There were three sisters in total: Euryale, which means far-jumping, Stheno—mighty—and Medusa, who was the guardian. All three had snakes instead of hair, but Medusa's gaze held a special magical power. When a Gorgon flew over a lake, the surface would freeze, and when she looked at someone, they turned to stone."

"Ice, stone, flying through the air ... You think it's all metaphors? And was Medusa the first infected?"

"Exactly!" Marian's voice ignited with sparks of hope as Raymond paid a drop of trust to her speculations. "I lean toward the idea that myths are allegorical. In ancient times, nearly every phenomenon was attributed to the actions of gods, especially unexplainable illnesses with equally mysterious sources. Just imagine how an ancient Greek might describe the airborne transmission of a virus. Perhaps he would say 'far-jumping,' and for an extremely short incubation period, 'mighty.' Not to mention the term 'immortal'—of course, no one at the time had the slightest clue how to deal with such a destructive force as an epidemic."

"Yes, I can picture that." Raymond smiled. "But the third millennium BCE and the time of our meteorite's fall are centuries apart. This, perhaps, is the most contradictory element in an otherwise seamless tale."

3:13 AM

"Raymond!" Marian exclaimed, and El, exhaling a cold breath of annoyance, turned to the conspirators. "Raymond," she continued much more quietly, "you know that even dinosaurs suffered from malaria. The oldest bacteria ever found, was discovered in salt crystals buried 650 yards deep during the construction of radioactive waste shafts in New Mexico and has a strain that's over 250 million years old. It likely pre-dates the dinosaurs. But a close relative of this very bacteria thrives in the salt of the present-day Dead Sea in Israel."

"But Greece and Alaska are worlds apart!"

"Apart in distance, apart in time. Yet they share the same realm. Brought forth by two meteors, once parts of a single world. One arrived on Earth earlier, while the other lagged behind by a couple of millennia. Is it really beyond the realm of possibility?"

"So you're suggesting our Gorgon could be a later iteration of an ancient human affliction?"

"Exactly! All these ancient bacteria, microbes, and viruses—they somehow survive, transfer, migrate, and they ..." Marian paused for a moment. "They endure indefinitely. And who else could endure indefinitely if not ..."

"Gods." Raymond finished the sentence, sensing a shiver of cold spreading down his spine.

The sound of slamming doors echoed from the roadside, and the travelers hastened their pace.

Thorny branches struck Raymond's wounded face and tore at Marian's disheveled hair as they sprinted. Before long they burst onto the rocky shore, facing the dark water.

"El." Catching her breath, Marian gripped her lover's strong shoulder." Somewhere around here, I saw a hunter. He was on the opposite shore."

"There?" El straightened his arm.

"There."

"Hmm, then his boat must be around here. We might be able to reach the opposite shore just by swimming. It's an island." El squinted, making out the dark silhouettes of rocks against the steadily brightening northern sky.

Twenty minutes of intense running later, a dock appeared on the lake, and beside the dock—a small motorboat.

El quickened his pace, sprinting along the wooden planks before descending into the small vessel. Following him, glancing back, came Marian. Last, trembling hands untying the mooring line, Raymond leaped into the boat. An armed group of people emerged from the forest—they were closing in.

A gunshot rang out, and all three dropped to the ground, which was littered with fishhooks. El lifted his head and peered into the gap beneath the helm. Of course, the key was missing.

"Can you start it?"

3:13 AM

Raymond nodded subtly and closed his eyes, recalling the straightforward ignition mechanism. He vividly imagined connecting the terminals in the starter cylinder, yet nothing happened. He wiped his sweaty forehead and peered beneath the helm.

"Well, of course, it's the fuse," he whispered and closed his eyes once again.

A bullet struck the port side.

"Come on already! They're targeting the fuel tank!" El panicked.

At last the boat roared to life and started moving. The gunfire from the shore suddenly ceased. Everyone watched as the fishing boat, controlled by an unseen force, pulled away from the shore and glided across the water's surface.

"It would be frustrating if the lake was a dead end," Raymond confessed, rising to the helm.

"This is Favorite Channel. It washes Juneau and flows into the Pacific Ocean," said Marian.

"Yeah, you're a walking encyclopedia, Doc." Raymond chuckled.

"I just have a good memory."

Meanwhile, El opened a narrow compartment amid the gear, ropes, and buckets, discovering a nautical chart of the local waters. He spread it out in front of Raymond and leaned over the intricate landscape of the southern part of the state.

"Everything would be splendid if only this coast was labeled with massive letters like the map. I've never driven in my entire life without a navigator." Raymond extended his arm, indicating a verdant hill emerging from the still-dark waters, now illuminated by the rays of dawn.

Maintaining speed, the boat aligned itself with the green-bathed island and the scattered low cranberry-colored houses along the shore. This peaceful magnificence was adorned with a row of moored motorboats, rowboats, yachts, and even seaplanes, one of which bore a bright red sign reading "Lincoln Island."

All three froze, their gazes fixed on the dock where, in less than twelve hours, Louis Rapshmir would be waiting for them.

"El!" Marian grabbed his hand. "Perhaps—"

"No, Mari, it's out of the question," he interjected.

"But how can we—"

"We can't!"

"But I set him up ..."

"I'm sure he'll find a way out," El replied coldly.

Raymond bypassed the residential part of the island and steered the boat through a narrow strait. Suddenly the roar of engines echoed from around the cape.

3:13 AM

"Your friends, Agent," Raymond called out. "El, take the helm."

"Mari, go to the compartment," El ordered.

"I won't!"

"Please." He softened his tone, but his stern look remained.

Marian gathered the bags and disappeared into the cramped, wood-paneled space. Raymond settled into a vacant corner and closed his eyes.

The cold air tickled his nostrils, while his ears caught the distant chatter from the islands. He had stirred up the birds, and he soared high with them. He ascended so far that he glimpsed Port Alexander, washed by the Pacific Ocean and swept by relentless winds. Raymond memorized the uncomplicated route and then instructed the clouds to descend.

When he opened his eyes, a white haze had enveloped everything.

"You certainly came up with a clever plan," El remarked. "But how do we avoid running into some cape ourselves?"

"Pursuit is futile if we can't shoot to incapacitate, wouldn't you agree?"

"True. But it's a six-hour journey to Alexander. They'll just cut us off from reaching the ocean wherever it suits them."

"El, just look at this!" Raymond waved the map under the agent's frozen nose. "There are at least a hundred routes, if not more. And we'll take the shortest one." He snatched the wheel from El's grasp and turned sharply to the right at full throttle.

El staggered and caught the airborne map, staring at it. "You want to go here?" He pointed to the blank spot along the coast of the shortest channel.

"Yes, exactly! Look—a two-hour journey and we'll be in the ocean."

"Damn it! If the CIA doesn't finish us off, you surely will." El's face grew almost as pale as the spot on the map. "That really is the shortest route, but tell me, for heaven's sake, why does no one sail there? Look, the map shows routes from all the islands and coastal ports. But there's not a single turn here. Not a single maritime path."

"How should I know? Maybe they just don't need to go that way." Raymond shrugged.

"This is the Glacier Valley." El traced a vast snowy expanse along the ocean's edge. "These glaciers never recede. Perhaps, in the middle of summer and clear weather, you could navigate through there without encountering an iceberg, but not in fog, Raymond, and not in spring."

3:13 AM

Chapter 20

"Ease off, slow down ... We've arrived."

Raymond obeyed. A deep silence enveloped the lonely boat. Only the water lapping against the stern and the cry of seagulls on the high shore broke the stillness. Emerging from the dense fog was a massive red buoy. Weathered by countless storms, it swayed wearily, signaling their entry into open waters. *Crossroads of the Winds*, the guardian had marked it. The buoy creaked, shrouded in a white mist, as if resting after a tumultuous night.

"The inscription sends shivers down my spine." Raymond's voice repeated El's thoughts.

"Looks like Marian has fallen asleep." El cracked the compartment door open. "Mari? What are you doing?" He squeezed through the narrow opening.

A minute later he reemerged on deck, a black backpack slung over his shoulder.

"El, please ..." Marian rushed after him.

"From now on it will be with me. It's better for everyone." El extended his arm, keeping the doctor at bay.

"What's going on?" Raymond turned around.

“I don’t know,” El grumbled. “But she was sitting there”—he gestured toward the compartment—“staring mesmerized into an open container.”

“Forgive me. I don’t understand what came over me,” Marian confessed, inspecting the red buoy. “But where are we?”

“Gateway to the ocean,” Raymond explained. He cast an inquisitive glance at Marian, causing her to quickly avert her eyes.

The swaying grew stronger, and soon the fugitives realized they were in open waters. “Now keep watch in all directions!” El whispered.

Raymond kept watch. So did Marian, but she saw nothing. No shoreline, no islands, no sun. Even the weathered lighthouse of the winds’ crossroads dissolved into thin air like a phantom.

“Left!” El suddenly shouted, grabbing the wheel.

Raymond turned it and the boat tilted, veering to the side. A low block of ice emerged from the fog.

“Harder left!” shouted El.

“What are you doing? We’re passing through!” Raymond resisted.

“Eighty percent of the ice is underwater. And it takes up much more space below than above. If this boat rams into it, the only thing we’ll be transferring to is an iceberg,” El snapped.

3:13 AM

“Dear Lord, what is this place?” Marian’s gaze followed the white hill where a pair of seagulls had just landed.

Suddenly the vessel emitted an unpleasant grinding sound and slowed down—its bottom had touched the submerged part of the ice floe. Everyone froze. It seemed like a mere bump from the northern sea, but the fear they felt in those seconds was immeasurable.

“Do you think we’re okay?” Raymond gasped, his nerves on edge.

“We’ll find out soon enough,” El responded tensely.

Raymond reached for the radio, ready to call out to any ship for help at a moment’s notice. El leaned over the side of the boat and froze.

“Well?” Raymond couldn’t wait a minute longer.

“This time we got lucky ...” Both let out sighs of relief.

Marian suddenly perked up, noticing the radio. “Raymond, how far into the ocean can this thing transmit?”

“Communication between ships takes place on short waves that reflect off the water. The quality of the connection suffers, but maritime radio signals can be heard as far as the horizon.”

“And the channel? Is it the same for everyone?”

"Everyone has different channels that need to be agreed upon beforehand. But channel 70 is reserved for special messages, like distress signals."

"We're in distress, Raymond!" Marian dashed to the equipment. "We're in distress!"

"You're not planning to call out for Rapshmir by name, are you? The whole of Alaska will be listening to us."

Marian didn't say anything. She just asked what to press, and after Raymond had pressed it, she started speaking: "Phorcys, come in! Phorcys, this is Medusa. Medusa Gorgona."

"Jesus Christ," El muttered, covering his eyes with his hand.

Phorcys didn't respond.

"What happened to Gorgona?" Raymond lowered himself onto the cold floor.

"Hermes, the god of knowledge, killed Medusa," Marian said, distracted from the radio.

"How?" El asked.

"He cut off her head."

"So no vaccination in sight," El quipped. Raymond chuckled.

Marian rolled her eyes, let out a sigh, and turned back to the radio once again. She coughed and continued to call out to Phorcys, her voice now hoarse. The cold seeped into her bones. Every breath was accompanied by white vapor just like that enveloping the fishing boat. Marian's legs ached incessantly, her eyelids drooped involuntarily, and her tired mind succumbed to slumber.

"Raymond!"

El's urgent call pulled him from his drowsy state. Marian recoiled, and El swiftly spun the wheel. Raymond jumped to his feet, wincing from the unbearable pain in his soles.

"Again?"

"Again," El grumbled. "Hold on!"

Marian and Raymond pressed themselves against the stern, gripping the ropes just in time. The boat veered as a shape grew, emerging from the mist—a gigantic block of gray ice.

Raymond lifted his gaze. An iceberg was sailing past a few yards from the schooner. Someone was standing motionless on its peak. Mist shrouded the figure's body, but its filthy, bare feet were unmistakable—far from the fluttering gulls, illusion, or mirage.

"What's there?" Marian whispered, her frightened gaze darting between Raymond and the iceberg.

"Nothing," he replied in a barely audible voice.

"Raymond! Damn you, what can you see up there?" Marian was losing control.

"Somebody standing ..."

"Can you see his face?"

"No ... only bluish legs and a blood-stained hospital gown."

Marian swallowed. A shiver ran down her arms, and she hastily rubbed her shoulders.

"I was down there and then this intrusive thought came ... It wouldn't let go of me. At some point I realized I no longer had control over my actions ..."

Raymond cast a worried glance at Marian.

"Imagine this—I was ready to chuck all the ice overboard. And if anyone tried to stop me, I was ready to grab the containers and jump into the water."

"Hey, hey, hey! Mari, we need to hold on!" El intervened.

The boat rocked one last time, and El finally straightened the wheel. The icy behemoth vanished into the mist.

"I don't know how to hold on!" Marian sighed heavily, releasing a cloud of vapor. "I can't even fathom how you manage to endure all this," she added, her disheveled head nodding.

"As long as we're on water, let the containers stay with El," Raymond said; this time his voice sounded much softer. "This guy is unbreakable. Sometimes it feels like he's deaf to his own inner voice."

"But you're not my inner voice, Raymond. And I hear you perfectly well," retorted El.

3:13 AM

Marian smiled, releasing her heavy thoughts. El picked up the transceiver and pressed the transmit button. "Phorcys. Phorcys. This is Medusa Gorgona ..."

Marian stood up and approached El. She buried her nose in his shoulder and whispered softly, "Let me do it. You are definitely a long way from the Gorgon's family."

He kissed her and turned to the helm. Soon Marian's voice resumed its chatter. "Phorcys, Phorcys ..."

Raymond closed his eyes. It was more comforting that way. He didn't want to peer any further into this dense fog. Marian's voice grew distant, replaced by the splash of water against the tired, scratch-covered stern accompanied by the hungry cries of gulls—the boat was sailing not far from the shore, where they seemed to feed. Raymond soared over the ocean. Somewhere in the distance, his worries and the freezing grip on his body were left behind. Amidst the clouds of spring green, jagged shores pierced through, and the craters of former volcanoes still gleamed white. Soon the water changed color, marking a clear boundary—here, the sea met the ocean and never seemed to blend with it.

In the distance, the ornate islands of Port Alexander appeared. They were like velvety patches on the ribbed water's gloss, captivating Raymond's gaze. He circled above the city, dotted with gigantic ships, and continued his journey into the open ocean. Somewhere out there, in neutral waters, a yacht was sailing. No, it was an entire ship. Three decks, a swimming pool, and a helipad. This pale *Tis* with its polished blue stern resembled a palace, stretching over a hundred yards in length and costing a quarter of a billion dollars.

Raymond landed on the middle deck and slipped through the wall. The opulent living room, equipped with a grand staircase, spanned two floors, as if it were a set for the movie *Titanic*. If that were true, Raymond wouldn't have been surprised. It looked the same: a bar, a grand piano, and instead of dining tables, gambling tables. A small dance floor, velvet sofas, and antique clocks that softly ticked at Raymond, "It's 9:10 a.m., Mister." He ascended the stairs and walked to the cabins, one of which housed Louis Rapshmir.

But which one? The psychic began checking them, yet the luxurious rooms stood empty. He reached the last door and attempted to enter but couldn't. Usually walls were no obstacle for Raymond, but not in this case. Here and now, he had no way of entering the last cabin. Everywhere he turned, he was met with walls, as if he had come to Rapshmir in the flesh.

"Damn you ..."

"Who else has been brought here?" A slender man opened the door.

Raymond met Louis's eyes. Both fell silent, studying each other with interest.

"What brings you here?"Rapshmir's astral body frowned.

3:13 AM

"It's about time to get up. Phorcys is being summoned on the bridge by Medusa Gorgona. It wouldn't hurt to go up and talk to her," Raymond said coldly.

"Medusa Gor ... Marian?" The billionaire suddenly realized. "But why summon me? Has something happened?"

"Something has."

"Where are you?"

"Can you fly?"

"I never leave the walls I raise before sleeping."

"Hm, then ..."

"But we agreed the location with Marian."

"Our boat is near the shores of the national park of Glacier Bay. We're making our way into the open ocean." Raymond gestured into the distance down the corridor. "We're being pursued, so I had to release fog onto the water."

Rapshmir for an instant looked disbelieving. "All right, I'll meet you near Kruzof Island," he rattled off, trying to dismiss the uninvited guest.

"The shores are covered in ice ..." Raymond continued to interrupt him.

Louis glanced wearily at Raymond. "Head into neutral waters. In three hours I'll be awaiting your coordinates on channel 86."

"We don't have a navigation system."

"My God!" Thin fingers with a gold ring touched Louis's dark forehead. "Fine, fine. Just get in touch with me. I'll locate you based on the outgoing signal … And now I strongly request you to leave my ship."

The man in the white silk robe lingered in Raymond's blue eyes for a moment longer before he closed the door. Raymond walked down the corridor, rushed to the upper deck, and took off at a run. Ripples spread across the dark surface of the ocean. He gazed at it and suddenly he understood—something was pulling him into the water. He resisted as best he could until he found himself just a couple of yards above the crests of the uncharacteristic waves.

Raymoooond, someone called from the depths, and hearing that voice could easily freeze one's blood if it were still in one's veins.

And so, just a moment later, Raymond was struggling weakly, already halfway into the water. When the emerald ocean closed above his head, he lowered his gaze. From the darkness of the depths, two glowing green dots stared at him. He felt uneasy. The lights were approaching, slowly fitting into the eye sockets of a face distorted by a scream. Thin, wriggling worms surrounded the pale skin, and finally he saw the creature, which was exerting an incredible force to draw him closer.

Hands descended into the water. Someone pulled Raymond to the surface with a strong grip.

3:13 AM

"Pull, pull him!" Marian screamed, and El pulled. Soon his heavy, soaked body collapsed onto the floor of the boat.

"What possessed you?" Marian sounded hysterical.

El stepped aside to catch his breath. He adjusted the backpack behind his back, wrung out his sleeves, and looked curiously at his friend.

"I flew to Rapshmir." Raymond's teeth chattered.

"And then?"

"Then the sea swallowed me."

"The sea swallowed you?" Marian was indignant. "You just got up and jumped overboard!" She was crying, unwilling to admit that the all-powerful Raymond had succumbed to the influence of the Gorgon, just like her. "Let's go—come on! You need to change. You don't need a chest infection on top of this." She began to help him up.

His legs slipped, and a puddle of seawater spread from under his sweater. El dragged him into the hold.

Marian squeezed into the room and started undressing Raymond. His lips had turned blue, and his hands were clenched into fists. There wasn't enough space for the three of them, and El returned to the helm, closing the door against the northern wind.

"Come on, Raymond, help me," Marian murmured, stripping off his heavy clothes.

Raymond wasn't embarrassed to be naked and didn't try to hide himself, but Marian did become embarrassed. She helped him stand and briefly averted her gaze, then stole another glance. She was drawn to him. Strongly drawn. Dressed in dry clothes, Raymond overcame the cramp and caught his breath, while the blushing Marian rushed out onto the deck as if scalded.

"Doc?" A rasp emerged from the hold. "Don't call Phorcys anymore. No need to attract attention. In three hours, Rapshmir will contact us on channel 86."

"Are you sure?" Marian was skeptical, not even turning her head toward the hold anymore.

Frankly, Raymond was puzzled by Rapshmir's behavior. But, pushing aside his confusion, he confidently answered, "Yes!"

El turned the boat southwest, and when Raymond had cleared the fog, he increased the speed.

***

"Raymond, wake up!" Marian touched his shoulder.

Raymond jolted awake and sat up. "How long was I asleep?"

"Two hours and forty minutes." Her eyes and cheeks were flushed from the cold, and her voice was hoarse.

"I'm getting up." He clumsily rose to his feet. An unpleasant stiffness spread through his body, causing him to collapse back onto the low bunk where he had been sleeping.

3:13 AM

"Yeah, moving is better in this cold." Marian coughed.

"How are you holding up?"

"I'll survive," she replied through her coughs.

Raymond rubbed his legs and exited the cabin. El didn't look much better, though he was considerably sturdier than the other two combined.

"To be honest, I don't know where neutral waters begin. There are no border ships around, and the boundaries aren't marked on the map," the agent admitted.

"We might already be beyond Alaska." Raymond took the helm. "And if our pursuers didn't spot us, we might have slipped away from the watchful eyes of the Feds."

"It'd be great if that's the case." El rubbed his hands together and blew warm air into his frozen palms.

Raymond switched on the radio and tuned it to channel 86. He sighed heavily, looked out over the ocean, and spoke clearly into the transmitter. "Phorcys, come in!"

Marian and El held their breath. Only a lifeless hiss came from the receiver.

"Phorcys, come in!" Raymond squealed through his teeth.

Again, only the lapping of waves and the monotonous white noise answered.

"Damn." El scanned the horizon, which was devoid of shores.

Phorcys, Phorcys, this is Medusa. Come in! Raymond's spirit remained unyielding.

Releasing the button, he opened the channel to receive, and through the static, a distant voice reached their ears. "Phorcys is here. Received Medusa's coordinates. Closing in ..."

"Louis!" Marian exclaimed, a smile cracking her wind-chapped lips.

They laughed in relief.

"I can't believe I'll be taking a hot shower and sleeping in a clean bed soon." Raymond lifted his gaze dreamily toward the sky.

"I don't think I'll believe it until I'm actually in the warm water and lying in that bed." El chuckled and shook his head.

Marian had just slipped into the hold and retrieved their bags ready for departure when the sound of an approaching helicopter echoed from behind. All three froze in place, not believing their ears. As a dark speck appeared in the sky, the doctor's travel bag slipped from her shoulder.

"How could they have gotten here so fast?" Raymond muttered.

El lowered his head and cursed under his breath. "Marian, hide in the hold," he ordered.

"What good will that do?" Marian shouted. "It's the end for all of us!"

3:13 AM

Raymond squatted down and shut his eyes tightly. Fog appeared like a wall from the Alaskan coast. But before it had engulfed the boat, a gunshot rang out. Raymond lifted his eyelids. Before him stood El. His black parka quickly soaked up the blood, covering the plastic floor with crimson droplets. A moment later, El collapsed. The shock blocked Raymond's ears and he failed to hear Marian's prolonged scream. The psychic's gaze rose to the sniper in the helicopter—now aiming at him.

None of them would ever forget what happened in the next moment. The helicopter's rotor blades suddenly ceased. It plummeted and crashed into the dark water.

Raymond turned his head toward El—Marian, sobbing, was bent over his body. From the mist like a ghost ship emerged the iridescent nose of a massive yacht. Raymond leaped to his feet and anchored the boat. The ship turned to provide support. Soon a pair of bodyguards appeared on the gangway and, seemingly on cue, leaped onto the blood-soaked deck, lifted El, and carried him away. Marian followed them, and after collecting their bags, Raymond trailed behind.

The yacht sailed away. And the last thing Raymond saw through the fog was three chilled federal agents, one after the other, climbing onto the abandoned fishing vessel.

Chapter 21

El found himself in a spacious cabin. Through tinted glass, the blurry silhouette of a woman could be discerned. She finished smoking, flicked the cigarette overboard, and entered the room from the narrow balcony.

"Rachel?" El croaked.

The woman rushed to the bed and leaned over him. The powdery fragrance brought him back to the present and assured him that Marian was by his side.

"El!" she whispered.

"Was I in bad shape?"

"You were. Your lung was punctured. But no arteries or heart muscle were affected ..." Marian smiled and held El's weak hands. An oxygen tube was under his nose, and sensors were attached to his chest.

"Louis has an excellent medical office and an operating room." Marian couldn't hold back, kissing his lips. "We're so lucky, El! So lucky!"

Large drops fell onto his skin. Marian was trying hard not to cry, but tears of joy occasionally slid from beneath her eyelids. El felt queasy. So many times Rachel had sat just like this by his side, cried, and reassured him that they were lucky. This time lucky … but he had never felt as sorry for her as he did for Marian right now.

"Okay, that's enough," he rasped. "No need to cry, Mari … It's all behind us."

"Promise me you won't leave me," Marian said, leaning over his shoulder.

"Who would I leave you for? Of course not. Of course I won't."

Today, El meant it. For the first time in his life, he believed what he was telling his Marian. He knew exactly what he was promising her, more than ever, and was certain he would keep his word.

"El, I need to confess something to you." Marian spoke, her eyes downcast.

"No need …"

"No, I want to!" she insisted. "A couple of days ago, at Ethan's house, I kissed Raymond. I … I don't know what got into me. You see, once I saw him in a dream. A long time ago, when I was just a girl. I saw Raymond exactly the way I saw him in the dossier photo they sent me before my flight to Thailand. Just like he first appeared in front of me on Bangla Road, when the two of you had had quite a bit to drink."

El frowned. He had never felt this sense of betrayal from a woman. Throughout his life, betraying Rachel, he had never truly understood the pain he had caused her for nearly ten years. Well, the day had come, and now every word Marian uttered pierced him like a bullet. She wiped away the tears that stubbornly reappeared.

"I was fifteen. A time of daydreams and secret diaries. One night I saw a guy in my dream. Handsome, well-groomed, and manly—far superior to my pimply peers. We were laughing; we were so happy, El. He smiled and threw a souvenir into the air. Suddenly it was in my hand. When I opened my fist, I saw a beautiful pink pearl. It was incredible. Nature had fashioned it into the shape of a droplet, and for years that symbol was a symbol of true love for me."

"Well." El averted his eyes, his heart heavy with an ocean of bitterness.

"But I don't love Raymond, El! I love you!"

El froze. After a moment, he let out a hoarse breath and embraced his Marian. His biggest fear was behind him.

"Where are the samples?" he remembered.

"With Raymond. Rapshmir is asking a lot about them ... He wants to see the ice."

El furrowed his brow. "I need to get back on my feet quickly," he whispered anxiously.

"We're heading to Vancouver. My parents' home is about twenty miles from the city. I talked to Father—he'll send a car for us."

"That's near Washington." El frowned.

3:13 AM

"Yes." Marian sighed. "We're going very cautiously, avoiding American waters."

Raymond's joyful face appeared at the door. He approached and patted El on the shoulder. Following him into the cabin was Rapshmir.

"The famous El Roberts!" Rapshmir raised a glass filled with fizzy drink.

"Not that famous," El hissed.

Raymond took a seat by the window, and the yacht's owner sprawled on a leather couch. "Champagne?" he asked. Before anyone could answer, a table laden with drinks and snacks was wheeled into the room.

"I suppose." Raymond nodded.

"So you're the third oracle?" El croaked.

"In the flesh." Rapshmir bowed. "Please, my dear guests!" The billionaire personally handed Raymond and Marion each a glass.

"I can't believe no one's chasing us." Marian squeezed El's hand and took a sip.

"It hasn't been easy for you." Rapshmir squinted, examining the drink against the light. "But it's all behind you. And so far, no special units have contacted the ship."

"That's good." Raymond exhaled. "These chases are terribly exhausting."

“To Louis!” Marian raised her glass. “To our savior!”

Raymond joined in.

“To your health.” Rapshmir waved his ringed fingers. “You three really surprised me.” He gazed lecherously at Marian and emptied his glass. “So where is she?” he whispered mysteriously.

“Who?” Marian didn’t immediately understand.

“The Medusa. The legendary Gorgon Medusa.”

“She—”

“Louis”—Raymond interrupted—“won’t you introduce us to your guests?”

“Guests?” He glanced at Raymond. “I’m here alone. Of course, not counting the crew and servants.”

“But this morning I was at your door.” Raymond bored a hole through Rapshmir with his gaze. “And I could have sworn there was someone else in your cabin.”

“Hmm, you know”—Louis paused—“what’s the point of keeping this a secret? No, I wasn’t alone. An attractive individual came to see me. However, she came out of her body. But then again, she hasn’t had a body for a long time ... so there’s nothing to worry about. More accurately, no one to worry about!”

“Hasn’t had a body for a long time?” Marian frowned. “How’s that possible?”

3:13 AM

Rapshmir swallowed, realizing he had said too much. "This lady is no longer alive. Her spirit came to me."

"On a date?" Raymond raised an eyebrow. "Did you lose someone?"

"I haven't lost anyone." The billionaire waved it off. "When she died, I wasn't even born yet."

"Even so." Raymond smirked and took a sip of champagne. "She was a famous figure, wasn't she?"

"Bingo," Louis mumbled. "That's an understatement! A real hottie." Rapshmir touched his lips, lost in thoughts of a night filled with pleasure.

"Tell us!" Marian's eyes lit up with curiosity.

"I can't, Doctor. You know better than anyone else—these aren't my secrets."

"Then give us a hint."

Rapshmir leaned dramatically on the armrest and sang a simple song.

"Her?" Marian whispered, covering her mouth.

"Louis, and how ...? Are they willing?" Raymond inquired carefully, so as not to offend the host.

"What are you thinking? They've been longing for this opportunity," Rapshmir responded, gathering astonished glances in an instant. Like a waiter, he refilled the empty glasses and once again started talking about the damned ice. "So, where is our Gorgon?"

Our! Raymond leaned forward. "Listen, Louis, this ice is dangerous."

"I'm not planning to touch it. I want to feel it ..."

"That aspect is no less dangerous than physical contact," Raymond confessed. "It hypnotizes, suppresses willpower, compels you not only to act oddly; the Gorgon is fully capable of making you think differently and believe in things that don't exist."

Rapshmir stared at his guest with a fox-like squint.

"It's true," Marian said. "First, in the middle of the night, Ethan wanted to kill all of us. Medusa spoke to him and then she appeared to Raymond, and while he was driving, he lost control. Afterward she spoke to me. Well, it wasn't really a conversation—she was giving very specific commands."

"Toward the end, in my dreams, when I was flying away from you, she dragged me underwater," Raymond added.

"In dreams and reality," Marian supplemented. "El was pulling him overboard to the sea." She nodded toward Roberts.

"Well then, by all means keep her to yourself." Rapshmir waved dismissively.

"How did you begin your journey as a psychic?" Marian hurried to switch to a less painful topic.

3:13 AM

Rapshmir reclined on the sofa in a leisurely manner and rolled his eyes.

"It was when I was fourteen. I was playing a computer game with a friend when my mother stormed into the room. 'Louis, we need you!' she was calling. My friend stayed behind and I followed her. We went downstairs into the living room, where about thirty guests had gathered. That evening I learned that my parents were members of the Masonic society."

"Good heavens," El murmured.

"Thank you, Agent Roberts!" Louis bowed sarcastically. "I know the CIA hates us. Their anger stems from their inability to control us. But we haven't done anything harmful. Moreover, Agent Roberts, your life right now owes its existence to our society. Which means we're not as useless as everyone thinks."

El clenched his lips to refrain from saying too much—things the Mason wouldn't be ready to hear.

"Louis, please continue! I'm really intrigued," Marian said.

And Rapshmir, sipping champagne, continued: "All these people, friends of the family and faces you'd see on the covers of global magazines, surrounded a round table. 'Is this your Louis?' An elderly lady smiled with impeccable teeth. 'Take a seat, my boy! The spirit pointed to you.' I didn't notice the divination board among the flickering candles right away. It lay there on the table, and the old lady's frail hand held the planchette—the teardrop-shaped indicator. That night, I first felt their presence. There were many of them, and they encircled me. I'll never forget this experience till the end of my days. I heard their whispers, felt their icy breath before I even placed my fingers on the planchette, and it slid across the board. But it got worse from there. Soon I could feel touches, know their thoughts and desires—I could even smell their ancient scents. When I finally realized that at the Masonic assembly, where the dead outnumbered the living, my sanity faltered. I lost consciousness, but it didn't save me from the visions. That night, the founders of the oldest society came to me. It was in a dream that I underwent initiation, and in the morning I made a promise to myself to never again contact the dead in the real world. My parents supported me in this decision, and I managed to divide my life into two—a life in the body and one beyond this beautiful shell."

To some extent Rapshmir was fortunate that Raymond had drowned his sarcasm in alcohol, and El hardly said a word.

"So it does exist after all!" The lone woman's voice pierced the room.

"What?" Rapshmir raised his head.

"Life after death."

"Of course it exists." He lowered his head back onto the plush armrest. "Have any of you ever seen a crab shed its shell?" No one answered, but Rapshmir didn't wait. "Death is an important necessity when it comes to things with varying expiration dates. That's why the death of the physical body should be perceived as no more terrifying than a seasonal molt."

"Louis"—Marian drained her glass as if it held courage instead of champagne—"there are rumors that the Masons are patronized by the very ..."

"The Devil?" Rapshmir was surprised.

"There are rumors." Marian nodded slowly.

"I implore you, if we were required to worship anyone, we would have chosen someone less controversial," Rapshmir assured her. "We worship ourselves, Marian. We are our own judges, gods, and even devils. Contrary to numerous legends, we have fairly simple principles and not-so-strict rules. As you can see, we admit people of color to the order. Moreover, our lodges are scattered all over the globe. Initially the order was formed as a small circle of people focused on studying the universe. Our prerogative is not faith; the strength of Masonry lies in knowledge."

"Terrible deeds are attributed to you," Raymond mused.

"Our most terrible deed over the centuries has remained unchanged—at the outset we slipped from the Church's control, and now we've escaped the grip of the authorities."

Suddenly El grimaced, clutching his chest, and asked Marian for water.

“It was a great pleasure to meet you, El Roberts.” Rapshmir moved to the edge of his bed and extended his palm. El didn’t say anything, but he shook Louis’s hand.

“I think we all need to rest.” The yacht owner bowed gallantly and left the room.

He walked down the corridor to his cabin and knocked. His bodyguard opened the door, leaving him alone. Low clouds shrouded the sky, and soon the window was streaked with slanted rain. The yacht rocked more as the storm intensified, lulling Louis. The last thing he remembered was the crystal chandelier swaying on his cabin ceiling. For the fifteenth time, he fell asleep.

“Louis,” someone whispered softly into his ear, rousing him from slumber.

Louis Rapshmir had a penchant for games. He glanced at the clock, which read 9:39 p.m., smiled, and rose from the bed. The storm had passed, and the yacht was cruising smoothly at a moderate speed.

“Marian?” Louis surveyed the dark room.

A shadow glided by the panoramic window—someone persistently beckoning Rapshmir to leave his warm bed. He slipped his feet into his moccasins, draped a blood-red velvet robe adorned with the family crest around his shoulders, and stepped onto the deck.

3:13 AM

An eerie mist spread across the black ocean—these waters were forever shrouded in fog, with or without Raymond. Rapshmir walked along a narrow balcony and reached the blue pool. A transparent black blouse had been left on one of the loungers, and a slender silhouette flickered, leading down the staircase.

"Dr. Flay, if I'm not mistaken." Louis tied his robe and had just sneaked down to the lower deck when every light on the massive yacht was suddenly extinguished.

Rapshmir jerked nervously—his sinful thoughts instantly gave way to anxiety. He couldn't tolerate such antics even from the living, let alone the dead. He turned and headed swiftly for the captain's bridge.

"Louis ..." Marian said sensually over his shoulder. Drops of cold sweat formed on his forehead.

Ever since that very night when he was not yet fifteen, he had despised that bone-chilling fear. For the remaining years he had preferred not to acknowledge it, and now something had lured him out onto the deck after sunset and turned off all the lights. It seemed that she had not only managed to cut the power to the illuminations but had also lulled the entire crew.

Rapshmir was breathing heavily, trying not to turn around, when he felt ghastly touches under his robe. Cold, moist hands wound around his torso, aiming to descend into his silken pajamas. He froze.

“You must set me free,” a tender voice whispered in his ear. “And you will know pleasures you never knew before ...”

Rapshmir mustered all his strength, but even that was insufficient to utter the word “no!” In that moment, he was only able to think about refusal.

The Gorgon breathed icy, noxious air onto the back of his neck, dragging his helpless body towards the edge of the deck.

The words “You’re already dead” resounded in his ears, and he felt the sensation of hundreds of thin serpents enveloping him, tickling repulsively and invading his ear canals. They crawled into his nose and throat, writhing there in living tangles. They filled his sinuses and coiled around his eye sockets, tormenting him incessantly with an endless itch beneath his trembling eyelids.

Medusa had ensnared him in her chilly embrace. He swayed weakly and leaned over the low railing. Now, instead of her voice, he heard the rapid propellers of a powerful engine. They were just an instant away from engulfing him, ready to chop his flesh to pieces.

“Louis!”

Rapshmir snapped awake, finding Raymond’s frightened face before him. He lowered his gaze—Raymond was holding onto his robe, attempting to pull him away from the edge. He grabbed his savior and took a step forward. He gazed at the churning waters—another second and they would’ve consumed him.

3:13 AM

“What was that?” His stare darted around the deck. “Why did the lights go out? Did you turn them off?” He glared fiercely at Raymond.

“Hey, boss, if I wanted to kill you, I wouldn’t bother saving you, would I?” Raymond raised his hands as if surrendering to an enemy. “And the lights didn’t go out. I’ve been chilling out here for about two hours.”

“Why?”

“I just didn’t want to share the same space with her.”

“With her?” Rapshmir tensed. “So it was her?” He looked terrified. He tried to wipe the horror from the face with his palms, but it lingered. “You must leave my ship,” he declared resolutely.

“But El—”

“I’m sure he’ll be fine!” Rapshmir interrupted, swiftly leaving the deck.

“Damn.” Raymond sighed and stared into the eerie darkness of the ocean.

And that was the last they saw of Louis Rapshmir. The crew lowered a motorboat onto the water and helped the wounded El aboard. Soon one of Rapshmir’s bodyguards appeared by the boat, extending a handheld navigator and a rectangular bag made of dense silvery material to Raymond.

“What’s this?” Raymond frowned, but the burly man offered no response.

Raymond opened the bag and was flabbergasted.

“What’s in there?” Marian called to him, but he had been rendered speechless.

Taking the backpack off his shoulder, he quickly unzipped it and peered inside. Instead of the containers of ice, a pair of ship’s thermoses stood in their place.

“Did he steal the ice?” Marian recoiled.

“He stole it and then returned it,” Raymond muttered.

“Why didn’t you check the backpack?”

“I was afraid to look inside!” Raymond yelled.

“But why did he return it?”

Raymond fell silent, checking the route on the navigator.

“Did something happen?” Marian inquired.

“Something did,” Raymond said indifferently.

“Did something happen to Rapshmir?” El raised his head. Raymond looked at Marian with tension in his gaze.

“Nothing,” Marian reassured El. “He just can’t continue the journey. The shore is within arm’s reach, so rest up.” She checked his pulse and breathing and pulled the blanket higher.

3:13 AM

Marian watched as the yacht's brilliant stern, now moving away from them, disappeared. The pain of betrayal tore at her. The truth was that Marian Flay had never interested Louis Rapshmir as a woman or as a friend. He hadn't sailed to Alaska to rescue her and her companion. He had undertaken the entire journey for one solitary purpose—to learn about Medusa and, if possible, to possess her.

Raymond started the engine. He cast an anxious glance into the darkness of the nocturnal ocean, which frightened him much less than the silvery bag resting peacefully at his feet.

Chapter 22

The cold seared her face. Marian huddled closer to the sleeping El. Raymond looked hopefully at the glowing navigator screen and then lifted his gaze back to the desolate darkness. He pushed the boat forward, straining to make out the lights of the first headlands.

"How much longer to the shore?" Marian turned her head.

The device showed 10:13 p.m., and Raymond, studying the map, audibly calculated their route.

"In about forty minutes we'll reach the Salish Sea. It's split in half, so we'll stick to the left bank, which belongs to Canada. From there, it's half an hour to Cape Victoria. Less than twenty minutes from there is the Moresby Passage. After that, we'll enter Swartz Bay and carefully skirt the waters that the States have laid claim to. Then, about an hour past Duke Point, we'll reach Tsawwassen port."

"Two and a half hours," Marian calculated, resting her head on El's shoulder.

Half an hour of monotonous ocean travel passed, and Raymond visibly calmed down. Ten more minutes and he would see the first beacon lights on the steep Canadian slopes. But suddenly Marian lifted her head. Maybe she'd fallen asleep earlier, Raymond couldn't help that. But now with horror she stared into the emptiness and, trembling all over, retreated towards Raymond.

“What?” he whispered. “What do you see?”

“She’s here ... She came for me!” Marian echoed as if in delirium.

Raymond turned off the motor, closed his eyes, and took a deep breath of the fresh night air. In the next instant a syringe, stolen from the yacht, glinted in his hand. He removed the cap from the needle and injected the clear liquid into the doctor’s shoulder without hesitation.

She twitched and looked at Raymond with huge gray eyes filled with horror. But soon enough, alarm gave way to oblivion. Her body went limp and slumped to the bottom of the boat. Raymond dragged her over to El, covered her with a blanket, and sped full throttle over the ominous black water. He couldn’t see the shore but suddenly felt the boat collide with something. The motor screeched and, emitting smoke, gave up. Raymond pulled a rope from his backpack, tied it around himself, and fastened the ends to the oarlocks. No matter what he saw that night, no matter what he heard, he promised himself that he wouldn’t leave the boat under any circumstances. Medusa had no physical form; she couldn’t kill him. The only person who could end his life was himself—Raymond Lee.

He listened carefully. The black water lapped against the hull of the skiff. From a distance, someone chuckled and splashed water at him. He turned sharply, shining his flashlight towards the sound. The light reflected off the surface, which foamed as if someone had dived beneath.

"Who's there?" he asked for some reason.

As if in response, glass shattered, and the next moment the lantern exploded, scattering into small shards. "Damn," Raymond muttered through gritted teeth, dodging the sharp glass.

Another second and he would have released his grip, losing his sole source of light into the sea. However, he merely shut his eyes and, with a raspy breath, placed the lantern in the boat. When he opened his heavy eyelids, he saw the lantern on the floor beaming a powerful ray into the night sky.

"Trying in vain! You can't deceive me!" Raymond laughed, and his laughter was echoed on the starboard side.

He fell silent when, from the dark ocean, someone splashed water at him again.

A splash won't kill me, he concluded, discovering a scattering of small crimson drops on his arms.

His frozen fingers rubbed mechanically at the dark spots on his skin. In an instant, he realized that instead of seawater, he was covered with blood.

Where could that have come from? He was nervously examining his clothes when the boat suddenly rocked.

3:13 AM

Raymond froze. He listened but heard nothing. That was when he raised the lantern and shone it on the water—corpses were floating on it, shaved and disfigured bodies ravaged by disease. He felt sick; the taste of champagne rolled up his throat, the same one he'd enjoyed on Rapshmir's yacht. He fixed his gaze on the blanket covering the sleeping El and Marian, but out of the corner of his eye, he noticed black fingers gripping the boat.

Raymond slowly turned. A dead man's hand had detached from its body and continued to lie just couple of feet from the psychic's horrified eyes. He took in a lungful of air, fighting back a wave of nausea, and, armed with an oar, struck with all his might at the decaying fingers. The flesh crumbled, releasing an innumerable swarm of hair-like worms. Black, wriggling threads cascaded into the boat, clinging to his trousers and easily infiltrating the gaps in his sneakers.

"Son of a ..." Raymond hissed nervously, stomping on the repulsive snakes.

His shoe slapped against the rubber floor, unable to crush the relentless creatures. Suddenly, a loud thud echoed. Raymond froze, afraid to lift his foot. Soon a black fog of worms enveloped his white footwear. It seemed as though they were surging forth with a speed that only water could match.

The parasites slipped in with their slimy ribbons, infiltrating his socks, slipping between his toes, and crawling beneath his nails. Panic gripped Raymond. Even if these sensations were unreal despite their vividness, could he have hit rock bottom?

Perhaps what he had taken for dreadful parasites was actually streams of cold water?

That would be terrifying. Truly terrifying. Raymond tried to calm himself and focus on the sensations. He remained still as the writhing creatures covered his body. Even when his skin became unbearably itchy, he didn't move. But when the worms, in perpetual motion, invaded his nostrils, slid between his lips, and descended into his throat, he couldn't take it anymore. Now he was desperately trying to rid himself of the ever-present parasites. He reached so deep into his throat with his hands that he retched. Blood rushed to his face, and an unbearable heat engulfed him. Water, only cold water, could save him—wash away all these creatures, relieve the itching, and soothe his nerves. Raymond leaned overboard. The black ocean called him, called him by name.

Raymond … He reached out to the icy sea. A snap came from behind, and the rope holding him in the boat tensed. He lay limply against the gunwale and looked at his friends. The worms covered the sleeping El and Marian, going through their bodies with uncanny agility. Raymond watched as the glossy sheet of moving worms sealed their faces, and with each breath it absorbed more, vanishing beneath their pallid skin. He wanted to move, to help them, but he couldn't. Desperation gripped his soul, and Raymond, once again regurgitating worms, burst into tears. He cried helplessly and bitterly. The tears forced his eyes shut, and as a cold hand brushed his left arm, he saw no more.

***

3:13 AM

Jerking convulsively, Raymond discerned El's face. Wounds gaped on his flabby skin. Nematodes dangled from his mouth, bathed in bloody rivulets; a white film covered his eyes.

"Raaaymooond," El's voice croaked.

"Damn it," Raymond sobbed, tears streaming down his face. "Damn you, El!"

A dead man's hand dug into living flesh. Raymond screamed in pain but didn't budge. If El was truly dead, his own death wouldn't be far behind. He endured as much as he could until the living corpse released him. El straightened up and, standing on the edge of the boat, leapt into the water. Pain contorted Raymond's face. He shut his eyes once more, unwilling to witness any more horrors.

A few minutes later, the silence was broken by sobbing. Raymond raised his head. Marian was seated on the bloodied sheet, facing away from him, gazing out at the pitch-black ocean.

"Doc?" he whispered in fear, but Marian didn't hurry to reply.

He pulled the silvery bag towards him and concealed it behind his back.

"He died because of you," Marian uttered unexpectedly. "Everyone died because of you."

Raymond frowned. He was doing everything in his power not to believe what was happening, but the empty space next to the doctor sank his soul to the ocean's depths along with El. Like El, he had grieved only for his mother.

"What do we do now? El won't come back," Marian cut in with a sharp edge to her voice. "No one will come back. And it's all your fault."

His father, Leslie, had always said that. Raymond remembered him in fragments; he hadn't appeared at home often. Nevertheless, the final moments of Leslie Lee's life were forever etched in his memory.

Twilight had fallen outside, and he was hurrying home. His mother always worried when he returned from his friends after dark. He stopped before the tall veranda and placed his bicycle on the ground. Shouts, furniture crashing, and the sound of breaking dishes emanated from the house. The teenager bounded onto the porch, opened the screen door, and froze in the doorway—Leslie's beefy fist was hovering over his spouse. Alicia's body was covered in cuts and bruises. She looked at her son fearfully—her eyes pleaded for him to run farther from danger, to hide in a neighbor's house or with friends. Before, Raymond had always fled. But he was tired of running, and that evening, he stayed.

"Look at yourself!" Leslie released the tormented mother and advanced toward his son. "You look like a girl. Come on, take off your pants; I'll turn you into a man right now!"

The closer his father came, the more clearly Raymond could smell the cheap alcohol. Leslie yanked the worn leather belt from his trousers and demonstratively tested its strength.

3:13 AM

"Leslie, leave him alone!" Alicia, limping, rushed to his tormentor and attacked from behind.

In one swift motion, Leslie tossed his wife to the floor and swung the belt over her tortured face.

"Hey, you, jerk!" Raymond called out.

Leslie slowly turned his wild gaze towards the young boy. "What did you say?"

"I said you're a jerk," Raymond repeated confidently.

The sadist clenched his lips and lunged at the boy. He grabbed his son by the collar and lifted him off the ground. The rare shade of blue eyes, which in the sunlight seemed bluer than ice, had been passed down to Raymond from Leslie. He looked into those merciless, perpetually intoxicated, world-hating eyes and for the first time in his life, he felt no fear. His father swung the belt and froze. Suddenly Leslie's eyes bulged, his fetid mouth opened slightly, and after a moment, he collapsed to the floor.

For a minute he convulsed in pain, but Raymond never looked away from him. Only when his father ceased twitching and blinking did Lee junior turn his gaze to his mother. Alicia rushed over to her son. She kicked Leslie in the side—his body swayed lifelessly. She turned to Raymond and held him tightly.

Once the doctors had confirmed his heart had stopped, news of Leslie Lee's sudden demise spread among their relatives and close friends. Alicia organized the funeral, not crushed by grief. She chose honesty; she enjoyed life without Leslie—calm, measured, free from fear. After that, the entire family turned away from the widow. Alicia and Raymond Lee were utterly alone.

"He's to blame for everything," Raymond retorted. "I warned him." He swallowed nervously, watching Marian. "And I'm warning you."

Her tousled hair took on an odd motion, as if a strong wind was blowing from behind. As though defying gravity, it rose into the air and twisted like a cloud of living snakes.

A cold wave of horror washed over Raymond. Marian slowly turned, sank to the bottom of the boat, and crawled to his feet. Her eyes burned with an eerie fire, and her mouth opened in a silent scream. Her movements seemed unnatural, as if her body had lost its bones yet still retained the ability to move. The Gorgon approached, and Raymond could discern the movement of thin worms beneath her skin. Infested with parasites, she rose and released a slimy mass from her black mouth. Raymond bent over, desperately scraping the repulsive creatures off his face.

This can't be real; none of this can be real! He gasped, struggling against the nightmare.

"Raymond, my son ..." Cold fingers touched him.

He hesitantly raised his gaze—his mother was before him. Alicia looked at him with the same loving gaze she had had seventeen years ago. He had missed her so much. Unbearably.

3:13 AM

"Mom," he whispered.

"You can do it, my golden boy! You can do it all ..."

"Yes, I need to endure tonight." He squeezed her pale hands and, trembling all over, kissed them.

"Raymond"—Alicia released her son and untied the rope from him—"follow me."

She stood up, straightened her hospital shirt, and headed toward the bow of the boat. Her warm smile spread, beckoning Raymond with a gesture, and she leaped into the water.

Raymond's heart shrank to the size of a pea but grew heavier than lead. Now he was truly alone, without the slightest inkling of what was happening in the real world beyond mirages and delusions. Not knowing when this nightmare would end and not understanding if it would end at all, he simply sailed through the pitch-black molasses-like ocean.

He listened—no sound except the waves and no light except the lantern. Suddenly the boat came to a halt. He leaned cautiously over the side and peered into the darkness. The sea was washing around rocks that protruded from the water for hundreds of yards, if not miles, around.

He could have sat there forever if he hadn't tried to push away from the stones. He leaned over and shoved one of the rocks. The slippery stones began to move. Now he saw—they were the dead standing in the water, submerged up to their heads.

He pulled back when one of the corpses grabbed his wrist. Black fingers dug into the space between tendons, tearing his delicate skin. Raymond screamed, writhing in pain. Another corpse grabbed his collar and tried to pull him into the water. Now hundreds of hands reached for Raymond, all aiming to pull him out of the boat. And this time he wasn't tied to it.

He pried apart the bruised fingers, gnawing at them with his teeth. He fell onto the bottom of the boat and caught his breath.

The dead turned their attention to tearing the sloop apart instead of Raymond. He heaved a sigh, examined his bloody, trembling hands, and rose again. Armed with an oar, he began chopping at the skulls of the afflicted. With every puncture, a splash of putrid blood shot into the air and the skull disappeared into the black water, only to be replaced by another. The sound of bones cracking was followed by agonized moans until Raymond had exhausted his strength. He stopped and raised the lantern. The shorn heads and blackened fingers of the corpses stretched for miles.

"It's senseless, all of it's senseless," he muttered as if in a trance.

He sat on the floor, tied himself to the stern, and embraced the silvery bag of containers. He couldn't defeat the dead; there were too many of them. All he could do was float downstream until they tore apart this accursed boat along with him.

3:13 AM

With unbearable longing, Raymond gazed at the solitary blanket splattered with bloodstains. Large tears rolled down the cheeks of the magnificent Mr. Lee. He had failed once again to protect the people he had grown so attached to—people he might even have grown to love.

Chapter 23

El heard cries and slowly lifted his heavy eyelids. Nausea swept over him, his head spun, and he couldn't feel his feet at all.

He leaned against the side of the boat and clumsily pulled himself up. He dragged his legs with his hands and finally turned around, catching sight of Raymond. The latter had tethered himself to the boat and, half hunched over, was fiercely battling the black waves with an oar.

"Raymond!" El croaked, but Raymond couldn't hear him. "Raymond!"

It seemed even if he could have shouted, Raymond wouldn't have heard him anyway.

El shifted his gaze to Marian. She lay motionless.

"What did you do to her?" El's forehead was creased with deep lines.

He leaned over the pale face of the doctor—she was barely breathing. El spasmodically felt her wrist and froze ... Faintly, the heartbeat echoed. He let out a hoarse exhale.

Meanwhile, Raymond sat on the floor, pulled the bag with samples close to him, and clutched it to his trembling body.

"Hey," El called out to him, but Raymond was gazing into the distance, staring through him.

3:13 AM

Tears filled Raymond's eyes as if an eternal glacier had suddenly decided to thaw. El pressed his palm to his chest, overcoming the pain, and crawled over to the psychic.

"Raymond!" El rasped, touching his terrified friend's leg. "Raymond! Come on, snap back!"

A horn sounded behind El. He started and turned abruptly—a massive cargo ship was approaching. It illuminated the skiff with a spotlight, its blaring horn demanding a change of course.

"Raymond!" El shouted, his voice cracking.

He tried to reach the tiller, but Raymond forcefully held him back. Seemingly in a trance, Raymond was steering the boat straight towards disaster. El winced with pain, but another powerful blast that reverberated in his gut forced him to rise. He approached Raymond again and, without wasting time on pleas, delivered a punch to his jaw. Raymond crumpled against the side, releasing the bag, one hand still clinging to the tiller. El froze—he could hear the massive tanker right behind him, mercilessly slicing through the ocean. Perhaps for the last time in his life, he exhaled, and he struck Raymond again.

Raymond howled in pain and raised his eyes to El, clutching his face, and his gaze cleared. In the ice-blue depths, a fleeting glimpse of happiness appeared, swiftly replaced by horror. Behind El loomed an iron behemoth. The slightly rusted bow of the colossal cargo ship, salt stained and towering, was about to collide with the skiff. El fell to the floor, tightly embracing Marian, and in the next moment, a piercing screech echoed above him. Afraid to move, he hesitantly lifted his head—over them loomed an inconceivably enormous bulbous shape. Streams of seawater flowed down from the massive formation, and high above, near the bow, swung a monstrous anchor.

El felt like he was either dreaming or losing his mind. But as he turned his gaze to Raymond, he understood—none of his fears had been true. The psychic's face had taken on a peculiar pallor; the veins on his temples bulged and traced beneath his thin skin like blue branches, while the whites of his eyes were washed with crimson. One by one, the vessels burst, revealing insane stresses.

Not only did Raymond halt the ship of horrifying dimensions, but with power unimaginable for a human, he lifted the ship's bow into the air. El, feeling no pain, lunged for the motor, started it, and sped away from the multi-ton behemoth that could have crashed down at any second. The skiff shot out from under the bow and raced across the black water.

Raymond released the tanker and collapsed onto the floor, utterly powerless. El was exerting all his strength, attempting to escape the colossal wave created by the ship. The boat was tossed around, but he managed to keep it afloat.

He shut off the motor, his labored breathing calming as he gazed at the thousand-ton monster disappearing into the dark ocean. He leaned over Raymond and felt a faint pulse.

3:13 AM

"Well, maybe this is for the best," El concluded, looking at the silent figures of Raymond and Marian.

El opened Rapshmir's silver bag, glanced inside, and took out the containers. He shifted them to his black backpack, which he slung onto his shoulders with a wheeze. He weakly pulled his sore body to the tiller and started the motor. The boat roared to life and sped through the foamy crests. It passed the black cliffs that surrounded the Salish Sea and entered the Haro Strait..

Golden lights warmly illuminated the cape, scattered along the waterfront, while a beckoning lighthouse stood a little way off. A warmth spread through El's chest when he looked at this view. He had never peeked into others' windows, never imagined himself in the place of those sleeping peacefully in warm beds. Never until tonight. Right now, he yearned to become someone else for just a while, to borrow the tranquil routine of one of the inhabitants of this isolated place and catch his breath. Contrary to his desires, he clutched his gunshot wound tightly and kept moving.

He glided past a cluster of islands in the Moresby Passage and from there into Swartz Bay. The navigator indicated that if he followed a straight line, he would need to navigate the waters belonging to America for twenty-six minutes. El sighed heavily—or as heavily as his punctured lung allowed. If he didn't venture into dangerous waters, he'd have to sit like this for a couple more hours.

His head was unsteady again; everything swam before his eyes. He found a water bottle in his bag and drained it. Whether it was the wrong kind of water or his attempt at drinking in large gulps was too early, he began to cough heavily. Choking waves tore at his lungs until he noticed his hands were coated in crimson drizzle.

"Damn it ... The last thing I need is to black out in the middle of the Georgia Strait," he whispered in fear.

El peered into the black sky with trepidation, turning the tiller strictly towards Tsawwassen. He watched on the bright screen of the navigator as the boat crossed, like a line drawn with a ruler, the straight boundary. Alarm coiled at the base of his throat. He sensed this eerie silence boded ill.

Ten minutes passed, and El calmed down. They had a quarter of an hour left to reach the port when a bright spotlight blinded him. A military ship turned on its lights and sounded a warning: "In the name of the United States Border Security, I order you to stop!"

El knew perfectly well what would follow in ninety seconds if he didn't obey such an order, yet without slowing down, he continued to drive the boat. A minute and a half later, to his surprise, a shot rang out. A bullet whizzed past his head and pierced the water.

"What the hell are you doing, you bastards?" he muttered and removed the backpack from his shoulders.

3:13 AM

He extended his arm over the side, guaranteeing that the containers would hit the water if the sniper moved from warnings to elimination. The ship remained silent, still illuminating the skiff with a powerful spotlight, and a helicopter appeared in the dark sky, its blades beating. Without flashing lights or search beams, it melded with the night air, offering no chance of identification.

"Agent Roberts!" blared a familiar voice from the loudspeaker—a voice that was painfully known to El. "This is Julian Turner speaking!"

Turner himself has arrived, El thought. *Now it definitely smells like kerosene!*

"I order you to stop the boat, lay down your weapons, and secure the samples," Turner's voice continued. "The border patrol ship will tow you. I guarantee ..." Julian paused. "Listen—I guarantee your safety." He fell silent again, the parts of his sentence separated by an unsettling hush. "And the safety of your companions."

El understood that Turner wouldn't stop at persuasion. And, seeing the red dot right on Raymond's forehead, he was once again assured of that. He shut off the motor; the boat drifted another dozen yards from inertia and came to a halt.

El had never seen Julian Turner—this dark horse, the puppeteer, or simply the man who, lacking an official position in the counter-terrorism department, was endowed with boundless capabilities. Some considered him a deranged fanatic; however, according to others, in the fight against terrorism, the ends always justified the means. Everyone knew that this scoundrel was elbow-deep in blood. Everyone knew that those hands didn't just clean up city streets but even the hallowed halls of the Bureau of Investigation. El, however, firmly believed that Turner had been combating terrorism for so long that he had become an inseparable part of it.

"El." Raymond's whisper broke the silence.

"Hmm?" El replied, not looking at him and keeping his lips sealed.

"Up there—Turner." Raymond still couldn't open his eyes. "What time is it?"

"What?" El asked again, as if he hadn't heard.

"Tell me, El, what time is it?"

El, having traced the sniper's red beam, looked up at the sky. There were no lights left, but he caught a glimpse of the laser's flicker.

"Exactly eleven," he declared confidently.

Raymond raised his palm slightly.

"The scoundrel's protected. I can't locate him," he muttered. "Let him talk. I need him to talk!"

"Hey, Julian! Do you know what's in these containers?" El rasped, feeling the sickly taste of blood filling his throat.

"Ice—ice from Alaska," Turner replied.

3:13 AM

"So why don't you fly over and get yourself some ice?"

"El"—Turner sighed—"what are these games for? We both know—"

Julian Turner fell silent. He fell silent as if someone had cut his throat. El looked at Raymond—he had clasped an invisible neck with his hands. Without loosening his grip, Raymond got down on his knees and leaned over the side. At that very moment, something like a sandbag dropped from above and splashed into the water. The helicopter's lights lit up, and the sniper's crosshair disappeared. Now a bright beam was slicing through the water in search of a body, but Turner, having plummeted like a stone to the bottom, hadn't resurfaced yet.

"Raymond!" El yelled, scanning the dark water. "Raymond!"

A hand emerged from the ominous waves. El flinched but quickly regained his composure—Raymond's head appeared on the surface. El pulled him into the boat, started the motor, and, taking advantage of the moment when there was no one to give orders, raced away from the scene of the tragedy. The blue pointer on the navigator screen approached the black line and crossed it. The lights of the port of Tsawwassen blinked ahead. El's chest burned like fire. He would gladly have taken such a sensation for happiness, but it was this feeling that heralded a severe hemorrhage in his lung.

The last thing he remembered was a strong guy in a tracksuit extending his hand to him. Then came the sirens. A bright medical flashlight briefly flickered, and an alarmed voice sounded: "Hold on, El. Don't go. We need you conscious!"

"Where's my backpack?" El snapped, splattering the medic with blood.

"Calm down, calm down." The doctors repositioned him and fastened tight straps around him. "All the bags are with your friend, Chris. He took care of you and called for an ambulance."

"Took care of ..." El grumbled dissatisfiedly.

"Don't worry about anything. Just focus on staying with us."

And El held on, observing in a delirium the hustle, the long silicone tubes, and the oxygen mask. He took a painful breath, as if gas had seared his chest, and then he blacked out.

Once, El had been shot in the abdomen. Seriously shot. By his partner's gaze, he understood that if he closed his eyes, he might never open them again. A coma is a cunning thing. It engulfs you, takes you further away from pain, but with the pain, it also takes you away from reality. Back then, El didn't know why he should fight against the shutdown; he heard the doctors' shouts, but he still gravitated toward the light.

His bare feet were seized by a biting cold. The bright light stabbed his eyes. The place where he had ended up was icy and foggy. As the mist thinned, he saw the sea. The cold northern sea. With no visible shores, without ships—frozen and lifeless, just like El himself. He strained his ears—only the distant cries of seagulls feasting on a dead fish on a desolate shore reached him. His pale body was covered with a thin surgical shirt with a massive bloodstain in the middle of his abdomen, and his legs had turned rather blue.

El stood on an ice floe jutting out of the water. A distant rumble sounded. Through the translucent haze, the bow of a fishing boat appeared. It was led by a grizzled, strong man in a black suit, and a couple of drowsy companions huddled at the side of the small vessel. El didn't recognize these people—in fact, he didn't even recognize himself standing at the helm.

On the dark blue water, frothy trails were left behind the boat, and when they dissipated, El spotted a strange figure following the vessel. The woman swam silently, concealed in the somber waters. Her hair seemed like a million intertwining snakes, and her tattered clothing enveloped her gray, corpse-like body. She extended her arms forward, attempting to grasp the stern as she felt his intense gaze. Her angular head jerked upwards, her face contorted in a scream, and the fierce gaze of her burning eyes pierced El with unbearable agony. He fell to his knees and clutched his wound, while the monstrosity emerged from the cold water, slowly climbing the ice floe. The scraping of her nails created waves of fear in El's abdomen—fear that made him want to vomit himself inside out. He spat a red-laden hark onto the white ice, and beside the puddle, the gnarled hand of the Gorgon struck the ice.

"Come on, El! Hold on! I'm begging you, don't leave—don't abandon me," Rachel sobbed.

Then El took a raspy breath, opened his eyes, and never closed them again for fear of finding himself in the horrifying midst of an unknown sea.

Once again, just like he had done many years ago, he departed his own body. He was transported through space. Now he stood on a lawn in front of a blue mansion. Yellow roses had once grown here, but now dry stems with sharp thorns lined the façade. He walked across the lawn to the inner courtyard—what had once been a stunningly beautiful garden was now neglected. El paused for a moment, remembering a summer day and a brand-new swing beneath a blossoming apple tree. The tree had grown considerably, and the swing seemed smaller now. Rotten leaves and last year's fruits lay on the wire mesh swing, and the rusty supports had noticeably tilted.

El opened the door leading to the spacious kitchen. He froze, for instead of the usual bustling and pleasant aromas, the room was empty. The countertop remained dirty, and a broken egg had frozen on the floor. Anxiety tore at his soul. He wanted to leave, to escape, but hesitated in the doorway.

"Rachel?" he called out, but there was no response. *Perhaps she's moved. Maybe other people live here now*, he thought hopefully.

Curiosity prevailed. El crossed the kitchen and stepped onto the soft carpet of the living room. The once impeccable cream color was marred by unsightly stains. The cozy couch, where he had enjoyed so many evenings, was sloppily covered with a frayed blanket. On the round table surrounding a flowery lamp, rows of medicine bottles were arranged, and a pink laundry basket stood against the wall.

El couldn't bear to look anymore. He fled. Fled with his unseen spirit just as he used to escape with his body.

He shifted again. This time, picturesque mountains surrounded the area, with rare patches of snow on their steep slopes. He found himself in front of a log mansion. The three-story house made of reddish-brown wood, nestling within a dense pine forest, looked inviting and welcoming.

El passed through the wall into the spacious, rustic-style living room and ascended the chic staircase. It was from here, through a partially open door, that the sound of Marian's crying reached him.

She was kneeling by the bed, weeping inconsolably.

"He's still in critical condition, and they won't let me see him," she whimpered.

Raymond half opened his bluish eyelids and immediately winced in pain. He felt the doctor's hand and squeezed it. Marian shuddered, looked up, and pressed Raymond's palm against her tear-moistened cheek.

Strange emotions visited El. He had missed Marian so much, yet he wished her a life free of pain and sorrow with equal intensity.

Chapter 24

Raymond adjusted the wave of his dark hair and activated the camera.

"My name is Raymond Lee, and I'm a psychic," he began, his voice carrying a weight that matched the gravity of his words. "I work for the government. I predict disasters, terrorist attacks, and even wars. But recently I foretold the demise of all humanity ... It wasn't my task to seek out the source of our impending doom"—Raymond's gaze momentarily faltered—"but fate led Dr. Flay, Agent Roberts, and me to discover it nonetheless. Risking our lives, we extracted a deadly bacterium from Alaska—a bacterium that will soon set off a devastating epidemic, claiming billions of human lives. Yet before it kills, it will enslave, changing us beyond recognition. The world's glaciers, like refrigerators of a bacteriological laboratory, hold within them millions of frozen assassins. Assassins no larger than a micron. These are the ones that science has yet to uncover. Microorganisms don't die in the cold; unlike humans, they're immortal. They're the stronger ones. Once reanimated, they will unconditionally seize the planet, turning us, the masters of the world, into insignificant slaves."

Raymond took a deep breath, his chest rising and falling with a heavy realization.

"I'm an American citizen seeking refuge under Canada's protection. The people I've supplied with information for many years have turned against me. And not just me—they're after Dr. Marian Flay, who gathered information on the epidemic for them, and Agent El Roberts."

Raymond averted his moist eyes and touched his trembling fingers to his brow.

"El wasn't just an agent; he became a true friend. This brave man, at the cost of his own life, saved Marian and me from certain death. Now El lies in a deep coma, his reflexes unresponsive. Furthermore, he can no longer breathe on his own. This has become the pretext for euthanasia, and if my friend doesn't wake up, he'll be disconnected from life support in two weeks."

Raymond wiped away his tears and let out a heavy sigh.

"El not only saved our lives, but he also safely delivered a monstrous cargo to the shores of Canada. It is solely thanks to him that samples of the Alaskan ice were transported to a laboratory in Vancouver. Marian, alongside the finest scientists, is working tirelessly around the clock to dissect the bacterium. Let each of you wish her strength in the comments of this video; even if she doesn't read them, her resolve will undoubtedly grow. Consider it a kind of magic—the magic of thought. Sadly, you can't slay a Gorgon by the power of thought alone. This is what scientists dubbed 'the enigmatic bacterium.' Perhaps a thousand years ago it arrived on Earth hitched to a meteorite, freezing in its icy embrace. Or maybe Earth itself birthed it. Buried beneath the layers of time, the bacterium slumbered through the ages, only to awaken anew one fateful day. Science remains ignorant of its origins. However, one undeniable truth is that the cells of this novel organism are voracious; with the right nourishment, they can grow up to a meter in length and eighty micrometers in diameter—precisely the diameter of a strand of human hair."

Raymond ran his slender fingers through his hair, then brought a glistening, resilient thread toward the camera lens.

"This bacterium, within a matter of days under terrestrial circumstances, can evolve into a parasite. Resembling a nematode parasite, it can infiltrate beneath the skin, occupying nutrient pockets, substituting our hairs with itself. Then it seizes the entire organism, infiltrating the tissues even of the still-living brain. Remember the depictions of the Gorgon Medusa from mythology? Well, those aren't mere myths. Humans have encountered the immortal Gorgons. We're faced head-on with the ailment of Medusa. 'So how did ancient man triumph over an epidemic?' you might ask. We don't know! According to the myths, they beheaded the only mortal, apparently the first infected ... It was the Gorgon Medusa, and Hermes, the god of knowledge, slew her. They say knowledge is power. Perhaps Hermes, like Marian, was a talented scientist, or maybe he symbolized human enlightenment and the dissemination of information. Who knows? Maybe in the twenty-first century, Hermes is the internet itself. Well, if the deciphering of ancient myths turns out to be accurate, then I'll know that I haven't shared this top-secret information in vain."

3:13 AM

He paused for a moment, lost in thought, then swiftly resumed:

“This outer space bacterium swiftly annihilates its host, radically altering its DNA in an extraordinarily short time. That’s precisely why it’s of utmost importance that this research is undertaken by a nation that has never engaged in warfare throughout its existence. While the laboratory hasn’t yet tested it practically, theoretically the Gorgon could rapidly transform us into true monsters. Although for those who were monsters before encountering the bacterium, there’s nothing to fear ...”

Raymond’s expression softened into a melancholic smile.

“I’m confident, ladies and gentlemen, that you’ll take samples from the glacier. I’m sure that your first move will be to test the bacterium on a human in your secret bunkers. And I’m even certain that one fine day, you’ll watch this video ... The only thing I truly wished for was that at the very moment you’re concealing your inhumane experiments, the entire world would know about it. Do you hear me? Your crimes are already exposed! You’re universally despised. And that too is magic—the magic of emotions. Moreover, I intend to infiltrate your minds, your thoughts, and bring to the surface all your secrets, all your sinister plans—every dirty case you’ve gathered over the years, complete with names and juicy details. Be cautious, for now the hunt is on for you.”

Raymond winked playfully and took a sip of water. His hand no longer trembled.

"In this world, there are countless secret oracles. I'm personally acquainted with two—individuals coerced into working for the special agencies, cloaked in secrecy and power. Extraordinary people possessing knowledge, and sometimes abilities, so vast that people endowed with immense power eliminate them behind the government's back, erase them from the face of the Earth, for controlling such unique individuals becomes increasingly intricate. And since these people are essentially engaged in control, we become strategically unfavorable entities to them ... and they take us down. Ruthlessly, under cover of night, they dispatch cleanup squads into our homes."

He let out a heavy sigh, as if reliving the horrors of persecution once more.

"You know, I genuinely believe that a life free from the grip of penitentiary oversight is what we need for true happiness. I believe that I could speak to the world about impending catastrophes right here on this internet channel. And Ethan could just as easily report on the weather, climate change, and what nature communicates to humans. What the Earth herself is saying! Wouldn't you be intrigued? And Louis could shed light on the most enigmatic deaths in human history. Transmit messages from the beyond, vocalize those often crucial unsaid words before passing. Our world would be liberated from deceit! Then each of us would finally know the truth. And on the day it happens, we could decide for ourselves what to do with that truth. How to handle it. Perhaps if we knew what the planet was saying, we would stop polluting it. Or maybe, discovering that there's an inevitable reckoning after death, we would cease to transgress. Maybe firsthand truth has become a remedy for us—a remedy for impunity. A salvation from irresponsibility. Because before the planet, there's no commander. Before Earth, much like before death, we're all equal; we're all accountable for how we treat it. How we treat each other. How we treat our future and the future of our children."

The psychic fell silent in contemplation. He lowered his gaze, fumbling with something in his hands.

"And you know, my story would be incomplete without proof of my words." Raymond jotted something down on the table.

He lifted his gaze, then picked up a piece of paper where a sequence of eight digits had appeared.

"Here are the numbers for the balls that will drop this Friday during the National Canadian Lottery draw at 9:30 p.m. Eastern Time. Its jackpot stands at thirty million Canadian dollars, meaning it could be a day of great luck for many. Look for tickets with these numbers if you want to verify my words and, of course, if you wish to claim your winnings. This has been Raymond Lee—prophet, telepath, but for the most part just a mortal man!"

He turned off the camera, paced around the room, and uploaded the video to the internet. Thanks to trending tags, within a couple of minutes about ten people had already watched it. However, this was just the beginning. Now people were transmitting information about the shocking video, exposing the methods of the most influential global security agencies and discussing the impending apocalypse at the speed of thought, passing it from one to another.

By the time Raymond had descended to the ground floor of the Flay family nest and brewed himself a cup of coffee, his video had garnered a hundred thousand views. By evening, two more zeroes had been added to that number. He smiled, observing how the truth, like a forest fire, spread across the world, but something else troubled him much more.

He sat in silence during dinner, just as Benjamin Flay wouldn't stop talking.

"Haha," chuckled Marian's father triumphantly, replaying the video over and over. "But what if I bought a lottery ticket too?"

The well-groomed silver-haired man picked up a shot glass of Yukon Jack from the table. Thanks to his recent business trip to Miami, Benjamin's skin had taken on a pleasant bronzed hue. Now his impeccably pressed shirt (and this was at the end of the workday) shone brighter than the cloudless sky. It was odd, but if it weren't for those blue eyes, Benjamin could easily have passed for El Roberts' older brother.

"Did Marian call?"

"No, but she wrote that she'll swing by El's after the lab. That means it'll be late again. You know what, Raymond, you could talk to her. Maybe she'll listen to you."

3:13 AM

"Talk? About what?" Raymond squinted.

"The lab is full of experts—the best of the best. I'm sure they'll manage without her. After all, she's my daughter. The only relative I have left after Emma's passing. Even if we don't find the antidote, even if we can't stop the ice melting. Even if nothing changes and we're all doomed, the remaining nine years, I'd want to spend them with Marian, alive and well."

Raymond didn't reply. He finished his dinner and retreated to his room, taking a bottle of wine with him. The house was silent when at around half past twelve he heard the front door slam. Quiet footsteps crossed the spacious hall, and someone ascended the wide staircase. Marian was tired, and Raymond could hear that clearly. He got up from his chair and peeked into the corridor.

"Not sleeping?" Marian froze on the last step.

"Can't sleep." Raymond leaned against the door frame. "Your father is worried—thinks you don't belong in the lab. I agree ... I suppose El wouldn't want you messing with that plague either."

Marian only let out a deep sigh and cast her gaze downward.

"The living organisms are being worked on by machines; we don't physically touch them. We've isolated the DNA of the Gorgon." She raised her weary eyes, red capillaries visible within. "Now I'm working with it on the computer, far away from the sample refrigerators. And on top of everything, we're constantly under observation and often replaced by other scientists. The Gorgon gains strength near water. In the lab, away from the ocean, its power is diminished. Right now its influence is manageable ... although I'm also there because it was the thing that took El away from me. I can't forgive her for that. I'm obligated to find a compound that kills her. Simply obligated ..."

Marian's eyes reddened even more, and thin rivulets ran down her cheeks. Raymond averted his gaze and took a sip of wine.

"Did you go to see him? Did you talk to him?" she asked.

Raymond nodded ever so slightly.

"And what happened?"

"Still nothing."

"Where is his soul? Why isn't he coming back?"

"I don't know, Doc. No matter which way I approached him, in the room there's only his body. I truly don't know where El is."

"It's been three months!" Marian wiped her reddened cheeks dry. "Emma will never know her father ..."

"Did you decide to name her after your mother?"

"I never really knew her; she left too early ..."

Marian clenched her lips, shot a brief glance at Raymond, and quickly ascended the final step, disappearing down the dim corridor. Raymond watched her until she reached her door.

3:13 AM

She didn't look back. She vanished into her room, leaving him in solitude.

Raymond took another sip of wine, breathed in the pine scent of home deeply, and jumped up. He rushed past the staircase and approached one of the bedrooms. He leaned against the wooden door, breathing heavily. Every night he spoke to El. Every single goddamn night he taught him how to return. But for the past month, he had lacked the strength to rejoin his body and wake up.

***

"Take care of her." El sat on the edge of the bed, where his frail body lay motionless, connected to machines. Raymond didn't respond. He had sat in that chair all night—where Marian sat every evening.

"I can't get out of this, my friend. I feel like I'm losing my connection to this world."

"El," Raymond began excitedly, "there's something I need to tell you—"

"No need." El cut him off. "I've found peace. Perhaps only you know the extent of my suffering. How I flew above her, inhaling her powdery scent, touching her hair, embracing her in my dreams. But it's all futile. No matter how much I yearn to return, I can't. It seems that's not within my control."

"Yours, El, yours! You've resigned yourself to this too soon."

"Too soon." He smiled sadly. "You never tell me how much time has passed. I've asked you again and again. And yesterday the doctors let it slip right in my room. Three months ... Three long months."

"You need to ignite a desire to live, then everything will work out—"

"No," El interrupted. "Enough tormenting everyone, and I've been tormented enough. I've said it: take care of her. Convey my dying wish—let her love the living, not the dead."

No response came. El turned around—the chair was empty.

He lay on the bed, adjusting his body into a simple posture. He tried to sense a tingling in his fingers but felt nothing. He attempted to recall the medicated scent that had once filled the room, but it eluded his memory completely. Even the tickle in his nose, as if on the verge of sneezing, was out of reach. To put it bluntly, he felt absolutely nothing! He would have closed his eyes and fallen asleep forever, but he couldn't even do that. Gray shadows filled the ceiling, stretching toward him, ready to consume him into eternity. And for the first time, El didn't resist.

He decided to die with the thought of Marian. He recalled her scent, the softness of her hair, and her body arching in ecstasy. Rapshmir's yacht had intoxicated her and rocked El's senses. His past indiscretions paled in comparison to possessing this woman. He had lived far too long to repeat that night. And now he was dying so that Marian could enjoy love with someone else.

3:13 AM

Suddenly a children's song began to play in his mind. He listened closely—it was the same song his mother used to sing to him. Yet now the voice sounded different—thin, childlike.

El lifted his head—there was a little girl of around five years old by the monitors. A floral-patterned headband adorned her light hair, and her denim jumpsuit clearly seemed bought for growth. The child curiously inspected El's life support devices.

"Hey! Who let you in here?"

The girl traced her small finger along the green zigzag of the heart rate indicators, paying no attention to the question.

El propped himself up in a sitting position. "Hey, I'm talking to you. Step away from the machines!"

"And what if I don't?" She finally spoke.

"Then you might break something, and I'll definitely die."

"Weren't you planning on dying anyway?" She showed no fear and, it seemed, had no intention of leaving.

"Hmm." El frowned. "What's your name?"

"Emma." The girl turned her head and looked at him with huge brown eyes.

He flinched at that gaze. Emma had his eyes, a slightly upturned nose, and Marian's thin lips.

"Where are your parents?" he managed to whisper.

"Mom's at home."

"And your dad?"

"Somewhere around here."

An overwhelming bitterness swept over El. He distinctly felt a sharp pang in his heart. Then a strong pain bloomed in his chest. It expanded, soon paralyzing his entire body. Alarms blared frantically from the sensors. El felt the weight growing. And the next moment he distinctly heard—heard with his own ears—the on-duty doctor bursting into the room, accompanied by the nursing staff.

3:13 AM

Chapter 25

Raymond burst through the glass doors, which had barely begun to open before him.

“Can I help you?” called the attractive young woman at the reception desk.

“To Dr. Flay! Marian Flay!” gasped Raymond.

“Dr. Flay is in the restricted area.” Her almond-shaped eyes widened. “You can’t go in there!”

“But it’s urgent! You have no idea how urgent it is!”

“Please go to the waiting room.” She pointed to the next set of glass doors. “We’ll inform her of your visit.”

Raymond entered the brightly lit room and slumped onto a couch.

“Coffee?” A lovely woman with the name Jenny on her badge appeared.

“Thank you.” Raymond nodded. “Tell her that El has woken up.”

“What? I’m sorry?”

“Tell Marian Flay that El Roberts has woken up!”

Jenny paused, then vanished behind the glass walls of the Vancouver Viral–Bacterial Research Center. Raymond waited patiently until suddenly the door swung open and Marian rushed into the room. She threw herself onto him—tears of joy soaked his shoulder. She sniffled and laughed.

"He woke up," Raymond repeated. "Can you believe it? He woke up!"

Marian looked at him with eyes brimming with happiness. Raymond pulled something from his pocket and tossed it into the air. A pink pearl, drop-shaped, landed in Marian's palm.

"What's this?" she croaked.

"A gift for Emma." Raymond squeezed her fingers into a fist. "She brought El back. She pulled him out."

Long ago, as a young girl, Marian had experienced this moment in a dream. Back then, she didn't know the true reason for her happiness, didn't even suspect the true recipient of this exquisite gift. How much we don't know, gazing inadvertently into our future. And when it seems everything is so obvious, still our future doesn't belong to us in the present. We never fully understand it from the past, even if we manage to catch a glimpse.

"I saw your video." Marian tucked the pearl into her uniform pocket. "Impressive."

"Thank you." Raymond smiled.

"So you're not afraid of them anymore?"

3:13 AM

"I'm tired of being afraid, Marian. People are stronger than any organization when they're together—when they believe in their strength. Just like a psychic is nothing without faith in his abilities."

"So you've chosen the path of war?"

"I've chosen the path of truth."

Behind the panoramic window, as if breaching defenses, people poured in armed with cameras.

"Truth is exceptionally popular these days." Marian frowned, observing the crowds of journalists and curious onlookers.

"Let's call it the price we pay." Raymond took her hand and led her out of the room. "I'm heading to El."

"Then try to shake them off." Marian gestured toward the paparazzi.

She headed to the laboratory. Raymond watched her for a few more seconds, then suddenly called out, "Marian?"

She turned.

"How's it going?"

She sighed deeply, glanced at the marble floor, and lifted her gray eyes to Raymond again. "We still have nothing."

"What? Nothing at all?"

"Absolutely nothing. The gods truly are immortal."

Raymond nodded in desperation and walked decisively out of the building. Amid the relentless cries of the crowd, he hopped into a taxi and sped away through the vibrant streets of Vancouver. By the end of summer, many trees had turned yellow, the weather was warm, and the bright sun blinded his eyes.

The artificially blue twilight of the Atlantic Ocean washed over him with melancholy. Gazing at the green-hued mountain peaks surrounding the rugged coastal landscape, Raymond inhaled the coolness of the Canadian evening. Now he didn't just have a premonition; now he knew for sure—the cure wouldn't be found. And soon even the most peaceful shores would be plagued by chaos and devastation. Inevitably it would come.

Just a minute ago the warm light had been glaring in his eyes. Raymond didn't ever want to witness firsthand all the images that surfaced in his thoughts. He didn't want to see the madness in people's eyes. He didn't want to see the world descend into insanity in just one day.

Bumping into the balding Aldridge in the corridor, Raymond entered El's room.

"This is ... What was he doing here?"

El tensed but soon relaxed his stern expression and gave a faint nod. "Well, of course you managed to recognize him. He came for negotiations."

3:13 AM

"Negotiations?" Raymond chuckled. "Too late for that! There can be no negotiations."

El silently observed the young man as he paced around the room, his tension thinly veiled. "Today's the lottery," he said slyly as Raymond finally settled into a chair. "They'll swap the numbers."

"But doesn't the Canadian government—"

"Everything's arranged," El interrupted. "No one wants these risks; no one desires chaos and loss of control over society."

"But what if I announce new numbers?"

"They'll change them again."

"So they're turning me into a fool?"

"I, Marian, and the entire government are aware of who you are. That's precisely why the truth won't be allowed to appear as truth, understand?" El sighed heavily. "Tell me, didn't you foresee this? Weren't you prepared for this?"

Raymond was silent. His usually pale face reddened, and his temples began to throb. "Will they let me leave?"

"You're safe here. Why fly somewhere?"

"Because I want to go home!" Raymond finally lifted his eyes, burning with anger.

"To New York?"

"To Koh An."

"Raymond, my advice to you is not to cross the Canadian border. At least not now." El looked genuinely concerned. "I'm telling you this as a friend."

"I can't stay here. Can't be among people. I need emptiness, with no one around, do you understand?"

El didn't reply. He simply covered his face with his hands. The yellowish silicone tube still protruded from his swollen vein, and the zigzag on the monitor sped up. "Listen ..." he began on an exhale.

"There's nothing to say, El. I've done my part of the deal. Now it's up to you."

"I'm no longer part of the department. I'm just a mediator between them and you."

"I know, El. I know ..."

***

Raymond struggled to fall asleep. He tossed and turned in the creaky bed, in a peculiar state. He felt unwell, as if he had caught the flu. His stomach churned, and so did his legs. His head was heavy as lead, yet, contrary to its weight, it remained devoid of thought. His eyes burned, and with each new breath, his chest felt more constricted.

"Don't close yourself off!" Margot used to shout, bringing a glass with a strange liquid to his parched lips.

"I can't anymore," Raymond moaned.

3:13 AM

"No one asked you to," the unnaturally thin girl with multicolored dreads growled. "It's a gift! You can't refuse it! Drink!"

Just yesterday his roommate had called all their acquaintances in search of a doctor or at least someone who worked in a hospital. Medical insurance in New York was just a dream for an ordinary waiter. Margot came to the rescue. She had never been a doctor, but Raymond was not indifferent to her. Not indifferent from their first meeting. He didn't reciprocate, but now this Buddhist polyglot had the unique opportunity to take care of a patient and practice all the dubious knowledge she had acquired in a year of living in Goa. Raymond resisted desperately, though he realized that Margot had somehow seen through him. Yes, he had shut himself off. Forbade himself to feel and see. What the girl called a gift was destroying his life, and when he locked it inside, it destroyed his body.

The final straw was the incident in the restaurant. On that rainy evening, there weren't many customers.

Edward burst in through the doors and yelled loudly, "Someone bring this guy in a coat an espresso!"

Edward was the best of the best and wouldn't work without tips, but no one would pay more than the regular price for a cup of coffee. Raymond clicked his tongue disapprovingly, wiped a tiny cup, filled it with Italian Lavazza from a narrow coffee machine, adorned the saucer with two chocolate candies in golden foil, and, with a practiced shoulder movement, opened the door. In the far corner of the half-empty restaurant, a man was sitting. His face was concealed by a dense shadow, and only the glint of ash from a puff of smoke indicated his living presence. Although living—was it?

Raymond approached. "Your coffee." He placed the order in front of the guest and hesitantly raised his eyes.

The cigarette lit up again, illuminating grotesque burn scars. Raymond only saw half of his face, but it was enough. The guest was practically devoid of skin, and what was left of it had twisted into intricate knots on his sunken cheeks. The desiccated lips released smoke, revealing holes chewed by something, as if worms had punctured the entire lower part of his face. Raymond recoiled, feeling the gaze of eyes devoid of eyelids.

"Raymond! That snob seriously lost it!" Edward flew over to the pale young man huddled in the corner of the kitchen. "What—didn't you serve him?"

"I ... I did ..." Raymond jumped from his spot and dashed into the hall, soon finding the distant corner empty. A cup of coffee sat cooling on the table. "Hey! Where did he go? Did he change places?"

"Yeah, who? What are you staring at?"

"Over there in the corner, the guy in the coat was sitting ..."

"Go get some rest! That table's been vacant all day!"

3:13 AM

Raymond felt a coldness, as if someone had splashed icy water in his face. The next morning he encountered the fire department in the restaurant. Two burly men with smoke detectors were bustling around the ventilation above the very table where the stranger had been sitting just the previous day.

“Raymond! Take this to the inspectors.” The chef greeted him from the doorway, handing over a tray with cups and a couple of sandwiches.

“Good morning,” Raymond muttered shyly.

“Morning, son!” One of the inspectors grinned, rubbing his hands.

“Is there something wrong with the restaurant?”

“Can’t you feel it yourself, kid?”

“Feel what?” Raymond choked.

“The smell,” the other explained, taking a sip of his coffee.

Suddenly a bitter stench reached him, suffocating his lungs. His throat constricted sharply, and he took a step back. “Where is it coming from?”

“We’re just trying to figure that out. A house at the end of the block was on fire last night, but how did this smoke end up here?”

“Did he survive?” Raymond asked in disbelief.

“Who? Do you know something?” The inspectors exchanged glances.

“The man who was burned.”

“Mr. Borgo died in the hospital yesterday evening. The press hasn’t been informed yet. Are you a relative?”

“No, no … I …” Raymond stammered, unable to find an answer.

He returned to the kitchen and approached the chef. “Hey, Lou, who is Mr. Borgo?” he exclaimed in disbelief.

The tanned Frenchman turned slowly. “He used to be the owner of this restaurant. When he started, this place was the best bakery in all of Manhattan.”

Fifteen years ago, Raymond had shut himself off. Shut himself off just like he was doing now. He no longer wanted to see the dead and unravel their post mortem mysteries. He wanted to belong wholly and completely to the world of the living.

Back then, he couldn’t do it. And he couldn’t do it today either. The breakdown only stopped when Raymond, in a daze, spotted a figure by the bed.

He sat up, his elbows trembling. He was too weak to dispel the mirage. The spirit world had once again triumphed over him.

“Hey,” he called out to the deceased.

The figure stood motionless, blending into the darkness.

3:13 AM

"Hey, I'm talking to you! How can we kill you?"

The figure remained silent, observing the room's owner. Raymond reached for the nightstand and switched on the bedside lamp. The apparition dissolved into the electric light, and the clock on the nightstand froze at 3:13 a.m. Raymond furrowed his brow and scanned the room suspiciously. He sensed a presence but couldn't detect it.

He rested his feet on the soft carpet and stood up, remembering that the bathroom had been locked since last evening. But now he stood before an open door, gazing into the black unknown.

Whatever was hiding in there terrified Raymond. Fear immediately spread through his body, paralyzing his movements. He took a step, pressed against the bed, and rushed to the light switch. The yellow tiles of the bathroom were illuminated even more brightly. Raymond inspected the corners and reached for the shower curtain. The rings clicked evenly, revealing the damp surface of the empty shower stall. He exhaled, but the act didn't alleviate the tension. He felt it on his skin—the dead hadn't left. The spirit was still here, perhaps right behind him.

His breathing grew deeper, and a stream of white vapor escaped from his mouth. The warm room transformed into a frozen necropolis within seconds. A frigid wave washed over him from head to toe as he finally turned around.

Now he was facing a nearly decomposed corpse. The familiar clouded eyes were surrounded by black bruises; the nose protruded from sagging flesh, a grotesque lump of cartilage. Strands of hair, dislodged, hung in bloody clumps as the monstrosity raised its cyanotic hands to its face. Its gnawed fingers plunged into its torn mouth and with two jerks, it ripped off its lower jaw. A parasite-eaten tongue dangled from its sinewy neck.

Raymond stepped back, his hands clammy as he found the cold edge of the sink and clung to it. He had seen many corpses in his lifetime, but this one frightened him more than any other. It evoked a genuine terror within him, for this dead body was none other than Raymond Lee himself.

Nothing is more repulsive than the stench of decaying human flesh. Nothing can make us suffer more than the sight of a tortured body. And even all of this pales in comparison to witnessing our own lifeless form. The fear of death is our utmost dread. It's encoded within us by evolution, safeguarding us from untimely demise and guiding us to the threshold of old age. Yet it's also what prevents us from peacefully savoring our allotted time. Each of us inevitably ends up in the garden of silence but secretly each of us hopes, for some reason, that we alone are endowed with immortality. That very immortality reserved only for gods. Gods the size of a grain of sand.

Their biomass surpasses the combined mass of all plants and animals, humans included. They constitute thirty-nine trillion cells in our own bodies, whereas the human body itself is composed of merely thirty trillion cells. And despite such infiltration, they don't hesitate to claim the lives of over two million people annually.

Who are the gods if not them? Bacteria! The ones from which life on Earth commenced and quite possibly the ones with whom this life will conclude.

***

"Are you sure about leaving?" Marian whispered, offering breakfast.

"I ..." He hesitated to say it aloud. "I saw myself dead, Marian. Nothing's changed; we'll all die in nine years. And if that's the case, I want to spend my remaining time at home on my island."

"But if they start pursuing you again?"

"Yeah, well, they will," he said with a sad smile. "Likely or not, I'm just a clown on YouTube to everyone!"

"Raymond!" Marian demanded a more reasonable explanation.

"El made a deal," he confessed. "They're letting me go home."

"You can always come back here, you know." She placed her hand on his.

Raymond froze, tightened his pale grip, and said softly, "Don't wait for the moment of infection. When El gets better and the kid grows up, come to me. Koh An is an island; we'll last longer there."

Marian nodded desperately. She lowered her gaze, unable to hide her tears.

“So I’m not saying goodbye ...” Raymond cast his gaze down.

Marian shook her head and wiped her cheeks dry. They finished breakfast in silence, pondering the inevitable.

A car pulled up to the house, and Raymond, slinging his beloved black bag over his shoulder, walked out into the yard. Marian had promised not to say goodbye but couldn’t resist following him outside. She raised her hand in the air, waving to the orange taxi. Raymond turned around. A strange unease flashed in his gaze, but he managed to smile. He was happy to return to the place he had been forced to flee so hastily.

The car disappeared behind the high fence. The street emptied. Marian cradled her morning tea and listened to the birds chirping. Swift clouds raced across the blue sky, driven by the easterly wind, while yellow leaves were plucked by rare golden rain and fell onto the stone-paved courtyard. A minute later, a deafening bang echoed. Marian dropped her mug, bent over, and recoiled toward the door. Birds fled from the treetops, and a cloud of black smoke rose above the forest.

“Oh God, oh God, oh God ...” Marian muttered, approaching the road.

She didn’t want to see it, yet when she finally saw the burning car in the distance, she collapsed in pain—both physical and emotional. She didn’t want to believe her eyes, but the taxi in which Raymond had just ridden had exploded.

3:13 AM

Chapter 26

"Hello?"

"Good evening!"

Recognizing the voice, Aldridge stopped swaying in his chair. "Good." He stood up and walked to the dark window.

"Have you finished the forensic analysis?"

"Yes, quite ..." The pathologist wiped his forehead with his fingers.

"Is it him?"

"Yes, the samples belong to Raymond Lee."

"Are you sure?"

Aldridge moved away from the window and, leaning on the table, froze over the microscope. "The materials they gave me fit in a shoebox. And all of this belongs to him," he concluded firmly.

"Thank you. I'll be waiting for a detailed report from you. Good night."

"Good night." Aldridge hung up the phone, took a trembling hand out of his pocket, and wiped his forehead with a handkerchief.

***

Marian wrestled with insomnia. The explosion on the road had dissolved not only Raymond Lee but also the peaceful life of the doctor. Moreover, her stomach had been steadily growing, causing all sorts of discomfort, from lower back pain to relentless heartburn.

El had long been sleeping, and Marian, armed with a somber mystical detective novel set in Ireland, stared at the cramped lines of text. Suddenly her gaze was drawn to the armchair by the window. She raised her eyes and froze, staring at the white velour. The sheer curtains danced in the night breeze, enlivening the space, but Marian felt something more. She could have sworn that someone was sitting in the armchair. Someone invisible yet so familiar to her and so dear.

"Raymond ..." she whispered.

Marian vividly remembered these sensations—the invisible presence of Mr. Lee. Her delicate fingers slackened, and she dropped the book. It slid down the blanket and fell to the floor. El jerked awake and opened his eyes.

"What's happened?" He frowned, looking at his wife.

"Raymond ... Raymond came to visit us."

***

"Mr. Johnson, where did you say you lost your tooth?"

"Iving o the acht ..."

"I'm sorry?"

3:13 AM

"I was diving off the yacht!"

"Hmm," the doctor pondered, palpating the patient's gums. "By God, it feels as if it was very neatly pulled out."

"Ih had een obly for ile ..."

"Excuse me?"

"It had been wobbly for a while," Liam Johnson admitted, opening his mouth again.

"Well then! Let's put in a new one!" One of Phuket's finest dentists grinned.

At the moment when Liam left the private clinic, he couldn't feel his lower jaw. It seemed that if he jumped without holding on to it, it would simply detach and fall onto the yacht's floor. He revved the engine and, skirting the jutting cape, flew over the azure ocean. Gray clouds amassed on the horizon—a rare moment when the sky turned darker than the shore, as if the world had turned upside down.

He darted between the towering hills of the islands and emerged onto open waters. He loved these places, adored the intricate landscapes of the Andaman Sea.

Docking the pristine white yacht at a short wooden pier, Liam stepped ashore. He sprinted along a winding path to the beach, kicked off his tennis shoes, and stepped onto the soft sand. A fragrant blend of curry and simmering vegetables wafted across the bay.

He reached the shore just as the tide was receding and settled into a woven chair. He touched his jaw—sensation was slowly, steadily returning.

A tanned Thai man burst out of the kitchen and hurried over to the island's owner. "Dinner, Mr. Johnson?"

"No, not just yet." Liam shook his head. "I'll start with some chilled wine."

"Yes, sir." Sunan hastened back to the kitchen.

The evening jungles were drenched in excessive moisture, each new wave of the tide swallowing the pristine white beach. Beyond the islands, a long motorboat with a vibrant canopy emerged and approached the shore. Sunan, spotting the guests, rolled up his trousers and, lifting his legs high, dashed across the shallows. Liam Johnson remained motionless, squinting as he watched the scene unfold.

The visitor said something to Sunan, who nodded in response.

"What's up?" Liam asked casually as Sunan returned to the shore.

"They were looking for someone named Mr. Lee," the servant said.

"Why?"

"A letter arrived for him at the Phuket post office. The address: this island. But I told them that Liam Johnson lives here; we don't know any Lee."

3:13 AM

"You did the right thing," the island's owner affirmed.

Liam Johnson stared into the gentle haze that, as usual, veiled the equatorial twilight. Soon enough, a foggy bottle of Australian white wine materialized on his table. The light, slightly tangy liquid spread through his body with the first sip, soothing him and chasing away his worries.

Who could be writing him letters? Moreover, sending them to this island? Clearly only someone who had a hunch about his miraculous rescue could do so, but surely not someone who knew him for certain.

It wouldn't be accurate to say that Liam was tormented by questions, but the following morning, right after breakfast, he handed Sunan a handful of bills and dispatched him to Phuket. Sunan sailed on Mr. Johnson's yacht to Ko Phi Phi, then took a scheduled catamaran to Patong and upon arrival managed to catch a minibus to Phuket. The servant disembarked at the central square, walked a few blocks, and hailed a young lad. He asked him to retrieve a letter addressed to Mr. Lee from the post office, generously compensating him. The lad, in turn, rewarded the postal worker, and in less than five minutes the letter was in Sunan's hands.

The Thai man gave his shirt to a street beggar and, strolling through the city, hopped into a passing rickshaw on the fly. Not five hours passed before he was back on the island.

"Your letter!" he exclaimed.

"Thanks." Liam hastily snatched the envelope, then hesitated. "Thanks, but it's not mine ..."

Sunan flashed a sly smile and hurried off, taking an empty tray from the table.

Liam entered his bungalow and pressed the button on the coffee machine. It spat into the grate and clattered loudly. The envelope bore the name of the city Vancouver, and Mr. Johnson paused for a moment before tearing it open.

Raymond, you can fool the entire world with your death, but not me!

Such a bold beginning belonged to Marian, and it brought a smile to Liam's face. He filled a bowl-like mug with hot coffee and stepped out onto the veranda.

Storm clouds hung over the island, and it wouldn't be long before raindrops started pattering on the surface of the blue pool. Mr. Johnson inhaled the pleasant scent of mango trees, took a sip of his hot drink, and reopened the letter.

If you haven't shown up yet, that means you have no internet or television. I'd like to inform you that after the video you made last summer, others have emerged. Eight more psychics who once worked for the government have spilled the department's methods, intimidation, and attempted purges, as well as the dire predictions that went unnoticed. They've sparked independent investigations—bloggers and journalists tracked down Ethan in Alaska, and California residents unearthed Rapshmir.

3:13 AM

Everything went as you wanted—the truth began to spill, and the common folk started to learn of it. The planet has become a canvas for countless demonstrations; citizens of all countries are demanding their governments admit to the existence of the micromonster that will soon bring the world to ruin. Yes, we had to admit that the bacterium was found, but there's no cure for it. Then a new wave swept across the internet. Bloggers, in unison, began to talk about the need to unite oracles to battle the Medusa.

You might say let them gather, let them search. But the truth is, Raymond, that you remain the strongest of them all. Without you, this venture is futile. To combat the impending evil, twelve magicians must unite, and the thirteenth must be resurrected ... just like in the holy scripture known throughout the world.

I'm not asking you to leave Koh An; I'm only asking you to connect to the internet. And who knows, maybe then, as in the ancient myth, the god of knowledge and foresight will once again triumph over the immortal monsters!

Liam lowered the letter. The unrelenting rain tapped against the broad palm leaves. The pool rippled, and a hunched silhouette flickered in the palm groves. He still saw them. The deceased came, incessantly reminding him of their presence. He wasn't afraid to see them, but he feared seeing children among them one day.

Who knows? Perhaps the secret of salvation lies within a child's body, Liam mused.

He hastened back to his bungalow, retrieved a laptop from the closet, and wiped off the dust. The psychic returned to the veranda and lifted the silvery lid.

On the pool's surface appeared a bloated corpse, swollen from putrefaction gases. Liam glanced at it and returned his gaze to the now-lightened screen.

"Damn, hardly catches anything in a storm," he grumbled.

Yet even from what he managed to glimpse, it was clear that the world had changed. National and private lottery companies had crumbled; crowds of people worldwide were taking to the streets demanding the secrets of secretive organizations be unveiled. "No more secrets," their slogans declared. "We're not in the Middle Ages anymore!" "We inhabit this planet, and we want the truth." "What did Raymond Lee die for?" "What will happen in nine years?" "Who will survive if we die?" "Have you already begun human trials?" "Are you preparing shuttles to the moon?" People of all ages, faiths, and nationalities. Of all wealth and education levels. Now something greater than just the inhabitance of our planet united them all.

The questions were indeed numerous, yet nobody was in a hurry to answer them. The overflowing Manhattan, brimming with protesters, captured Liam's attention completely, and he didn't even notice that the corpses had invaded his garden. For the first time in his life, the world of the living interested Raymond Lee far more than the world of the dead. Hope sparkled in his gaze. It seemed that right now, even while seeing the inevitable time ahead, he no longer floated along the currents of destiny. Today, he knew for sure that he was not only capable of glimpsing the future but also of changing it.

3:13 AM

HOIA BACIU: WOODS OF HORROR

Anton embarks on a road trip with his university friends, traveling from Minsk through Ukraine and Romania straight to a resort town in Bulgaria. After sunset, they leave the border road of Ukraine and enter Transylvania. Here the weather deteriorates, the road becomes slippery, and fog creeps onto the path. Narrowly avoiding an accident, the group suddenly comes across a wrecked car. They call for rescue services, torn by doubt about what to do next. Tolya leaves the vehicle to provide first aid, while Galia, sensing danger, succumbs to hysteria from terrifying visions. They know nothing about the passengers of the mysterious car, but they know even less about the forest where they've stopped. Hoia Baciu is aptly dubbed the Bermuda Triangle of Transylvania. Those who venture into these woods lose track of time and feel an overwhelming sensation of being under constant surveillance by unseen entities. Some of these brave souls have never come back.

Introduction

The novel *Hoia-Baciu: Woods of Horror* was pieced together over the course of six long months. It draws equally from the author's imagination and the stories of those who have faced death head-on. At the heart of the gripping plot are the accounts of individuals who have ventured beyond reality and managed to convey their experiences to a grateful listener. As a writer, I had to grapple with truly shocking revelations, realizing that they were probably not mere products of the storyteller's vivid imagination. Twice I seriously considered abandoning the project altogether—retelling things that defied any scientific explanation proved immensely difficult. Yet even when I stepped away from working on the novel, I felt the story continue to live within me, constantly seeking release. Today, as I penned the final line, I felt an unparalleled sense of relief. I set my ghost ship adrift, laden with a weighty, at times truly terrifying, cargo. The narrative is told from a male perspective, though the author is female. Purposefully choosing this challenging path, I embedded parts of real-life stories in the book, unwilling to alter a single letter.

The characters and names in the book are fictional; any resemblances to real individuals are purely coincidental.

3:13 AM

Chapter 1

I heard the pop of a beer bottle and someone greedily gulping down half of it in one go. Turning to the mirror, I caught sight of Tolya. His sparse, light beard still had foam clinging to it, which he didn't seem eager to wipe away.

"Tolya, that's just plain rude!" I snapped.

He had promised to take over right after midnight. Yet here he was drinking beer and grinning like a Cheshire cat, not bothering to hide his satisfaction as he looked at me with those sleepy, translucent eyes.

I couldn't fathom how this guy managed to be top of the class. It felt like some kind of magic trick. This long-haired hipster with not a gram of responsibility was acing all his exams. Did I envy him? Oh, you bet! Not only was he devilishly good-looking but he also seemed to get everything he wanted out of life. Tolya was always the opposite of me. I knew the hard work it took to have a good life and how you couldn't afford to let your guard down for a second. How did he manage to drink beer in the evening and ace all his exams the next morning? I had no clue. He didn't come across as nerdy or gifted. Every single professor looked wary as Kurt Cobain reincarnated walked into the classroom for the first time. But as soon as he opened his mouth, brilliant remarks poured out, showcasing his outstanding knowledge of the subject.

I remember we had this one professor with a strong bias against the younger generation. We dreaded his exams, let alone his quizzes. I came out relieved with a C; I didn't have to retake the class or face that demon in human skin again. Meanwhile Tolya had an A.

"How?" I fumed.

"How what?" He didn't get it.

"How did you manage that again?"

"Dude, you're speaking in riddles. Be clearer." He looked puzzled. This guy didn't even realize I was talking about grades!

"Bro, how did you get an A?"

He grinned sheepishly, revealing his devious dimples.

"Did you sell your soul to him? Come clean!" I chuckled.

"You mean about the grades? That's not all that important." He shrugged.

"What is important, then?" I pressed.

I was genuinely intrigued by what really mattered to someone who seemed to have it all figured out in life. He slipped his hands into the pockets of his jeans, which, annoyingly, fit him perfectly. Shrugging, he rolled his expressive blue eyes to the ceiling and replied, "I don't know, man, what's really important in this life. But it sure as hell isn't grades."

3:13 AM

To buy that car, I had worked weekends on a construction site for two years straight. I wasn't particularly fond of manual labor, but it could propel me towards realizing my dream. During those years, I hardly hung out with my friends, went to the cinema, or got much sleep. There was this one time when the crew was celebrating the foreman's birthday on a Friday, and to meet the Saturday quota and stay within regulations, I had to spend the entire day hauling heavy sandbags by myself. I earned a hernia that day, which was nagging me particularly annoyingly that evening. It was a dull pain across my entire lower back that radiated down my left leg. It would have been tough dealing with a manual transmission. Luckily my iron steed was equipped with cruise control, so on the highway I didn't even use the pedals. Mom had this great ointment for back pain—it quickly relieved any tension in the spine and smelled pleasantly of pine. However, I was in such a rush that I'd forgotten it.

My mother. She always scolded me as she rubbed the fragrant mixture on my skin. "You're wearing yourself out too soon! What's the hurry? You can't earn all the money in the world."

Well, yes. My parents never rushed, which meant I had to make up for lost time now. Our one-plus-one apartment had long forgotten what renovations were, and the wallpaper had probably witnessed the fall of regimes. Right up until college I slept on a kiddie couch, propping my feet up on a chair borrowed from the living room set. Every time I settled into that makeshift contraption, thoughts of my friends' stylish rooms depressed me. I could never invite anyone here ... So with my very first paycheck from the construction site, I took out a loan for a big plush yellow couch. I often found my mother on it; she'd come home from work and lie down to rest there. But my father never once sat on it. That couch seemed only to infuriate and irritate him. Perhaps it was too bold a color for his taste.

"Couldn't you have bought something less flashy?" he grumbled.

"I need something to sleep on! Or did you think I'd stay a teenager forever, not needing a bigger bed?"

"Your mom and I make as much as we can. Your grandfather slept in a damp trench at your age!"

"That's exactly why he's not around anymore!"

I never regretted the past. Everything in my life followed a meticulously crafted plan that inevitably led me down the path to success.

The landscape shifted. Mountains surrounded us. The temperature outside was dropping rapidly, and the road began to twist smoothly. The evergreen forest loomed over us, and through its canopy, the snowy peaks of the mountains gleamed. I turned on the seat warmers and, once again, reminded everyone to buckle up.

I was probably the only one among us who, every time they got into the car, buckled up and remained completely sober. There were two fake clicks from the back seat. Well, I couldn't care less about those two, but because of Zhenya, I could get fined. I asked her again to use the seatbelt, since the car was equipped with it. In response, she just pursed her lips and stared out of the window. Similar behavior had caused our arguments before. The car beeped desperately for twenty seconds, futilely trying to reason with this beautiful but stubborn girl but, getting absolutely no reaction, falling silent just like me. But today, setting off on a long journey, I demanded a promise from her to ride buckled up, and that was my little victory. But just an hour ago, while exchanging chips and beer with Galia, Zhenya had sighed demonstratively, showing how the hated seatbelt tightened around her fragile body. Not seeing any understanding in my eyes, she unbuckled again. I turned away, tired of this endless war.

Striving to cool down, I glanced at the cold peaks of the mountains. Against the dark sky they glowed, their whiteness like lanterns. This contrast mesmerized me. I wanted to be there, at the very top, and look at this world from above, free as a bird, far from all the worries and the heavy burden of responsibilities.

The dense forest began to thin out, interspersed with clearings and small fields. We had escaped the noisy city for the holidays. Spring was already in full bloom there, but here it seemed like nature had not yet awakened. The fields were darkened by last year's crushed grass and bare bushes. Beside the road, remnants of dirty snowdrifts were still visible. The windows began to fog up, making it harder to see the road. Of course, it was precisely at this moment that Zhenya and Galia felt a strong urge to tickle each other.

"Zhenya, stop fidgeting and buckle up. I can barely see the road," I said, my frustration rising.

"Why do you even need to see it? There's no one on it," she retorted.

"There are turns and trees next to it!" I exclaimed. "And at the end of the day, you promised ..."

Zhenya, essentially, was backwards all the time, and I knew perfectly well why. When I had suggested we go on a trip, she had mentioned she was flying to Italy with her parents. But upon learning that Tolya was joining me, her plans had immediately changed. Clearly she was interested in him. Why use "interested" instead of "had feelings"? Because Zhenya and genuine feelings had nothing in common—that is to say, they were very distant from each other.

Zhenya, as far as I remember her, was always a very beautiful and vibrant girl with a mass of curly red hair and slanted gray eyes. She achieved a lot, but she always wanted to achieve even more, and in that, we were very alike. Last year she had earned the title of Miss University and was sent to the city competition. From an ordinary cheerful student, in just days she transformed into the epitome of kindness, morality, and prudence. A sweet smile never left her face; she was considerate and modest, gracefully playing the role of the best of the best. For a long three months she lived in the future, where she won the love of the whole of Minsk and became the embodiment of unearthly beauty. But by a twist of fate she didn't even make it to the top ten, and it completely crushed her. Only thanks to me did she emerge from her prolonged depression and return to her studies. That incident became my chance to win such a luxurious girl and become her boyfriend. Under no other circumstances would fate have presented me with such a gift. However, now, without a trace of guilt, she flirted shamelessly with my best friend. The only remaining mystery for me, and maybe even for her, was whether he truly evoked feelings in her or if she was simply trying once again to be the best and conquer the unconquerable.

I recalled the silent scene of her emotions as we drove to pick up my friend, who had suddenly announced that he wouldn't be alone. She incessantly twisted the rings on her slender fingers the whole way to Tolya's house. And when Galia was introduced to us, Zhenya couldn't take her eyes off her. But soon suspicion turned into unbridled joy, and they quickly became friends. This girl was vastly different from the redheaded model. Galia's slender body in loose overalls and boyfriend jeans looked entirely adolescent. A gray hoodie covered her rather short haircut, and her nearly transparent eyebrows vividly hinted that Galia had recently undergone chemotherapy. The shape of her pale lips was graceful and quite attractive, but I couldn't remember the color of her eyes upon first meeting. I always felt awkward looking sick people in the eye. Inside, for some reason, a false sense of guilt arose, as if I should be the one suffering instead of them. Zhenya, apparently, didn't suffer from such complexes and conversed with Galia on equal terms.

Well, *equal*! It's a strange word. They could never truly be equal—not even close to resembling each other in any way. But let's start from the beginning.

I think Galia's appearance instilled in Zhenya a confidence that she simply wasn't Tolya's type. They were probably just friends or even relatives. This question bothered me the least, although their extremely friendly relationship was hard to miss. They didn't exchange kisses, didn't embrace with romantic fervor. Only occasionally did Tolya gently place his hand on Galia's fragile shoulder.

To be honest, I wasn't even particularly bothered by my girlfriend's hyperactive behavior toward those sitting in the back. It had happened before, and I knew it was all about her desire to showcase herself to society, although initially I was genuinely puzzled by it.

One day Zhenya was invited to perform on the stage of our uni theater. She was thrilled with the offer and soon discovered the actress within herself. I can't say she nailed every role, but the ones she truly felt, she excelled in. The audience applauded her, adoring fans brought bouquets to the stage, and during intermissions there was a line to take pictures with her. Soon enough, I caught her studying casting schedules for film auditions. She wasn't looking for youth shows or a minor role in a series. Setting her sights on an upcoming movie by a famous director, Zhenya printed out the main character's script and diligently started working on it.

I volunteered to help, but it turned out I only annoyed her. She prepared for almost two weeks, stubbornly ignoring my existence. Once I tried to take her to the cinema and it nearly ended our relationship. Creating a scene out of nowhere, Zhenya kicked me out and didn't answer my calls. I was deeply troubled. A lump of indignation and pain rose in my throat every time I entertained the thought of us breaking up. However, a day before the auditions, Zhenya suddenly called me. I hesitated before answering her second call, but I still answered. With a cheerful voice, she asked if I could pick her up tomorrow to take her to the studio. I agreed. On one hand, I sometimes even liked this kind of relationship, where I carefully planned every move like a chess game just to stay with her. On the other hand, I realized that sincerity was lacking in our romance. But what is sincerity in the modern world, which is built on lies from the very beginning?

Ascending the grand staircase of contemporaries, we found ourselves in a long corridor. Along the walls, sitting on folding chairs, were some rather attractive young ladies, whom I shamelessly began to scrutinize. Some of them also seemed interested in me, for which I received an elbow jab in the side. Next to a tall door sat another girl, this time with a badge labeled "organizer." She handed Zhenya a paper with a number and filled in the form with her name. We patiently waited our turn. Zhenya didn't get nervous or rehearse her role; instead she studied each of her competitors, trying to behave as kindly as possible. In her mind, she was already a winner. Right now, the last thing she wanted was to provoke aggression and slander among her rivals when the results were finally announced.

Unlike her, I wasn't so sure. Beauty isn't a talent; it's just a pleasant addition to it. Eugenia had no clue how to move toward her goal. She was convinced she deserved everything, and all at once, not gradually. She believed all the skills needed to become a star were innate and didn't require acquisition. Sure, this girl had a fire that ignited the audience. But her mischievous gaze and lovely copper curls became tiresome, the artificial sweetness settling heavily on the palate. Versatility and authenticity inevitably demanded effort and refinement of skill, which never occurred to her.

When the last girl had left the auditions, the door swung open, revealing the famous actor—at least by Minsk city's standards, with a population of around just one and half million. It was with him that the heroine of the new movie would experience all the joys and sorrows and deliver long speeches. He announced that he would answer questions about the film while the director made such an important decision for all present. We followed him into the spacious, brightly lit hall and arranged our chairs in a circle. Zhenya had never looked at me with the same eyes as she looked at the screen star then. Never! It seemed like her gaze emitted light, sending little sunbeams around the room. The actor, in turn, bestowed his attention on everyone, not lingering on anyone. A professional! I envied him.

3:13 AM

"Idiot! Who did he choose? No, did you see? Did you see her?" Within an hour, Eugenia was screaming in hysterics. "That pompous peacock! He didn't understand anything either. Or didn't see! I bet he's got minus five vision, no less! He can only see his own reflection, and that's when he's kissing himself in the mirror!"

Her indignation knew no bounds. Soon aggression gave way to depression, and Eugenia, staring at her computer screen, didn't even notice when I left her apartment.

Unlike Zhenya, Tolya never bluffs. He doesn't play games or conquer girls to validate himself. He harbored absolutely no feelings for Zhenya beyond friendly sympathy and risked earning an unfavorable reputation once that fiery redhead figured it all out. I waited. There was no jealousy in me. I simply waited for the veil to lift once again from her gray eyes and for her to run into the only embrace ready to accept her for who she was—mine.

Through all her ups and downs, her bouts of depression and bursts of ecstatic joy and futile attempts to conquer everyone and everything, I was always there. Over time, I became her sturdy anchor—the lifeline that kept her afloat in the storms of her stormy life.

I flicked on the windshield wipers and cranked up the defrost. Whether it was the alcohol or the fluctuating temperature, the windows fogged up even more. I desperately needed visibility on this already dark road. The snow-capped peaks drew nearer, their triangular shapes suspended between sky and earth in the piercing darkness. Lost in contemplation of one of them, I felt the steering wheel suddenly veer, and the wheels skidded.

“Zhenya, sit down and buckle up!” I yelled.

The road was becoming treacherous. She fell silent for a moment, then erupted in fury.

“Anton, seriously, enough already! You’re like an old man. We just escaped from uni. Let’s have some fun for once!” she snapped, then turned to Galia and repeated, “I hate all of this! I hate it so much ...”

We were fighting again. Honestly, in the few months of our romance, this was the one thing we’d gotten exceptionally good at. I’d urge her to keep things in order and behave reasonably, while she would lament that her happiest days were being spent with a bore like me.

I was angry. Angry and driving. I felt like just dropping everything and having a beer too, but Tolya beat me to it.

“Do you think seatbelts were invented to restrict your movements?” I couldn’t help but snap.

“Oh my god!” came the response.

“Would you please, for once, switch on your brain? Even in the phrase ‘safety belts’ there’s a clue for you—safety!”

Perhaps that came off too harshly. I don’t know. Maybe I did often pressure her and genuinely didn’t let her have fun, depriving her of the chance to experience truly wild moments, the ones you're supposed to tell your grandchildren about. Who knows, maybe I really was pushing it too far. My voice softened, but I stood my ground. "Buckle up, that's all I'm asking."

Zhenya silently slumped into her seat with a sigh. Jerking the belt, she clicked it into place with a loud snap and turned away to stare out of the window.

Judging by the silence that hung in the cab, the company was dissatisfied with me specifically. In their eyes, I could never truly relax and enjoy our adventures.

As soon as I entertained the thought of my wrongness, muffled laughter came from behind. Tolya was miming something with the air of a silent film professional, while Galia was giggling like boiling water under a lid. I didn't feel hurt or offended, just a little sad. Sad that no one could understand me here and now, or at least show some respect for my requests.

I heard them empty another bottle of beer and toss it into the trunk. It clattered noisily among the suitcases, spreading the smell of hops in the stiff air. My friends knew perfectly well that I disliked sloppiness in the car. It was their protest against my fussiness, and now all I could do was grit my teeth and swallow my discontent.

Realizing that I had finally retreated and ceased my moralizing, the passengers in the back seat started throwing peanuts at Zhenya. At first she ignored them, which gave me hope.

However, as if catching some airborne virus to which I personally had a strong immunity, she began stealthily throwing peanuts back. But when the virus invaded her brain through the respiratory tract and completely took it over, she quickly unfastened herself and lunged at the offenders with a tickle.

Silence and order only emerged when they all ganged up on me. But, sensing my indifference, my comrades resumed their ruckus. Zhenya slipped between the seats and whacked me on the arm with her sneaker. The car veered sharply to the left. I yelled, struggling to regain control, and desperately tried to steer back onto the road. With jerky movements I pressed on the brakes, barely managing to regain control of the car for a split second. But it continued to slide, and the landscape in the windshield swirled counterclockwise.

"Oh god, no, nooo!" Zhenya shouted.

Only after the car had made three full turns did it come to a stop.

"Is everyone okay?" I asked, choked with concern.

"I'm fine," replied Tolya, "but ... Galia!"

I turned sharply and saw him shaking his friend, who had lost consciousness, probably from fright.

"Does anyone have any smelling salts?" Tolya shouted. I shrugged; the car kit only had iodine and brilliant green.

3:13 AM

"I have whiskey!" Zhenya unexpectedly confessed and, perking up, unzipped her bulky bag.

Fetching a miniature Jack Daniels, she hastily unscrewed the toy-like cap. Tolya carefully took it, but Galia came to before the sharp scent filled her lungs. She twitched and cracked her eyes open.

"How are you?" Tolya whispered.

"What happened? Are we all dead?" She looked alarmed.

"No, no, no ... What are you talking about? Of course not." Tolya hugged her and kissed her forehead as gently as if she were a child.

"Someone decided to send us to the afterlife ahead of schedule," I said, shooting a glance at Zhenya, "but thankfully the plan didn't work out."

"Anton, I didn't mean to—"

"Just stay there now," I practically ordered, glancing over my shoulder at the back seat. "I've had enough!"

Because of that stupid stunt, we could all be lying in a ditch inside a wrecked car by now. And then what? Only God knows. Everyone fell silent. It was clear that we were terribly scared and especially worried about Galia. We had a sick person with us. And even in remission, she still seemed to be very weak. The invisible responsibility for this fragile person fell on my shoulders, and I began to seriously consider whether it was Tolya's best idea to bring along a girlfriend with cancer.

Losing control of the car on such a road, especially at night and in these weather conditions, wasn't surprising. Gradually my frustration ebbed away; I didn't want to sour the trip by blowing the incident out of proportion. After all, we were alive and unharmed, and that was what mattered most.

The weather worsened, and I felt relieved when Zhenya leaned back. The fog enveloped the highway, crawling out of the lowlands like a living thing and hurling itself under the wheels. Within five minutes of driving, it rose to full height, completely blocking visibility. I slowed down. The beams of the headlights were lost in this dense veil. Eventually it became abundantly clear that the fog was far worse than Zhenya. She was still silent, and the thought of apologizing even crossed my mind. But if I did, she would just start everything all over again without drawing any conclusions. *No way! Not now ...*

Suddenly a strange glow appeared ahead. I gently braked three times and approached the scattered beam. About five meters in front of us was a car. From inside our vehicle it was only possible to distinguish the doors and one working headlight. I parked and turned on the hazard lights.

"What's up with that car?" Tolya leaned forward.

"I don't know. I can only see one headlight. I think they got turned around too, but they weren't as lucky as us. Looks like they crashed into a pole."

3:13 AM

"We need to call an ambulance and the police," concluded my friend.

Galia and Zhenya were silent as fish. Tolya dialed the ambulance number. I called the police. A male voice came through the speaker in an unfamiliar language. I had almost forgotten that we had crossed the border from Ukraine and were now in Romania. Tolya effortlessly switched to English, and I repeated his words verbatim. The dispatcher calmly replied, "Thirty minutes away. Stay there."

Everything happened so quickly that I didn't realize immediately—we had stumbled on the scene of an accident. The realization flooded my mind with blood, pulsing in my temples. What to do? How to proceed?

Perhaps we should stay and wait for the ambulance, give our statements to the police. But we didn't witness how it all happened—we just found the wrecked car. In any case, we were stuck here. And it would be a relief if no one crashed into us in the zero visibility. The rear door swung open.

"Tolya, where are you going?" the shocked girls practically chorused.

"Maybe someone needs our help," he replied shortly.

"No, you're not going anywhere!" objected Galia. "They should be thankful we found them! It's not our responsibility to go further; you're not a doctor."

She now sat in the middle between Tolya and Zhenya, and I could clearly see her face in the rear-view mirror. Tears welled up in her transparent blue eyes. She hung on to Tolya's neck, burying her face in his hair.

"No one is getting out, you see? We must help, we are obligated ..." he said softly, trying to release Galia's hands.

"I can't lose you again! I just can't bear it, you understand?" she pleaded.

They were indeed in a relationship; now it was clear to everyone. But what did she mean by *again*? Personally, I didn't think we would lose Tolya if he went to check on the passengers of the wrecked car, although I would have voted for staying in the car and waiting for the professionals. Those guys were already lucky someone had found them!

"What do you mean by 'lose'? I'm going to check if emergency assistance is needed! If someone there is bleeding out, every minute counts. It's a matter of life and death, don't you know?" he said gently, stroking her knitted cap. "If you're afraid to stay, come with me. But there are people ... You understand? And they need help!"

"No, I saw ... I saw you dead! This cursed place. Please, let's go further," Galia cried.

"What are you talking about? Where did you see that?" Tolya was puzzled.

3:13 AM

The girl started sobbing, her hysteria escalating as none of us could understand the reason behind such strange words. "I saw that we're all going to die! We mustn't get out of the car ... We mustn't stop here ..." She covered her face with her hands, unable to calm down.

Galia started making her way towards the instrument panel, trying to turn on the ignition and prompt the car to move. Actually, I agreed. I had no desire to linger here for long. We had called the right people, and thankfully there was phone reception.

"Listen, I'll just check if my help is needed. It's two minutes, okay?" Tolya couldn't stop his altruism.

"I've seen it a hundred times in movies—cars exploding after a collision. Don't go, I beg you. The ambulance will come and help them." Sobbing and clutching his jacket, Galia continued.

"Galia, five minutes ago we could've been in their place, praying to God for salvation, just like them. If you want to be saved someday, you have to know how to save. Everything will be fine. Come on, take my hand and let's go check on the passengers in that car."

"What if someone's in there with a knife waiting for you? I saw you all cut up!"

"What are you talking about? You're scaring me." He backed away.

Her words weren't just strange; they were downright terrifying.

"I know how it sounds ... but ... but I don't know how I saw it all when I lost consciousness. What if I somehow caught a glimpse of the future? What if, for instance, he's a criminal and wants to kill us?"

"That's nonsense! Okay, enough. I'm outta here." Tolya released his beloved's hands and opened the car door.

Turning around, I finally glanced at Zhenya. She was huddling in the corner of the car and had tucked her hands between tightly clenched knees. Her gaze seemed fixed somewhere among the tree trunks hiding in the fog, while tears streamed down her cheeks. I didn't know what was going on with her. Was she in shock from witnessing the accident, from my harsh tone, or from some sudden news? The next moment, I heard Tolya kiss Galia and step out onto the road. Leaving the car hadn't been part of my plan, but I followed my friend. Opening the door, I lowered my feet into the dense fog, which momentarily receded, revealing the wet asphalt.

Around us, a murky haze blanketed the scene, limiting the visibility to just a few meters. Turning to Tolya, I watched as his figure disappeared into the mist. Tears filling her eyes, Galia pulled her legs up beneath her and slammed the car door. Lost in her own world, she stared blankly at the windshield. She must be wrestling with some sorrow seemingly much deeper than I had initially imagined.

3:13 AM

Suddenly Zhenya slammed the door. I turned to see her walking toward the wrecked car. Silently, I followed her. After a few meters, her figure vanished into the fog as well. I didn't rush to approach. I must confess, I dreaded the thought of seeing mangled bodies. And what if they were still alive? Oh god! I would have to do something then, seeing a sea of blood, exposed bones, and perhaps much more. My limbs went numb at those thoughts. I was literally paralyzed, unable to make the slightest move. Suddenly I heard Zhenya's soft voice: "Tolya, what's going on here?"

I froze, waiting for a response. A response that would determine whether my legs would move from this spot today or not.

Printed in Great Britain
by Amazon

42794114R00228